MW01514751

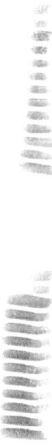

The
WAIT

Ms. Kalodimos,
I hope you enjoy
this walk through old Nashville.
All the best,

The
WAIT

A NOVEL

+ by +

LISA KAYE PRESLEY

Lisa Kaye Presley

Inquiries may be directed to:

Lisa Kaye Presley
P.O. Box 140907
Nashville, TN 37214-9998

ISBN categories
Literature & Fiction – Literary Fiction
Literature & Fiction – Literary Fiction – Historical
Literature & Fiction – Literary Fiction – Military & War

ISBN: 978-0-9988550-0-4 Ebook
ISBN: 978-0-9988550-1-1 Paperback
ISBN: 978-0-9988550-2-8 Hardback

AUTHOR'S NOTE

This book is a novel. Although some of the characters in this novel actually existed historically, they are fictional representations. Having gone to great lengths to maintain historical accuracy as to the events and persons of this time period, it is noted that THE WAIT is strictly a fictional novel.

DEDICATION

There are so many people I need to thank for their help in the creation of this story. Too many to list here, but without some, I wouldn't be writing this dedication for a story that is so near and dear to my heart.

In the early days of the writing of this book, I did more research and interviewing than writing. Some of those people are not with us any longer. People such as Jack Norman, to whom I will ever be grateful for recording his memories of the Nashville he knew. To the door greeter at the Office Depot in Belle Meade, who recounted his days in the Eighth Army Air Corp to me. To Jay Sanders for his painful, yet vivid memories of serving in France after D-Day, and to all of the Nashvillians who lent their voices to the interviews, which came to be known as SPEAKING OF UNION STATION, without whose recorded memories I would have never been able to write this book.

I'd like to thank Donnie Creighton for sharing her memories of Nashville, especially Loveman's Department Store, Fletch Coke for her extensive knowledge of the city's history, and to all of the countless people I've met over the years who have been willing to share their memories with me. These Nashvillians, who remember an America in gentler times, who remember the sacrifices they and their parents made to supply this nation with the men and machinery needed to defeat an evil that threatened the very existence of their freedom, are owed a debt of gratitude. I'd like to thank those who sacrificed in order that their children and their children's children would live in peace. I dedicate this book to them and the sacrifices they made for us all.

On a personal note, I'd like to thank a few co-workers, Tawnya and Ginger, who read this story, fell in love with Bonnie and Calvin, and gave me the courage to share it with others. To my guru, Ed Massey, who never let me give up, who kept pushing me toward the finish line. To my boss and my friend, Aubrey Harwell, who took the time to read this story, to get behind it, and help me see my dream come true. But, above all else, to my own Bonnie Girl, my little-redheaded angel, my daughter, my best friend, Jennifer Marie, my muse. If she wasn't who she is; I would never have never met Bonnie McCaverty.

PART I
Smithville, Tennessee

∾

PART II
Nashville, Tennessee

∾

PART III
World War II

PART I
Smithville, Tennessee

CHAPTER ONE

"Did the sickness come and git her?"

"THERE'S ONE THING everybody knew about Bonnie McCaverty," Pippin said as a mischievous grin wrinkled the tough skin of her dark, leathery face. Memories of her old friend always made her smile.

"That girl never gave up on nuthin'; not on a sickly calf or a stubborn pony, not on gettin' her way . . . and not on Calvin Wade," she continued, all the while shaking her head as though it was a thing that still, all these years later, she couldn't convince herself actually happened.

"Oh, she tried a might few times, but it never lasted. Always did come back and even stronger than before.

"Them two locked horns from the minute Calvin came to live with the McCavertys that awful winter," Pippin said, rearranging her body trying to make her old bones more comfortable in her rocking chair. She had quite the story to tell, and better than that, there were two women sitting across from her leaning in with the eager ears of youth who had traveled all the way from Nashville to hear the story of the Wades and McCavertys.

The chair, worn to the shape of her body from years and years of the same repetitive motion, came to a stop as Pippin sat straightening her spine trying to quiet the pain that never left her tired body. Her head creaked on its axis as she turned slowly to face her audience.

Old Pippin, dressed in her favorite long gingham skirt, still wrapped in the worn apron she wore every Sunday, tilted her chin toward her chest, peering over her spectacles. A grave look now replaced the joyful look of remembrance. This part of the story always brought a coldness to her body; one that she couldn't shake after living it. She began in a whisper that barely parted her thin, papery lips.

"That sickness came in and killed so many people we knew; Mrs. Marsh from in town; the teacher, Miss Dowd, and her papa. It was just runnin' all about pickin' and choosin' who it was gonna take. Took Calvin's ma and pa," she said vehemently as if she still held a grudge about the epidemic that took the lives of so many.

"Mr. Wade went first. After that, Lizzie and Jessie stayed with Mrs. Wade, hopin' for their son's sake she'd make it, but poor Miss Sarah left in a heap of fiery fever.

"It was the coldest winter we'd ever seen out 'chere on the plateau that winter. I believe it was in nineteen hundred seventeen or eighteen," she said, resting back in her chair.

"The temperature dropped down well below zero most days, and the snow, well I tell you, it never did stop."

The old woman carefully pulled her spectacles from behind her ears with fingers stiff and crooked from years of cutting tobacco and picking cotton and held them in one hand. With the other, she waved across an imaginary scene only she could see with her memory, not with the dimness of her weary, faded eyes.

"The gray sky swallowed up the whole countryside in a heavy blanket of despair and fear.

"It was the influenza, so they said. Most of us didn't know, but what little news we could get out of the neighbors From time to time, or from Doc Morgan when he'd come 'round. They said thousands across the country were dyin' because of that black devil plague.

"Even as far as we is from Nashville, our quiet, little community out 'chere in Smithville wudn't immune to its deadly hand. Men, women, and children jest died at random. That deadly haint crept in and out of homes pickin' and choosin' its victims just as it had in Nashville and just as it had at the home of Sarah and John Wade."

Pippin placed her spectacles back on her nose, carefully threading them behind her ears, taking a long, ragged breath, turning to look at the two women staring at her with wide eyes. Her eyes narrowed to slits in her dark face. Her mouth drew into a determined pout. She pulled in a long draw of breath, and in a rough whisper, she spoke. "I remember it all. No amount of livin' or the passin' of time can dull the memory of something so evil steppin' across life's threshold into this world."

The beads of sweat that trickled down Sarah Wade's forehead reappeared almost as soon as Lizzie wiped them away. Her fever had persisted for three days now, and Lizzie feared the worst for her best friend if it didn't break soon.

"You should go get Calvin," Lizzie said to Jessie, her husband, who pondered silently against the frame of the bedroom door.

"He should see his mother one more time." Her voice cracked on the last word, now on the verge of tears, an unusual occurrence for Lizzie McCaverty.

She was tired. She and Jessie had been at the Wade farm for five days tending to Sarah. Jessie's task had been to build a makeshift coffin for John from what wood he could find that wasn't buried in the snow. For the last three days, the coffin sat in the barn, the snow too deep to move it and the ground too frozen to bury him.

"I don't think so, Lizzie," Jessie replied. He stroked his chin, now covered in gray stubble, his eyes fixed on Lizzie's ashen face.

"It's no use him seein' all a this. Anyway, we promised John we'd keep him away. We'll just do the best we can do." He tried relighting his pipe, failing as a result of hands stiffened from the cold.

When Lizzie turned back to Sarah, her eyes were closed. She lay still. Her struggle had ended. Sarah Wade had gone to be with her beloved John.

A loud knock on the front door startled Lizzie and Jessie.

"Who could that be?" Lizzie asked, making her way down the stairs. Even though thick, gray clouds promising more snow shrouded the afternoon sun, it was enough to illuminate the silhouette of Calvin Wade, Sarah and John's son, peering through the glass of the front door. He was trying to see through the lace sheers that hung just inside. He stepped back when he saw Lizzie coming toward the door.

Lizzie threw her shawl around her shoulders, stepping out into the bitter cold.

"What are you doing here, Calvin?" she asked, covering her mouth to prevent the torturing cold from stealing her breath. "You're supposed to be at home with the girls."

"I just wanted to see how Mother was," he said with a nervous tremor in his voice Lizzie had never heard before. *Understandable*, she thought, under the circumstances.

"Is she any better?" he asked.

Lizzie shook her head, struggling to maintain eye contact. "There's no reason for you to be here, Calvin," she said. "You go on back to the house now."

Calvin's chest hitched. His lower lip trembled.

"She's dead, too. Idn't she?" he asked, stomping around nervously on the porch in front of the door to his own home.

Lizzie stared at her feet. Her frame, although thin and fit, was stooped a bit from all the farming, but she could outlast any man in the field and never break a sweat. Brought up from tough and taught to be so; Lizzie never cried much. If she did, no one ever saw it. She also never raised her voice. Lizzie knew all those things about herself and how it caused people to be unable to tell what she was thinking. She faltered at what to say next.

Lizzie cast her eyes down, unable to answer him directly. She realized that by not answering his question, she had actually answered.

"There's nothing more for you to do here now, boy," Lizzie said without tone. "Get on back to the girls. It's getting late, and they'll be needin' some firewood." She wiped her brow with the back of her hand, trying to put the worry for her own children out of her mind.

"Yes'm, Miss Lizzie," Calvin answered. He hung his head, wringing his hat in his hands.

Her heart broke for him, knowing the grief he felt couldn't be taken away by anyone. She watched as Calvin stood looking at his home, knowing an empty hole had opened up on the inside of him—an open, empty void that could never again be filled. It wouldn't do him any good to stay there. Lizzie knew it, and she was sure he knew it, too.

Although only sixteen, Calvin acted much older. He was an only child and had never been around other children much, except for Jessie and Lizzie's three girls, so he was accustomed to acting older than he actually was. He knew strength would be expected of him. Slowly, Calvin turned and descended the steps of his front porch as Lizzie watched. All he'd ever known lay behind him in that house. Now, every step he took drew him closer to an unfamiliar life, the life of an orphan.

After a few steps, he turned, looking back at his home, shrouded in a frozen, white cloak of icy death. He knew his mother lay upstairs dead, and his father lay in a pine casket in the barn waiting for warmer weather so he could be buried.

Lizzie remained on the porch, looking back at him, even though the fiercely cold wind whipped through her skirt and the thin shawl gathered around her, prickling her skin beneath. Calvin opened his mouth as if he'd had the same thought, but he made no sound. Maybe he wanted to scream, but couldn't. Maybe he wanted to cry out, but didn't. He simply fixed his eyes on Lizzie, and hers remained fixed on his.

Calvin drew his hands into fists. He was struggling, trying to fight back tears forming in his eyes, but it was a losing battle. They began to trickle down, spilling out of the corners of his eyes, stinging his face as they hit the cold air.

Lizzie moved toward him. As she did, Calvin turned and struggled to run hard through the thick snow. He sped across the yard and up the hill to the footpath that connected the two farms. Lizzie watched him go without calling after him. When he was gone, she turned and made her way back into the house, steeling herself for the many unpleasant duties that awaited her.

The McCaverty farm lay only a mile southeast of the Wade farm as the crow flies, but by wagon, it was quite a bit farther. Through the years, the families had mostly used the footpath to visit. Foothills forming a ridge in the shape of a horseshoe surrounded the valley where the Wade home stood. The path descended into the valley on the east side at its lowest point. Even there, the climb was steep and uneven. Calvin fought the icy path like a racehorse stretching for the finish line. By the time he reached the top, his lungs were on fire.

From the summit, the path ran along for another quarter of a mile before he would enter what the children called The Dark Forest. The trail cut through a deep thicket of trees by the elders, Wade and McCaverty formed an even arch of tree limbs above the path, sparking childhood imaginings of a magical tunnel winding its way through enchanted woods. The Dark Forest provided hours of entertainment for the children of both families. Now, it was his escape.

When Calvin reached the trees, he slowed to catch his breath. His mind reeled as he trudged along in the deep snow, trying to make sense of all that had happened during the past five days. The silence, compounded by the thick layer of ice and snow, was maddening. His father was gone. Now, so was his mother. It was an odd feeling to be all alone, so completely alone; no father and now no mother. The only family he had, other than his mother and father, were his family's best friends, the McCavertys. He had practically grown up with them, and their three girls were just like his sisters.

What would he do? Where would he live? Would he stay here? Would he be forced to go up north to Boston where distant family lived? When would he have to decide? Worse, would someone decide for him? Rage welled inside him. He felt as if he might explode out of his body at any moment, although he knew he mustn't show anger. Anger wasn't strong. He was supposed to remain calm and responsible. That is what his parents would want.

Calvin's eyes darted about looking for something to hit or kick, something he could lose this anger on, but there was nothing. He kicked at the snow instead. He pulled his hat off, threw it onto the ground, stomping on it for lack of anything better to do, until he was quite out of breath. He stopped, observing his hat now covered in wet, icy snow, the memory of his father on the day he gave Calvin the hat flooding his mind.

The weight of his memories brought Calvin to his knees. Reaching for the brimmed leather hat, he gripped it to his chest. The extreme pain he felt finally made its way from his lungs, over his vocal cords, and into the air.

"Noooo!" he screamed, the steam from his breath clouding the air around him. Calvin buried his face in the cherished gift as his scream reverberated off the surrounding hills, escaping into the cold, empty hollows.

It was his one expression of grief.

It never reached the ears of another human being.

"Nettie, when's Mama and Daddy comin' home?" Bonnie asked.

"Soon, I'm sure they'll be home soon," Bonnie's oldest sister answered. Nettie was seventeen and in complete charge of the household, while Lizzie and Jessie held vigil at the Wade farm.

Nettie sat stitching Bonnie's pinafore, which had mysteriously ripped while playing upstairs. Things like that often happened to five-year-old Bonnie McCaverty. Rambunctious and impetuous, Bonnie was always acting before considering the consequences. Nettie knew that. She also knew that the rip came from Bonnie's playing in the attic where she wasn't allowed to play. She thought about scolding her sister, but then decided she was in no mood. The cold was unbearable, and they had been cooped up in the house for days. Without her mother there, Nettie's chores had more than doubled. She had neither the time nor the energy to solve the mystery.

After mending the pinafore, Nettie set it aside and stood. She placed the palms of her hands against the small of her back, arching backward, her muscles grateful for the stretch.

"I have to fix supper now," she said to Bonnie. "Please, please behave. Okay?"

"Okay, Nettie," the little redhead answered, her pouty bottom lip extended. "I'm sorry."

"Now go find Emma," Nettie ordered. "We'll eat soon. Wash your face and hands, and you two come help with supper.

"And be sure to use fresh water," she warned.

"Okay, Nettie," Bonnie called over her shoulder, racing up the stairs to find her older sister.

Nettie pushed open the door that led to the kitchen. Reaching for the apron that hung on the wall, she instinctively threw it around her neck, tying it at the back. She lifted the metal plate on the stovetop to light the fire, striking a match before realizing there was no wood. The sulfurous plume barely made its way to her nose when the back door opened. A fierce blast of cold air quickly extinguished the flame. Tiny flakes of snow whirled about the kitchen, the figure of Calvin emerging from among them. He carried an armload of wood. Nettie noted he must have been walking for some time. His hat and coat carried a thick layer of snow.

"Oh, fine," Nettie said, smiling. "Thank you, Calvin. I was afraid I'd have to go out in this dreadful cold," she said, closing the door behind him, struggling against the cold wind that tried to force its way into the warm house.

She turned to face Calvin, who stood quietly, the wood grasped tightly in his arms, his steel blue eyes glistening, seeming distant, revealing to her something was wrong.

He laid the wood beside the stove, removing his coat and hat, sitting quietly at the kitchen table, saying nothing. Nettie stoked the fire, adding more wood, and began to prepare supper. Calvin hadn't told her where he was going, but she figured he had probably gone to his house even against her parents' wishes.

"Mother died today," he said, his voice unemotional, matter-of-fact.

Nettie pulled her apron to her face, spinning around to look at him. "Oh, Calvin, I'm so sorry."

Calvin sat staring at his hands folded on the table in front of him. She moved to sit in the chair next to him.

"Your father and now Mrs. Wade? Oh, Calvin," Nettie cried. "What will you do?"

"I don't know," he replied, never looking up from his hands.

Just then, the door burst open. Bonnie and Emma entered the kitchen. Bonnie, who was particularly fond of Calvin, gasped when she saw him. She bound over, putting her arm around Calvin's shoulders.

"Why are you sad, Calvin?" she asked, her tiny face an exaggerated mask of concern. "Did your mama die, too?"

Calvin looked up from his hands. "Yes, Bonnie. Mother died, too."

"Did the sickness come and git her?" the little girl asked.

"Yes," he said, his gaze returning to his hands. "The sickness came and got her."

"It's okay, Calvin. You can come and live wiff us. I'll take care a you," she said, patting him on the back. Calvin's lip quivered as he fought back a swell of confusion and sadness. Pulling the little girl up onto his lap, he felt her instinctively lay her head on his shoulders, wrapping her chubby arms around his neck.

Emma, who had been watching the exchange with sad eyes, sat next to Nettie as they held onto one another. The four of them sat quietly for some time in the dimness of the room, the winter sun beginning to set beyond the kitchen window. The color of the room mirrored the changing of the sky outside from dismal gray to a mysterious haze of purple.

As the blackness of night began to swallow up the very air around them, Nettie lit the lamp on the table and started supper. Moments later, Emma and Bonnie got up to help. Calvin stared at his hands.

Chapter Two

"It might git you, too!"

C ALVIN AND JESSIE stopped their work on the corral
fence for a drink of water when Calvin caught a glimpse of
something out of the corner of his eye. He squinted in the
afternoon sun to get a better look.

"Someone's comin'," He said.

Jessie straightened slowly, giving himself a chance to stretch his
back. "It looks like my Bonnie," he said.

"Yep, I think it is," Calvin added, slapping his worn hat against his
pants trying to rid it of the dust and sweat that had soaked in during
the day's work

"She's not due home from school for another two hours. Wonder
what happened this time?" Jessie pondered aloud.

"Well, *somethin's* wrong. She's got that look on her face," Calvin
said, knowing they were both just going to have to wait to find out.
There was no telling with Bonnie.

That look was the one Bonnie wore when she became angry. Even as
far away as they were, they could see it. Her lips tightened against her
face, forming a determined pout. Her eyes became angry slits in her
face, her nostrils flaring, stomping her feet as she walked. The afternoon sun shining on her reddish-blond hair turned it the color of a
wheat field against the sun—shades of red, gold, and orange.

Neither Jessie nor Calvin made another acknowledgment of her other than watching her approach. There was no use guessing. They could never tell with her. Calvin crossed his hands over the butt end of his shovel, propping his chin on top and waited.

"Well, if it isn't my little Bonnie," Jessie said when she was within earshot. "What are ya doin' home from school so early, girl?" His stern Irish accent was meant to be intimidating, but it didn't appear to faze Bonnie. She was far too angry.

"The teacher sent me home early," she said, her pout becoming more pronounced. She folded her arms one under the other as she plopped down on a hay bale near the barn.

"And why is that?" her father asked.

Bonnie didn't look at him. "'Cause I got in a fight with that Joshua McCallister!" she exclaimed.

"Josh? He's bigger'n you, Bonnie," Calvin said.

She jumped up, wagging her fist at him. "So what? I'd a whupped him if Emma hadn't a pulled me off him!"

Calvin looked at his feet, trying to swallow his laughter. He glanced at Jessie, who was doing the same. Evidently, Bonnie was less upset about having gotten into the scrap than she was about the fact that she didn't get to finish it.

"What'd he do to you?" Calvin asked.

Bonnie sneered.

"Well, he kept pullin' my hair while I was tryin' to do my problems," she shouted. "Then, when play time come, he kept pokin' at me with a stick. I warned him to quit, Daddy. I did!"

"I'm sure you did, girl. I'm sure you did," Jessie said with a slightly prideful smile.

"Then, he said he was gonna whup me," she continued, "'cause we didn't need no redheaded, Irish trash in this school, and I'd have to go somewheres else.

"Well, that was it, Daddy! I jumped onto him from the porch and knocked him onto the ground. Then, I pounded him in the right eye! I's about to go for the left one when Emma had to go pull me off him! That rat!"

"Now, now, don't go talking about your sister like that. She probably saved you from getting bad hurt, girl," Jessie said. "I don't quite know why that boy would make such remarks to you, Bonnie. Obviously, Joshua McCallister knows nothing of his own lineage to throw such slander at the Irish."

"He couldn't hurt me," Bonnie added exuberantly. "I'd break his knees first. I told him I didn't understand why his daddy named him after a man in the Bible when he didn't act Christian at all. Then, he tried coming at me again. That's when Miss Vickers sent us home."

"You better go on and play now before Mother comes out here and finds you home early," Bonnie's father warned. "She told you she'd get the paddle out next time. Remember?"

"Oh, Daddy, don't let her," Bonnie pleaded. "What was I supposed to do? Was I supposed to let him call me names?"

Calvin laughed. "You know Emma's gonna tell."

Bonnie's face soured. "She's the one ought to git a whuppin'," she said. "She's the one 'caused me to get in trouble. If she hadn't a pulled me off of him, I'd a just whupped him and that would a been it!"

Just then, Lizzie's voice echoed to them from the front porch. "Jessie . . . Calvin. C'mon and eat now." Bonnie winced, crouching at the sound like a small bunny trying to hide from a fox.

"You better go, girl," Jessie whispered. "Get on to the barn. I'll send Calvin out with something to eat."

"Thanks, Daddy," Bonnie said, replicating her father's stealthy tone as she ran to the safety of the barn. Calvin and Jessie made their way inside for lunch.

"Wudn't my fault. Mean, old Josh McCallister," Bonnie declared. "It's not fair. I'm always the one gets in trouble. Just 'cause I take up for myself and no one else does."

She picked up a hay straw and chewed on the end as she strolled through the barn. "Why should I be punished for takin' up for myself? It's not fair. Just 'cause I'm a girl 's all. If I was a boy, they wouldn't a sent me home. They'd just make me dust erasers or sump'n. If I had a horse, I could ride into The Dark Forest and hide. No one would find me there."

Bonnie grabbed a pitchfork that had been leaning against a nearby mound of hay, beginning to stack the hay, for a place to sit. The early afternoon sun laid bright streaks across the ground as it snuck between the wallboards of the barn. As she worked, Bonnie began to sing the song she always sang to herself whenever she felt bad. Jessie had been singing it to her since she was a baby. It was an old Irish folk song, he had said. It always managed to make her feel better.

"As I get to end of the meadow I'll see,
A big, fine, white house for my Bonnie and me.
We'll sit on the front porch and watch the sun set,
A fine time we'll have that we'll never forget.

We'll have ten fine children and all with red hair,
To match with their mother's so bright and so fair.
We'll sit on the rooftop and watch the moon glow,
As me and my Bonnie together grow old.

"Don't you ever get tired of that song?" she heard just as she jumped up, landing on top of the pile of hay she had been making. Dust and chaff from her impact spewed into the air around her. Little flecks of dried grass slinked to the ground, shimmering in the air as they floated in and out of the streaks of golden light that shone between the boards of the rickety old barn. She looked up to see Calvin standing against the stall doorframe.

"Nope," she said. "And you shouldn't sneak up on a body like that."

Calvin chuckled. He handed her a napkin with a warm biscuit inside, which she eagerly accepted. She had missed lunch and, in her rage, had left her bag at school.

"I hope that dumb Emma doesn't forget my schoolbag," she said through a mouthful of biscuit. "I'll for sure get in trouble if she does."

Calvin leaned against the wall of the barn. It was a familiar pose to Bonnie, who often sat talking with Calvin in this same spot or in the treehouse Calvin built for them. Mostly they talked about fishin' and mules and horses, things of that nature.

"Bonnie Girl," Calvin said.

"Don't call me that!" she spat comically, picking up a handful of hay, pitching it into his face.

"I have something to tell you," Calvin said. His voice was soft, but serious.

"What?" Bonnie asked, chewing more slowly on her biscuit, her eyes trained on him. Calvin shifted uncomfortably against the wall, kicking his left heel against the toe of his right boot.

"Well, you know Mama made Lizzie promise to make me live here until I finished my schoolin'," he said.

"Yeah," Bonnie answered slowly, sensing that something was wrong.

"Well, you know I've finished," he continued. "I've learned all I can from Jessie," hesitating before delivering the blow.

"It's time for me to go home."

Bonnie drew a surprised breath, causing the biscuit she was eating to travel down her windpipe. As she coughed, trying to open her airway, chunks of biscuit spewed from her mouth. Quickly, she scrambled to her feet.

"Home?" she screamed, "to your house? Why would you want to go there?"

"It's *my* house, Bonnie," Calvin explained. "It's my home. I have to go back. It's been sittin' empty for a long time now. I've been going over there, working the land some, trying to get it ready for planting. It's almost ready. Soon, I'll have to be there full-time."

Bonnie turned to face him. "Home?" she asked again. "You're gonna leave?"

"I have to," he answered.

"But, Calvin, I didn't think you'd ever go back to that house. What if that sickness is still there? It might git you, too," she argued.

"The sickness is gone, Bonnie," Calvin said, trying to present her with a reassuring smile. "Besides, you can come over and visit me. I'll let you help me plant my first garden, okay?"

Calvin knelt, meeting Bonnie at eye level just as tears began to leak down her face.

"Bonnie Girl," he said softly, "please don't be mad at me. I have to go."

"You don't have to go!" Bonnie shouted at him, wagging a finger in his face for emphasis. "You *want* to go!"

"That's not true. I have to," he argued, his words trailing off as Bonnie ran out of the barn ending the confrontation. Calvin straightened, shaking his head.

Bonnie raced into the house and up the stairs to her room, forgetting that she was home from school early and was supposed to be in hiding. Downstairs, Lizzie and Jessie still sat at the kitchen table eating lunch.

"Who is that going up the stairs?" Lizzie asked Jessie, whose mouth was full of food.

He swallowed hard. "That would be Bonnie," he said, not looking up from his plate.

"Bonnie? What's she doing home at this hour?"

Jessie met her eyes. "Don't be too hard on her, Lizzie," he pleaded. "She got into a fight with the McCallister boy and the teacher sent her home. 'Supposed to be hidin' from ya. I can't see how that would send her flying up those stairs, though."

"Well, if that wasn't the matter, tell me what it'd be then?"

"I'm guessing Calvin just told her he'd be moving home soon."

"Oh." Lizzie softened. "I didn't know he was going to tell her today."

"He's decided to go on home as soon as we finish with the corral."

"Well," Lizzie said, pushing away from the table, "she'll just have to get used to it 's all. He's a grown boy now. He can't stay around just to entertain her." Lizzie tried covering her surprise with her statement of fact.

Calvin, Emma, and Jessie loaded the wagon with all the belongings Calvin had collected during his years with them. Bonnie watched from the upstairs window. She had carefully avoided Calvin since their confrontation in the barn. It had been a quiet week.

"Don't forget your quilt, Calvin," Lizzie called to him. "Did you get it already?"

"Yes, ma'am. I did."

"How about your books out of the room downstairs? Did you get all your books?"

"Yes, ma'am," he repeated.

"Well, okay then," she said, wiping her hands on her apron.

Over the few days leading up to Calvin's move, Lizzie spent her afternoons at the Wade farm, ensuring the place was clean when Calvin moved back. It was one activity Bonnie hadn't had the luxury of boycotting. Lizzie recruited both Bonnie and Emma to help her. At times, Nettie helped, too. In no time, the women had the farm looking the same as it had before—before that awful winter.

"Well, I guess I have to say goodbye to you then," Lizzie said to Calvin.

Calvin forced a smile. "You don't have to say goodbye," he said. "I'm only a stone's throw away."

He would keep the goodbye simple. He knew that was the way Lizzie wanted it.

"I can expect to still come to Sunday dinner. Right?"

"Well, of course, boy," Lizzie replied, "but only after you go to church."

"You don't believe I think you'd let me get away with missing church now, do you?"

"Well, just don't you go getting any bright ideas," she said, using her Irish lilt to hide her pain.

"I won't," Calvin said, leaning down to hug her.

"Thank you for everything," he whispered.

Lizzie allowed him the hug for a moment, then gently nudged him away.

"Oh, get on now," she said. "You have a great deal to do before nightfall."

"Okay, here we go."

Calvin lifted himself up onto the wagon. Jessie gently tossed the reins against the old mule's back, giving a gentle clicking sound. With that, Calvin began his journey home.

As the wagon pulled away, Calvin glanced at Bonnie, who still sat watching from the second story window. He blew her a kiss. She didn't acknowledge it. Instead, she stared in silence as the loaded wagon rolled out of the yard and down the dirt road.

Beyond the glass of her bedroom window, Bonnie sat alone. She felt a tightening in her chest. Her throat felt as though it were swelling shut. *What is this strange feeling?*, she thought. *Am I dying?*

It was an odd feeling. One she wasn't sure she understood. She was sure about one thing; she didn't like it. She was sure she didn't like it at all.

Chapter Three

"It's about time you took yourself a wife."

WEEKS TURNED INTO months. Bonnie never visited, or so Calvin thought. Bonnie found a suitable lookout on a ridge from where she could see the farm, but Calvin couldn't see her. She visited. She watched from the ridge as Calvin plowed the fields his father once plowed. She watched as her best friend grew into a man and grew away from her. Bonnie felt a sadness she had never felt in her short life.

Bonnie took Calvin's move hard. She missed him. As time wore on, she began to visit more in person than from the ridge. She would take food from Lizzie or come by in the evenings after finishing her chores and talk to him while he worked in his tool shed. Even so, it never felt the same as it had when Calvin lived in the same home. There was an uncomfortable space between them, and Bonnie felt like she'd lost her best friend forever.

Months became years, and Calvin did well with his farm. His namesake, Calvin's uncle, had been fortunate enough to stake his claim on some of the richest land to be had near the Caney Fork River near Cove Hollow. Now it was Calvin's, and he had made up his mind long ago that even if his mother and father weren't there to see, he would become one of the best farmers in the state of Tennessee. Now he was doing everything in his power to do just that.

Calvin decided to grow tobacco in addition to his corn, making use of every available piece of land he owned, which was a mighty lot at around four hundred acres. About two hundred and fifty of that four hundred was the best land for farming any man could hope for. He reserved another hundred or so for grazing because it was either too hilly to farm or too stony to plow. The last fifty or so was mostly the woods that comprised the whole of The Dark Forest.

By the time Calvin Wade reached his mid-twenties, he had become a respectable farmer in DeKalb County and had everything any respectable society believed a man could want. Everything, that was, except a wife, someone to take care of him. At least that was how Lizzie saw it. She had made up her mind she was going to tell him that, too. Late one Saturday afternoon, she paid Calvin a visit.

Calvin walked out of the barn just in time to see Lizzie pulling up in the wagon. He wiped axle grease from his hands as he moved to greet her.

"Well," he asked, stepping over to help Lizzie down from the wagon, "to what do I owe this honor?" When Lizzie stood safely on the ground, he hitched the mule to the post in front of the barn.

"Afternoon, Calvin," Lizzie replied. "I brought you more of those pickles you wanted."

"Ah, yes. Lizzie McCaverty's fine, Irish pickles." He laughed.

"Oh, get on with ya now. No such thing as Irish pickles. Let's have some coffee." She smiled as she turned to make the short walk to the house. Calvin instinctively followed. Lizzie enjoyed their afternoon coffee breaks whenever they could find the time to take one.

She sat at the table as Calvin made fresh coffee. He poured a cup for each of them.

"Calvin, I been thinkin'," Lizzie started. She was ready to get to the point.

"Oh, Lord, I'm in trouble now," Calvin teased.

"No, now listen to me. I'm serious about this thing I have to say to ya."

Calvin sat. Lizzie's voice was slipping in and out of the Irish. She caught it herself and supposed that he should know as well as anyone that it meant she was serious.

"I been thinkin', Calvin. You ain't gettin' no younger, ya know?"

"Yes . . . I know," he answered, rubbing the stubble on his chin.

"Well . . . I was a thinkin'. You know it's about time you took yourself a wife."

Calvin's eyes bulged. "A wife!" he barked, standing straight up from his seat at the kitchen table.

"Now, now hear me out," Lizzie added quickly. "Calvin, you need someone to cook and clean. Someone to take care a ya. You know, son, won't be long 'til you'll be in your thirties, then what? Why, you'll be tagged an old bachelor. Won't none of the girls in the county want nothin' to do with ya. You know that. Don't ya?"

He retreated to the kitchen sink, crossing his arms defiantly, tucking a hand under each of them. "Lizzie, I don't want no wife, least not right now."

"Don't go gettin' all upset on me now. I just want you to think about it. You know that girl at church, the Simpson girl? I happen to know she has a fondness for ya," Lizzie said with a sly smile. "Oh, and she's a mighty pretty thing."

Calvin smirked. "Are you trying to play matchmaker, Lizzie McCaverty?"

"No, no. I just know the family. They're a fine family. You couldn't go wrong. Why don't you just ask her to the church picnic?"

"The church picnic? I hadn't planned on going. I have so much to get done. Spring's almost over and—"

"Calvin Wade," Lizzie interrupted, standing from the table, her voice loud and sharp. "Don't you think for one moment I'm going to let you put this farm above the Lord. You'll go to the church picnic, and you'll enjoy it!" she said with emphasis as both hands landed defiantly on each hip.

"Fine," he said, conceding. "I'll ask her to the church picnic if you think I should, but don't go planning my wedding yet. Okay?"

"Good. You'll need to ask her at church tomorrow. She's well liked, and someone else might ask her before you get a chance."

"I'll do it tomorrow."

"Thank ya, dear. You'll not regret it. I'm off now," she said, turning to make her way to the door.

"What about your coffee?" Calvin asked.

"I've got things to do," she yelled back over her shoulder.

"Things like going to visit Mrs. Simpson?" he added in a loud voice as she made her way down the hall.

"Oh, get on back to your workin'," Lizzie called on the way out the door.

Calvin smiled as he picked up the coffee cups. He stood over the sink for a moment thinking about what Lizzie had said. It was true. He did need someone to help him around the farm, although he didn't relish the idea. He'd gotten used to living alone and fairly liked it. He didn't see any need in changing things. If it made Lizzie happy, Calvin would walk to the ends of the earth.

The next day, following the church service, Calvin found enough nerve to walk up to Rosalee Simpson. He then found enough nerve to ask her to the church picnic. Rosalee Simpson accepted.

"Why is Calvin talking to Rosalee Simpson?" Bonnie asked her mother as they climbed into their wagon for the ride home from church.

"Maybe he's askin' her to the church picnic," Lizzie said, smiling.

"The church picnic? I thought he wud'n goin'! Told me he had work to do."

"Well, I guess he changed his mind," Lizzie said. She set her jaw and looked her thirteen-year-old daughter directly in the eye. *Be careful*, that look said.

"Mama, did you make him ask Rosalee to the picnic?"

"Now, Bonnie," her mother warned.

"Mama, how *could* you? He dudn't want to go to no picnic with a girl like her. You made him ask her. Mama, how *could* you?"

Lizzie rolled her eyes. "Now, Bonnie, don't you go sayin' a word to make Calvin feel bad. He has to ask some girls out his own age. It's time Calvin Wade thought about a wife."

"A wife!" Bonnie stood in the back of the wagon. "Calvin can't get married!"

"And why not?" Lizzie said sharply.

Bonnie recognized the last straw in her mother's voice and sat back down. How could she tell her mother he couldn't get married to Rosalee because he had to wait until she was old enough, then *she* would marry him? How could she tell anyone that? It seemed awful dumb if you said it out loud, but to feel it in your heart was another thing entirely. He was eleven years older than her, and most people probably thought of them as brother and sister, but not Bonnie.

How could she let anyone marry him? As Bonnie sat in the back of the wagon on the ride home from church, she realized she'd have to come up with something. The church picnic was only a week away. She would have to think of something—and fast!

After school Monday afternoon, Bonnie ran lickety-split through The Dark Forest to Calvin's farm. Her mother had made her promise not to say anything to Calvin that might get him to change his mind. That didn't leave her with many options to break up his date with Rosalee Simpson, so Bonnie decided to use the indirect approach.

Calvin was riding in from the field on his mule when he saw Bonnie racing down the hill.

"What are you doing here?" Calvin asked. "You look like you haven't even been home since school."

"I haven't. I thought I might come and see if you needed any help today. I could help in the house if you want me to."

Calvin smiled. Bonnie walked along beside the mule as they made their way toward the barn.

"Bonnie Girl, don't you ever get tired of coming around here? I know you have plenty of chores to do at home. If you keep this up, you'll get me in trouble with Lizzie."

"She dudn't mind, Calvin. Long as I get my chores done 'fore dark."

Calvin slid off the mule, leading him into the barn with Bonnie following behind. She threw her schoolbag onto the ground falling right into place alongside Calvin, helping him with the chores. She grabbed the water bucket, drew some water, filling the mule's trough while Calvin pitched hay into the stall.

When they were both engrossed in their chores, Bonnie saw her chance.

"You going to the church picnic with us, Calvin?" she asked without looking up from her work. It's at Cross Roads this month at the Hampton farm.

Calvin smiled. "You know I'm going to the church picnic, and I bet you know who I'm going with, too." He looked up at Bonnie, who now wore a scowl. She couldn't hold back any longer.

"Oh . . . okay. I know sure nuff. You're going with that fat, old Rosalee Simpson girl. Why are you going with her, Calvin? Why don't you just tell Mama you don't want to take her and come with us?"

"I can't, Bonnie. Besides, Rosalee isn't fat, and I want to take her. She's pretty."

Bonnie twisted her nose in disgust. "Ewwww! She's about as pretty as a wart on a frog's nose."

"Bonnie," Calvin warned. His smile had faded.

"Okay, well, maybe she's not that ugly," Bonnie conceded. "I just don't understand why Mama has to go and be so nosy."

Calvin stopped pitching hay. He stood the pitchfork on its prongs, leaning on the handle. "Did you just come over here to try to talk me out of going to the picnic with Rosalee," he asked, "or did you really want to help me?"

Bonnie's face reddened. "Oh, go on to the silly, old picnic with her then. You won't have any fun, and you know it!"

Calvin laid the pitchfork aside, wiping the sweat from his brow. He ushered Bonnie out of the barn, shut the barn door, and started for the house.

"Maybe not, Bonnie Girl," he said. "Maybe not. We'll see."

"I'm going home," Bonnie said with a pout. "And don't tell Mama I came over here, or she'll be mad at me."

Calvin stopped to look at her. His face brightened. "I promise you can have the first dance, okay?"

"Okay," Bonnie conceded, unable to continue to be mad.

Calvin leaned down, kissing her on the cheek. Bonnie glowed. She stretched upward, quickly pecking him back before running for home.

Sunday came. After church, Rosalee rode with Calvin to the Hampton's farm, where the picnic was being held this month. The truth was that Calvin had been looking forward to Sunday. Since he had first summoned the courage to talk to her, he realized that Rosalee was a pretty girl. All week, Calvin thought about her dark skin, her hair, and her deep brown eyes. Now that the picnic was upon him, he could feel his stomach twinge with anticipation.

Rosalee brought a basket with enough food in it to feed an army. They spread out under a shade tree, and Calvin was indeed having a good time.

"Bonnie, why don't you go over and play with the other girls? You've just been sitting here all afternoon," Lizzie said, noticing Bonnie's bad mood was getting increasingly worse.

"I'd be having fun if you wouldn't a forced Calvin into taking Rosalee. I bet he's just bored silly."

Lizzie smiled as she glanced over to where Calvin and Rosalee sat spread out under an immense oak. Rosalee's cheeks were flushed, and Calvin wore a broad smile. He looked anything but bored.

"I think you're wrong, Bonnie. Calvin is enjoying his company very much."

Bonnie's face crinkled unapprovingly, her lower lip shooting forward, pouting at her mother. "He couldn't be enjoying *her* company. Besides, he promised me the first dance."

Just then, the band struck up the music, and couples from every corner of the field drew together on the lawn for the first dance of the afternoon. Bonnie's face lit with the remembrance of Calvin's promise.

"It's time!" she squealed.

Bonnie stood, looking around for Calvin. He was walking in the direction of the other couples with Rosalee's hand in his. Bonnie's face fell.

"He forgot," she whispered. "He forgot his promise."

Lizzie watched her daughter watching Calvin.

"Bonnie," Lizzie said, draping her arm around the girl's shoulder. "Come, girl, let's take a walk." Tears welled in Bonnie's eyes.

"Bonnie, I think it's time you must realize that Calvin is much older than you. He has different wants and different needs than you do. He's probably going to want to marry soon, and you're just going to have to let him go. I know he's always been more than just a brother to you, but eleven years is a big difference. You're just thirteen. He's twenty-four. He's a man, and you're still a girl to him."

Bonnie broke away from her mother's grip. "But I won't always be a girl, Mama," she shouted. "When I'm sixteen, he'll only be twenty-seven. That's not that big a difference."

Lizzie folded her arms. "You have to get that idea out of your head," she said in her stern Irish. "Calvin doesn't feel that way about you, girl. You're like his little sister."

Tears streamed down Bonnie's face. "He's my best friend. How can I let him go?" she asked as she put her hands to her face, beginning to cry from a wound Lizzie could tell came deep from her heart. She wrapped her arms around her daughter.

"Oh, Bonnie, things will change," she said soothingly. "You'll see. In another year, you won't even be thinking about Calvin. I promise. It's all part of growing up."

"I'll never be able to let him go, Mama. Never!" Bonnie cried out as she broke away from her mother running away to be alone. Lizzie let her go, figuring it would be best to let her be for a while. A girl with a broken heart needed some time to herself.

Spring came and went. With most of the planting done, Calvin and Rosalee spent the entire summer together. She brought his lunch to him in the middle of the day as Bonnie watched from her perch on the ridge high above unnoticed by anyone.

Bonnie's regular visits with Calvin became less frequent. When she did visit him, he seemed different, distant and preoccupied.

On one of those extraordinary Saturday afternoons when the temperature was just perfect, the air was thick with promise, and everything was right with the world, Calvin rode up to the McCaverty farm on his old mule. Bonnie and Emma were on the front porch stringing beans with Lizzie when they saw Calvin riding toward the house.

"Well, hello stranger," Lizzie said, accepting her usual kiss on the cheek from Calvin. "You seem to be keeping yourself busy lately." She grinned at him, continuing to snap the beans into the big bowl lying in her lap.

Calvin returned her grin, looking at his feet. "Yeah, I guess I have," he replied. "Listen, I came by to talk to you about . . . something." He glanced at the two girls, and Lizzie took the hint.

"Girls, go inside and start those beans," Lizzie instructed.

Bonnie started to object. "Mama," she said.

"Bonnie, do as you're told." Lizzie had a feeling she knew what Calvin was going to tell her, and she didn't want Bonnie hearing it straight from the horse's mouth like this.

The girls shuffled inside. Lizzie listened, waiting until she heard Emma dragging her younger sister away from the door and into the kitchen.

"Now," she said to Calvin, "what did you want to talk to me about?"

Calvin sat in front of Lizzie taking the bowl from her lap. He held her hands in his.

"Lizzie, I've never thanked you for taking me in like you did when my parents died," he said to her.

"Oh, get on . . ." Lizzie tried to interrupt.

"No, hear me out, okay?" Calvin said. "You've been my mother for near thirteen years now and, well, I just felt like you should be the first person I tell."

Lizzie's eyes widened. She had been right. He had come to tell her he was getting married. "Should tell what, boy?"

"I've asked Rosalee to marry me," he said with a wicked grin.

Lizzie leaned forward from her rocker hugging him tightly. "Oh! Glory be!" she exclaimed. "I knew you'd get along. I just knew it!"

Calvin beamed at her happiness, but his face turned sullen.

"I do have one thing I want to ask you, though," he said, walking to the end of the porch. Lizzie stood taking a place beside him.

"What is it, son?"

"Well, I'm . . . well, this may sound strange considering I just told you I asked Rosalee to marry me, but . . ." He paused, pursing his lips. "But, I'm not sure I'm in love with her, Lizzie.

"I mean, don't get me wrong," Calvin continued. "She's a beautiful girl and, well, I know I love her, but it doesn't feel like the same kind of thing my parents had. I mean, I can remember how my parents acted toward each other, and I'm not sure if it would be right if I married her, you know, knowing I don't fully love her like that.

"Oh . . . I don't know," he added, shoving his hands into his pockets. "Maybe I do love her more than I know. I guess I've just never been in love before."

"Calvin," Lizzie said, turning him around to face her. "What your parents had comes from years and years of being together, side by side through the thick and the thin of it. No one said love has to be instant. Most of the time, people grow into it. If you have a mutual respect for one another, the rest will fall into place. I promise." She laid a reassuring hand to his cheek. Calvin put his own hand over hers.

"Okay," he said, looking embarrassed. "I feel better now that I've got that off my chest."

Lizzie smiled at him. "You'll be fine. Oh, I'm so happy for you," she said, standing on her tiptoes giving him a quick peck on the cheek. "We've got so much to do! When's the wedding?"

"Not until next spring, maybe April or May."

"That gives us plenty of time."

Calvin cleared his throat. "Lizzie, what about Bonnie?" he asked.

"I know she's protective, and I'm not sure how she'll take it. She hasn't been too keen on Rosalee so far."

"I know," Lizzie replied. "It's something she'll have to deal with, Calvin. Everyone has to grow up. She'll be okay. You let me take care of Bonnie. You just be happy. Have you told Jessie yet?"

"No, just you."

"Well, get on with you then. He'll be happy to hear."

"Thank you," Calvin said. He kissed her on the cheek again and descended the steps.

Lifting the bowl of beans from her chair, Lizzie stood for a moment, allowing a proud smile to linger on her face. As she entered the kitchen, Lizzie caught Bonnie's glance as she set the bowl on the table. Before she could mask her smile and explain things to Bonnie, she ran for the back door.

"Bonnie," Lizzie started, but she never got the chance to explain. Her youngest daughter had, no doubt, run off somewhere to lick her wounds.

When she finally returned to the farm late that evening, Bonnie vowed to her mother that she would never speak to Calvin again.

Lizzie, however, was certain that would pass, too.

Winter settled in on the Plateau. The McCavertys didn't see much of Calvin. He and Rosalee were busy making arrangements for their wedding.

Lizzie spent a great deal of time at the Simpson farm, helping to plan the nuptials. She and Mrs. Simpson got along well and were naturals at the detail work. At times, Lizzie would think about Sarah. She could imagine the two of them together, planning a wedding for Calvin. Now, she alone would stand as Calvin's mother as she had done for so many years. It had been so long, it was difficult to imagine life without Calvin. He was as much a son to her as any of her girls were daughters. Even though Calvin wasn't Lizzie's blood, the pride she felt for him was just as strong as Sarah's would have been.

Bonnie's fourteenth birthday came that February of 1927. Calvin showed up to present her with a riding blanket. He said she would need it for the gift she was going to receive from her parents. The entire family led Bonnie outside to the barn where a small chestnut horse stood in the corral waiting for her. Jessie had decided to buy it for her at the same time he and Calvin went to Lebanon to buy a new pair of horses for spring plowing. The small horse had been stashed away in Calvin's barn for over a week.

The spunky chestnut wore a ribbon between his ears, which he didn't seem to care for much. He tossed his head up and down, trying to loosen it.

"Look, he's trying to talk to me," Bonnie said, delighted. She named him Danny and, shortly after that, seemed to return to the Bonnie they all knew and loved.

Bonnie even began to visit Calvin again. Every now and then, she would ride by on the ridge top and wave to him down in the valley. What Calvin didn't knowl was that sometimes Bonnie would sit in the cold on her perch, tucked away on the ridge that ran between the two farms, and watch him in silence. She knew that marrying Calvin was impossible, but no one could take her dreams away. Not even a wife.

Calvin and Rosalee rode to church together every Sunday now. He would drive out and pick her up early. They always took the long way to church and the long way home.

The wedding was scheduled for April, and March was upon them in no time. As Rosalee grew more excited, Calvin seemed to grow more apprehensive as they prepared for their wedded bliss.

On the way home from church one particularly warm day toward the end of March, the two of them stopped for a picnic. Out of nowhere, a sudden spring shower blew up over the plateau, pressing itself against the hills that surrounded the valley. The previously clear sky blackened with thick, rolling clouds, threatening more than just a light rain. Calvin glanced at the sky, the smell of rain wafting in the early spring breeze.

Heeding the warning, Calvin urged Rosalee as they hastily gathering the remnants of their picnic to begin the long descent down the already muddy country road that led to the Simpson's farm.

The patters of light rain rapidly became spears dropping violently from thick clouds. Calvin's new horses grew increasingly more frightened by the thunder and lightning crashing around them. Calvin became alarmed and decided they had better wait out the storm. The roads in and out of the hollows in that part of DeKalb County were steep and treacherous at times, so he pulled the team over to the side of the dirt road, stepping down to help Rosalee out of the wagon.

Wind whipped the remnants of last year's leaves in furious circles upward toward the darkening sky. As he stepped down out of the wagon, Calvin grabbed his hat, pushing it heartily down on his head. He then made his way around the horses, trying to calm them. The next thing he heard was the boom of thunder as the air was suddenly charged with electricity. A flash of light filled the air around them followed immediately by the crack of splitting wood. The next thing he felt was the frame of the wagon jerking away from his grip as the horses bolted from the thunderous explosion.

Calvin reached out for Rosalee's hand as she turned to reach for him. The only thing he gripped was thin air. The sound of her screams as she turned to him in terror was barely audible through the confusion. Calvin ran as hard as he could to catch the wagon, Rosalee reaching out for him screaming for help. The wagon raced away too fast. All Calvin could do was watch in horror as it slammed against the side of the hill that flanked the road and overturned. When the horses finally slowed to a halt, the wagon was a twisted, busted up pile of lumber. Rosalee lay pinned underneath.

Calvin stopped dead in the middle of the country road, the pelting rain trying to force his steps backward. He played back the last few minutes through his mind. What had just happened?

"Rosalee! Rosalee!" Calvin yelled to her as he frantically raced around the wagon, trying to figure out a way to get it off her.

"Oh, God. Oh, my God! Rosalee!" The rain beat down even

harder, filling the brim of his hat. It rolled off in streams whenever he looked down.

He stood unhitching the team, which were spooked and not easy to handle. He quickly tied the lead onto the side of the wagon and made the horses pull until what was left of the wagon stood upright, then he ran back to where Rosalee lay.

He stood over Rosalee's muddy, tangled body falling to his knees beside her. Rain mixed with his tears, forming ruddy streaks down his face. He knew Rosalee was dead. Slowly, he lifted her limp body and walked the rest of the way to her home. Death had visited Calvin Wade once again.

CHAPTER FOUR

"I'd do the same for him as I would if it were one of you."

C ALVIN RETREATED FROM everyone after Rosalee's death. Jessie hired two hands to plow the fields for him, ensuring he get his crops in before it was too late.

Meanwhile, he drank, trying to forget. He sat for hours drinking himself to sleep. When he did sleep, he would wake covered in sweat. The look on Rosalee's face as she reached out for him, the wagon tumbling over and over until she was underneath, playing across the screen of his mind every night, searing into his memory. The only time he ever left the farm was to make a trip into the hills to fetch a jug of corn whiskey, the only thing that gave him any relief.

Bonnie had her own demons to face. Guilt consumed her. She had wished that Rosalee would die, and her wish had come true. Now she felt horrible, mean, and ugly. She pleaded with God to forgive her, but couldn't feel the burden lift from her soul. She wanted to run to Calvin and help him, but because she had wished this to happen, Bonnie couldn't even think about Calvin without feeling an overwhelming sense of shame.

Lizzie, by contrast, mourned for Calvin. Three times she had watched death come to him. Three times she stood by watching him grieve.

They say everything comes in threes, she thought, so maybe it was over for him now.

Lizzie did everything she could to comfort him at first. Only after he didn't respond did she realize that coming out of his mourning was something that would have to happen when *he* wanted it to happen. All she could do for him was take care of him, wait, and pray.

One Sunday afternoon, almost a month after the accident, Lizzie sent Bonnie over to the farm with food for Calvin.

"Mama, don't make me go," she begged.

"And why not? Only a short time ago you couldn't stay away from him."

"I just can't, Mama. You take it. I'll do something for you here, okay?"

"What is it, girl? What's got you so scared to go around Calvin?"

Bonnie's body began to tremble, tears welling in her eyes. "I can't go! Please don't make me!"

"All right, Bonnie. What is it?" Lizzie said, motioning for her daughter to sit at the kitchen table.

"I wished it to happen," Bonnie admitted. "It's all my fault. I didn't want her to have Calvin. I wished something would happen, and now Rosalee's dead.

I didn't mean it. I didn't!" she said, burying her face in her hands.

Lizzie put her arms around her youngest daughter. "Bonnie. You didn't cause this to happen," she said. "It wasn't your fault. I know you didn't particularly like Rosalee, but I know you wouldn't wish something like that on anyone. It's not your fault.

"Bonnie, look at me, girl."

Bonnie lifted her tear-stained face to look at her mother. Lizzie pulled away strands of hair that stuck to her tears. "Calvin needs us. He needs the people who love him to be around him as much as possible. He's in a place where none of us have ever been before, a desolate place. I, for one, don't want him to stay there. I want him back. The only way to do that is to pray for him, love him and help life to go on around him until he decides to join us again.

"I know how you feel about Calvin, but now is the time for us to put all our feelings aside and do for Calvin what Calvin can't do for himself.

"So," she said, standing, "you'll take this over to Calvin, and you'll clean for him if you have to. You'll wash for him if you have to. He's part of this family. I'd do the same for him as I would if for one of you. Do you understand?"

Bonnie surrendered, dropping her hands from her face, and sighed. "Yes, ma'am," she answered quietly.

"It's not a pretty sight there," Lizzie said. "Don't expect to see the same Calvin we've always known. He doesn't even talk the same. He's got a bit of a mean tongue on him these days, but don't pay him no mind. It's just the bitterness talking. Just do what you have to do and come on back."

"Okay," Bonnie said as she stood, grudgingly lifting the basket off the table.

Outside, Bonnie saddled Danny and rode over to Calvin's farm with the basket precariously balanced across Danny's neck. She rode slowly through The Dark Forest, occasionally craning her neck to scan the forest around her. The McCallister boy's coon dogs bayed in the distance.

"Those boys are huntin' on Calvin's land again," she muttered, "and him not able to run them off." She kicked Danny's pace up a bit, making a mental note to tell her father about the dogs when she returned home.

Bonnie managed to dismount Danny with Lizzie's basket in one hand. She eyed Calvin's house warily. It was a beautiful spring day in Dekalb County, but not for Calvin. Bonnie knew somewhere in that house, he sat alone and unhappy. The thought made her heart squeeze tightly in her chest.

She knocked. Once. Twice.

There was no answer.

She peered through the lace curtains and didn't see anyone, so she went around back to the kitchen door. She called to Calvin several times but received no answer. Finally, she pushed the kitchen door open and went inside.

Bonnie laid the basket on the table and began to empty its contents.

The kitchen was a mess. Remembering her conversation with Lizzie, she started to clean. Just as she looked into the stove to see if there was a fire, Calvin entered the room.

Startled at the sight of him, Bonnie quickly recovered and straightened to face him. A full beard hung from his face, his clothes hung ragged from head to toe. He had also lost a good bit of weight. His eyes and cheeks were hollow and discolored. His overalls hung loosely on his body.

"What are you doing here?" he mumbled almost as if he didn't have energy to even speak.

"I brought you some food," she answered softly.

"I don't want no food," Calvin said. It sounded distant rather than mean. "Go back home, Bonnie. I don't want no company."

"Nonsense," Bonnie replied. "Everybody has to eat. Calvin, this stove hasn't been used for a while. I need some wood. Go outside and . . ."

Suddenly, Calvin thrust forward, lightning fast in contrast to his initial heaviness upon entering the room raking his giant right arm across the kitchen table, knocking most of the food onto the floor in one fell swoop.

"I told you I don't want any food!" he screamed at her. His face became bright red, his eyes steel blue burning coals of fire. He glared at her like a crazy animal standing between her and the kitchen door.

Bonnie dropped the pan she was holding, slinking back against the sink. She folded her hands under her chin, holding her arms close to her chest, making herself small.

Calvin spread his hands out on the table leaning over it. His breath came in hard gusts. His eyes were fixed on Bonnie. For a moment, she feared he might climb over the table, clawing at it like a wild dog, then just as suddenly as the rage had come, it was gone. Something inside him seemed to break. He pulled his body away from the table, his big arms falling at his sides as if some great weight were pressing them down.

"I don't want any food," he said softly, averting his eyes from her trembling frame. "I just want to be left alone."

Bonnie's paralysis broke. She knelt and began picking up the food piece by piece that was strewn across the floor. She retrieved the jars he hadn't broken and set them back on the table.

"Bonnie . . . Bonnie," Calvin repeated tiredly. "Bonnie, go home. You got no business here."

Bonnie stood, looking defiantly at Calvin. Her jaw was set, her eyes unyielding. "I need some firewood," she ordered through clenched teeth, slamming a jar down onto the table, glaring at him. He opened his mouth to argue, and she cut him off. "If you don't go get some firewood, I'll have to get it myself. I ain't goin'a like it if I have to, Calvin Wade!"

Calvin stared at her a moment longer, but Bonnie didn't flinch. He grumbled under his breath as he stumbled outside to bring Bonnie the wood she insisted upon.

He let the wood fall slowly out of his arms, clunking onto the floor beside the stove, then walked out of the kitchen and upstairs to his bedroom. Bonnie heard the door slam. She knew he'd gone back to his bottle.

When he finally left, the tears she held during the ordeal began spilling out. She cried softly to herself so that Calvin wouldn't hear. She cried for the man locked away upstairs, the man she had loved all of her life. She knew there was nothing she could do to ease his pain, nothing she could do to help. She knew he felt responsible for what had happened to Rosalee. She also knew Calvin well enough to know that he would never forgive himself.

Bonnie made a fresh pot of coffee and left it on the stove. She made a plate from the food she could salvage after Calvin's display of anger, and left it on the table. She knew better than to go upstairs, so she left the meal there for him for whenever he decided to come down and eat. Mentally, she prepared a list of things she needed to bring on her next visit. She also made a mental note to get there earlier, hoping she could avert this version of Calvin, the one who had been drinking all day.

Bonnie and Danny cantered toward home through The Dark Forest. Night was falling fast, and there was no moon. The foreboding

Dark Forest became ever more so as darkness settled in. Bonnie was anxious to get home.

Once there, she told her mother how Calvin had reacted to her presence there. She agreed with Bonnie that, no matter his reaction, he needed their help and care until he could once again take care of himself. It was then that Bonnie finally began to deal with her guilt.

Before school the next morning, Bonnie rode to Calvin's, made a pot of coffee, and cooked breakfast for him. She saw no sign of him. Just as the night before, Bonnie left the food on the table for him. She hoped it wouldn't be waiting there like the one she left the night before was.

From then on, Bonnie and Lizzie took turns visiting the Wade farm to cook for Calvin. Most of the time, the previous meal would still be sitting on the table, untouched. Other times, they would find themselves tasked with cleaning up the mess after he had flung the food against the wall.

Lizzie did manage to get him to take a bath one day. He also let her shave him. Bonnie helped Buttermilk and Shorty, the two hands Jessie had hired to plow and plant for Calvin. She knew that farm as well as Calvin did. She knew what he planted and where and when. She relayed all that information to the men and, teenage girl or not, they readily followed her orders.

The two horses that had been pulling the wagon on the day Rosalee died had become great plow horses. In his grief, Calvin had wanted to shoot them, but Jessie stopped him. Together, Bonnie, the horses, and the farm hands, had Calvin's corn and tobacco planted just in time.

Summer finally came. School was over. Bonnie's visits to Calvin's home became more frequent. Each morning she would clean and make breakfast, then go back home and do her chores. She would return to Calvin's in the evening to fix his supper. Since Rosalee's death, Bonnie seemed to lose her selfish nature. Over time, her guilt slowly gave way to concern for people other than herself, a sure mark she was growing into a young lady.

Bonnie was also growing in ways other than helping out at Calvin's. She began to play the piano at church. She had learned the instrument from Pinkie McCaverty, Jessie's mother. Pinkie had continued to teach Bonnie, right up until her death. As a result, Bonnie could play piano better at seven than most people at twenty-seven. The Reverend and Mrs. Parker were glad of that, too. Since Mrs. Lewis took arthritis and could no longer play, they hadn't had a piano player.

Calvin was still drinking three months after Rosalee's death. One evening, he stumbled downstairs in a particularly drunken rage as Bonnie stood cooking bacon and quietly singing her favorite song.

"As I get to the end of the meadow I'll see, a big fine white house for my Bonnie and me . . ."

"Stop," Calvin yelled. His speech was slurred, but nonetheless reverberated against the walls of the kitchen.

Startled from the harshness of his voice, Bonnie's body cringed from the sound, but managed not to turn around. Instead, she kept cooking in silence.

Calvin fumbled his way to the table and sat down. "I don't want you here," he said. "Please get out." His previous outburst seemed to have depleted his drunken body of any remaining energy to argue further.

"You have to eat," Bonnie replied. "I made some coffee and—"

Calvin's fist came down hard on the table. "I DON'T WANT YOU HERE!" he yelled. "Can't you understand that? I don't want you here! I want you TO LEAVE!"

Bonnie turned around to face him. "I'm not going to leave," she said defiantly.

Calvin's bloodshot eyes widened. "Yes, you are! Yes, you are!" He stood quickly, moving toward her, grabbing her arm with his right hand pulling her toward the door. Bonnie's eyes grew wide with fright. He yanked open the kitchen door with his left hand shoving her little body through the opening. Bonnie stumbled out the door, tripping over her skirt, and slid across the ground.

Calvin stood silhouetted against the light from the lamp that shone around him from inside the door. He breathed hard, his eyes glazed over with confusion. When the result of his actions made their way to his fuzzy brain, he moved toward Bonnie. She turned around on the ground to face him and held up her hand, halting him from moving any closer.

"Bonnie," he said hoarsely. "Bonnie, I'm sorry . . ." he said, stepping toward her again. She backed away from him in the dirt on all fours.

"Stay away from me!" she screamed, not because she was hurt from the fall, but because of his meanness. Calvin stretched out his arms, offering to help her to her feet. She scoffed at him scrambling to her feet on her own. She stood brushing herself off with bruised hands. Her long hair shook loose from its pins, falling across her face, sticking to the dirt and tears there. She brushed the loose strands away with the back of her dirty hand.

"You want me to leave?" she screamed at him. "Fine! I'll leave. You pig-headed, mean old . . . I hate you!" she said, stomping her foot. "All you do is lie around and feel sorry for yourself. Go ahead and die if you want to! Drink yourself to death. I don't care!

"You think no one cares about you?" she cried. "Well, I'm tired, you hear me, tired of coming over here every day, cooking for you and trying to help. I'll never come back!"

It was almost as if her anger split him wide open. Bonnie watched as Calvin grabbed his chest knowing the pain from the realization of what he had done had hit him. He fell to his knees in the yard, his hands covering his face. Bonnie knew he was ashamed. She knew he would never have done this horrible thing to her had the liquor not clouded his mind. She watched as the pain and shock became evident on his face. He had never intentionally harmed anyone, until now.

He bent over in the dirt and began to sob. Softly at first, then the pain that began to pour from inside him made his body wrench violently. He looked up at Bonnie, tears streaming down his face and neck.

"Bonnie," he pleaded. "Please forgive me. I'm so sorry." He doubled over, clenching at his heart.

Bonnie stared at him. Finally, the chaos inside him had reached its boiling point. Maybe now he would get it all out, maybe the demons would leave him forever. She moved toward him, quietly. He felt her skirt brush against his face. He reached out for her hands. Bonnie helped him stand. Calvin looked at her, his eyes, hollow and bruised. With trembling fingers, he brushed the stray hairs away from her face.

"I didn't mean to hurt you, Bonnie Girl," he said, his voice quivering. "Please forgive me." He cried softly, wrapping his arms around his little friend. They stood in the evening breeze holding onto one another as Calvin cried the tears he had held inside for so long.

When the crying finally subsided, Bonnie led Calvin back inside and sat him down at the kitchen table. She poured him a cup of coffee, then went to the sink and began to wash up from her fall. She sat with him for a long time in the quietness of the kitchen, then helped him upstairs and put him to bed. As soon as he was asleep, Bonnie mounted Danny and rode home.

When she returned the next morning, she was surprised to find that Calvin was clean, shaven, and standing outside talking to Buttermilk and Shorty. She saw them from her spot on the ridge and waved. With great excitement, she rushed Danny down the path.

Today, Bonnie thought, would be a good day.

She spent the entire day at Calvin's. He didn't stay outside long. He was weak and malnourished from replacing his meals with alcohol. He went inside to take a nap after lunch while Bonnie helped Buttermilk and Shorty with the garden.

Calvin's healing finally began.

Bonnie and Calvin spent a great deal of time together the rest of the summer. Bonnie took it upon herself to nurse Calvin back to health, but she had to be patient. Sometimes he would slip into a bad mood, and Bonnie would struggle to pull him out of it. One step at a time, though, Calvin began to rejoin the living.

The spring following Bonnie's fifteenth birthday was the anniversary of Rosalee's death. Not unexpectedly, Calvin withdrew from everyone for a short while. Bonnie was fearful at first, but relieved when he didn't resume drinking. Although a year had gone by, Bonnie knew why he still couldn't force himself to go to church. The thought of facing Rosalee's parents was too much for him.

CHAPTER FIVE

"It's a deal with the devil you're making, and it ain't no good!"

⁂

TIME FLEW BY during Calvin's recovery. The hands Jessie had hired to help with the planting stayed on, and Calvin's farm produced better than ever. Calvin planted more tobacco than corn, and it wasn't long before Buttermilk and Shorty were asking their benevolent boss, Mr. Wade, to hire more help. He did, and the Wade farm slowly came back to life.

Emma got married that year. Nettie had another baby. That left Bonnie as the only girl at home, and she was enjoying every minute of it.

Before anyone realized it, Bonnie turned seventeen, and Jessie and Lizzie were faced with the sudden realization that it wouldn't be long before they would find themselves all alone in their house. At least not if Bonnie followed the same path her older sisters had forged. Bonnie, however, hadn't dated a single boy. Even though she had lost her tomboyish ways, she was every bit as independent as before. Lizzie liked to say that she was just like Pinkie McCaverty, Jessie's mother—smart and witty, yet gently beautiful. How could this little town ever present Bonnie with anything big enough to keep her attention?

Had they asked her, Bonnie might have pointed out that the only man who had ever kept her attention was Calvin Wade. They went on picnics, often wading the cool streams of the Caney Fork. Sometimes they would go fishing and sit for hours, never saying a word. The bond between them had strengthened again, and Bonnie found herself hoping and praying that it would last forever.

In 1930, shortly after the stock market crashed, the land began to dry up. Boll weevil infestation devastated cotton crops. Depression and drought began to beset farmers across America, and just as with the influenza epidemic, Tennessee was not immune. Crops withered in the ground; cattle were unable to feed. Many people lost their homes.

At the Wade and McCaverty farms, everyone pulled double shifts. Although Calvin sent his extra help over to help Jessie and Lizzie, it seemed as though the work was never-ending. Lizzie and Bonnie had even more to do now that Emma was gone.

Bonnie wasn't able to see Calvin as much as she had in the spring. She found herself becoming impatient for the fall when the growing and harvesting would be done, and she could relax a little. She had finished her schooling and was looking forward to spending more time with Calvin. Finally, her dream of becoming his wife seemed to be more possibility than fantasy, even amid the chaos of the beginning of the new decade.

One crisp fall evening, after all the work was done for the day, Bonnie informed Lizzie that she was going to ride over to Calvin's. As she rode Danny down the footpath into The Dark Forest, Lizzie and Jessie sat on the front porch enjoying the cool, evening air.

"I don't know," Jessie said. "I don't see much good coming out of their relationship. She's only eighteen, and Calvin's almost twenty-nine. She's still a girl, for God's sake."

Lizzie sat in her rocking chair knitting a sweater for Nettie's baby.

"A girl? Where have you been, Jessie McCaverty? Bonnie's anything but a girl."

Jessie chuckled humorlessly. "I don't know. I don't think Calvin will ever think of Bonnie as anything but his little sister."

"Well, I think you're wrong," Lizzie replied. "There's something deep there, Jessie. Deeper than I think we both realize."

"Deeper than we realize and deeper than Calvin realizes," Jessie shot back. "He just doesn't know how Bonnie feels. I believe he thinks she's over him, and they're just good friends now. I really do."

Lizzie settled back in her rocker. "Well, I hope for Bonnie's sake you're wrong."

"Me, too, Lizzie. Me, too," Jessie said shaking his head.

Bonnie and Danny took their time traveling through The Dark Forest enjoying the fall colors and the cool, crisp air. Danny's reins lay on his neck. Bonnie sang to the trees:

> *As I get to the edge of the meadow, I'll see,*
> *A big, fine white house for my Calvin and me.*
> *We'll sit on the front porch and watch the sun set.*
> *A fine time we'll have that we'll never forget.*

> *We'll have ten fine children and all with red hair,*
> *To match with their mother's so bright and so fair.*
> *We'll sit on the rooftop and watch the moon glow.*
> *As me and my Calvin together grow old.*

She smiled to herself as she finished the song. As soon as her last note faded away into the hollows, she heard another sound, baying hounds, and they were close.

"Those McCallister boys!" she whispered. "They're down here huntin' again! I'll just have to tell Calvin." She grabbed for Danny's reins, but before she could reach them, a gunshot reverberated through the dense forest. Danny bolted at the sound. Bonnie, unable to grasp the reins, grabbed a handful of mane instead.

The next thing she knew, Bonnie was lying flat on her back in the middle of The Dark Forest. Danny continued at a gallop down the familiar trail. Bonnie could only listen as the hoof beats faded away into the darkness.

As soon as she was able to gather a thought, she began trying to move her body. She tried to lift her head and found she couldn't. Carefully, she tried to move her arm, bending it at the elbow finding that she was able to do so. She stretched the arm toward her right side, gently touching the spot where she felt a strange burning. When she brought that hand up to her face, she saw it covered in blood.

Bonnie now realized she was bleeding badly. She could feel the warmth soaking her clothes and sticking to her skin. She tried to move and couldn't. She could only stare upward at the tops of the trees that surrounded her. Her head began to spin, her eyes blurring the dark shapes overhead.

"My God," she whispered to herself. "I've been shot!"

She cried out first for Danny, then for Calvin, but was too far away from either farm to be heard.

The Dark Forest quickly became just that, dark and terribly so. As familiar as Bonnie was with the trail and as often as she had played there as a girl she still never liked to go through it at night. It could have been because of the stories Calvin used to tell her when she was young about the headless horseman, or the one about the witch that lived up on Beaver Ridge that would come down into the valleys at night looking for prey.

Bonnie's body began to shake uncontrollably. She couldn't tell whether she shook from fear or from the cold, but she couldn't control it.

"Calvin . . ." Bonnie tried to scream, but the pain in her side wouldn't allow it. She placed her hand firmly on her waist where most of the blood was leaking out. With her other hand, she grabbed the upturned root of an ancient tree, trying to pull herself to her feet. Sharp pain struck her midsection like a branding iron. She screamed into the night air. It was a sound she had never heard before, and somewhere in her mind, she realized it was coming from her.

"Oh . . ." Bonnie cried, faltering against the root and sliding back to the ground. "Mama . . . Daddy," she whispered, tears rolling down her face. She laid her head on the dried carpet of fallen leaves below her.

"Daddy, come help me. I don't want to die . . ." Her voice dropped to a whisper. "Someone please come and help me . . . Calvin?

"Calvin . . . you didn't save your first dance for me."

As night fell in The Dark Forest, Bonnie's body relaxed as she slipped into the quiet dark of unconsciousness.

Danny's right side was bleeding, and he was limping a bit when he arrived at Calvin's farm. As usual, he went first to the spot at the top of the ridge where his rider often sat peering down at the farm below. Weak and hungry, he paused only for a moment, then headed down the path to Calvin's barn.

A spectacular autumn evening had settled itself on the Wade farm. The sky shone a pale yellow through low, overhanging clouds as they cast a lazy warmth over the valley. Buttermilk and Shorty were just coming in from an evening of fishing down at the Caney Fork. Calvin stood in the tool shed, sharpening and oiling his tools as he always did this time of year. It was a peaceful night on the Wade farm . . . at least for the moment.

Buttermilk and Shorty washed up after cleaning their catch, then planted themselves outside their little house to enjoy the beautiful weather. Buttermilk was first to see Danny limping down the hill. In the twilight, he thought it might be a wounded deer. He stood carefully monitoring it quietly until he recognized Danny's form. He yelled for Calvin.

"Mr. Wade, come out 'chere. Miss Bonnie's horse comin' down the hill," he yelled. "What you reckon that horse doin' comin' over here so late, Shorty?"

"I dunno," Shorty answered, pushing his chair forward off the two legs that held it up as he leaned against the house. The clank it made against the wood of the porch startled the little horse. It stopped in its tracks.

Calvin walked out of the shed bringing his lantern with him. "What'd you say, Buttermilk?"

"Lookee there comin'. It's Miss Bonnie's horse," he said again.

Calvin held the lamp low so that his eyes could adjust to the darkness. When his pupils finally focused on what was in front of him, he saw Danny limping toward the barn to meet him. Danny stopped directly in front of Calvin, his head hanging low from his long neck. Calvin set his lantern down. Behind him, Buttermilk and Shorty were making their way across the yard.

"What you doin' here, boy? You step on a rock or something?" Calvin asked the little horse as he made his way around to the side he was favoring. As he stooped under Danny's neck to take a look at his other side, Calvin saw blood dripping from the small holes made by the buckshot.

"He's been shot!" Calvin heard himself say. "Danny's been shot!" he said again, this time with urgency.

Buttermilk and Shorty's last few paces to Calvin's side were at a run.

"He's been shot!" Calvin shouted again. He raised his head toward the cliff and shouted, "Bonnie!"

There was no answer.

"He's saddled. Bonnie must've been on him! Oh God . . ." Calvin whispered, the blood draining from his face.

He left the horse with his men and tore out for the barn. He bridled the faster of his two plow horses and, in a matter of seconds, shot out of the barn toward Buttermilk and Shorty.

"Take care of Danny," he said to them. "One of you ride over to the McCavertys' and tell them what's happened."

"Yes, sir, Mr. Wade," Buttermilk answered, nodding, but Calvin never heard him. When Buttermilk looked up from under the brim of his hat, Calvin was almost to the top of the ridge as his old plow horse was pushing and sweating his way to the top, giving Calvin way beyond what a normal day's work asked of him. It was almost as if he knew the importance of getting to the top.

Calvin inched slowly down the path toward The Dark Forest looking for any sign of Bonnie in the increasing darkness among the crinkling thickness of the forest floor.

"Bonnie!" Calvin yelled. "Bonnie!"

He rode into the dark tunnel. It quickly became too dark to see, and he worried that he might miss something from his position atop the horse. He dismounted and led the animal instead. Just as he was about to lose hope, he saw her. Bonnie lay still on the ground among the dried leaves. He dropped the horse's reins and ran to her side.

"Bonnie!" he screamed when he saw the dark colored liquid on her hands. A large puddle had pooled on the dry leaves at her side. Even in the darkness, her skin appeared ghostly white.

"Calvin . . ." Bonnie whispered. "Calvin."

"Don't talk, Bonnie Girl," Calvin said, lifting her out of the leaves. She was still alive. He felt some sense of relief mixed with his panic. Bonnie screamed in pain with the movement of her body. Calvin held her steadfast, stepping carefully over the soft crunch of dried leaves against the earth to where his horse stood waiting.

Calvin managed to pull himself up onto his horse with Bonnie's limp body grasped tightly in his arms. He adjusted her carefully as he steadied himself in the saddle. She cried out once more, then slipped back into her delirium. Calvin kicked the horse into a fast walk mindful of her pain, riding quickly for the McCaverty farm. Every now and then, Bonnie spoke in whispers. Calvin couldn't make out what she was saying and pulled her closer. He propped her head gently on his shoulder, her face buried in his neck.

"Calvin?" she whispered faintly.

"What is it, Bonnie?" he answered.

"Calvin, could we dance now? You broke your promise to me. You didn't save your first dance for me." She faded away again.

Tears welled in Calvin's eyes. The memory of he and Rosalee gathering together for the first dance, with Bonnie looking on waiting with anticipation played across this mind. He hadn't remembered his promise, hadn't known he'd forgotten until that moment. His heart suddenly ached, as if strained by the memory. He winced at how that broken promise must have hurt her.

"Bonnie," he said. "Stay with me, girl. Everything will be okay."

Shorty had taken the road instead of the trail through The Dark Forest and relayed Calvin's message to the McCavertys. Jessie met Calvin and Bonnie on the trail.

"She's been shot," Calvin told him as he rode up next to them.

"Dear God," Jessie said. His mouth was drawn, and his eyes stared unbelievingly at his youngest daughter's limp body. "I'll ride for the doctor." He snapped the reins, and his old mule leaped into a gallop.

"I'll get her home," Calvin shouted after him.

Jessie turned and rode like the wind for town.

Lizzie and Shorty were waiting on the porch as Calvin rode up with Bonnie. Lizzie gasped, placing her hands over her mouth at the sight of her daughter pale white and covered in blood. "Oh, dear Lord! Bring her inside. Oh dear Lord, how could this have happened?"

"I don't know," Calvin answered. "I heard some shots earlier tonight. Probably just the McCallister boys. Then, I saw Danny coming out of the trail, and I thought . . ." he stopped mid-sentence. "I . . . I thought he was a deer. As drunk as those boys stay, they could have mistaken Danny for a deer," Calvin spoke to himself, piecing the puzzle together as he climbed the stairs.

"Take Bonnie to her room," Lizzie instructed. Following on Calvin's heels, she folded her hands in prayer.

Calvin carefully laid Bonnie on her bed. Lizzie came right behind him with a pair of shears and began cutting her blood-soaked dress away from her body.

"Calvin, get the fire hot on the stove," Lizzie said. "I need hot water as soon as possible."

There was no response.

"Calvin!" she shouted.

Lizzie turned away from Bonnie to discover Calvin standing flush against the far wall, apparently in shock as he saw Bonnie lying there. He was ghost white, his struggles with the loss of Rosalee written all over his face.

"Calvin!" she snapped. His eyes blinked signaling the rest of his body to move from the crippling effect of those memories.

He turned and ran down the stairs to do as he was told, quickly returning with the hot water rushing into the room carefully averting his eyes from Bonnie's still form, which lay open and naked in front of him. Lizzie carefully adjusted Bonnie's sheets so that she was mostly covered.

Lizzie bent over to dip a cloth in the hot water to wash away the blood from her daughter's pale body. Calvin watched as she glanced out the window at the thin moon on the horizon.

"It'll be a long ride for Jessie into Smithville, and it would be just as long for him to get back to the farm with Doc Morgan." Calvin knew what she was thinking—that she might just have to get those pellets out herself if she wanted her youngest to live through the night. Lizzie rolled Bonnie over to get a better look at her side. Her little girl shrieked in pain.

"Calvin, we're going to have to get these pellets out and compress these wounds until the doctor gets here."

"O-Okay," Calvin replied shakily.

"Okay, girl, stay with me now," Lizzie said, her voice strong and confident. "I mean it, Bonnie. Do you hear me?" Bonnie didn't answer.

It was nervous work, but Lizzie skillfully pulled open her daughter's wounds one at a time, feeling around with her bare fingers for the buckshot pellets. Lizzie dug until she hit bone causing Bonnie to wake in intervals of horrific screaming as if a haint had settled on the inside of her.

As soon as Lizzie indicated that she felt confident one wound was emptied, Calvin applied pressure so she could move on to the next. The sight of Lizzie's hands covered in her own child's blood would not be an image that would soon leave Calvin's memory.

Lizzie and Calvin managed to get most the pellets out of Bonnie's side, all except one that had lodged deep in her thigh. Lizzie couldn't get to it without causing Bonnie a great deal of pain. All they could do was try to stop the bleeding until Jessie returned with Doc Morgan.

After what seemed an eternity, Doc Morgan finally arrived. He immediately went to work on the one pellet lodged deep in Bonnie's leg muscle. The pellet had, in sort of a game of hide and seek, slid deeper into the tissue of the girl's taut muscle, moving around at will. Doc Morgan, versed in buckshot wounds from years of hunting accidents, in no time removed the stalwart pellet and had Bonnie's wounds sewn up and bandaged.

"She's lost a lot of blood, Lizzie," Doc Morgan said, turning to the basin across the room to wash up. "Being out in that cold didn't help none either. I'm hoping she doesn't develop pneumonia." He pulled his glasses off, wiping them down with his handkerchief. "All we can do is wait and pray. I'll be sure to let the Reverend and Miss Annie know as soon as I get back to town."

Lizzie stood next to Jessie, holding his hands. Calvin sat next to the bed, his bleary eyes fixed on Bonnie.

"Any idea how it happened?" Doc Morgan asked.

"No, not really," Jessie said. "Calvin heard gunshots earlier in the day. He said it could have been the McCallister boys, but we're not really sure."

"Well, if we could have gotten to her before she laid out in the cold . . ." he added, trailing off quietly.

"Let's go downstairs and have some coffee, Doc," Jessie said.

The doctor wiped at his tired eyes. "Yes, yes. That sounds good."

Lizzie sat on the other side of the bed across from Calvin. He sat staring at Bonnie, not diverting his eyes to any other matter.

"Calvin," she said softly, knowing what was going through his mind.

Calvin's lips began to tremble. "She was on her way to see me, Lizzie," he said as tears rolled off his cheeks and onto his hands.

"Calvin, it's not your fault," Lizzie said. "Now don't you go thinking that way, boy. Bonnie's been down that path thousands of times. Someone raised a gun into the air and shot her. It wasn't you who pulled the trigger. Do you hear me?"

Calvin acted as if he didn't hear. He lifted Bonnie's pale, fragile hand, resting it between his and waited.

A few minutes later, Lizzie went downstairs, returning with coffee for the two of them. She didn't plan to leave Bonnie's side and suspected Calvin felt the same. Doc Morgan went home after informing them that he had done all he could do for now, promising to come back first thing the next morning.

Jessie slept in a chair.

Calvin sat holding her hand. They waited.

Lizzie cooked breakfast, although no one really felt like eating. Mostly they all picked at their food, not talking. Afterward, Jessie rode off to round up Bonnie's sisters. Soon, the house was full. Each of them took a turn sitting with Bonnie except for Calvin. His turn never ended. He only sat holding her hand. His bloodshot eyes and pallid face revealed to Lizzie that he hadn't slept at all during the night.

Doc Morgan came by that morning as promised. He stayed for the remainder of the day, regularly checking Bonnie for signs of infection. Later that afternoon, her fever soared. Her face was hot to the touch. By late evening, her breaths were short and raspy.

Calvin paced the room while the doctor listened to Bonnie's lungs.

"They're congested," he said matter of factly. "I'm afraid she's developed pneumonia."

"How serious is that, Doc?" Jessie asked.

The doctor ushered Lizzie and Jessie away from the bed.

"I'm afraid it could be fatal."

Lizzie's eyes filled with tears. "No! Oh no, Jessie," she cried. Jessie pulled her close wrapping his arms around his wife, his own eyes wet and stinging. Bonnie's sisters cried as well. They huddled together in the corner of the room.

"Now, now," he said. "Let's not give up hope. I said it *could* be fatal. She could also pull through it. Bonnie is . . . well, a strong girl, to say the least. This can't beat her, but we have to be vigilant and help her as much as we can." He tried to manage a smile. "I'll be back tomorrow morning, Lord willin'. I got to get to half the county before lunchtime."

He handed Lizzie a small bottle, which he retrieved from his bag. "Here," he said. "Get this down her if she wakes up."

Jessie walked Doc Morgan to the door as everyone else gathered around Bonnie's bed. Lizzie dampened a sponge, dabbing gently at her blazing skin. She instructed the other two women to go make supper, adding that she would be down soon to help. When everyone else had gone, she turned to Calvin.

"You must go rest, Calvin," she said. "It's been two days now. You've got to eat something, son."

"I ain't leaving her, Lizzie."

"What good are you going to be when her fever breaks if you're too exhausted to know it? I'm going downstairs to get you some food, and you're going to eat it."

Lizzie stood. On her way out of the room, she removed the globe from the lamp, instinctively grabbing her snips to trim the wick. Even in the dimming light of the room, the sight of Bonnie's dried blood clinging to the edges made her shiver. It was a memory that wouldn't soon fade from Lizzie's mind. Pulling herself back to reality, she struck a match, adjusting the flame.

Outside, Lizzie could hear Jessie and Doc Morgan. Moving to the window, she saw Doc Morgan's hack trundling down the drive toward the road. She didn't envy him; he traveled home under a moonless sky. Lizzie went downstairs, giving Calvin some time with Bonnie.

In the light of the lamp, Calvin sat maintaining his hold on Bonnie's hand, his memory flashing images of her through his mind. He saw her shining face running up to greet him as he came out of the field. He saw her sneak up behind him in the barn. He saw the look on her face when he told her he was moving back to his farm. He saw the day of his drunken stupor when he shoved her out his kitchen door.

Calvin raised his little friend's hand to his face, pressing the smooth back of it against his sandpapered cheek, and began to cry.

"Bonnie Girl, you have to get better," he cried softly. "I'm sorry I forgot about our dance." There was no response.

Calvin became angry. His big hands wrapped around her delicate pale hand.

"You should have stayed away from me," he snapped. "You should have stayed away. I should have made you. It's just like Mother and Father, then Rosalee . . . now you. Oh, God!" he cried, the sobs shaking his whole body.

He slid out of the chair onto his knees beside Bonnie's bed, his hands holding Bonnie's between his in prayer. "God, if you'll just let her live, I'll stay away from her," he said, his voice quavering. "They've all gone away, but not Bonnie. Not my Bonnie Girl. If you let her live, I'll stay away from her. I promise I'll stay away!"

Just then, the door to Bonnie's room swung open wide, Lizzie stood in the entryway carrying a tray of food.

"Calvin," she said sharply. "Get up and come here."

Calvin didn't move.

"Calvin!" Lizzie said, the stern Irish creeping into her voice. She set the tray of food on the table beside the door, grabbing Calvin by his arm, yanking him to his feet, ushering him into the hall outside the bedroom.

Lizzie put a hand on each of Calvin's broad shoulders, forcing him to look her in the eye. "I heard what you said. Now you have to listen to me. Bonnie didn't get hurt because she loves you. It's got nothin' to do with that now. I know everyone who ever loved you has passed on, but you mustn't think this has anything to do with Rosalee or your mother and father.

"You don't have to talk God into letting her live. It's not the Lord who caused her to get hurt. Why, if the Lord's in the business of shootin' young girls, then you can just bury me eight feet under 'cause I won't be servin' a God that kills. Do ya hear me? It's a deal with the devil you're making, and it ain't no good.

"The Lord will help her get well, Calvin, but what then? Why do you want her to live? So you can turn your back on her? Is that any reason for her to live? You want her to live so she can be an empty shell of a woman, the man she loves never loving her back because of some silly superstition?"

She let him go, her face softening.

"Calvin, Bonnie's loved you since she was a girl," she whispered. "She'll always love you. It's just time you faced up to that. What are you going to do about it? Run her off; tell her you don't love her?

"I know you do," Lizzie said softly.

Calvin stared at his feet. "I know you mean well, Lizzie, but you can't change my mind. Everyone I've ever loved has died. The only way she'll live is if she stays away from me. If I stick around, some-thing's sure to happen to her."

Just then, a weak voice called to them from just beyond the half-shut door.

"Mama . . ."

Lizzie rushed through the door to her daughter's side.

"Bonnie!" She turned to yell for the others. "Jessie! Nettie! Emma! Come quick! Oh, Bonnie, you scared me somethin' fierce, girl. Thank God!" she said as she stroked Bonnie's brow. The fever hadn't broken just yet. She was still hot to the touch.

"Mama," Bonnie whispered again. She winced in pain. Her lips were dry, her voice weak.

"Don't try to talk," Lizzie told her.

Jessie and the girls trampled into the bedroom at the same time gathering around the bed. They smiled at Bonnie and at each other, wrapping their arms around one another. Emma cried.

Calvin, however, retreated taking a place by the door.

"Bonnie, who was it done this thing to ya?" Jessie asked. "Do you know?"

"Hush!" Lizzie warned him. "Don't you go makin' her try to talk.

"You rest, dear," she said to Bonnie, but Bonnie's eyes opened wide with fear. Everyone watched as the realization of her trial reached her mind, the horror showing on her face.

"I heard a gunshot 's all," Bonnie said, struggling to maintain her breath. "But first, I heard them dogs, them McCallister boys' dogs."

Calvin retreated to the shadows of the lamp-lit room quietly slipping out of the bedroom door. That was all he needed to hear.

Bonnie seemed to sense his departure. "Mama, where's Calvin?" she whispered. Lizzie looked around. "Why, he's right . . .

"Lordy be," she finished, "he was just here." She looked up at Jessie. "Oh, Jessie, you don't think he's gone after them boys, do ya?"

Jessie scratched his chin. "I don't think he'd do that," he said. "Who even knows where they live? Never seen it, but I'd guess it's up there in that holler somewheres."

"Calvin knows," Bonnie whispered through parched, dry lips.

Lizzie shot Jessie a worried look, then remembered the bottle of medicine that the doc had left for her. She gave Bonnie a bit of the liquid. A short time later, Bonnie was asleep again.

Below Bonnie's window, Calvin mounted his horse and galloped into the darkness, his face grim, his brow furrowed. Yes, he knew where the McCallisters lived. He headed for the hollow with one thing on his mind.

After searching for some time in the dark, Calvin finally stumbled onto the path that led up to the hollow where the McCallisters' cabin sat perched in a deep gorge. The path was small and easy to miss. Calvin was certain he had ridden past it more than once without noticing. It amounted to little more than a hint of a clear path between two steep ridges. A quarter mile or so farther up, it opened into a good-sized hollow.

Calvin had never traveled all the way down the path to the cabin, but he had followed the dogs' tracks plenty of times to the entrance after he had run them off his land to know that was where they were coming from. Until now, he had never had a reason to pursue the path any farther than its opening.

Calvin's heart burned at the thought of wrapping his hands around the throats of those boys. Joshua McCallister had given Bonnie a hard way to go since their school days. Their mean, shiftless ways were known far and wide, but they were about to come to an end as far as Calvin Wade was concerned.

These days, Calvin stood almost six foot and then some. He had built up a broad barrel chest and huge arms from working the farm and was quite stout for his twenty-nine years of age. He weighed nearly two hundred pounds now and was pure muscle. His narrowed crystal blue eyes below his coal black hair gave him a menacing look. When he became angry, those eyes became long slits on his face where only the blue of his irises shown.

His horse carefully picked his way through the narrow opening between the hills. Before long, the path opened up and widened as he rode deeper into the hollow. Calvin squinted against the darkness of the moonless night. Finally, he saw a dot of light ahead, then the sound of barking dogs. He had found the McCallister cabin.

"Pa!" Calvin heard the younger McCallister yell as Calvin approached. "Somebody's comin'!" Calvin rode into the clearing where he could be seen. The front door of the McCallisters' cabin flew open.

Light from the lamps inside spilled out into the blackness of the night, illuminating Calvin's face.

"'Night, Calvin," the elder McCallister said as he walked out onto the porch, the butt of a shotgun resting in his right hand. The barrel leaned against his massive shoulder. The boys peeked out from behind their mountain of a father, hiding behind his bulk.

Calvin leaned forward, resting his arms on the horn of his saddle. "Hello, Ben," he said tonelessly. "Been awhile."

Ben McCallister cleared his throat and spat on the ground in front of Calvin. "Whad ya come up here fer in the middle of the night?"

"I need to talk to you about these boys, Ben."

"What about 'em?"

Calvin steeled himself. "They shot Bonnie McCaverty a couple days ago," he said. "My bet is they mistook her horse for a deer. She took a spray a buckshot on her right side. Now she's took pneumonia. We're not sure she's gonna live."

Ben McCallister ran the finger of his left hand under his nose and sniffed loud. "That so?" he said in disgust. He lowered his shotgun, rubbing the back of his stubby hand against the stubble of his chin as if he were trying to think.

"Yeah, that's so," Calvin replied, pointing a finger at the boys cowering behind the eldest McCallister. "I've told them time after time not to hunt on my land, Ben. There are too many people coming and going through that path. I knew someone was bound to get hurt."

Joshua McCallister spoke up from behind his father. "I thought it was a deer, Pa," he whispered, then his eyes gleamed at Calvin from the darkness. "Besides, what's one less Irish girl to worry 'bout, right, Pa?"

The three boys laughed and poked at each other in sheer jest. Ben's eyes remained trained on Calvin as he shoved Joshua behind him with a powerful swipe of his left arm.

"Idiot," he said under his breath, then turned back to address Calvin. "Well then, I'm guessin' you came up here to take care a some bidness. That right?" the old man said as he straightened, hiking his pant britches up a bit with the thumb of his left hand.

"Yes, sir," Calvin said. He dismounted his horse. "That's right."

"Well, night, Calvin."

"Night, Ben," Calvin answered.

Ben McCallister stepped nonchalantly away from the trembling boys who had been using him as their personal shield and turned for the cabin door. His three sons, stunned by their sudden vulnerability scampered to follow him. Instead of allowing them to do so, Ben McCallister turned on his heels in the doorway glaring at Joshua. Without saying another word, he closed the door against them. Calvin and the boys all heard the wooden beam slide into place and lock behind it.

Joshua banged on the door.

"Pa! Pa! Let us in, Pa!"

Calvin rolled up his sleeves.

The younger boys scattered to the four corners of the clearing, leaving their older brother Joshua to fend for himself.

It was early morning by the time Calvin returned to the McCaverty farm. Doc Morgan's buggy, along with his dedicated old mare Martha, was tied up outside. He was early today. Calvin mouthed a silent prayer.

The entire family gathered around Bonnie's bed again. The doctor stooped over, examining her.

"Her lungs are still congested," he said. "That fever must break today."

"She woke up for a bit last night, Doc," Lizzie told him. "I gave her that stuff you told me to give her."

"Good, good," Doc Morgan said. "That should help a great deal. I must see some other patients today. I'll return before nightfall."

"Thank you, Doc," Jessie said. "Come, I'll walk ya to the door."

Lizzie sat next to Bonnie taking her hand. She began to cry softly. "Mama, she'll be fine. I know she'll be just fine," Nettie said. She knelt beside her mother. Emma sat on the other side.

Calvin, who was standing in the doorway, cleared his throat. Each of the women turned to look at him.

"Calvin!" Emma exclaimed. "Where did you go last night? And

what happened to you?" She nodded at his tattered and blood-stained shirt.

"I had something to take care of," he said coldly.

"I hope you took care of those McCallister boys," Nettie said.

"Nettie, stop that now," Lizzie warned.

Calvin strode forward and took his seat next to Bonnie's bed. "What did the doc have to say?"

"He said the fever would have to break today. He was glad to hear that we got liquid in the bottle down her last night. Said it would help a great deal," Lizzie told him. "Calvin, you look awful tired. Why don't you go lie down?" She wiped her nose with her hanky. "I'll wake you if there's any change."

Calvin stood slowly, shaking his head. He was tired all right, tired of thinking. Tired of wishing things could be different, but this was no time for sleep.

"I'll just go down and get some coffee," he said.

Lizzie sighed. "Nettie, put some fresh coffee on and start some breakfast," she instructed. Nettie and Emma stood and quietly left the room. Calvin remained beside Bonnie, staring at her.

"Where have you been?" Lizzie asked him. "Did you go up into that hollow after those boys?"

Calvin nodded.

"Calvin Wade, that was a fool thing to do," Lizzie said. "You could have got shot or something. Lordy, don't you think we have enough trouble on our hands?" She glared at Calvin from across Bonnie's bed.

Just then, Bonnie stirred.

"Mama . . ." she whispered.

"Bonnie." Lizzie placed a hand on Bonnie's forehead. The burning seemed to have subsided. Calvin stood, backing away from the bed as the two women embraced. Lizzie held Bonnie for a long while. Finally, Calvin left the room, joining the others downstairs.

"She's awake," he said, at which point the rest of the family ran up the stairs making joyful sounds. Calvin could hear them as they surrounded her, talking to her, loving her.

He walked outside, mounted his horse, and rode home.

CHAPTER SIX

"Lord, I'll be needin' your help again."

ONNIE DIDN'T TAKE time recuperating. She had no intentions of lying in her bed all day, everyone waiting on her hand and foot. She missed her old life. She missed riding Danny, but most of all she missed Calvin.

Calvin came to see her only twice during her recovery. It had been a long time since she had spent that much time away from him. Bonnie couldn't understand what kept him away. Whatever it was, she planned on fixing it, and quick.

A month after the shooting, she was out of bed and as far as she was concerned, good as new. Lizzie wouldn't let her lift a finger, and Bonnie had simply had all she could take.

Lizzie stood taking the wash down from the line when Bonnie walked outside. She was dressed in one of Lizzie's brown wool skirts and a matching vest with the gold buttons. Underneath she wore her best white shirt, her hair piled high on her head. Her Sunday boots clad her feet.

"And just where do you think you going, girl?" Lizzie asked, after trying to hide the shock of Bonnie's appearance. Lizzie's hands automatically went to her hips. The stance she took when she meant business.

"I'm going visiting," Bonnie replied. "Mama, I can't stand staying inside any longer. I'm fine. I want to go visit Calvin." She looked down at herself sheepishly. "You don't mind if I borrow your dress. Do you?"

Lizzie sighed. "No, I don't mind if you wear my dress, but you don't need to go traipsing about the country. You're not strong enough yet."

"I'm strong as a horse," Bonnie argued with the familiar stomp of her right foot.

She certainly looked it, Lizzie thought. The dress made her look older than her actual age, but every bit as beautiful as she was at five years old.

"Mama," Bonnie continued, "I want to go see Calvin. I know it was him that found me on the trail. Nettie told me he sat with me for two days, then went after those McCallister boys." A smile curled her lips. "I have to go see him."

Lizzie looked at the ground trying to think of what she could do to spare her daughter the pain she was about to cause herself. She knew Calvin and knew he would stick by what he had said about staying away from her. That was why he hadn't visited.

"Bonnie," Lizzie said, putting her arm around her daughter and directing her to the porch. "Bonnie, you have to know that Calvin is busy. He has a farm to run."

"I know," Bonnie replied, "but I've waited long enough. Don't try to talk me out of it. I have to tell him how I feel."

Lizzie gripped her daughter by both arms.

"You're making a mistake, girl," she admonished. "I told you a long time ago, Calvin is much older and he . . ." Bonnie didn't let her finish. She shook off her mother's grip setting her eyes with determination.

"I don't care," she said. "I love him. I can't help that. I know he loves me, too. I know he does. I can feel it in here." She held her fist to her heart. "I know you don't think it's right. I know you think he's too old, but I have to know. I can't go another day without knowing . . . without knowing how he feels.

"Can't you understand that, Mama?" she said with eyes that pleaded for understanding.

Lizzie dropped her hands to her side surrendering. "Yes, I can," she said.

"Good. I knew you would. Wish me luck," Bonnie said as the

disturbed look on her facing changed quickly to one of excitement. Kissing her mother on the cheek, she ran to the barn.

Lizzie watched as Bonnie hooked up the wagon, mounted it, then drove down the road to Calvin's, no doubt with dreams of a future marriage and long life of love rolling around in her young head. Lizzie knew what lay ahead for Bonnie. She hoped against hope that Calvin wouldn't be able to say what she knew he would.

Bonnie drove the wagon to where Buttermilk and Shorty were working by the barn.

She reigned in the mule greeting them with a broad smile. "Hi there, boys."

"Miss Bonnie!" Buttermilk said, helping her down from the wagon. "Sho is good to see you up and about."

"Yes, ma'am. Sho is," Shorty agreed, removing his hat wiping sweat from his brow with the back of his hand.

"It's good to be out again," she replied. "How's my Danny boy?" Danny had been in Calvin's barn since the shooting. Buttermilk and Shorty nursed him back to health in the weeks following the accident.

"He's okay, Miss Bonnie. Jest fine. You ready to take him home?"

"No. Not today, Buttermilk. Where's Mr. Wade?"

It was Shorty who replied. "Believe you'll find him in the tool shed, Miss Bonnie. He's takin' care a them tools. All he does is take care a them ole tools." He mumbled the last sentence almost to himself as if afraid Calvin might overhear.

"Thanks," Bonnie said, turning to face the tool shed. With a resolute mind, she set her chin as she began walking toward the shed. She straightened her hair pinching her cheeks just a little for color as she walked.

The doors to the old tool shed stood open wide. Bonnie lingered in the doorway allowing her eyes to adjust. Calvin stood at a table against the far wall with a rag in his hand and some part of some tool in the other. His overalls were dirty and smeared with grease. Bonnie squinted until her eyes adjusted to the dimness in the shed, then she walked inside.

"Calvin?"

Calvin turned slowly with his rag in his hand. "Well, hello. What are you doing out and about?"

Bonnie watched as Calvin tried to hide the surprise on his face. He quickly turned back to his work.

"I'm feeling better," Bonnie replied. "I just couldn't stay in that house another day." She stepped closer to him.

"I'm glad you're better," he said, not turning to look at her again.

"Calvin . . . I haven't seen much of you."

He laughed nervously. "Well, we had a lot to do this fall. I've been keepin' the boys busy."

"Nettie told me you went and took care a them McCallister boys. I just thought I should thank you."

"No need to thank me." He jerked a thumb in the direction of the McCallister house. "They've been trespassing for a long time, Bonnie. I'd say they had it coming. Wouldn't you?" He rummaged around on the worktable for some piece of something he was looking for still not meeting her eyes.

It wasn't exactly what Bonnie had wanted to hear, but she agreed. Calvin kept on working.

She paced a bit behind him, trying to think of something else to say.

"Calvin?" she finally stammered.

"Yeah?" He continued working.

"Well . . . I just want to thank you for saving my life. I know it was you who found me."

Calvin waved a dismissive hand in the air. "It wasn't me, Bonnie. It was Danny that saved your life. If that horse hadn't a come down that hill, we'd a never known you were up there. He's a smart horse all right."

Bonnie's heart sank. "Yeah, he's a smart horse," she said, nervously rubbing her hands together, rolling her eyes. This conversation was going nowhere.

"Calvin? Calvin, please stop working. I got to talk to you."

Calvin stopped what he was doing pressing his eyes together before turning to face her.

"What's a matter, Bonnie Girl?" he asked.

"Calvin, I know how you felt about Rosalee." She stopped pacing and turned to face him. "I know you must've loved her a great deal, and it was a great loss when she died."

"Bonnie . . ." Calvin tried to interrupt.

"No, don't interrupt me, Calvin. I got something to say, and I'm not leaving here 'til I say it. Now, I know you loved Rosalee but, well, Rosalee's dead. I mean, well, she ain't comin' back and, well—"

"Bonnie," Calvin interrupted again, almost whispering as he stared at his feet.

"I said don't interrupt me!" The sound of her voice reverberating through the barn causing a barred owl startled by the sound to flee its roost on the shed rafters. Calvin turned away from her, staring at his work.

"Calvin," she continued, recovering herself. "I just have to tell you. I know you saved my life, and I know you were there for me. I just can't stand it any longer. I just have to tell you—"

"Bonnie . . . stop." He turned to face her again.

"I know I'm not Rosalee, but no one, no one could love you as much as I do, Calvin! No one!"

"Bonnie!" Calvin's face grew taught. She could see his shoulders tense beneath his work shirt. Veins stood out on his arms below the border created by his rolled-up sleeves.

She walked up to him, placing her hands on his forearms. "Calvin, I know you might not feel as strong as I do, but, you will. I . . ."

She felt Calvin relax under her touch. "Bonnie," he said softly.

"Calvin, I have to know!"

"Bonnie!" He shouted this time, but she didn't pull away. She only looked at him with the innocence of the little girl he knew so long ago. Even in the dimness of the shed, her hazel eyes flashed bright green. The honey-colored tendrils of her hair fell loosely around her milky white face. The few freckles left over from her younger days perched on her nose, a constant reminder of the splendid child in her.

"Listen to me," Calvin said. He laid the tool he was working with down on the table. Bonnie smiled. Calvin took a deep breath. "You've got to listen to me."

"Okay." Bonnie agreed with a smile, certain she had gotten through.

"Bonnie, you've got to realize something. I'm too old for you. We're eleven years different, you and me. People look at us as brother and sister."

Bonnie's face fell.

"I know how you feel," Calvin continued, "but it . . . it just won't work." He turned his back to her again.

Bonnie could only stand behind him in complete disbelief, the edges of her mouth quivering against every ounce of will she could muster. Little by little, tears began to leak down her face as the words Calvin spoke made their way first to her brain, then to her heart, causing a familiar tightening in her chest.

"Why?" she finally asked. It came out as a whimper. "Why?" she asked louder. "Why? Because you don't love me? Is that why?"

"Bonnie," Calvin said. He sounded exasperated.

"Look at me, Calvin Wade." She stomped her foot. "Look at me! I'm not a child anymore. You can't turn your back on me. Turn around and tell me to my face that you don't love me!"

She waited, her words hanging awkwardly between them, but Calvin didn't turn around. The silence whirled about her like flies around a pierced peach. It soon became too much for her to bear. She pounded her fists against his back.

"Turn around and look at me! Turn around and face me!" Tears streamed down her face, making their way down her neck, ultimately spilling onto Lizzie's Sunday shirt.

Calvin whirled and caught her by her wrists. "Bonnie, stop it!"

She wrenched free from his hold. "Stop? You want me to stop? Okay, I'll stop." Her breath was heavy, fuming. "You might not be able to admit it, Calvin Wade. That's fine, but I know it. I don't understand why you won't admit it, but if that's the way you want it, fine. I'm leaving, and I'll not be back again ever. I can't stay here knowing . . .

knowing." Her mouth quivered again; her still weak body trembled. Calvin stepped toward her.

"Bonnie, I . . ."

She backed away. "No. You're not going to treat me like a child anymore. I won't let you." She raised a hand to stop him. "I won't stay here. I won't!"

She turned, running towards the wagon, slowing down, then stopping halfway there, squaring her shoulders and wiping her eyes, determined to leave the Wade farm with her head held high. She unhooked the mule and stepped up onto the wagon. Snapping the reins hard, she rode off, thinking that it would probably be the last time she ever set eyes on the Wade farm.

Calvin labored toward the doors to the barn, shading his eyes watching Bonnie tear down the dirt road resisting the urge to go after her. He knew better. Calvin felt in his heart no matter how much he loved Bonnie she was better off away from him. At least, she would be safe.

His big arms dropped to his side as a heaviness pressed him. Inside his chest, his heart actually hurt. He knew what he had just done to Bonnie would change everything between them. He knew he just lost his best friend.

Lizzie stood at the sink, washing dishes. She heard the clanging sound of the wagon before she ever saw it. Craning to look out the window, she saw Bonnie tearing down the drive faster than she ought to have been toward the barn. She watched as Bonnie unhooked the wagon, her movements quick and intentional. Lizzie held her breath.

Bonnie led the mule into the barn. When she came out, she stormed across the yard straight for the house. Lizzie knew by the look on her face she was upset. She let out her breath, shaking her head. "Lord, I'll be needin' your help again," Lizzie whispered.

The kitchen door flew open. Bonnie stomped past her mother as if she didn't even see her running up the stairs. Shortly, Lizzie heard the bedroom door slam. Wiping her hand on her apron, Lizzie slowly ascended the stairs. She stood at Bonnie's door listening for any sounds, she knocked gently.

"Bonnie, may I come in?"

Bonnie didn't answer.

Lizzie opened the door. Bonnie sat in her chair at the window, staring out. It was the same spot from which she sat and watched when Calvin moved back home. Her hands were folded in her lap, and tears fell down her face onto Lizzie's brown wool skirt.

"Bonnie," Lizzie said softly, "are you okay?"

Bonnie shook her head slowly, back and forth.

"You tried to warn me," she said. "I wouldn't listen. I just went barrelin' out of here with nothing on my mind but what I wanted. I guess you want to say I told you so."

Lizzie walked over to her daughter, sitting on the edge of the bed. "No, I don't want to say that 'tal, girl."

Bonnie looked at her mother. "At least now I know. At least I won't waste another minute dreaming about something that doesn't exist." She looked down at her hands just as she had a thousand times before imagining the wedding ring that she would one day wear. Tears continued to fall.

Lizzie stood next to her with an arm around her shoulder. Bonnie leaned into her mother's embrace. Lizzie's heart ached for Bonnie. She knew that Calvin really loved her. The fact that he refused to tell her was mighty disappointing. He had caused Bonnie to lose faith in something she believed in all of her life. How could she fix that? Lizzie didn't know.

"It'll be all right, Bonnie. I promise. Someday, you'll look back on this and laugh. It won't hurt forever."

Bonnie pulled away from her mother and stood to face her. "You told me that once before remember, the day at the picnic? Mama, it won't go away. I love Calvin. To know, after all of this time that he doesn't feel the same way . . . it hurts. I don't think I'll ever be able to face him again."

"Oh, yes you will. Time takes care of everything."

"I can't stay here. I can't stay here around Calvin. It just hurts too bad."

Lizzie gasped. "What do you mean you can't stay here? And where do you think you'd be going?" she said, taking a step back from Bonnie.

"Well, Reverend and Miss Annie have accepted the church in Nashville. They're going to be leaving here soon."

"I know that. What has that to do with you?" Lizzie asked, placing her hands on her hips, slipping into her Irish.

"Well, I want to go with them," Bonnie said, turning to face her mother.

"What?" Lizzie stammered. "Go *with* them? Bonnie, have you lost your mind?" She stood face-to-face with Bonnie. "You can't just up and leave when something doesn't go your way, girl. You can't run away from your problems."

"You don't understand," Bonnie pleaded. "It's never gone my way with Calvin. I've loved him since I can remember. I can't just stay around and watch him marry someone else or act like I never loved him."

Bonnie took her mother's hands. Lizzie thought how grown up she looked.

"I have to go," she continued. "I love you and Daddy, but I have to go. If I have to put these feelings behind me, I'll have to do it somewhere else, not here, not seeing Calvin all the time. I'll always feel this way, but if I'm going to be forced to put my feelings aside, I'm going to have to do it somewhere where I won't see him all the time.

"Last Sunday after church, when we visited the Reverend and Miss Annie, they mentioned they needed a piano player and someone to keep their books. Mama, I thought about what I'd do if Calvin . . . well, if Calvin didn't want to admit his feelings. I just couldn't stay here, Mama! I just couldn't! I asked them if I could go to Nashville with them. They said they didn't mind at all, but you and Daddy would have to approve it. Nashville's not far. Please try to understand. I can't just stay here." She balled her fists, striking angrily at her sides.

Lizzie pulled Bonnie close and held her. She knew she had thought long and hard about confronting Calvin. She was grown up now. She wasn't the precocious little girl they had all come to know. She'd thought this out carefully, and now she'd have to face the consequences. Lizzie knew she couldn't stand in her way.

"All right, Bonnie," she said at last. "I understand. You'll have a fine time convincing your father, though. I don't see him lettin' any of his girls move to the city even if it is with the Reverend and his wife."

Bonnie looked at her mother with bright eyes. "Will you help me?" she pleaded. "He listens to you. If I have to stay here, I'll just die!"

"Okay, I'll talk to him, but you have to ask him yourself. I'll talk to him afterward."

"Thank you," Bonnie said to Lizzie as she kissed her cheek. "I'll be okay. You know I will."

"Yes . . . I know," Lizzie said, quickly turning to make her way out of the room so Bonnie wouldn't see the tears forming in her eyes.

Bonnie took her seat by the window. She pulled her picture of Calvin out of her pocket, holding it gently. It was her most prized possession. She knew she would have to stop looking at it, stop wishing and dreaming, but for just a little while, Bonnie told herself, she could dream. Just for a little while longer.

Leaning her head against the frame of the window, she held the picture to her chest, the gnawing feeling in her gut only growing worse. Knowing she had to get permission from Jessie wasn't something she was looking forward to.

That night at supper, Bonnie proposed the idea to her father.

"Daddy, I need to talk to you about something."

"Okay, girl. What is it?" Jessie said, chewing his food.

"Well, Daddy, I . . . I . . ."

"Out with it, girl. What is it?"

"Daddy, I've been out of school now for a while and, well, I guess I need to be thinking about what I'm going to be doing next."

"You need to be finding you a beau, that's what you need to be a doin'," Jessie said, grinning at his daughter as best he could with his mouthful of food, then swallowed.

"If you didn't stay hidden over at Calvin's place all the time, maybe someone would be asking you to go somewhere," he said, shoveling another forkful of potatoes into his mouth. Lizzie shoved her foot into his shin under the table, causing him to swallow the mouthful without chewing. He looked up at his mate as she narrowed her eyes at him.

"Daddy, I want to ask you something if you'd let me finish."

"Go on, girl," Jessie said.

"Well, Daddy, I need to do something now. I think it's time for me to be growing up and maybe get a job."

"A job? What do you need a job for?"

"Daddy, if you don't let me finish, I'm never going to be able to tell you!" Before he could interrupt again, she added, "I want to move to Nashville."

"What?" Jessie shouted. "What do you mean, move to Nashville?"

"Now Daddy, let me explain," Bonnie said as she began to stuff as much information into one sentence as she could before he stopped her. "Reverend and Miss Annie got their new church in Nashville. You knew that, and well, they said I could go with them if I had a mind to, and I could play the piano and help keep the books. I could get paid for it. You know I'm good with numbers, and they kind of aren't, so I'd be helping them, and they'd look after me. I could live in Nashville. Oh, Daddy, it would be so exciting. There's so much to do and see there. Things we can't imagine. There's plays and concerts and parks." She stopped to draw breath, then turned her sad eyes to him beckoning for his approval.

"Please let me go, please."

Jessie stood from the table, wiping his mouth with his napkin. Dropping it onto the table, he looked at his wife then his daughter. His face was as blank as stone. "I can't see it, Bonnie. I just can't see it." He walked out the kitchen door and made his way to the barn.

Bonnie exchanged a glance with her mother. Her bottom lip quivered. "Oh, Mama. He'll never let me go."

"Let me go talk to him," Lizzie said. She set her own napkin on the table, following him so fast that she entered the barn at almost the same time he did.

"Jessie McCaverty!" Lizzie said, her Irish clearly audible.

"What is it, woman?"

"Don't you *woman* me. I've never seen you be so stubborn. You need to think on this thing." She sighed. "I should have warned you, I guess."

Tears filled her husband's eyes. "Do you want her to go, Lizzie? Do you? Do you want our girl to move away to the city where we'll never see her? Have you both lost your minds? Do you not know how bad things are?"

Lizzie reached lovingly toward her husband, placing her arms around him. "Jessie, Bonnie's not a little girl anymore."

"She'll always be my little girl, Liz."

"I know, but you've got to let her grow up." She said, backing away so that she could look him in the eye. Jessie wiped his face on his shirtsleeve.

"She went to see Calvin today," Lizzie explained. "She said she just had to. I tried to stop her, but she wouldn't listen. She went over there with dreams fillin' her head, and Calvin turned her away. I know he loves her, and you know he loves her. What I can't make him understand is that just because he loves her doesn't mean she's going to die. He just won't listen."

She folded her arms, looking thoughtfully at the ground. "So, now we have them both with their minds made up. Calvin refuses to let Bonnie in, and Bonnie's determined to put him out of her mind. That's why she wants to move. She wants to get away. She says she wants to put this behind her."

Lizzie looked up to see Jessie's attention drifting toward the back of the barn. "Jessie, look at me," she said, gently tugging at her husband's chin. "I don't want to let her go either, but how can she get over Calvin? She loves him right down to the core, she does. I know that feeling. I was a young girl taken by a young man at one time."

At that, they both smiled. "I've put myself in her place, Jessie. Thinkin' about how I'd feel if I would have come to you with my feelings on a silver platter and you turned me away. I don't know that I have the courage to do what she's doing. We can't know how she's hurting. How can we stand in the way of the only thing she knows to do to get it behind her? How can we?"

"I don't know," Jessie grumbled. "I've just got to think on it." He led his mule from the stall, pulling his bridle over his ears. Lizzie watched as he threw the saddle onto the mule and mounted.

"Where you goin'?" Lizzie asked.

"I'll be back. I have some things to tend to."

With that, Jessie kicked his mule, hurrying out onto the road. Although he'd never said so, Bonnie was his favorite, and Lizzie knew it. Nettie and Emma were practically grown by the time Jessie could quit working so much and enjoy his children. He loved all of his girls, but Bonnie was special. She was independent and spirited, just like he'd been when he was a child. He loved all his children, but he loved her in a different way, and Lizzie was sure that it was nearly impossible for him to imagine letting her move so far away.

Reverend and Mrs. Parker were just settling down after supper when they heard a knock on the door. Reverend Parker answered, opening the door to see a rather ruffled Jessie McCaverty standing in the deepening darkness of the evening.

"Why, Jessie," he said amenably, "how are you? Please come in." He smiled as Jessie brushed past him, removing his hat in the process.

"Evenin', Miss Annie."

"Evening, Jessie. How are you?"

"Fine, fine . . ."

"Can I get you a cup of coffee?"

"No, no. I just came by for a moment. I won't be keepin' you long."

"Jessie, come and sit down." Reverend Parker offered a chair.

Jessie got right to the point. "Reverend, I understand that you've asked Bonnie to move to Nashville with ya."

"Well, she said she might want to move on in her life, Jessie. We offered her an alternative. I hope we haven't offended you. I know it's an awkward situation, but she asked us."

Jessie shook his head. "No, no, I just want to understand what's going on. Bonnie wants to leave for different reasons, and I want to make sure I let her make the right decision."

Reverend Parker smiled. He was a kindly man, straight and tall with a bit of silver in his hair, Well liked by the community.

"Bonnie has confided in us about some of her feelings," he said. "She's a complex girl."

"Why would she want to move so far away from her family?" Jessie asked.

Miss Annie spoke up. "Jessie, Bonnie is not the kind of girl who can settle for just anything. She has to have things just so. If they're not, she's going to try to change them. I think if she's decided to move to Nashville, she needs that change. There's a big world out there for her to discover. She's a bright girl. There are plenty of things out there for her to do, and you know she'd be safe with us. You know she would. She's like part of our family."

Reverend Parker interjected. "Jessie, we don't want to try to make up your mind. This is something for your family to decide. We just want you to know, if that is what she decides, and you approve, that we will be there for her. She is more than welcome. The church we've accepted is wonderful. It's in an exceptional part of town. There would be plenty of people for her to meet." He stood. "But this is a decision for you, Bonnie, and Lizzie to make."

Jessie stood to meet the Reverend, twisting his hat in his hands as he did. "I know. You're right." He freed his right hand from his wadded hat extending it to Reverend Parker. "Well, good night. Good night, Miss Annie."

"Good night, Jessie."

"Godspeed," Reverend Parker said as he opened the front door to show Jessie out.

Jessie mounted his old mule and rode toward his farm. He had one more stop to make along the way. He took the path away from home at the fork in the road and headed toward the Wade farm.

Through the prevailing darkness, Jessie could see Buttermilk and Shorty sitting in their usual spot in front of their little house watching the evening settle over the farm. Calvin was nowhere in sight. Jessie waved to Buttermilk and Shorty as he tied the mule in front of the house.

"Evening, Mr. McCaverty," Buttermilk yelled across the yard.

"Evening, Buttermilk. Shorty."

Jessie knocked on the front door. Through the windows, he could see Calvin making his way to the door. The front door opened, and Jessie brushed past Calvin in a rough manner, as if he were afraid Calvin might try to shut the door on him.

Outside, Buttermilk and Shorty scratched a chin and a forehead, respectively. "You reckon that's got anything to do with Miss Bonnie gettin' so upset over here today?" Buttermilk pondered aloud.

Shorty continued to rub the stubble on his chin. "I sho hope not. Them two's like father and son. But Miss Bonnie, she sho was upset when she left here."

"You know, I think Miss Bonnie and Mr. Calvin make a fine pair. You don't reckon that would upset Mr. McCaverty, would it?"

"Naw," Shorty answered. "But I don't think that's it. I think Miss Bonnie done tole him how she feels, and he done turned her down on account of what happened to the last girl he fell in love with."

"You been eavesdroppin' again?" Buttermilk asked.

"I just heard a little bit over by the shed 's all!"

Buttermilk shook his head. "This just don't look too favorable 'tall. No, it don't."

Calvin closed the door against the rest of their whispers.

"Jessie?" he asked. "Anything wrong?"

"Well, you tell me," Jessie said, dragging his hat off his head.

Calvin looked down at the floor. He had an idea it might have something to do with Bonnie. This part, he knew, would be hard.

"I'm not sure I know what you're talking about," he said as he strode by Jessie to stoke the fire.

"Calvin, what's going on with you and Bonnie? She wants to move to Nashville!"

Calvin whirled around to face Jessie. "Nashville? What do you mean?"

"I mean she's so upset she wants to move to Nashville with the Parkers!"

Calvin started to say something, then took a deep breath and sighed. "Maybe it's for the best," he added, staring into the orange glow of the warm fire.

Jessie felt outraged. "For the best? How can that be? How can my girl moving so far away be for the best?" His Irish was noticeable, and veins protruded from his neck.

Calvin walked over to his chair and sat down. The last words Bonnie said to him echoed in his head. *I'll never come back. I'll never come back.* Jessie kept shouting, but Calvin wasn't listening.

"What do you plan on doing about this? You can't let her go," Jessie said as he sat across from Calvin.

"I have to, Jessie," Calvin answered quietly.

"What does that mean? You can't," Jessie pleaded. "Do you not see that she loves you? You know she does. She always has. I know maybe you don't love her as much as she does you, but I know you have feelings for her.

"You can't let her leave," Jessie begged.

Calvin's eyes darkened. "Listen to me, Jessie," he answered coldly. "Would you rather have her alive in Nashville or dead here? If she stays here, something will happen to her." His eyes softened as he stared back at the floor. "Just like it has to everyone else."

"Just because you love her doesn't mean she's going to die!" Jessie thundered.

Calvin waved his hands in front of his face. "Stop it! Just stop it, Jessie. Don't you remember how you felt when you thought that gunshot might have killed her? Don't you remember? Well, I do," he said pointing at his own chest. "She got shot coming to see me. Me! If I have to turn her away, make her go away, then so be it. I can't put her life in any more danger. I just can't!"

The two men stood facing each other like father and son, Calvin's nostrils still flaring with anger. He watched as the old man that stood across from him seemed to shrink, the loss evident on his face. It was as if Calvin had stuck a pin into him and let all the air out. He had lost. Calvin's mind was made up, and his daughter was going away where he might never see her again.

"Well . . . I guess that's it then," Jessie said, the pain apparent in his voice. "I don't guess there's anything more to say."

Calvin shook his head. "No, there's not."

Jessie gripped his hat, slowly making his way to the door. He turned back once as if to say something else then, decided against it. He walked out, letting the door close slowly behind him. He looked across the yard at the Wade farm. He thought about Sarah and John. He thought about how sad they would be to see how things had turned out. He shook his head as he went down the steps.

Jessie untied his mule after retrieving Danny from the barn. He walked slowly home through the shortcut leading both horse and mule, pausing at the spot where Bonnie had been shot, remembering. Dried blood still clung to leaves that scattered about the trail.

Lizzie was mending clothes when Jessie walked in the kitchen door. "Where's Bonnie?" he asked.

"She's upstairs in her room," Lizzie answered.

Jessie looked up the stairs toward his little girl's room and thought about her not being up there anymore. He turned, looking at his wife.

"What's it going to be like around here, Lizzie, just me and you? What's it going to be like?"

Lizzie smiled at Jessie. "It'll be quiet, Jessie . . . too quiet."

Jessie looked down at his hands. "Yes, quiet. Something an old man usually looks forward to." He grimaced as he started up the steps.

Jessie knocked softly, then entered Bonnie's room. He found her sitting in her chair by the window. He thought how grown up she looked, how he almost didn't know how to talk to her anymore.

"I . . . I went to see the Parkers," he said as he entered her room.

"You did?" she asked, matter-of-factly.

"Yes," Jessie answered, walking over to her bed and sitting next to her.

"Bonnie, I understand why you want to leave, I . . . I just don't, I . . ."

"Daddy," Bonnie began softly, leaning closer to her father. "I know you don't want me to go. I know that. I don't want to leave you and Mama. I don't, but I can't stay here. I just can't. I have to do something with myself. I've never seen anything of myself other than being married to Calvin. I always thought that was my future. I always thought that one day . . . one day we'd be married. I really did. I lived for that dream. Now, I feel lost, Daddy. I feel all alone without my dreams. They've been my whole life, and now they're gone. I can't stay here without them. What would I do?"

Jessie smiled at Bonnie. "You're so grown up, girl. When did this happen?"

Bonnie smiled back. She slipped off her chair onto her knees, folding her arms on her father's lap. She looked up at him with the happy face of his little girl. "It happened while you were out working so hard to take care of me."

"Aye, that it did," he said, replacing lost strands of her golden-red hair to their rightful place.

"Daddy, I love you. Please don't worry about me. You know I'll be fine. After all, I am a McCaverty, right?"

"Yes, that you are, girl. That you are," Jessie answered, laying a hand on her head, stroking her hair. Bonnie laid her head down in his lap. Jessie, wishing she was a little girl again before things became so complicated, stared out the window seeing in his mind a young, wild little girl tearing out across the meadow, her sun-drenched hair flowing out behind her. He thought about the song he always sang to her and, unconsciously, the words made their way to his lips.

"*. . . we'll sit on the front porch and watch the sun set. A fine time we'll have that we'll never forget.*"

Bonnie lifted her head joining in on the next verse.

"*We'll have ten fine children and all with red hair. To match with their mother's so bright and so fair. We'll sit on the rooftop and watch the moon glow. As me and my Bonnie together grow old."*

Tears slowly rolled down the old man's face. He tried his best to hide it from Bonnie. Jessie McCaverty never cried. He hadn't cried at Sarah and John's funeral, not at Rosalee's funeral, not even when Nettie and Emma got married.

Bonnie was special to Jessie. He knew that, as did Lizzie, but always tried to hide it.

As Bonnie pulled herself up to face her father, tears fell down her face onto his lap. Jessie's lips began to quiver against his will. Bonnie laid her head down on his shoulder as he wrapped his big arms around her. Out of the blue, a thought made its way to her lips.

"Daddy, can I ask you something?"

"Of course, girl," Jessie answered, trying to blink back his tears.

"Why would someone sit on a rooftop and watch the moon glow?"

Out of his deep sadness, Jessie began to laugh. It started down somewhere deep inside him, building slowly like a locomotive working up a head of steam.

"What?" Bonnie asked. She began to giggle as well.

"What? Don't laugh!" she said, giving her father a hard shove. "I've always wondered that. I've always wanted to ask, but I was afraid to!"

Jessie bent over double, unable to answer. Bonnie was laughing so hard she fell backward onto the floor. Lizzie's brown, wool skirt spread out all around her.

They laughed for some time until Jessie was finally able to talk.

"Oh . . . dear Lord, I haven't had a belly laugh like that since you fell out of the hayloft! Oh . . . you've always wanted to ask me that, have you?"

"Yes," Bonnie said as she tried to gain her composure. "I always thought you'd laugh at me . . . and you did!"

Jessie chuckled again, and both were unable to contain another round of full belly laughs. Finally, he wiped tears from his eyes, drawing in an exhausted breath. His eyes grew distant as he looked beyond Bonnie to a long ago memory. As he spoke, his thick, Irish brogue overcame his speech, the way it always did when he spoke of his homeland.

"In Ireland, sometimes the cottages are built right into the hills. The land grows over 'em, and the rooftops are covered with grass just as the hills are . . . so green. On a clear night, people sit out on top of their houses to look at the sky. It's sort of like their front porch."

"Oh, that sounds so beautiful, Daddy," Bonnie said.

Jessie smiled. "Eye, it is." Bonnie pulled herself up to look at Jessie. "I love you, Daddy."

"I love you, too, Bonnie Girl."

Bonnie's heart leapt a little at the sound of Calvin's nickname for her. As she hugged her father, she closed her eyes, struggling to fight back the ache trying to take over her heart.

"Come on. Let's go tell Mother you're moving to Nashville."

"Oh, Daddy! Daddy, thank you." Bonnie jumped up off the floor. She bent down to hug her father, kissing him on the cheek. She took him by the hand, pulling him off the bed, throwing her arms around him. "I love you! I love you! Thank you!"

She dragged him downstairs to tell her mother the news.

It was Sunday, December 15, 1930. Reverend Parker had preached his last sermon and introduced the new pastor to the congregation. There was a big going away party after church, and everyone in the county was there except for Calvin Wade.

Later that afternoon, Bonnie saddled Danny for one last ride. Before she knew it, she ended up at her perch on the ridge, overlooking the Wade farm one last time. She saw Buttermilk and Shorty puttering around, doing the work that winter always held in store for them.

Bonnie smiled as she watched them arguing over something. Calvin walked out onto the front porch to see what the ruckus was all about. Bonnie's heart fluttered at the sight of him. She blinked back tears. Two weeks had gone by, and he hadn't even come to say goodbye. Now it was time to leave, time for her to go. The reality of her leaving felt like a hot branding iron pressing against her chest. She was scared, but as she watched Calvin, watched him move, watched him walk, watched him laugh, she ached inside.

He stood on the front porch, leaning against the railing, surveying his property. Bonnie wondered if he was thinking about her. He looked up toward the path and the Dark Forest that led to the McCavertys' farm. Was he thinking about going to say goodbye? Did the chance he might beg her to stay stop him from going? Bonnie didn't know. She could only hope.

Bonnie watched Calvin as he looked up at the hillside. She felt as if he was staring right at her. She knew he couldn't actually see her, not from her hidden watchful position. She blew him a kiss. Danny nudged her from behind.

"I know . . . we have to go," Bonnie said, wiping tears off her face as she turned walking toward her house with Danny following behind.

"Now, Danny, you have to be a good boy, okay?" Bonnie said to her little companion as they walked along. "I'm going to miss you." Bonnie stopped on the path, putting her hands to her eyes, trying to hold back the inevitable tears. They came pouring down her face like a rainstorm. Danny nudged her arm. She buried her face in his mane.

"Oh, Danny, how can I leave this place? How can I leave?" The little horse neighed softly as if he was telling her not to be afraid. Bonnie laughed quietly. "You're right, I have to be brave. C'mon, let's go home."

At the edge of The Dark Forest, Bonnie allowed herself one longing look over her shoulder. She said goodbye, at least for a while.

When she got back to the house, Nettie and Emma were there with their families. The children were playing on the front porch. Inside, Emma's husband Sam and Nettie's husband Tom were getting ready to load Bonnie's trunks onto the wagon. They'd be leaving for the station early in the morning, and the trunks were mighty heavy. Jessie couldn't lift them by himself.

"Okay, boys. Load the trunks onto the wagon and pull it into the barn in case of rain," Jessie instructed as they made their way inside the house for a going away celebration.

"Daddy, I thought Doc Morgan was going to drive us to the station in his car?" Bonnie asked.

Jessie nodded. "He was, but the Parkers have their trunks and all of their belongings, so there's just not enough room. We'll have to take the wagon."

"It's going to be so cold!" Bonnie said, thinking about the early-morning trip to the McMinnville station.

Lizzie spoke up. "Well, that's why we got you this," she said, producing a big package wrapped in white paper.

"A present!" Bonnie squealed.

"We all pitched in, Bonnie," Emma said.

Bonnie sat down to open the package. Her mouth dropped open.

"Oh, my goodness! It's lovely!" Bonnie said, pulling the wool coat out of its wrappings. It was a gray, wool traveling coat with a black velvet collar and fashionable velvet cuffs. It had come directly from the Sears catalog.

Nettie soon arrived with another package from the kitchen. "I brought something else for you."

"Nettie!" Bonnie felt like it was her birthday. She opened the package. It was a black velvet hat to match her coat.

"It's so beautiful. Thank you all," Bonnie said, making her way around the room hugging everyone.

"Well, time to eat," Lizzie announced from the kitchen doorway. It was their last Sunday afternoon together. Bonnie would be leaving in the morning.

After nightfall, Lizzie found Bonnie on the front porch looking toward The Dark Forest. Lizzie put her coat on walking outside to talk to her.

"Bonnie, what are you doing? It's freezing out here."

"I just can't believe he's not going to come and say goodbye."

Lizzie put her arms around her daughter's shoulder. "I don't think he knows what to say. Or maybe he's afraid of what he might say."

"What do you mean?"

"It's just his stubbornness that's keeping him away."

"I can't think about it anymore, Mama. I'm so tired of thinking about it."

"I know. It'll all be behind you soon."

"Will it? Will it ever be all behind me?"

"It'll have to be, Bonnie. It'll have to be. Come on. Let's go inside now. Tomorrow will be here in no time."

The train for Nashville was scheduled to leave the McMinnville station at 8:45 a.m. Hating goodbyes as she did, Lizzie stayed behind. After breakfast, she went up to say goodbye to her youngest daughter.

"Well, how do I look?" Bonnie asked her mother twirling about in her new coat and hat.

"Like a grown young woman, you do." Lizzie stood. "Well, I guess this is it," she said, attempting to not sound sullen. "By nightfall, you'll be in your new home. It's all so exciting. Don't you think?"

"Yes, it is. Although I think I feel more scared than excited."

Lizzie wrapped an arm around her. "You'll be fine, Bonnie. The minute the train leaves the station you'll be so excited you won't be scared at all."

Bonnie hugged her mother. "Thank you, Mama. Thank you for understanding. I'm going to miss you so much."

"I'll miss you, too, girl. You better promise me to take care of your-self and write me every day. Do you understand?" She gently pushed Bonnie away, forcing her to meet her eyes.

"Yes, ma'am. I promise," Bonnie said.

"Now the Parkers are doing something special for you. You have to promise you'll do as they say and help them as much as possible."

"I will, Mama. I'll be so busy helping with the church, and during the week I'll be helping Miss Annie with her Christian work. I won't have any time for anything else much. I promise I'll stay out of trou-ble." Bonnie smiled.

"Yes, well, we know how that goes," her mother replied gently returning her smile. "I love ya, girl."

"I love you, too, Mama."

Jessie called to Bonnie from downstairs. "Bonnie! Get down here. We've got to get going!"

"C'mon," Lizzie said. "I'll get your grip. We better hurry."

Bonnie stopped, turning to look at her mother. "Mama, I'd like for you to make me a promise."

"What is it?"

"Will you look after Calvin?"

"Of course, as I always have, Bonnie. I promise. Now let's go."

Bonnie and Lizzie made their way downstairs with her carrying bag and one suitcase. It was time.

Daughter and mother held each other for a long time saying good-bye, but not wanting to let go. Lizzie wave from the front porch until Bonnie was completely out of sight.

They met Doc Morgan and the Parkers at the station at exactly 8:30 a.m. fifteen minutes before the train scheduled to leave. Hurriedly, they checked the baggage and prepared to board the train.

"All aboard for Nashville. All aboard!" the conductor yelled.

Bonnie looked at Jessie. "I guess I need to get on the train."

"I guess you do," Jessie agreed.

Bonnie threw her arms around her father. "I'm going to miss you so much!"

"I'll miss you, too, girl. Now, get on that train, and don't you forget to write or I'll come get you and bring you home. You hear me?"

"Yes, Daddy. I love you," Bonnie added with a mixed feeling of excitement and heartbreak.

"I love you, too, Bonnie."

Bonnie turned, looking down the road from which they had come. Jessie looked, too. He knew what Bonnie was thinking.

"C'mon, girl, get on the train before it leaves ya now."

Bonnie hugged her father one more time, stepping up to get onto the train with the help of the conductor. Even though she felt a great rush of excitement toward her new journey, she knew getting onto this train meant leaving a part of her behind; leaving Calvin behind.

Bonnie blew him a kiss from her window. "Bye, Daddy. I love you," she yelled, knowing Jessie couldn't hear her, but hoping he could read her lips.

The train slowly began to pull away from the station as the wheels fought hard against the weight it carried to turn. The engine spit and sputtered. Bonnie watched her father stand there with his hat in his hands until the train rounded a corner. A single tear rolled down her face. Miss Annie pulled out her handkerchief, handing it over to her.

"Now, now, Bonnie dear," she said. "Don't cry. You're going on an adventure. Smile now."

Bonnie looked up. "You're right. I'm sorry." She looked out the window at the scenery now speeding by. "Oh my, we're moving so fast!"

"Have you ever been on a train before, Bonnie?" Reverend Parker asked.

"No, sir. I haven't."

"Oh, you're in for some fun," Mrs. Parker said. "Look out the window. See how the countryside goes by so fast?"

Annie Parker was nothing more than an overgrown child herself, although a bit adventurous for a preacher's wife. Her brown eyes sparkled when she was excited about something or when she talked about the Lord's work. That was one thing the Rev. and Annie Parker had in common, their love for people and their love for the Lord. They had worked many years together through many hard times helping many people. Finally, they would be in the city again and could enjoy all the amenities of civilization, which meant that the adventurous Mrs. Parker could take it a bit easier.

"The fields look so bare," Bonnie said.

"Now they do, but in the summer when you go by this fast, and you pass a cotton field, they look like one big white cloud lying on the ground. And the cornfields, they look like one huge sea of green."

Bonnie rested her chin on her knuckles continuing to watch the countryside pass by. She thought about Calvin. Bonnie still couldn't believe he hadn't come to say goodbye. She fought hard not to cry each time the reality surfaced in her mind, but it was becoming more difficult as the miles between them slipped by uncounted.

Jessie let the mule walk on slowly down the country road toward home. It was a good drive back, and he was in no hurry. He felt he needed to deal with this sadness before he got back to Lizzie.

A few cars passed him on the narrow road. He waved at each one, then he heard the sound of hooves pounding against the packed dirt road. He looked up to see a rider tearing down the road at breakneck speed. He pulled the old mule to a stop.

"Whoa now, whoa," Jessie said, squinting against the sun to see if he knew the rider. When the rider was finally within his clear field of vision, he realized it was Calvin. He pulled the reins, stopping his horse directly beside Jessie.

"You're too late, boy," the old man said. His voice was gruff, defensive. "She's already gone." He turned to face the road in front of him. "Here now, get up now!" The wagon pulled away, leaving Calvin's horse prancing in its place.

Calvin slid his hat off, slapping his leg with it. "Damn!" he shouted. "Damn!" He spurred his horse and rode as fast as he could toward the station. When he arrived, no one was there. There was no train, nor were there any people waiting on one. Nothing greeted him but silence. Calvin looked down the tracks. The train was nowhere in sight. He had missed it.

"Bonnie Girl . . ." Calvin whispered.

PART II

Nashville

CHAPTER SEVEN

*"If I have to drink another cup of tea with
those dried up old bags, I'll scream!"*

T
HE TRAIN EASED its way into Union Station as scheduled.
Bonnie stood in awe as she stepped off the train gazing at the
massive roof of the train shed and the ornate stairs that led to
the entrance of the huge stone building.

"It's so big," she exclaimed.

"Come now, girls. Go up to the ladies room and wait for me. I'll
get the baggage and come get you. Boy," he yelled to one of the nearby
porters, "show these ladies up to the waiting room. You go on now. I'll
come for you soon."

Annie squeezed Bonnie's gloved hand as they made their way to
the stairs that led to the lobby of the station. Trying to take in all of
her surroundings, Bonnie almost bumped right into two carts loaded
with baggage.

"Miss Annie, look at those beautiful windows."

"Yes, dear, I've seen them before. You should watch where you're
going," she advised. Annie retrieved her handkerchief from her sleeve
covering her mouth and nose to protect them from the smoke and
steam lingering underneath the shed.

Completely and utterly fascinated, Bonnie watched people rushing past her. The ladies, she noticed, dressed so fancy. Some even wore

fur coats. When they entered the door to the lobby of Union Station, Bonnie stopped dead in her tracks.

"Look at the Christmas decorations!" she exclaimed. "They're so beautiful!" Bonnie gasped at the thirty-foot Christmas tree, which stood next to the fireplace.

"Look, Miss Annie," she squealed pointing to the enormous tree.

"Come along now," Annie admonished her. "We have to get to the ladies waiting room and wait on Reverend Parker."

Bonnie barely heard her. Scanning the walls of the railroad station, her eyes tracked every detail all the way to the immense ceiling. Craning her neck all the way back, there she stood in the middle of the lobby, mouth open, gaping at the ceiling with its brilliant colors.

At the ticket counter, an employee noticed Bonnie. He nodded toward her, nudging a co-worker in the ribs. "Hey, Jimmy, look," he said, "another country girl come to town." They both shook their heads laughing. Miss Annie glared at both of them urging Bonnie to the waiting room, where she promptly inspected every inch of the room with its pink roses and plush seating.

Finally, Reverend Parker came to fetch them. "Our car is here. Let's go, girls," he said, ushering the women out of the side entrance to the car, which was loaded down with trunks and suitcases.

"Oh my, we're quite loaded. Aren't we?" Mrs. Parker asked.

"Yes, well, we'll manage," Reverend Parker assured her. "Mr. Pollock, this is my wife, Annette Parker. Annie, this is Mr. Pollock. He's been instructed to bring our car and take us to our house. Mr. Pollock, this is a friend of the family, Miss Bonnie McCaverty."

"Is this your car Reverend Parker?" Bonnie asked in amazement.

"Yes, Bonnie. It's our car."

"You mean they gave you a car?"

Reverend Parker let out a chuckle, opening the door for the women. "It's for our use as long as I'm at the church. Just like the parsonage. Come on now. Let's get out of this dreadful cold."

Mr. Pollock drove them across the viaduct up Broadway toward their new home in the west end of town. As they drove by Centennial Park, Bonnie gawked at the sight of the large building perched in the center of a lovely park. It was a stone building surrounded by tall columns that led to the pediment, which featured images of people who seemed to be engaged in some sort of contest.

"What is that?" Bonnie asked as she pointed at the colossal structure.

"That's the Parthenon, Miss McCaverty," Mr. Pollock explained. "It was built for the Centennial Exposition that we had here in 1897." He spoke with a click in his voice, the click he had acquired from repeating the same thing over and over again, fast, emotionless, memorized.

"That's the one exhibit building left. I believe it was the Fine Arts Building. It's an exact replica of the Parthenon over there in Greece. There were buildings spread out all over this area. It was quite a big deal. They had a giant seesaw that rose two hundred feet into the air," he said with great enthusiasm. "It was a crane sort of thing with two cages at each end that would go up as the other came down. You could see forever up there, or so they tell me."

Silence filled the car as Bonnie craned around trying to get one last look at the massive building, her eyes bug wide in amazement.

"This here's Sylvan Park," Mr. Pollock continued as they made their way off the main road. "It's a nice neighborhood. We have a park here with a lake, and the people are wonderful. The church isn't very big now, but we have some prominent people in town who attend.

"Here we are now," he instructed as he entered the driveway of a stone cottage.

"Is this where we'll be living?" Bonnie asked excitedly.

"Yes, this is the parsonage. That there's the church," Mr. Pollock said, pointing toward the sanctuary.

"Come on, I'll help you with your things. This here's the key to the church doors and here are the keys to the house. Oh, and here're the keys to the car," he added, dropping the keys into Reverend Parker's open palm.

"Well, you folks settle in now. I'll be back tomorrow to show you around the church and get you familiar with everything. Mrs. Pollock put some supper in the icebox for you. If you need anything, our number is on the pad next to the phone."

"We have a phone!" Bonnie exclaimed as she disappeared inside the front door. Mr. Pollock looked after her, a wry smile on his face.

"She's never been to the city," Reverend Parker said.

"So I see. She's excited."

"Yes, she is."

"Well, she has plenty to see if she's never been to Nashville," Mr. Pollock continued in his clipped tone.

Mr. Pollock waved goodbye. "I'll see you folks in the morning."

"Thank you for your help," Reverend Parker said as he and his wife stood on the step of their new home.

"Well, Annie, let's go see what Mrs. Pollock made for supper," he said.

Visitors descended on the Parkers and Bonnie first thing the next morning. Well-wishers and snoopy old wives came by unannounced with cakes and pies, anything they could think of to be one of the first to meet the new pastor and his lovely wife.

Reverend Parker was almost too handsome to be a preacher, some said, but his charm immediately put all the ladies at ease. After the women had decided that Annette Parker was a suitable preacher's wife and they all gave her their silent approval, she was immediately flooded with invitations for tea from all the good ladies of the community.

Bonnie was another thing. Try as they may, the ladies of the church welcoming committee couldn't figure out why this attractive young girl had come to Nashville with this childless couple to play the piano and keep the church books.

The Reverend's first sermon came and went. The congregation welcomed him with open arms as had all of the congregations in his thirty years of service. As they settled in, all three of them fell in love with this new community. The Parkers finally had their city church where they could take it a bit easier, and Bonnie, so fascinated with the city, found much to occupy her time and kept homesickness at arm's length.

After a month of endless teas and social gatherings, being social began to grate on Bonnie.

"If I have to drink another cup of tea with those dried up old bags, I'll scream," she said to Mrs. Parker after returning one afternoon from tea at Mrs. Emily Simms' house. She was the leader of the prayer group that met every Thursday. They did more gossiping than praying.

"Bonnie! Don't talk like that," Annie said, removing her gloves. "You know it's not ladylike."

"I know, Miss Annie. I'm just so tired of their gossip. I don't think they like me very much."

"They just don't know you yet, dear. You're different, Bonnie. They just can't figure out why you're here with us is all. It's a bit of an odd situation for them. They're having trouble understanding it."

"I'm eighteen," Bonnie said, pouting. "Most girls are married by now or gone off to college."

Annie put her arms around Bonnie's shoulders. "Come on, dear. You're just a little homesick I bet. What you need is something to occupy your time. I'm sure you're tired of sitting around with us old women.

"I've been thinking," Annie continued. "I have a friend at the Red Cross whose always looking for volunteers, girls like yourself to help her out. You could do so much to help her. Things as tough as they are, I'm sure she'd love to have the extra hands."

"Miss Annie, that's a wonderful idea! I could ride the streetcar to wherever I needed to go, and I'd never have to drink another cup of tea."

Annie laughed. "Well, thank you for your honesty! I'll call her tomorrow. Now, let's go get supper ready, okay?"

In no time at all, Mrs. Parker's friend had put her in touch with Mrs. Betty Greenfield, one of the field leaders at the Red Cross. Soon, Bonnie completed training to become an official Red Cross volunteer. One of her first assignments was to help with the home visits. The first of those was a tenement house near the Cumberland River.

One cold, February morning she and several other volunteers

ended up on Gay Street, where the poor lived in less than desirable conditions. It was the first time Bonnie had seen the other side of the city; the poor, the unemployed. She was plainly shocked.

"Mrs. Greenfield, are we going in there?" she asked, pointing to the rundown old house.

"Yes, we are, and wipe that look off your face," Mrs. Greenfield answered sternly. "These people don't need your pity; they need your help."

Bonnie felt flush. "I'm sorry," she said.

"It's okay. Come on," Mrs. Greenfield said, leading the band of volunteers to the front stoop of the first house.

"Bonnie, take these coats and shoes," she said, handing off a bundle of clothes. She gave the other women instructions for some of the other houses on the block. Since it was Bonnie's first field assignment, Mrs. Greenfield told Bonnie to stay with her.

Mrs. Greenfield knocked on one of the apartment doors inside the house. It had been transformed to hold more than one family, and from what Bonnie had seen so far, in less than desirable conditions.

"Hello, Mrs. Sutton. How are you today?" The woman was at first suspicious, glaring at them through the crack in the door. She recognized Mrs. Greenfield and opened the door.

"How's Mr. Sutton? Has he found a job yet?" Mrs. Greenfield asked. She ignored the rat scurrying across the floor. Bonnie's eyes widened as she moved closer to Mrs. Greenfield.

"No, he's looking today, though. Pray he finds one, Mrs. Greenfield. Please pray," the lady replied, her eyes downcast.

"I will, dear. Where are the children?"

"They in the back playing," she answered.

"Call them. I have a few surprises for them."

"Well, my Polly, she's sort of sick right now."

Mrs. Greenfield became alarmed. "Where is she?"

"Well, she's . . ." Mrs. Greenfield didn't wait for the rest of her answer. She went looking and found the girl in the bedroom pale as a ghost.

"How long has she been like this?" Mrs. Greenfield asked the little girl's mother.

"Since last night." Mrs. Sutton began to cry. "I don't know what to do! She's been spittin' up, and her stomach hurts real bad. I can't take her to the doctor. I don't have no money."

Bonnie stood in the corner of the room aware that she wasn't being helpful. She watched the story unfold, a feeling of helplessness in her heart. How could someone not have enough money for a doctor? It was unheard of where she came from. If you didn't have enough money to pay the doctor when you were sick, you paid him after you were well.

"Do you know what made her sick, Mrs. Sutton?"

"No, I just know she's been getting worse."

Mrs. Greenfield observed the child. "Can you move your arms and legs, honey?" she asked.

The child merely looked up without speaking and shook her head. The gesture appeared to have required quite a bit of effort.

"I'm afraid she don't move too well."

"Mrs. Sutton, my guess is she has some form of poisoning. I'll see about getting a doctor over here. Don't you worry, okay?"

Mrs. Sutton began crying softly. She sat on the bed and lifted the child's limp body into her arms.

"I'll leave the coats for the children, and we'll be back to check on you, okay?"

"Thank you, Mrs. Greenfield. God bless you."

Mrs. Greenfield and Bonnie left the unhappy apartment. Bonnie leaned against the hallway and covered her face. "I think I'm going to be sick," she said.

Mrs. Greenfield pulled Bonnie's hands away from her face. "Listen to me," she said. "That child is very sick. Believe me, you'll see worse."

"Why is she so sick? Why can't they afford a doctor?"

"Mr. Sutton lost his job when the hosiery mill had to cut half of its employees. He's been doing enough odd jobs around the city to keep a roof over their heads, but that's all. They were farmers before the drought, but they lost their farm. They hadn't been here long when Mr. Sutton lost his job at the mill."

"Why is this place so awful? Why don't they fix this place?"

"Honey, that's not the way it works."

"Whoever owns this house should be ashamed," Bonnie said quite indignantly. "What will happen to the little girl?"

"I'll call and see about getting a doctor down here to look at her. Maybe it's not as bad is it seems. You go upstairs and help the other ladies."

Bonnie nodded. After Mrs. Greenfield left, she started upstairs. Just then, a smartly dressed man entered through the front door. Bonnie cast her eyes on him, causing her to slip on the third step, falling to her knees. The man rushed to her aid.

"Are you all right? Here, let me help you," he said.

"Yes, I'm fine. I just scraped my knee." Bonnie lifted her dress a bit to examine the damage. "Oh no, look. I've ruined my stockings. This place is horrible!" she said with a characteristic stomp of her foot. "The person who owns this place should be hung up by his toes. I ought to make him repay me for my stockings."

The man reached into his pocket pulling out a stack of cash. He unfolded a few bills and handed them to Bonnie.

"Allow me," he said smiling.

"Oh no, I didn't mean you," Bonnie blushed. "I meant the man who owns this building."

"One and the same," the man replied. Pulling his hat off, he tucked it under his arm and offered his hand. "Ned Bass at your service, Miss . . ."

"You mean *you* own this place?" Bonnie asked, astonished.

"Yes, I do."

She stood, straightening her skirt. Her mouth tightened. Her hands made fists at her sides.

"You should be ashamed of yourself!" she spouted to him.

"I should?"

"Yes. This place is horrible. Look at these steps. I could have broken my leg. There are rats in here. Rats! Did you know that? Rats!" Bonnie exclaimed her confusion at everything she had just witnessed causing her voice to rise to a heated pitch.

"Well, I . . ."

"There's a sick little girl in that apartment, and they can't even afford a doctor. You should be ashamed!" Bonnie shouted, turning again to mount the stairs and find the other volunteers.

Ned Bass watched until she was out of sight.

"Boy, I wonder what she's like when she's *really* mad," he said, pulling his hat from underneath his arm, fanning his face.

Bonnie came home around four o'clock in the afternoon from her first day of volunteer service with the Red Cross. She was tired and decidedly upset. She walked into the living room and plopped down onto the couch.

"I thought I heard you come in," Annie said, entering the living room. She slowed her walk when she saw the look on Bonnie's face. "Are you okay?" She sat next to Bonnie, who began to cry.

"Miss Annie, it was awful! Just awful!" She buried her head on Annie's shoulder.

"Now, now, what happened?"

Bonnie sat up and blew her nose, then began to tell Annie about the whole day, hardly taking a breath.

"We went into this house, and this little girl was so sick. She couldn't even move. They think she might be poisoned or something, and there were rats right there in their apartment! I saw one! It ran across the floor. Then, I almost broke my neck on a broken step. I ruined my stockings, and on top of that the awful man who owns that building helped me up when I fell." Bonnie sat up, looking at Annie. "I told him a thing or two!" She blew her nose again. "It was just awful."

"Oh, dear, come on. You go upstairs, and I'll get you a hot bath and something to eat. You can go to bed early. You've never seen anything like this before. Honey, many people live like that, especially now with the depression and all. There are so many people out of work. They have no one to depend on but themselves."

"I feel so sorry for the children. They just look so pitiful," Bonnie said. "The little girl was so sick, and the baby just cried and cried."

"Come on, Bonnie. Forget it for tonight. It'll be better in the morning." Annie patted Bonnie's hands. "Maybe I shouldn't have gotten you into this so soon. We'll see about you doing something different," she said as she stood.

"No!" Bonnie shouted. She shot to her feet, facing Annie. "No, I don't want to quit! I want to help. I really do! Oh, I'm sorry I complained, Miss Annie.

"Please don't make me quit," she begged.

"All right, dear," Annie said, looking a bit perplexed. "Now, c'mon upstairs and get ready for a hot bath. You'll feel so much better."

"Okay, Miss Annie," Bonnie answered, relieved Annie hadn't decided to make her quit. Something woke inside Bonnie that day. As bad as the day had been, an excitement grew inside her, and Bonnie realized she even looked forward to tomorrow.

CHAPTER EIGHT

*"But tomorrow, I'm going to visit that rat
and give him a piece of my mind.*

ONNIE SPENT MANY days at that tenement house on Gay Street. She spent a great deal of those days with Polly, the four year old at the Sutton apartment who had been so ill. Bonnie did the one thing Mrs. Greenfield told her not to do since the beginning of her training, not to get emotionally attached, and now she was attached. So attached, Calvin Wade never entered her mind.

Little Polly reminded Bonnie of herself when she was a girl, although Polly had seen much more at the tender age of four than Bonnie had in her entire lifetime. She had long blonde hair that she kept in a single braid down her back. Her azure blue eyes seemed to change colors with her moods. They always lit up when Miss Bonnie visited.

Bonnie had been told not to present gifts to her charges unless she could take one for all of the children, so every now and then, Bonnie and Polly would take a walk and Bonnie would give Polly a piece of candy or a hair bow or some little unnoticeable item. She would tell Polly to be sure not to tell anyone. It was always their "little secret."

The two of them became fast friends and, contrary to her training, Bonnie became emotionally attached to little Polly Sutton.

It was now November, and Bonnie had been so busy that she didn't notice Thanksgiving was right around the corner. It was already bitterly cold in Nashville, and her volunteer work was taking her all over the city.

Bonnie began losing weight from overwork, becoming thin and frail. She knew it caused Miss Annie to worry.

"Please stay home and get some rest today, dear," Annie pleaded as Bonnie eyed herself in the mirror one last time before leaving to catch the streetcar. "You're looking so thin and worn out."

"I can't. I have a family I have to visit today. If I don't go, they won't eat. I think that's more important than my rest," Bonnie quipped.

Annie folded her hands, her eyes aimed at the floor. Bonnie could see she'd spoken a bit too harshly to her friend. She took Annie's hands in her own. Annie had seen much in her life, but she had refused to go to the tenement houses with Bonnie, who assumed that Annie just couldn't bring herself to see any more suffering.

"I'm sorry, Miss Annie. I just, I can't seem to separate myself from these people. They have nothing, and I feel as though I have everything, and I . . . I would feel guilty if I just sat here and didn't do anything. Please don't be angry with me. I promise Sunday after church we'll spend the whole afternoon together, okay?"

Annie looked up from the floor. "All right, dear, I understand how you feel about them, but you're not going to do anybody any good if you overwork yourself and are forced to take a rest. Then, who would help them? You say they're already understaffed as it is. Just promise me you won't make yourself sick."

Bonnie walked back over to the mirror adjusting her Red Cross uniform once more. She rearranged a long stray hair that had wormed its way out from underneath the rigid white cap. Even though all the girls Bonnie worked with had long ago done away with their long locks, Bonnie refused. Always at the end of each urging by her friends, she would admonish, "If God would 'a wanted me to look like a boy, he'd a made me one." She removed the hairpin from her mouth, pinning the loose hair back.

"I promise, okay? Now, you have fun today, and I'll see you back at suppertime," Bonnie said as she pecked Annie on the cheek. She grabbed her bag and headed for the door.

"Oh, dear, I'm going to miss the streetcar! Bye," she yelled back to Annie, tearing down the steps heading for the street.

Mrs. Parker parted the curtains watching as Bonnie hurried down the sidewalk to her destination, shaking her head. It was time she contacted Lizzie. Bonnie had to get away or she would drop from exhaustion. Lizzie McCaverty was the only person who could get Bonnie to do something she didn't want to do.

Bonnie arrived at the Red Cross office at 7:30 a.m., received her instructions for the day, preparing herself for the day's task. She would ride with Henry to deliver dry goods to some of the tenement houses she had put requests in for earlier in the week. Usually, it took longer than a week to get a request such as a truck full of dry goods, but Bonnie had become a master at this game. She knew just which strings to pull.

The night before her request, Bonnie would bake the cookies she had promised to Henry if he would hurry her route along. The day before that she brought Mrs. Ross fresh honey for her tea; the fresh honey her father had sent to her. She figured it was going to a good cause so he wouldn't mind, then there was Mrs. Greenfield. Although she tried to be stern with Bonnie, most of the time she gave in to Bonnie's pleadings. Even Mrs. Greenfield was beginning to worry about Bonnie. She had been at this for a year now almost every day except for Sundays. Mrs. Greenfield also knew that Bonnie often snuck over to visit the Sutton girl even on her day off. She knew it was about time for her to insist Bonnie take a trip home to get some rest. After Bonnie left her office that morning, Mrs. Greenfield decided to take a drive over to see Mrs. Parker. The two of them would have to come up with a plan to convince Bonnie it was time to go home for a visit.

Bonnie knocked on the first door to the right when she entered house on Gay Street. Behind the door of the first apartment, she heard the scurrying of little feet approaching. As the door cracked open, a little blue eye peered out to see who was knocking. Bonnie knelt so That she could be eye to eye.

"Hello," she whispered.

A finger appeared in front of the lips that went with the blue eye. "Shhhhh . . . Mommy's asleep. I can't wake her up. She dudn't feel good."

"Okay," Bonnie whispered back. "Why don't you get your coat, come outside, and we'll take a walk?"

"Okay, but we have to come right back. If the baby wakes up, she'll wake up Mommy."

"You get your things, and I'll wait out here."

"Okay, be wight back!" the little lips whispered with excitement.

Minutes later, the body that went with the blue eyes and the little lips squeezed through the doorway, pulling it quietly to shut behind her.

"Miss Bonnie!" Polly said, wrapping herself around Bonnie's neck. Bonnie bent down, scooping the little girl up into her arms. "I missed you!"

Polly wrapped her legs around Bonnie's midsection at Bonnie's direction as the two of them headed for the door. "How could you miss me? I was just here yesterday?" Bonnie teased.

"I always miss you when you're gone," Polly said buttering Bonnie for her next question. "Did you bring anything for me?"

"Oh, you little rat. Did you look in my pocket?"

"No, no," the little girl said, laughing. "I promise, I promise!"

Bonnie placed Polly gently onto the ground outside of the house, as they proceeded to take their walk. Henry waited in the truck. First, she'd take the kid for a walk, give her something special, then they'd take Polly's secret gift, along with the dry goods allotted for the Sutton family, inside. Henry smoked a cigarette in the cab of the truck watching the pair as they walked by.

Polly looked up and waved. "Hi, Henry!"

"Hi, Kitten!" Henry answered. As they made their way past the truck, he shrugged at Bonnie and shook his head. Bonnie gave him a look of admonishment. He had already warned her more than once that this was not going to turn out well. Henry took one last draw off his cigarette and tossed in onto the street.

"Tell me, what did you do last night?" Bonnie asked Polly.

"Mommy cried all night, Miss Bonnie. Daddy didn't come home.

She says she doesn't know where he is or whether he's coming back at all," the little girl said, the inevitable sadness returning to her face.

Bonnie knelt beside her. "Don't worry, dear. They're looking for him. I'm sure he's just working hard, and can't get home until he gets lots of money to bring back to you."

Polly cast her eyes downward, her bottom lip extending showing her sadness. "I guess so, but Mommy sure is sad. She says we can't go much longer if'n he don't come back."

Suddenly, her eyes flashed upward to Bonnie. "And that mean old man in the suit says he's gonna kick us out if'n we don't pay!" she said, kicking her chubby little leg into the air. "He wouldn't do that to us, would he Miss Bonnie? We don't have nowhere to go."

Bonnie's blood boiled at the mention of Mr. Bonnet, the man who collected the rent at the houses on Gay Street and generally terrorized its tenants. She attempted to quash her anger with a soft smile.

"Don't you worry about that, Polly," she said. "I'll take care of him. Now, come over here and sit down. You know I have something for you."

"What is it? What is it?" the little girl squealed as she sat on the step next to Bonnie.

"Well, let's see."

Bonnie reached into her pocket drawing out a silver hairbrush with a pink ribbon tied around the handle. Polly's eyes grew to the size of saucers as she slowly reached toward it, touching its fine handle.

"It's beautiful! Is it yours?"

"No, silly, it's yours. I got it for you."

"Miss Bonnie . . . my Mommy's not going to want me to keep it. She'll say it's to 'spensive," the little girl said, a forlorn expression passing over her face.

"Well, she has to let you keep it because it didn't cost me anything. It was my grandmother's, and I want you to have it."

Polly threw her arms around Bonnie's neck, hugging her tight. "I love you, Miss Bonnie," she whispered into Bonnie's ear. Henry sat in the truck with his hat tucked down over his eyes as if he wasn't watching. He shook his head again, rubbing the stubble on his chin.

By the time Bonnie and Polly came back to the Sutton apartment,

Polly's mother was awake. Bonnie unloaded the dry goods, then she and Henry headed back to Red Cross headquarters.

Annie Parker had written her note to Lizzie McCaverty as promised to Mrs. Greenfield. It was on its way to Smithville before Bonnie arrived home that day, which was just in time for supper. Bonnie wearily pulled her cape from her shoulders, draping it on the coat rack near the door.

"You look tired," Reverend Parker said.

"I feel tired. I'm just so frustrated!" Bonnie said rapping her hand on the table, causing a few spoons to go astray from their bowls. She closed her eyes, ashamed of her actions, then opened them slowly, squinting at the Reverend.

"I'm sorry" she said, standing to reach the sideboard for a cloth. As she dabbed the few spots off the tablecloth replacing the spoons in their bowls, Annie watched intently as Reverend Parker sat with his hands folded in front of him.

Bonnie quickly took her seat. She folded her hands in her lap, then sheepishly turned toward Reverend Parker. "Forgive me. I guess I'm just tired. I feel like I could explode inside, though. You don't understand. Polly's father, he's nowhere to be found, and that despicable Mr. Bonnet says he's going to kick them out if they don't pay their rent. What will they do?" She looked pleadingly at Reverend Parker, who quietly picked up his fork and began to eat.

It was a gesture Bonnie knew all too well. It meant "eat first, talk later." She followed suit, trying to eat what she could, patiently waiting to see if he was going to offer to help her.

Finally, Reverend Parker laid his napkin on the table, leaning back in his chair. "How is Mrs. Sutton? Is she still sick?"

"Yes," Bonnie answered eagerly. "She sleeps all the time, and she's so pale. The doctor says she has some sort of heart trouble, but that she should be all right in time."

"She should be under normal circumstances," Reverend Parker interjected, "but her husband disappearing and two children to care for isn't normal circumstances."

"I know, and now they want to make her leave because she doesn't have the money to pay for their home. What will they do?"

"Well, there aren't many places for a woman and two children, least of all now with everything as bad as it is. The church has taken in all the families it can take care of right now, Bonnie. I guess I could make some calls and see if anyone else has any room."

Bonnie leapt out of her chair Reverend Parker kissing him on the cheek. "Thank you so much! I knew I could count on you to help me. Now you make those calls. I'm going to pay someone a visit."

Miss Annie caught up to Bonnie in the entrance hall where she was already pulling a coat from the closet. "Where are you going?" she asked in amazement. "It's already dark out, and you're exhausted."

"I'm going to pay that Mr. Ned Bass a visit," Bonnie replied. "How can he be so cruel? Having that mean old Mr. Bonnet threaten to kick Mrs. Sutton and those children out into the cold with nowhere to go and their father missing! That's some kind of brotherly love I tell you." Bonnie began wrapping a scarf around her neck.

"You're not going anywhere!" Annie shouted, tugging at the scarf.

"What?"

"I said you're not going anywhere, Miss Bonnie McCaverty, even if I have to sit on you myself. You are going upstairs. You are going to take a hot bath, and you are going to bed."

"But . . ."

"No buts, young lady. You're staying home," Annie said, firmly standing her ground. "I've been quite patient with you, dear, but you've simply gone too far. You have to slow down.

"Now, Reverend Parker and I are responsible for you, and if your mother saw you with this weary look on your face and these dark circles under your eyes from working these long shifts, she wouldn't be happy with us. Your visit with Mr. Bass will have to wait until morning!" Annie said, her chin jutting outward indicating to Bonnie that she expected no less than a *yes, ma'am* from her.

Slowly, Bonnie removed her coat, hanging it back in the closet, glancing at Miss Annie out of the corner of her eye. Annie stood firm with her arms folded in front of her. Bonnie tried to hide a giggle as she stuck her head in the closet. It was a hard thing for Annie Parker to be stern, and that uncharacteristic behavior somehow made it funny.

"Yes, ma'am," Bonnie answered slowly. She put her arms around Annie. "I'm sorry. I just can't help but worry about them. I guess I got carried away, and I haven't been very considerate. The last thing I wanted to do was cause the two of you to worry." She kissed Miss Annie on the cheek. "I promise I'll go upstairs and rest."

Bonnie turned, walking to the bottom of the stairs. As she rested her foot on the first step, Bonnie turned around, shaking her fist in the air. "But tomorrow I'm going to visit that rat and give him a piece of my mind." Just as quickly, she scrambled up the stairs.

Reverend Parker was still sitting at the supper table with his back to the scene. He chuckled quietly. Annie walked back into the dining room and sat at the table. "Can you believe her? What are we going to do with her?"

"Oh, I think she'll be just fine. Bonnie can take care of herself!"

Annie reached out slapping his hand. "Oh, and you just encourage her. You're just as bad."

"Look," Reverend Parker said, reaching for Annie's hand. "Bonnie is a head-strong girl. You knew that when we asked her to come live with us. What she's doing is noble, Annie. Granted, it's more than most nineteen-year-olds would do, but she's doing all the right things." He put a hand on his wife's cheek, forcing her to look at him. "You can't keep her from getting her heart broken. You can't protect her from experiencing life. You and I both know that Bonnie McCaverty will experience life to the fullest, and nothing or no one can stop that from happening."

Annie pulled away from her husband, turning her head upward toward the ceiling. Bonnie was above them in her room preparing to take a bath. "That's exactly what I'm afraid of," she said.

The next morning, Bonnie arose early already preparing to leave when Annie came down the stairs.

"Where are you going so early?"

"Well . . . I slept for ten hours, and I feel glorious! I'm going to see Ned Bass before I go to the Red Cross."

"Bonnie, now don't go into that man's office acting foolishly. These are businessmen, dear. You have to remember that."

"I know that, Miss Annie, but that doesn't give them the right to be inhuman to people who are less fortunate."

Annie placed her arms on Bonnie's shoulders, turning her to face her. "These are hard times for everyone, Bonnie. Even the businessmen are having a hard time. Their problems may not be where to live or what to eat, but they do have their own kind of problems. Just promise me you'll remember that."

"I'll remember," Bonnie acknowledged. "But those problems couldn't be as bad as Polly's." With that, she opened the front door, trotting off to catch the streetcar.

By the time Bonnie reached Broadway, where the Bass family conducted its business, she was cold and quite irritated. She opened the heavy doors at the Bass Building and made her way inside.

The lady at the desk noticed Bonnie standing there in her freshly starched Red Cross uniform looking rather puzzled. She walked over to greet her.

"May I help you, Miss?" the lady asked.

"Yes, you can tell me where I can find Mr. Bass," Bonnie said curtly.

"Which Mr. Bass are you looking for?"

"He's about so high, big shoulders, and he's about, oh I don't know, I think his name is Ned. He owns some houses down on Gay Street. I want to talk to him."

The lady frowned at her.

"Well, I'm not sure where you'll find Mr. Bass this morning. You can check his office. It's on the fifth floor."

"Thank you," Bonnie said. "Where are the stairs?"

"You can use the elevator. It's right over there." She pointed the way.

"Elevator?" Bonnie whispered, swallowing hard. She had never been on an elevator and wasn't looking forward to it. Slowly, she inched toward the doors where the lady had pointed, sizing up the problem at hand. Suddenly, the big brass doors began to slide to the side. Bonnie jerked backward.

"Oh my goodness!" she said.

The boy in the uniform smiled at her. "Which floor, Miss?" he asked.

Not without some trepidation, Bonnie walked inside the box and turning slowly to face the boy.

"Mr. Ned Bass's office. The fifth floor, I believe."

"Yes, ma'am, fifth floor coming up!" the boy said as the doors closed.

"Oh my goodness!" Bonnie shouted, reaching for the railing as the box began to rise. "Oh my goodness!" The young boy smiled. Bonnie was sure he could tell she had never ridden an elevator.

The car eased to a stop at the fifth floor. The doors slowly parted. The young man stepped across the threshold waving his hand, ushering her to move outside the car.

"Here you are, Miss. The fifth floor."

Bonnie straightened her Red Cross cap. "Yes, so it is," she said. She felt rather weak in the knees.

Glancing from right to left, she wondered in which direction to go when she noticed the directory straight in front of her. "Bass & Bass, Attorneys-at-Law," she whispered. "Suite 501 . . ." Bonnie decided to go right. Her white padded shoes squeaked against the marble floor as she made her way slowly, squinting at the rows of doors along the underlit hallway. At the very end, she found Suite 501 secured by a walnut stained wooden door with an opaque white windowpane. Printed in black letters on the pane were the words "Bass and Bass, Attorneys at Law." She opened the door and walked slowly over to where a woman sat at a desk.

"May I help you?" the older lady asked.

"Yes," Bonnie answered, purposefully extending her chin a bit to let her know she meant business. "I'm looking for Ned Bass."

"I'm sorry, he's not in right now," she said.

"Isn't this his office?" Bonnie asked. "I came all the way from Sylvan Park, and I want to see him."

"I'm sorry, Miss. Did you have an appointment?"

"No, I didn't have time to make an appointment," Bonnie said. The old lady sitting behind the big wooden desk was beginning to get on Bonnie's nerves.

"Well . . . you could wait for him here. He should be along soon. He's having breakfast right now, but I'm not sure he'll be able to see you."

Bonnie grew more frustrated. She had to get to the Red Cross office, but she also wanted to talk to Mr. Ned Bass and get the things she wanted to tell him off her chest.

"Where is he eating?" Bonnie asked the old lady.

"I can't tell you that!" the secretary answered. "Who are you?"

Bonnie stomped her foot. "I'm from the Red Cross, and I have a few things to tell him about his buildings and turning children out on the street!"

"Now, Miss," the secretary said as she came from behind her desk, "why don't you make an appointment, and I'll tell Mr. Bass why you'd like to see him."

"Oh . . . I don't have time to come again!" Bonnie's mind was racing, trying to figure out what to do. "Never mind, I'll come back later, and he better be here," Bonnie said. In her mind, a man who worked at a particular place should be in that particular place. What she didn't realize was that young Mr. Bass was second in line at Bass & Bass after his father, Carlton Netherly Bass, Senior. Although highly educated and a devoted son, the young Mr. Bass did tend to go about business in his own leisurely sort of way.

Bonnie headed back to the elevator. She stood in front of the doors and waited for them to open, not aware that she had to press the down button to call the elevator to that floor. The secretary grinned, walked over, pushing the button for Bonnie, whose face flushed. The doors opened, and she saw the young elevator operator standing there. Bonnie's face softened to a warm smile as she entered the box to go down to the lobby.

"Lobby, Miss?" the boy asked.

"Yes . . ." Bonnie said with a smile, turning on her McCaverty charm. "You know, I just can't believe I missed him. I traveled all this way, and I missed him! Land sakes, you know I could have telephoned first. I just forget sometimes that I should do those kinds of things."

"Who did you miss?" the operator asked.

"I missed Ned, of course. I came all the way down here from Smithville to volunteer to help the poor. I'm Ned's cousin, Bonnie!" she said, extending a hand out from underneath her cape.

The operator's cheeks reddened. He extended his hand to shake Bonnie's as the elevator slowly descended to the lobby. Bonnie looked up, watching as the floor indicators flashed past the fourth floor, the third floor . . . she knew she had to think fast.

"He went out to eat breakfast, they say. Well, I guess if I would have called, he could have taken me. Oh, I wish I knew where he was!" Bonnie exclaimed, trying to act aggravated at herself.

"Well, Mr. Bass—the young Mr. Bass, that is—always eats at Underwood's up on the square," the operator said. "He's been eatin' there for years. Everyone knows that!"

Bonnie smiled triumphantly. "Underwood's. Well, I should have thought about that. Just exactly where is that now?" she asked.

"It's up on the square."

"Oh, thank you. Now I'll get to see him before I have to go off and do my duties. Thank you so much. I just don't know why I didn't ask his secretary to tell me where he was. You've been such a big help," Bonnie said as the big brass doors slid apart opening onto the lobby. Bonnie took a few steps out, turned around to face the operator, and waved.

"Thanks again," she said as the big doors closed in front of her.

Suddenly, Bonnie relaxed her charm, and headed for the street. It was practically empty of pedestrians. Frustrated, she looked around for someone to ask directions. Usually, Henry drove her around town or she rode the streetcar. She was usually too busy talking to pay attention to where she was.

A man in a nice gray suit emerged from the building behind Bonnie and turned slightly to tip his hat. She seized the opportunity.

"Excuse me," she said, placing her gloved hand gently on his arm. "Can you help me? I'm looking for a restaurant called Underwood's. I believe it's on the Square?"

The man turned and smiled. Bonnie noticed he had a leather case in his left hand. "Underwood's? It's on the square," he answered.

"Yes . . . the square," Bonnie said, turning on every ounce of charm she could muster. "I'm sort of new to town. Could you point me in the right direction?"

The man smiled back. "I'll do better than that. I'll walk you there. I'm going to the courthouse myself. Underwood's is in the same building."

"Oh, wonderful . . . thank you so much!" Bonnie said, placing her hand in the crook of the arm he offered her. They walked up Fourth turning right to go to the square. The gentleman who walked along with her showed her to the door of Underwood's Restaurant.

"Here we are, Miss Bonnie, safe and sound. Now, you be careful out here. When you get ready to go to the Red Cross, just go right down to that corner and catch the streetcar there," the man said as he tipped his hat again.

"Thank you so much for your help," Bonnie said. She offered her hand. He took it in his, shaking it delicately.

"You're very welcome. Now you be safe out here on the street," the gentleman warned.

"Oh, I will. Thank you again."

Bonnie straightened her collar, stuck out her chin, pushing open the heavy door to the restaurant.

It took a moment for her eyes to adjust to the dimness as she looked around the dining room. Nothing but men, and they all looked the same. She walked over to the man behind the counter.

"How do you do? I'm looking for Mr. Ned Bass. Is he still here?"

Frank Underwood looked up from his newspaper and pointed a finger toward one of the tables in the back. Bonnie recognized the man she had met over a year ago in the hallway of Polly's apartment house. She took a deep breath and walked to the back of the restaurant. Ned Bass was just finishing his coffee.

"Mr. Bass?" Bonnie said. The young Mr. Bass looked up from his coffee cup.

"Yes . . . I'm Ned Bass," he said with a puzzled look. "Have we met before?"

"Yes, we have," Bonnie said, twisting her gloves in her hands, "at the houses on Gay Street. I fell and ripped my stockings on the stairs."

"Oh, yes, yes . . . well, I'd offer you a seat, but . . ." Mr. Bass nodded toward the three other men who sat at his table. One well-dressed gentleman was shoveling a forkful of eggs into his mouth, while one of the others precariously leaned out over his plate slopping his biscuit through a pile of gravy. The third stared coolly at Bonnie over his stoneware coffee cup.

"May I help you?" Ned Bass offered, standing.

"Yes. You can," Bonnie started. She looked around the room. All these men, it was so smoky in there, and they were all staring at her. "Well . . . first of all, you should be ashamed! Throwing innocent children and sick mothers out on the street! These people have nowhere to go, but you don't care. You just work down here in your fine buildings, eating a fine breakfast and driving fine cars. But Polly, she doesn't even know where her father is!" Bonnie began to spout at him. Ned Bass' eyes grew wide as Bonnie's voice grew louder. He backed up a bit every time she dug her finger into his chest.

"That awful man who works for you, that Mr. Howell, is so cruel. How could you employ someone like that?"

Ned attempted to recover control. "Hold on there, Miss. Let's you and me go outside and let these men finish their breakfast in peace. Why it's not very ladylike to interrupt men in the middle of their breakfast. Now is it?" Bonnie suddenly became aware of everyone staring at her and went silent waiting for him to say something.

"Let me get my hat and coat, and we'll go outside and talk, okay?" he asked. Bonnie nodded in agreement. Ned Bass winked at the other gentlemen at the table as he turned his back on Bonnie to get his things. They walked toward the door.

"Put it on my tab, Frank," Ned said, walking past the check-out counter.

"Sure thing, Ned. Now you be careful out there and try to have a nice day," he said sarcastically.

"I'll try," Ned said, leaning over the counter. The two men smiled at each other. Their patronizing interaction infuriated Bonnie even more. When they got out on the street, she let go on him again.

"You can try and embarrass me all you want, but I came here to say something, and I'm going to say it!" Bonnie said to him as Ned whisked her around the corner of the building for more privacy.

"Listen, I don't care what you say; you just don't have to say it in front of the whole world! You wanna put me outta business?"

"If I could!" Bonnie answered, jerking her arm out of his grip. "You should be out of business. People shouldn't have to live in places like you rent. You should be ashamed of yourself."

"Listen, why are you here? Why have you tracked me down at breakfast to start my day off like this? What have I done to you?" Ned asked as he drew a Chesterfield out of its pack and lit it.

"It's not me," Bonnie told him. "It's the family Mr. Howell is going to kick out on the street if they don't come up with some money. Their father is missing, and they don't know what to do. I don't know what to do." She turned away from him, facing the street.

Ned threw his match onto the street and leaned against the building. He drew his collar up closer around his neck. The November weather was beginning to turn cold. "What house?" he asked.

"The first one on Gay Street," Bonnie replied, facing him again. Suddenly, the young, fiery girl looked worn and tired. She rubbed her neck. "Look, their father is missing. He may be dead. He may have run away, but Mrs. Sutton is sick, and she has a four-year-old and a baby. She has no family and nowhere to go. Mr. Howell wants her to come up with the rent. She can get a job as soon as she gets better, I'm sure."

"Yeah, sure. Where's she gonna work? Where's anyone like that gonna work right now? If you haven't noticed, there aren't a lot of jobs to be had. You're right about one thing; the father is probably dead . . . probably killed himself." Ned flipped his cigarette butt into the alley.

Bonnie's hands went to her mouth. "No . . . he just can't be dead! What will they do?" she asked. She grabbed Ned by his coat, pleading with him. "What will they do?"

Ned instinctively covered her hands with his, which were still wrapped around the lapel of his coat, the alarm in her eyes caught his gaze. Just as sudden, they turned sad and misty.

At twenty-five, Ned Bass not only practiced law, but he also ran the real estate ventures for the family. Now here was this innocent young girl standing there facing him, pleading for the lives of some stranger and her children as if he was an executioner. He slowly pulled her hands away from his coat releasing them.

"What do you want me to do? I have to have money coming in from those rooms. Where would I be if I let every person who lost his job live there free? I'd be without a job, I tell ya," Ned said. He stepped away from her, rubbing his hands together against the cold.

"I just want you to give them some time," Bonnie pleaded. "We're trying to find a place that will take them in until she finds her husband, or gets better. Just give them a month, just a month. If I don't have them out by then, your Mr. Howell can do what he does best."

"Oh, don't blame him," Ned said. "He's just doing his job."

"Well" Bonnie said. "He doesn't have to enjoy it so much."

Ned smiled as he turned to face her. "That you're probably right about." He paused a long moment. Bonnie waited. "Okay, I'll give them one month. One month and that's all! After that, they have to go. I wouldn't be able to explain it otherwise."

Bonnie was ecstatic. It had worked. She had bought them thirty more days. She threw her arms around Ned, hugging him.

"Thank you. Thank you. I promise I'll have them out in thirty days. Wait and see. Reverend Parker is already looking for them a place to go. You'll see. It'll be fine. Thank you!"

"Okay, okay," he said, smiling. "Just don't tell anyone. It could be my head if my father finds out."

"Your father . . ."

"Yes, you know, Bass and Bass? He's the older one," he sarcastically informed her.

"He's your father . . . the one who owns the building?" Bonnie asked.

"Yes, and you might say he doesn't like it when someone goes soft. I must be crazy. If he finds out . . ."

"Oh," Bonnie said. "Oh my, well, I don't want to get you into any trouble or anything."

Ned waved her away. "Don't worry about it. I can handle it."

Bonnie checked the time. "Well, I've got to be going now," she said, moving toward him offering her hand. "Thank you again."

Ned slowly reached for her hand, took it in his, and shook it. "You're welcome. What are their names anyway?" he asked.

"Oh," Bonnie said. "I almost completely forgot." She pulled a card out of her pocket with their names written on it.

"Here," she said, handing it to him.

"Thanks, I'll take care of Mr. Howell."

"Well . . . thanks again. Oh . . . and, I'm sorry about your breakfast," Bonnie said, smiling.

"It's okay. We all need a little something to wake us out of our slumber every now and then."

"Well, goodbye," Bonnie said. "Thank you again."

Ned remained leaning against the building, watching as Bonnie walked down the street and around the corner toward the transfer station to catch her streetcar. He shook his head, slowly pushing himself off the wall, brushing off his sleeve. He had forgotten to ask for her name. Quickly, he walked down to the street corner where she had already disappeared. A streetcar rocked along down Charlotte and out of sight. She was probably in it.

Ned stood on the corner watching it for a moment longer, a broad smile making its way across his face. He wasn't sure why, but he lingered thinking about the fiery redhead and her bravely entering Underwood's to give him a piece of her mind.

"You don't see that every day," he spoke to himself as he stubbed one last cigarette butt out in the street with his foot.

CHAPTER NINE

"The poor guy didn't have a chance."

B
ONNIE STEPPED OFF the streetcar and entered the Red Cross office. She saw Henry as he was leaving to pick up his deliveries at the warehouse on Broadway and waved him down.

"You comin' back here at lunch time?" Bonnie asked, leaning into the cab of the old truck.

"Probably not," he answered.

"Henry . . ." Bonnie pleaded.

"Miss Bonnie, you're going to get me in trouble with Miss Greenfield if I keep takin' you down there to see that girl and get off my route."

"I'll bake you some more cookies," Bonnie promised.

"Don't want no more cookies, Miss Bonnie," Henry said, eyeing her warily.

"Henry," Bonnie said, lowering her voice, "you know I have to see her. I have to! Besides, I have some good news for them."

"They find Mr. Sutton?"

"No, but I did talk to that young Mr. Bass who owns the building, well, his father owns it, but it don't make no nevermind. He's gonna tell Mr. Howell to leave them alone for thirty days! Thirty days, Henry! That'll be enough time for us to figure out somethin'. What do you think about that?" Bonnie gave him a gentle shove. Her face was beaming.

Henry shifted, sitting straighter in his seat, removing his hat. "Why, Miss Bonnie, how did you do that? No one can't afford to go without their rent in these hard times."

"I just went down there and asked him. That's all."

"The poor guy didn't have a chance," he said.

"Why, Henry Stokes, what do you mean by that?" Bonnie grinned.

Henry put the truck into gear. "I'll be at the corner at twelve-thirty, and don't you be late!"

"Thanks, Henry!" Bonnie yelled after him, blowing a kiss as he drove away then hurried inside to see what her assignment was for the day.

At twelve-thirty, Bonnie stood on the corner of Fourth and Church waiting on Henry.

Together, they made their way to Seventh and on toward the house on Gay Street. There, Polly sat at the window in the lonely apartment. Her mother was in the bedroom with the baby sleeping again. When Polly heard the knock on the door, her heart leapt! She quickly ran to the door, opening it only a few inches, peeping out with one blue eye to see if it was Bonnie.

"Hi!" Bonnie whispered.

"Hi!" Polly whispered back. "Mommy's asleep."

"Well, open the door. I have to wake her up. I have some good news for her."

Polly's blue eye widened. "Did you find Daddy?" she asked.

"No, honey, I didn't, but I have some good news for your mommy. Unlock the door." Polly quietly unlatched the lock. Bonnie leaned down scooping the little girl up into her arms.

"I missed you," Bonnie whispered.

"How could you miss me? You just saw me yesterday," the little girl replied.

"Wise guy, huh?" She swept the little girl in her arms, tickling her as she sat her back on the floor, bending down to talk with her. "Honey, I have to talk to your mother. Go and wake her up."

"Miss Bonnie, she'll be mad at me. She's so tired."

"She won't be mad. I promise. I have something important to tell her."

Polly turned to make her way back to the bedroom where her mother was sleeping. The baby began to cry.

"Oh, Polly, you woke the baby."

"I'm sorry, Mommy. Miss Bonnie made me," she said in a whine, the combination of hunger, exhaustion and worry apparent in the little girl's tone.

"Okay, okay. Tell her I'll be right there." Polly walked back to where Bonnie was pacing back and forth. She didn't have much time. If Henry got caught taking the truck out, Mrs. Greenfield would severely reprimand them both.

"Polly, come and get the baby," Mrs. Sutton yelled from the bedroom. Polly scrambled to the bedroom to get the baby as her mother made her way to the other room.

Bonnie gasped when she saw Polly's mother appear at the bedroom door. She wore a housecoat and her nightgown. Her face was sunken and sallow. It was the middle of the day, but Bonnie knew she hadn't been out of bed since she'd been there yesterday.

"Hello, Bonnie. I'm sorry to keep you waiting, but I don't seem to have much energy." Bonnie moved to help her to a chair.

"Are you feeling any better?" Bonnie asked.

"No, I'm just so weak. I can't seem to do anything but sleep."

"Mrs. Sutton, why don't you think about going to City Hospital? You really need to be checked out again."

"Who would be here with the girls, Bonnie? What am I going to do?" She began to weep. Polly came to the entrance of the bedroom with the baby in her frail little arms, handing the baby to her mother.

"Is there no word on your husband?" Bonnie asked.

"No. Nothing. I can't imagine what could have happened to him. Where is he? Why would he just leave?"

"He didn't just leave. I'm sure he found a job somewhere and just can't come home yet. He knows you'll be all right until he gets back."

"All right?" She spread her free arm wide looking around her. "Do you call this all right? We're about to be kicked out, Bonnie. We have nowhere to go."

"That's why I'm here," Bonnie interrupted. "Listen, I talked to the man who owns the building. He's going to give you thirty more days here! Isn't that wonderful news? He said he'd take care of Mr. Howell so you can bet he won't be coming by here bothering you for a while." Bonnie smiled proudly.

"How? How did you do that?"

"Don't think about that right now. I have to go, but Reverend Parker is looking for a place for you and the girls to stay until we find Mr. Sutton. Everything will be okay for a while. You just try to get stronger, all right?"

Mrs. Sutton stood, trying to extend her frail hand. "Thank you, Miss Bonnie. What would we do without you?" She began to cry. Bonnie reached around the frail woman and her baby. Polly wrapped her arms around Bonnie's legs. Bonnie looked down to see little Polly's blue eyes looking up at her brimming with tears. She quickly bent down, pulling the little girl to her.

"Don't cry, Polly. Everything will be all right."

"Thank you, Miss Bonnie," Polly told her.

"Oh, don't thank me. Thank the Lord. He's the one working it all out. You just be a strong little girl for your mother, okay?"

"Okay," the little girl answered with a sniff. Bonnie wiped tears from the little girl's face before she stood.

"I have to get back to work. I'll try to get by tomorrow to see you." Bonnie left the apartment hurrying to the truck. Now, she and Henry were running late.

Bonnie arrived home that night just at supper time. She walked right into the dining room after hanging her coat. She sat at the dinner table, not even bothering to wash up. She was too eager to hear if Reverend Parker found anyone who would take Mrs. Sutton and the two girls.

"Well, did you find them a place?" she asked.

"Bonnie, Reverend Parker's trying to eat his supper. You go and wash up now."

"But—"

"Bonnie!" Annie said sternly. Bonnie knew better than to argue. She got up from the table, hurried upstairs, and was back sitting at the table in less than five minutes. She rushed through her blessing then eyed Reverend Parker expectantly.

"Well?"

"I've called all around today, Bonnie. No luck. I called everywhere. All of the churches are full."

"Darn!" Bonnie said.

"Bonnie McCaverty! I won't have kind of talk in this house," Reverend Parker admonished.

"I'm sorry."

"I've got calls in to many places around Nashville that help the poor. Something will turn up. Father Moore thinks he may have enough space for them soon. He'll keep trying," Reverend Parker said. He patted her hand. "Don't worry, Bonnie. God will prepare a place for them."

"Well, He'll have to come git me if we don't find them a place soon. I've practically promised them. I sure hope He comes through soon." Bonnie dug at her food. The Reverend and Annie exchanged glances. They ate the remainder of their supper in silence.

Sunday came and Bonnie spent the day with Annie as promised, however, her mind was on Mr. Bass' tenement house on Gay Street. She couldn't wait for Monday to come when Bonnie would make her regular monthly rounds. She knew she'd get to spend more time with Polly.

She was staring into the flames that were licking and popping at the logs in the living room fireplace late that evening when Annie found her.

"Bonnie . . ." she said softly.

Bonnie forced herself out of her thoughts.

"I'm sorry. I was somewhere else," Bonnie admitted.

"Gay Street?" Miss Annie asked.

"No . . . back home," Bonnie said. She looked down at the mending she was trying to finish.

"Home?" Annie asked, surprised.

Bonnie looked back into the fire. "Yes, ma'am. I guess I was thinking about Mama and Daddy. I miss them. You know, thinking about Polly and her family, I guess I never realized how lucky I am and how God's always been merciful to me and mine. Miss Annie, I never meant to sound sacrilege the other night at the supper table." She turned in her chair to face Mrs. Parker. "I just, well, I've just never seen how some people have to live with no place to go and no family. You know, Miss Annie, most of those poor people have never been to church. They don't know nothin' 'bout Jesus or Angels or nothin.' I know it sounds funny, but it makes me miss home."

Annie smiled, sitting across from Bonnie. "It doesn't sound funny, dear. You're homesick. You realize all the wonderful things you've had, and the people you try to help don't have those things. It makes you thankful for your family, so you want to see them. I'm sure they miss you."

"Miss Annie, after I get Polly's family in one of the churches or wherever we can find a spot for them, I'd like to go home for a while, just to visit, of course."

"I think that's a wonderful idea, Bonnie. I was going to suggest that very thing. I believe you should go for Thanksgiving and stay clear through until after Christmas."

Bonnie shot out of her chair. "Oh no, Miss Annie. I can't stay that long! I just can't! There's so much to do, and Polly would be so disappointed. I just couldn't!"

"Bonnie, you need to rest. I can't tell you how tired you look. Your mother and father will be so alarmed when they see you."

"Then, I just won't go!"

"Now, Bonnie . . ."

Bonnie leaned closer to Mrs. Parker. "Miss Annie, you don't understand. Polly has no one. Her mother is deathly sick. Her father is God knows where, he may even be dead, and half the time she doesn't even know where her next meal is coming from." Tears filled her hazel eyes, pooling onto her face. "I can't leave, not for more than a few days. I have to come back. She's so alone."

Bonnie began to cry. "I just can't stand it, Miss Annie. I just want to take her out of there, away from that awful, dreadful place. I want her to play in the sun like I did at her age, to run through a hay field when it's plum tall over your head."

Bonnie stood. "I want her to ride a horse like Danny and play in the hayloft or see a rainbow end right smack dab in the middle of a green cornfield in a spring rain. She just has to know that life is like that, Miss Annie. She just has to know." Bonnie paced around the room lit by the amber of the fire as she spoke.

"She has to know it's not sitting up at night with an infant crying in your arms, and your mother won't wake up because she's so weak, and you have no food to give the baby, and you're only four years old. She has to know that people live in places where the rats don't crawl in your bed at night!"

Annie stood quickly, wrapping her arms around Bonnie's frail body, pulling her close. Bonnie's thin frame shivered in Mrs. Parker's arms.

"Now, now, dear, it's okay," Annie said consolingly. Bonnie pulled away, walking toward the crackling fire.

"It won't be okay. Not 'til I get her out of that place."

"Bonnie, you can't do everything. Reverend Parker is trying his best . . ."

Almost as if summoned, Revered Parker walked in. "Bonnie," he said, "I found a place for your friend and her children."

Bonnie looked at Annie, then at the Reverend, her face still damp from crying, her mouth opening wide in disbelief.

"Where?" Bonnie asked, pulling away from Annie, wiping her face with the back of her hands.

"Well, the First Presbyterian will take them in a few days. They're taking over a small house that was left to them by a widow woman, and it will be ready in a few days.

"Hallelujah!" Bonnie squealed as she threw her arms into the air.

"This calls for a celebration," Annie added. "I'll make some coffee, and we'll have some cake." She sprinted for the kitchen.

Bonnie walked over to the Reverend, slipping her arms around his neck. "Thank you. I know you've been working really hard to find them a place."

"I had to promise the Pastor the moon, you know," the Reverend said, smiling down at Bonnie, the fine silver of his hair glistening in the light of the fire.

"The moon? I didn't know the moon was yours to give?"

"Youuuu . . . always a wise guy," he said, giving her chin a fake right hook.

Bonnie hugged him while breathing a sigh of relief. Tonight, at long last, she would sleep well.

On Tuesday, Bonnie received a letter from Lizzie, instructing her to come home for Thanksgiving. Her father was going to borrow a car and would be there to pick her up on Saturday.

Bonnie was upset that her mother hadn't phoned first, but knew she had better be packed and be ready to go come Saturday morning. She was anxious because she hadn't yet been able to move Polly, her mother, and sister over to the house in Flat Rock. The house was old and needed some work before it would be ready to occupy.

On Wednesday morning, the Reverend received a call the house was ready, and they would even send a truck to load their things.

"That's mighty fine. Bonnie will be so pleased. Now, you let me get that address from her, and I'll phone you back.

"That's fine, yes . . . okay. Thank you again," Annie heard Reverend Parker say as she walked into the room.

"Who was that?" Annie asked.

"That was Pastor Mooney. The house is finished, and they're even sending a truck to pick up Bonnie's friend."

"That's mighty Christian of them. Don't you think?"

"Yes, it is. I've got to get back to the church. You tell Bonnie if she phones that you need the address on Gay Street, and they need to be ready to move by tomorrow."

"If I know Bonnie, she has them packed already," Annie said, grinning. "At least she'll go on to Smithville in peace now. Maybe she'll even enjoy herself."

"I hope so, dear," Reverend Parker said. He kissed Annie's forehead. "Just think, we'll be alone again. How 'bout that?"

"How 'bout it, you old coot? Get out of here and get to work!" Annie said, waving her kitchen towel at him. Reverend Parker blew her a kiss, grabbed his hat, and made his way out of the kitchen.

Bonnie obtained permission from Mrs. Greenfield to spend most of Monday and Tuesday with Polly and her family helping get them ready to move. She noticed Mrs. Sutton's spirits beginning to rise a bit.

Bonnie had also made a claim for them at the Red Cross for the rent money they owed for the few weeks they had been there. Mrs. Greenfield was able to drum up the money and have it in Bonnie's hands by Wednesday morning. Bonnie walked right over to one of the other buildings, where Mr. Howell lived, to give him the money.

The burly, old man opened the door observing Bonnie sourly.

"Oh, it's you," he said. "What do you want?" he said, turning to take his seat in a beat-up old chair, leaving the door open. Bonnie remained on the other side of the threshold.

"I have the remainder of the money Mrs. Sutton owes you," She said very business like. "I have found a place for them to move. They'll be leaving today."

"Oh, they are? Are they?" he said.

"Yes. Would you kindly take this money and tell Mr. Bass I appreciate the time he was so nice to give us?"

"You tell him. Leave the money on the table."

"I won't," Bonnie said. She wasn't about to give in to his test of her will. "You come and get this money."

The old man looked up at her from his chair by the window, an evil grin on his face. Bonnie's heart thumped hard in her chest. She swallowed hard. The smell alone of the musty old room made her feel sick.

"Mr. Howell, I don't need to tell you how much I disapprove of your treatment of my client, Mrs. Sutton. I also don't need to tell you that I'm an acquaintance of your boss, Mr. Bass. If you don't behave yourself and come get this money, I'll have to take it to him. While I'm there, I'll be sure to tell him you wouldn't take the money from me."

Mr. Howell stood from his ragged chair, walking over to the doorway where Bonnie stood holding out the money in her gloved hand. He went to reach for it. Bonnie pulled away.

"I'll need a receipt please," she said firmly.

"Receipt . . ." the old man mumbled. He floundered around, looking for his receipt book. He scribbled something on it and walked back over to Bonnie, then took the money, handing her the receipt.

"Thank you," Bonnie said.

"They're your responsibility now. I hope you're happy."

"What do you mean by that?" Bonnie asked.

"I mean their Pa, he ain't comin' back," the old man said as an evil grin spread across his face showing teeth stained by tobacco. He sneered at Bonnie.

"How would you know?" she asked.

Mr. Howell put his arm against the doorframe leaning toward Bonnie. She could smell the liquor on his breath. The smell of him nearly choked her.

"Because he's dead," the old man exclaimed with a evil edge to his voice.

"And how do you know that?" she said, hoping she sounded defiant.

"'Causin' I seen it. He was a coming down through Black Bottom, and they jumped him. I heard they dropped him into the river."

Bonnie's hand went to her mouth.

"Why didn't you tell the police?"

"Weren't none of my business. I didn't know it was for sure him or not. Besides, I don't like cops."

"You horrible person!" Bonnie shouted. "You horrible, horrible person."

She dashed off. Mr. Howell stood in the doorway in his undershirt. She could still hear him laughing as she scurried out of the building.

Outside, Bonnie took a deep breath. Between the liquor on Mr. Howell's breath and the thought of Polly's father being dead, she thought she might be sick. Henry, seeing her pallor, came rushing to her aid.

"What's wrong, Miss Bonnie? I told you to let me give him the money! What'd he say?"

"Nothing, I'm okay," she said. "I guess it was the liquor on his breath; turned my stomach. Come on let's get back."

Bonnie didn't tell Mrs. Sutton what she'd heard from old man Howell. It wasn't certain anyway, and she wasn't sure Mrs. Sutton could take that kind of news. Besides, she was so much better since they had gotten the news they were moving. Henry and Bonnie helped the mother and children finish loading their things into the truck sent over by the Presbyterian Church., then they escorted Polly and her family to an area of Nashville that most folks called "Flat Rock" to their new home.

The family wasn't allowed to take much with them, mainly clothing and a few pieces of furniture. There would be three other families living in the house, too, so they were only allowed one room of the place for themselves. Mrs. Sutton and the girls didn't care. It was clean, and they would be with other people. Polly even had other children with which to play.

When they were all moved in, Bonnie steeled herself to tell Polly she would be gone for a while. The happiness everyone was feeling following the move seemed to provide the perfect time to tell her.

"Polly, I have something to tell you," Bonnie said, taking a seat on the top step to the back yard.

"Okay, Miss Bonnie," Polly answered, tucking her little hands under her chin, cocking her head to one side looking at Bonnie, her unkempt hair framing her little face.

"You know, my mother and father live in another city," Bonnie said.

"Ah huh," Polly answered, squirming in her seat.

"Well, Thanksgiving is coming up, and they want me to come

and visit them. I haven't seen them for a long time, and I miss them very much."

"Kind'a like I miss Daddy?" Polly asked.

"Yes, honey, like you miss your Daddy. So, I have to go visit them this week, and I'm going to be gone for a while. I didn't want to leave until you and your mother and sister were in a better place, but since you have other people to help you now, I have to go and see my parents."

Polly's bottom lip began to quiver. "Are you not coming back, Miss Bonnie?" the little girl asked with a pout.

Bonnie put her arms around the little girl, pulling her close. "Yes, Polly. I couldn't stay away from you if I tried. Can I tell you something?" she asked as she turned Polly around to face her. She reached over and wiped tears from her pouty cheeks.

"Yeah," the little girl quietly answered.

"Polly, you know I never had a little sister. All my sisters were bigger than me, and well, I always wanted a little sister."

Polly's eyes lit up. "Miss Bonnie, I could be your little sister," she said, pointing her fat little hands at her own chest.

Bonnie smiled. "You know, that's a good idea! We could be sisters!"

Polly stood and wrapped her arms around her new big sister. "Will you have a tea party with me and everything?"

"Yes, I'd love to." Bonnie hugged her back. "Ohhhhh . . . Polly, I love you so much," Bonnie said fighting the lump forming in her throat.

"I love you, too, Miss Bonnie. Let's go have a tea party now," she said as she pulled Bonnie up the stairs to the back door, which led into the kitchen.

"Okay, okay." Bonnie laughed as she and Polly raced into the crowded house.

Bonnie saw Polly again on Thursday. Mrs. Sutton wasn't feeling well, but there was a kind woman who had moved into one of the rooms and was helping her with the baby. Bonnie was relieved and felt somewhat better about leaving them. By Friday, she was excited about going home to see her folks. Friday evening Bonnie was standing out on the front porch of the parsonage when Annie came out to join her.

"What are you doing out in this cold?" she asked. "You need to come in and get ready for bed. Your father will be here early in the morning.

"Can't you just see Daddy driving a car?" Bonnie said. "I guess a lot can happen in a year."

"Yes, it can," Annie agreed.

"I think some things will never change, though," Bonnie said thoughtfully.

Annie grinned. "Bonnie, are you thinking about Calvin?"

"A little, I guess. I've been so busy that I haven't thought much about it, but now, going home . . . knowing I'm going to see him again. I guess I'm just a bit nervous," Bonnie admitted.

"You never talk about him anymore. I guess I assumed you were over him. Are you?"

"I don't know. I thought I was, but now, thinking about seeing him again . . . oh, what am I thinking? He probably has a girl by now. I'm just being silly."

"Bonnie," Annie said, "feelings are not silly. You'll always have feelings for Calvin. He was your first love. Believe me, you never forget that."

"Wait a minute," Bonnie whispered. "Was Reverend Parker not your first love?"

Annie smiled. "No, dear, he wasn't. There was a boy near our farm where I grew up in Georgia. His name was Thomas."

"Thomas," Bonnie whispered.

"Yes. We were childhood sweethearts."

"Well, what happened?" Bonnie asked excitedly. She saw a side of Annie she'd never seen. As far as she'd ever considered, Annie and Reverend Parker had been together since the beginning of time.

"He took sick. Influenza. He was eighteen when he died. I was sixteen. I never thought I'd love anyone ever again," Annie said wistfully. "Then, along came Frank Parker, the traveling preacher. Oh, he was so handsome and tall, straight, self-assured. I'd never met anyone so refined, yet so gentle.

"Well, needless to say, Frank Parker stayed in Peach Grove for quite a while, and you know the rest of the story. I'll never forget Thomas. I think about him from time-to-time. I still have a small place in my heart that will always be his, but it doesn't mean that I don't love Reverend Parker. You'll get over Calvin. I have a feeling when you get home, it won't be as hard to see him as you've imagined."

"Well, I guess if there was hope for you after Thomas, there's hope for me!" Bonnie replied.

The two women had a nice laugh, then went back inside the warm house.

Chapter Ten

"Our little girl has grown up and has a different life now."

A KNOCK ON THE door of the parsonage came early Saturday morning. Bonnie raced down the stairs, her heels cracking against wood, making all kinds of racket.

"I'll get it! I'll get it!" she yelled.

She yanked open the door and there, bigger than life, stood Jessie McCaverty.

"Bonnie!"

"Daddy!" Bonnie flung herself into her father's open arms. "Daddy, I missed you so much!" She kissed him. Jessie had to push her away to get a better look at her.

"Let me look at you, girl. My goodness, you're all grown up!"

Arm in arm, they walked inside and into the warm living room.

"Jessie!" Reverend Parker said. "Jessie, it's good to see you." The two men shook hands.

"Miss Annie, why you're looking beautiful as ever," Jessie said, pulling his hat from his head.

Annie gave him a quick hug. "Come on in, sit down and have a cup of coffee with Reverend Parker while we finish with Bonnie's things."

"Okay, okay. Don't mind if I do. I tell ya. I'd rather sit on the back of an old mule all day long than sit in a moving automobile." The four of them laughed at the comment. Hearing the lilt of her daddy's voice again brought a certain peace to Bonnie's heart and made her all of a sudden eager to get back home.

Jessie and Reverend Parker went into the living room by the fire. Bonnie and Annie started upstairs.

"I'll be right back, Daddy. I'm almost ready."

"Okay, girl, okay." The two men took a seat near the fire.

"Jessie, I want to talk to you for a moment before Bonnie comes back down," Reverend Parker said rather urgently. "Annie and I believe Bonnie is working too hard with her Red Cross duties. We've tried to get her to slow down, but she's gotten attached to a little girl in one of the families she helps and, well, she's worried sick about her. She hasn't gone out with anyone except for a few of the volunteers she works with. We're worried about her."

Jessie nodded. "Yes, her mother read Annie's letter to me. You know, Bonnie was always bringing home strays, even when she was a young girl. That girl never gives up on anything. Every animal she found that was hurt, she'd bring home, nurse it to health, then, of course, she'd have to let it go. Oh, she would be so upset." He looked thoughtful. "She'd eventually get over it, though."

"I'm not so sure she'll get over this little girl, Jessie. Bonnie talks about her all the time. I'm not sure it's healthy. She should be going out with boys, dating, going to shows at the park, and here she is constantly worrying about this family. I know it's just Bonnie's nature, but we thought maybe you could try to keep her in Smithville as long as possible, you know, to get her mind off everything."

"We'll do just that, Reverend. We want her to stay at least through Christmas."

"Don't mention that to her," the Reverend said quickly putting his index finger to his lips. "She says she's only staying until after Thanksgiving, then she's coming right back."

"Reverend," Jessie said seriously, "I want to thank you for everything you've done for Bonnie. I know Bonnie is a handful, and if you and Miss Annie, well, if she's—"

Reverend Parker didn't let him finish his sentence. "No, no, Jessie, it's not that. We're happy with Bonnie here. It's been good for Annie to have her here. Having someone other than me to fuss over and take care of, well, it's been wonderful for her. You know that. We're just worried about Bonnie. We're aware she needs some rest."

"Truly, she does look tired, but not to worry. You know Lizzie. She'll have her rested up in no time at all."

"Good, good." Reverend Parker smiled. The girls came down the stairs at that time. Bonnie wore her gray coat and velvet hat that they had given to her almost a year ago.

The two men stood.

"My, my, hasn't she grown?" Jessie asked.

Annie put her arms around Bonnie's shoulders. "She's not a girl anymore, Jessie. She's a beautiful woman. All the boys at the church just flock around her, but she won't have anything to do with any of them. Talk to her, Jessie."

"That I will, Miss Annie. Come, girl, let's get going. It's a long drive back to the farm."

Jessie extended his hand to Reverend Parker and gave Annie a kiss on the cheek. "Okay, we'll be going. Let's get these things into the car."

The men took the bags to the car. Soon enough, Bonnie and Jessie were waving goodbye as they drove down the street and back to Smithville. It would be most of a day's drive to the McCaverty farm. Jessie would be exhausted but had refused to stay the night. He said Lizzie was too anxious to see Bonnie. Bonnie knew the reason though. Jessie had never spent a night out of his own bed, except for hunting and such, in over fifty years.

As they drove down the long dusty road that led to the two farms, Bonnie glanced at the fork to the left that led to the Wade place.

"We've been all this way from Nashville and you haven't even asked me about Calvin," Jessie said.

"Why should I?" Bonnie asked stubbornly.

"Bonnie McCaverty, a year away hasn't dulled your tongue."

"I'm sorry, Daddy. How is Calvin?" she relented.

"His farm is fine. He's doing well. He's working every acre. He's a fine farmer, Bonnie."

"I'm happy for him," she remarked coolly.

"He's put everything he has into that farm. He don't do nothin' else."

"He never did," Bonnie said.

Jessie rolled his eyes. "What I'm trying to tell you, girl, is he ain't seen nobody since you left."

Bonnie straightened defiantly, glancing sideways at her father. "Daddy, I didn't come back to see Calvin. I left to forget him. Remember? Please, don't bring it up again."

"Okay . . ." Jessie grumbled. "I just didn't know whether you wanted to know or not."

"Well, I don't. Now you know."

Jessie grinned. He knew his Bonnie. For her to be so stubborn about it only meant one thing. It was bothering her. Jessie hoped it bothered her real bad. He wanted his daughter back home.

As they pulled up to the farm, Lizzie sat waiting on the front porch in her shawl.

"What's she doing out in this cold?" Bonnie asked, jumping out of the car.

"Mama!"

Lizzie greeted her daughter with her arms open wide. Bonnie ran into them as Lizzie wrapped her arms around her youngest daughter.

"I'm so glad to see you, girl!"

"Mama, what are you doing sitting out in this cold?"

"I couldn't wait to see you. Come inside and let me look at you."

Jessie looked on from the car. "Don't mind me," he mumbled. "I'll get the bags."

Once inside, Lizzie twirled her shawl from around her shoulders and latched it to a nearby hook.

"Look at ya! Just look at ya! You're so grown!"

"Mama, it hasn't even been a year. I haven't been gone that long."

"It's been plenty long, believe you me. Your father and I have missed you terribly!"

"I've missed you, too," Bonnie said, hugging her mother again. 'C'mon, sit down. Coffee's on. We have so much to talk about. Tell me all about Nashville." Lizzie poured the coffee just as Jessie stumbled in the front door with Bonnie's bags.

"Daddy, put those down and come over here. We'll tend to them later." Jessie dropped the bags and willingly took a seat. Lizzie poured the coffee.

"Well," Bonnie began, "Reverend and Miss Annie are wonderful. The church is great. At first, I couldn't get used to the people. They seemed so uppity and all, but then I realized they were different. When I first got there, Lordy, all the women in that community invited Miss Annie and me to tea. Every day, we'd go to tea here and go to tea there. They'd just sit around and talk about the unlucky person who wasn't there that day. At first, I liked it 'cause we got to dress up and all, but then, I just plain got bored.

"I went to the park there and saw a band playing. I rode the street-cars all over town. Even with so much to do, I still was bored. So, Miss Annie, she has this friend who volunteers at the Red Cross, and she got me trained to become a volunteer. I've got my own uniform and all. I brought it just for you to see!

"Things are bad in the city. There's lots of people there with no jobs, no family. It's so sad, Mama. Little children with no food to eat."

"Well . . . I declare," Lizzie said. "We've got our share of poor folks here, too, but they know they can always come to the church for help."

"All the churches there are helped out, Mama. They've got families living right in the church buildings, in the basements and donated houses. Some of the congregations have even taken families in themselves, them that have the room to do it," she said, slipping quite naturally into her native accent.

"Well, that's the Christian thing to do," Jessie said, pulling out his pipe.

"But, Daddy, you can't imagine how bad it is. This one family that we been helping, the Suttons, when I first met them, the oldest girl was real bad sick. They thought she had some kind of poisoning. They didn't have no money to take her to the doctor. Her daddy got laid off from the hosiery mill where he was working, then they had another little girl. Well, Mrs. Sutton, he goes off looking for a job and never comes back. Mrs. Sutton, they found out something is wrong with her heart. Mr. Sutton has been gone for months, and nobody knows what happened to him; nobody 'cept for their mean old landlord, Mr. Howell. He told me that he saw him get jumped and he heard they killed him. But who knows? The police don't know nothin'."

By now, Lizzie and Jessie were staring at Bonnie, their mouths hanging wide open.

"My Lord!" Lizzie exclaimed. "That's horrible!"

After taking a moment to draw breath, Bonnie continued.

"Well, the landlord, Mr. Howell, he was going to kick the mother and the two girls out on the street and her so sick with those two girls. So, I went downtown to the office building where the owner works and finally found him eating breakfast up on the square. I told him a thing or two, and he gave me an extra thirty days to find them a place to live. Turns out, we didn't need it, though, because the next week, Reverend Parker found them a house to live in through one of the Pastors in town. He moved them into a little house over in Flat Rock, and there's also three other families living there with them. That's why I came on because we finally got them taken care of. I had a real hard time leaving Polly, though. That's the oldest girl who was so sick. We're sort of close and, well, I just wasn't sure I could leave while they were in such a state, but everything's okay for right now." Bonnie smiled and paused for a sip of her coffee.

"What's wrong?" she asked, looking up from her cup.

"My goodness, girl," Lizzie said. "You've been the busy one, haven't ya?"

"Well, I guess. The time just goes by so fast. There's so much to do."

Lizzie nodded. "But not right now. You're going to rest. You hear? I mean rest. Why, you look like you took sick or somethin'. I never seen you so pale."

"It's nice to be home." Bonnie smiled as she reached out for her Daddy's hand. Lizzie stood and poured more coffee.

"There's a whole bunch of people can't wait to see you. The girls will be over first thing in the morning with their families. And Calvin will be over for Thanksgiving dinner," Lizzie carefully added.

"Calvin?" Bonnie asked.

"Yes, Calvin," Lizzie said. "Boy's always been part of this family, Bonnie."

"Yes, Mama," Bonnie said, attempting nonchalance. "He has been. How is Calvin?"

"I done told ya how he is. He don't do nothin' but stay on that farm and work," Jessie said.

"Jessie," Lizzie said in a warning tone.

"Well, I can't help it. He don't! Never leaves the place 'cept come time to sell the crops or get seed or supplies. Don't see it, I don't. Makin' all this money for what? Sits on that front porch and don't ever go nowhere!"

"That's what he wants, Daddy," Bonnie said solemnly as she rose from the table. "Anyway, I can't wait to see the children. I bet they've grown."

"Yes, they have. You won't recognize them," Lizzie said.

Just then, a soft neighing sound came through the kitchen window from outside.

"Danny," Bonnie cooed.

"That little mongrel," Jessie said, smiling. "Gettin' meaner all the time, he is. No one can hardly ride him since you left." Bonnie barely heard the last of his sentence before she was out the kitchen door headed for the corral.

"Danny Boy!" she yelled, running toward the little horse in the corral next to the barn. Over the fence she went dress and all as the little horse pranced over to her.

"Danny," she said again, burying her face in his mane. The memory of the night in the Dark Tunnel lurched from her memory. Tears welled in her eyes as she furiously blinked them away. Once the lump in her throat subsided, she spoke softly to her old friend.

"Danny! Oh, I've missed you, boy. How have you been? Daddy says you're being hard to get along with. Is that so? Now I told you to be a good boy while I was gone, didn't I?" Danny nudged his face against Bonnie's chest, waiting for his ears to be rubbed.

"Oh, you haven't changed." Bonnie laughed. "How about a ride early tomorrow morning?" The little horse neighed with contentment. "You rest. I'll be out here early in the morning." She lifted the latch on the fence and let herself out of the corral and made her way back to the house to unpack.

There was much work to be done at the McCaverty house on Thanksgiving Day, but at five o'clock that morning Bonnie had Danny saddled and ready to ride, even before her mother had coffee on. She took the road and made her way through the old familiar trails that cut from one part of the community to the other.

Bonnie made a quick stop at the old mill where everyone used to go swimming. As she headed back to the barn, Bonnie eyed the opening that led through The Dark Forest. The urge to visit her lookout over the Wade farm overwhelmed her senses, but Bonnie had learned a bit about restraint since she'd been away. When combined with her Irish pride, those lessons kept her from revisiting something that had no influence on her any longer.

As Bonnie passed the entrance to the forest and put Danny in the corral, Lizzie, who watched Bonnie's indecision from the kitchen window, felt sad for her daughter.

Bonnie came straight into the house to help Lizzie with the Thanksgiving fixings; Jessie was about his regular chores. Even on holidays, the cows still needed to be seen to, the eggs gathered, the hogs slopped. Life never stopped on the farm, even to give thanks.

Soon enough, the whole family gathered in the living room; Nettie and Tom, Emma and Sam and their children, all with their ears tuned to Bonnie and her endless stories of the city with its carnival rides and circuses, the zoo, and especially the streetcars. The children couldn't get enough of hearing about the streetcars.

Only Calvin hadn't shown up yet, and it was getting close to time for the Thanksgiving turkey to be carved. Bonnie tried not to think much about it, occupying her time with talk of Nashville and thoughts of Polly and how much she wished she was here with her to see what a real family is; to experience the togetherness and love Bonnie had known all of her life.

They were all gathered around the table when the sound of a automobile tearing down the drive to the house caught their attention.

"Who could that be on Thanksgiving Day?" Jessie said.

"It looks like Doc Morgan's truck, Daddy," Bonnie said as she joined him at the window.

"Why, I believe it 'tis," Jessie said.

They all watched as Doc Morgan's son, Chad, got out of the driver's seat and quickly made his way up onto the porch. Jessie opened the front door and let him in.

"Hello, Chad," Lizzie said. "Have you come for Thanksgiving dinner with us?" Lizzie smiled at the young boy as he removed his cap from his head.

"No, thank you, Mrs. McCaverty. I've come with a message for Miss Bonnie," the young boy said.

"For me?" Bonnie spoke up from the table where she stood helping to set the places.

"Yes'm, Miss Bonnie. I'm afraid it's bad news."

The relaxed smile on Bonnie's face quickly turned to concern as she quickly dropped the plates onto the table, making her way over to the boy.

"What is it, Chad?" she asked.

"Well, Pa said to come over quick and tell you that Reverend Parker phoned and said to tell you that a Mrs. Sutton has died and you better come quick."

Bonnie's hands went to her mouth. "Oh, my God!" she said, the news causing her knees to go weak. Lizzie moved to steady her.

"Pa said to tell you if'n you wanted to go back to Nashville, for you to come with me and he'd take you as far as Carthage Junction first light in the mornin'. You can catch the train there and get the rest of the way, Pa says."

"Oh, Polly! She must be so scared!" Bonnie cried. "Chad, you wait right there, and I'll get my things together quick, okay?"

"Yes'm, Miss Bonnie. Pa told me to wait on you."

Bonnie turned to her mother. "Mama, please don't be upset with me. I have to go back. Little Polly's all by herself. I can't even imagine how scared she is."

"Did Reverend Parker say anything about the children?" Bonnie said to Chad.

"No, ma'am, I don't think so. Or Pa didn't say."

"I have to go back," Bonnie reiterated to her mother. "Please don't be upset."

"I won't, dear," Lizzie said.

"Daddy, you understand, don't you?"

"Well, Bonnie, we hadn't seen you in so long, and Calvin's not even here yet."

"Daddy," Bonnie said, walking over to him. "I know you don't understand, but Polly is only four, and her mother has just died. She has a baby sister who's not old enough to walk yet, and her father is missing. She's all alone." Tears began to fall down her face. "I have to go."

Jessie nodded, wrapping Bonnie in his big arms. "I understand, Bonnie Girl," he said. "I just missed you so much. I guess I'm bein' a bit selfish, aye?"

"Just a bit," Bonnie said, forcing a smile, "but I love you for it."

"Chad, I'll be right down with my things." Bonnie went for the stairs, her two sisters following on her heels to help her with her things.

"Bonnie?" Jessie said. Bonnie turned on the stairs and looked back at her father.

"Yes, sir?"

"What'll I tell Calvin?"

"Tell him someone needs me. I had to go," Bonnie answered solemnly.

In no time at all Bonnie's bags were repacked. The men loaded them into Doc Morgan's car. Everyone stood on the porch and waved good-bye as Chad drove the old truck out of the driveway and down the dirt road.

As they all moved to go back inside, Jessie stood leaning on the railing of the front porch watching the dirt settle back to the ground in the wake of the old truck. Lizzie walked over to his side looking toward the road, too. They stood there for a few moments in silence.

"She'll never come back, Lizzie," Jessie said. "She'll never come back. Our little girl has grown up and has a different life now."

"Oh, don't say that. She just had to leave unexpected. She'll be back."

"No, I think Bonnie knows her life is in Nashville now. She'll never come back."

Lizzie breathed a sigh. "Well, it's a good life she has, Jessie McCaverty. What would become of those two girls had God not put Bonnie in their life? He knows what He's doin', Jessie. We just have to try not to stand in the way."

"You always know what to say to me, don't you, woman?" Jessie said. He straightened up and put an arm around his wife.

"That I do, and don't you ever forget it. Come in for dinner now," Lizzie said with a pat on his chest. Together they turned to go in out of the crisp, November air.

Chapter Eleven

"Land sakes, Miss Annie, the Reverend is going to commit me for sure."

B ONNIE PHONED AHEAD from Doc Morgan's that night. He would drive her to Carthage to catch the Central. Reverend and Mrs. Parker were at stationto pick her up the next morning.

"Bonnie. Dear, I'm so sorry you had to come back so soon," Annie said. "We were so worried. We just weren't sure whether to phone you or not."

"No, I'm glad you did," Bonnie assured her. "Poor Polly, I know she has to be so scared."

Annie led Bonnie to the living room as soon as they arrived at the parsonage. They barely got their coats off before Bonnie began her questioning.

"What do you know, Miss Annie?" Bonnie asked eagerly.

"Well, Mrs. Carter died in her sleep, God rest her soul. Polly tried to wake her up to tend to the baby. Finally, one of the other ladies in the house came in and saw she had passed."

Bonnie began to cry. "Poor Polly. Can we go over there now and see her?"

"Well, I'm afraid we have some bad news that we didn't want to tell you while you were so far away," Annie began.

Reverend Parker walked into the room just then. He sat across from Bonnie. There was more to tell her.

"Now, Bonnie, there are rules here in the city that they have to follow when something like this happens."

"What's wrong?" Bonnie asked as Annie reached out for her hand. "What's happened?"

"They had to put the two girls in an orphanage," Reverend Parker said. His voice was as soothing as he could manage.

Bonnie leapt from her chair. "An orphanage! They can't!" she shouted. She began to pace back and forth in the small living room.

"They had to, Bonnie. It's the law."

"Well, it's a stupid law!" Bonnie said. She tried to sit down, but was back on her feet again almost as soon as she'd hit the chair. Her face was stained with tears. Annie handed her a handkerchief.

"I'll go get them. Where are they?"

"You can't get them, dear," Annie said. "It's not that easy."

"I can't go get them?" Bonnie asked in amazement. "Why can't I?"

"Well, you aren't kin to them," Annie said.

"But I love them. Doesn't that count for something?" she pleaded.

"Yes, it does. You can try to get custody of them, but they have to try to find the next of kin first. They're trying to find any family they have now."

"But they don't have anybody. That's what Mrs. Sutton told me. They neither one had any kinfolk to fall back on when times got hard. That's what she told me!"

"I know, Bonnie, but there's still their father."

"Their father?

"Yes, they're checking with the police to see if there was any word yet."

"There's no word," Bonnie whispered as she stood to walk to the fireplace. "There won't be no word. Nothing. He's dead."

Reverend Parker gaped at her. "How do you know that?"

"'Cause that Mr. Howell, he says he saw him get jumped down in Black Bottom right before he disappeared. Rumor has it they dumped him into the river." Bonnie's voice was calm and even.

Annie grew pale as though she was going to be sick. "Oh, dear!" she said, covering her mouth with her handkerchief.

"Why haven't you told that to anyone?" Reverend Parker demanded.

"He won't say nothin' to the police. That's just what he told me. Said he don't like the cops, and he ain't sayin' nothin'."

"Well, the police need to know."

"Oh? Why?" Bonnie screamed in her frustration. "Why? He's gone, isn't he? They're not going to find him now. They never did really even try. He's just another person who never came home. Oh, I'm so sick of this I could scream! Nobody cares about nobody. Those two children are the only ones who are getting the bad end of the stick! Doesn't anybody care what *they* want?"

Bonnie looked up at Reverend Parker. "Can't I even go and see them?" she asked.

"I'm not sure, Bonnie," he replied. "Get your things, and we'll go try."

Bonnie had her coat and hat on in no time at all. She was pulling on her gloves when Annie walked into the entrance hall.

"Now, Bonnie," she said as she pulled Bonnie's collar up around her neck, "remember that Polly is scared. You must show strength and reassure her. In that kind of situation, if they know they have someone on the outside, they're usually okay."

"You seem to know a great deal about orphanages, Miss Annie."

"I've done a little work in orphanages," she said.

"Don't let her kid you, Bonnie. She's done plenty of work in orphanages, years worth."

Bonnie glanced at Miss Annie with a puzzled look. "Why don't you go with me then?"

"No, dear, I can't. I'll stay here and listen for the phone. You two go on now."

"Okay, we'll call or be back soon," Reverend Parker said as he bent over kissing his wife on the cheek, rushing Bonnie to the door before the questions he knew were forming in her mind came out of her mouth.

As Bonnie and Reverend Parker reached the car, Bonnie stopped short of getting in, the perplexed look still on her face.

"Reverend," Bonnie said, "why doesn't Miss Annie want to come with us? If she's been in and around orphanages before, she could help."

"Get into the car, Bonnie," Reverend Parker said. He looked up at the living room window where his wife stood peering out.

Reverend Parker turned the key and put the car into reverse, backing the car out of the driveway in silence. Bonnie wasn't sure what she'd done, but she sat quietly, waiting to see if Reverend Parker was going to explain. As soon as they started down the street, he broke the silence.

"A long time ago, maybe ten or twelve years now, Annie volunteered at an orphanage in Georgia, close to where she's from. I was away doing some missionary work, so she enjoyed helping with the children. She loves children, Bonnie. I've never seen someone so good with them. She'd been helping out there for about six months or so when this one-year-old little girl was brought there. She'd been saved from a house fire, but her parents had been killed. Her name was Elizabeth. She had dark eyes and dark hair. It was eerie how much she looked like Annie. And Annie must have looked just like her mother because Elizabeth thought she was her mother. Annie loved that baby so much, just as if she were her own.

"So, when I returned, we decided to adopt her. I knew soon we'd have another church to pastor, so we did it. We adopted her."

"Reverend Parker, she never told me," Bonnie said, her eyes wide with surprise.

"That's not all of it, I'm afraid," Reverend Parker said. "We brought her home, and soon she was the happiest little girl you could ever meet. Big smile, the cutest laugh you've ever heard." His eyes began to mist over. "We loved her so much."

He cleared his throat, shifting in the seat.

"Right before her second birthday, Annie was out hanging clothes and Elizabeth had climbed up onto the back porch. Before Annie could catch her, she had crawled up onto the banister. She fell . . . she died shortly after that."

Bonnie sat looking at Reverend Parker with her gloved hand covering her mouth. Tears filled her eyes. "Miss Annie! Oh, how awful!" she cried. "No wonder she won't go with me on visits!"

"Yes, and she sees you getting attached to Polly just like she did to Elizabeth. I guess I should have told you about it already. It's just that, well, Annie doesn't like talking about it at all. She's scared for you, Bonnie. She doesn't mean to be unfeeling. On the contrary, she has too many feelings, and you're the closest thing to a daughter she's had in quite some time. She just doesn't want you to get hurt. That's all."

Bonnie folded her hands in her lap and looked down at them. "I wish I would have known."

"She doesn't want anyone to know. Don't ever bring it up to her or let her know that you know. She's protective of her memories of Elizabeth. She likes to remember her alive, not dead. Talking about it only reminds her that she's gone."

"Yes, sir. I promise. Poor Miss Annie," she whispered.

They drove the rest of the way to the orphanage in silence, Bonnie thinking about Polly while assuming that Reverend Parker thought about Elizabeth.

Soon, the red brick building loomed in front of them. It was late afternoon, and some of the children were playing in the yard. Bonnie and Reverend Parker went up the steps and down the hall to the office.

"May I help you?" a young girl said from behind an old wooden desk.

"Yes," Bonnie said, "I'd like to see the Sutton girls. They haven't been here long. Their mother died two days ago."

"Oh yes. Polly and her little sister, right?"

"Yes, yes!" Bonnie smiled, beginning to get excited at the thought of seeing them.

"I'll have to get the director. Wait here."

"Okay," Bonnie said. Reverend Parker put his arm around Bonnie. Her thin body shook.

A small man with round glasses and slick black hair appeared from within the office the girl had entered. He extended a hand to Reverend Parker.

"Hello, my name is Jordan, Mr. Jordan. What can I do for you folks?" he said with an air about him Bonnie didn't like.

"Reverend Frank Parker, Sylvan Baptist Church," Reverend Parker answered, extending his hand. "This is Miss Bonnie McCaverty. We're here to see the two Sutton girls."

The small man's face turned to a frown. "Yes, yes. Polly. She's not doing too well here I'm afraid."

Bonnie interrupted. "Why? Where is she? Can I see her?"

"She's fine, Miss McCaverty. She's fine. She's just not adjusting well. See, we keep the children separated by age groups and, well, she wanted to sleep with her sister, and we just can't have that, so I'm afraid she doesn't want to eat."

"She hasn't eaten?" Bonnie screamed at the little man. He jumped backward when Bonnie leaned over the desk to present her question to him.

"Well, no, but . . ."

"I want to see her right now," Bonnie instructed.

"Well!" the little man exclaimed, trying to regain his authority. "First, I have to ask a few questions," he said firmly.

"Mr. Jordan," Reverend Parker said, stepping in front of Bonnie. "I know you have quite a lot on your hands, but you see Bonnie here is the Red Cross volunteer who has been helping Mrs. Sutton and her children for quite some time. The children know her well, so maybe Bonnie could get Polly to eat."

Mr. Jordan brightened. "Well, you should have told me you were with the Red Cross! Right this way. I'll show you to the visiting room, and Alice here will have someone fetch little Polly and tell her she has a visitor."

"Yes, sir," Alice replied, hurrying off to carry out his instructions.

Mr. Jordan showed Reverend Parker and Bonnie into a large living room where he asked them to wait. In a few minutes, the door opened, and Bonnie saw Polly's little face light up when she realized it was Bonnie. They ran to each other.

"Miss Bonnie!" Polly yelled.

"Polly!" Bonnie said, stooping down to her knees wrapping Polly in her arms. They held each other for quite some time before Polly began to cry.

"Miss Bonnie, I went in to wake up Mommy, and she wouldn't get up. They told me she's dead. Why did they tell me that, Miss Bonnie?"

Bonnie sat on one of the chairs and pulled Polly into her lap. "Polly, your Mommy's gone to heaven. She's up there with Jesus and the angels. Did you know she's not sick anymore?" Bonnie said, remembering the words of advice Annie had given her, to be strong for Polly.

"She's not?" Polly asked curiously.

"No, she's happy and laughing, and she's not tired anymore."

"That's how she used to 'fore we came here to live. She was fun!" Polly smiled.

"You're the head of the family now, Polly. You're going to have to be strong for your sister."

"Miss Bonnie." Polly began to cry again. "They won't let me sleep with Cora. I can't sleep without her. Why won't they? She's my sister."

"I don't know, honey, but I'll see what I can do about it."

"Miss Bonnie, can't we come with you? Don't you want Sissy and me?"

Tears welled in Bonnie's eyes as anger grew inside.

"Yes, honey. Yes. I want you both, and I'll try to see if the people in charge won't let me take you myself. It's just that I'm not part of your family, Polly. Right now, they're trying hard to find someone who was kin to your mother or father. Can you remember anyone who used to come visit or anything?"

"No, Miss Bonnie. I want to go wiff you!" the little girl said. She buried her face in Bonnie's neck and cried. Bonnie rocked her gently until the crying subsided. Reverend Parker got up and left the room.

"Polly," Bonnie said as the little girl looked up rubbing her eyes.

"I'm awful sleepy, Miss Bonnie. I want to see Sissy."

"I know, honey, but listen to me. Look at me, okay? Now listen, I'm going to try to get you out of here so you can come and live with me, but until they let you go, you've got to be strong. Okay? Promise me, Polly. Be a good girl and eat for Bonnie. If you don't eat, you'll get sick. Please don't get sick." She pulled the child to her and tried to fight back her conflicting emotions.

"Okay, Miss Bonnie, I'll be brave. Like one a those Injans you told me about who used to fight with them cowboys," she said, continuing to rub her eyes. Bonnie stood and carried her out the door. The attendant, Mr. Jordan, and Reverend Parker stood just outside.

"Polly, you go with this lady and go to sleep. They'll bring Cora in to see you *after* you wake up and *after* you eat, okay?"

"Okay, Miss Bonnie," she said as she reached out and hugged her only friend.

"I'll be back soon," Bonnie whispered.

"Okay," Polly whispered back.

The attendant carried Polly to her room. She fell asleep in her arms. Just like Bonnie had suspected, Polly hadn't been able to sleep until she saw her. The poor thing was exhausted. Bonnie waited until the attendant turned the corner before she spoke.

"Mr. Jordan, that child wants to see her sister. She's just lost her mother, and you go and separate them! No wonder she won't eat. She's scared to death! Her sister is the only thing she knows that's hers and you go and take that away from her. How could you do such a thing? No wonder she wouldn't eat!"

"I'm sorry, Miss McCaverty. We just have to follow the rules. We have so many children here, you know," he said rather meekly.

Reverend Parker saw that Bonnie was about to explode. He intervened quickly.

"Thank you for letting us see her, Mr. Jordan. When can Miss McCaverty come and visit both girls?"

"Tomorrow in the afternoon after their lunch they have some time for visitation."

"I'll be here, and I hope Polly doesn't tell me that she hasn't seen her sister!" Bonnie stormed down the hall and out the door.

Reverend Parker forced a smile. "You'll have to forgive her," he said. "She's been through so much with the family. Mr. Jordan, has anything been found out about the girls' next of kin?"

"No, I'm afraid not. It looks like they'll be up for adoption if someone isn't located soon. We have a few couples who want the baby, but the girl, I'm afraid she may end up being with us awhile with her attitude and all," he said with a smirk. "Of course the baby would go as soon as we get the word that there's no next of kin."

"Would the couple take both girls?"

"My, no. I doubt that very much. People can't afford to take in more than one in these hard times, Reverend. It would be a miracle if someone did want both of them. Just a miracle."

"Yes, I guess it would at that," Reverend Parker said absently. He shook Mr. Jordan's hand, turned and walked slowly down the dark corridor toward the doors that opened to the outside. Bonnie waited in the car.

"Well, what did he say? Anything?" Bonnie asked as Reverend Parker slid into the driver's seat.

"Yes, I'm afraid so," Reverend Parker answered.

"What?" Bonnie asked, unaware that she was mimicking the concerned look on Reverend Parker's face.

Reverend Parker faced her. "Mr. Jordan says there's no sign of family and, unless they get word, the girls will be up for adoption."

"No, they can't have them. I won't let them!"

"That's not all. Mr. Jordan says that the couple wants the baby, but not Polly. Bonnie, it's a good chance the girls will be split up."

"No! That can't happen! No! What can we do?" Bonnie screamed.

"I don't know. Let's get home, and we'll discuss it further."

The drive to Sylvan Park was quiet and sad. Bonnie's heart was breaking for the girls.

Over supper that night, they decided to contact Jessie and Lizzie to make sure that Bonnie could bring both the girls home. Bonnie knew her parents, and she knew their hearts, but still Reverend Parker decided Bonnie had to get a message to them as soon as possible.

Next, Bonnie decided she needed a lawyer to help with what to do next, and the only lawyer Bonnie knew was Ned Bass. She tried to phone his office, but it was late, and everyone had gone home. She would make another unannounced visit to Mr. Ned Bass. She had another favor to ask. She hoped that he wouldn't be able to refuse one more time.

Bonnie rose early the next morning and began rifling through her closet. Annie came up to see why she hadn't made it down to breakfast yet. Bonnie had an array of dresses sprawled out across her bed.

"What's going on here?" Annie asked as Bonnie lifted her head out of her trunk at the end of the bed.

"I'm trying to decide what to wear! I can't seem to find the right suit."

"Bonnie, what are you up to now?" Annie asked in a low, suspicious tone.

"I want to be properly dressed when I meet the young Mr. Bass again," Bonnie said with a mischievous smile.

"Just what does that mean?" Annie asked.

"Miss Annie, I just need to look serious. You know, older," Bonnie said. She held up a dress in front of her body. "How's this?"

Annie shook her head. "If you want to look like someone's grand-mother. Bonnie, don't get yourself all worked up over this visit. He's a busy man. He may not have time to help you."

"He has to. That's all there is to it." She raised another dress up to her thin body. "I think this will do."

"Bonnie, the green suit dear, and put that hair up and wear a hat. If you want to look older, Bonnie, you're going to have to get rid of all that hair. You need one of those stylish waves all the girls are getting." Annie cleared a space off the bed and sat.

"Maybe I should. Maybe I should cut my hair. Oh, my mother would skin me alive; that is, if God don't first."

Annie laughed. "God doesn't care whether your hair is long or short."

"He don't?"

"No, He *doesn't*. It doesn't matter to Him what you look like. Let me ask you a question. If He cared whether you had long hair or short hair, wouldn't it only go to say that it made a difference to Him if you had a long body or a short body?"

"Why, that's silly, Miss Annie. God don't love tall people more'n He loves short people." She said it slowly, realizing what she'd said. She turned around to face Annie, her face lighting up. "Oh, I get it. If it don't make no difference if I'm short or tall, then it don't make no difference if my hair is long or short! Right?"

Annie laughed. "Yes, dear. That's right."

"Well, I want to go get one of them fancy hairdos then."

"One of *those* fancy hairdos," Annie corrected. "Bonnie, if you don't try to speak correctly, you never will."

"Can we go? Can we go after breakfast? I want to look like one of those office workers downtown when I go see Mr. Bass. I've got to look older than nineteen. He won't never take me serious."

"He won't *ever*, Bonnie. *Ever!*" Annie said, exasperated.

"He won't ever what?" Bonnie asked.

"No, dear. I mean that *won't never* is not correct. It's *won't ever*, not *never.*"

Bonnie held the green dress in her hands as she looked at Annie with a puzzled look. "Won't ever what?" she asked quietly, knowing Annie was growing impatient with her.

"Never mind, Bonnie. Just hurry up and come down to breakfast," Annie said, leaving the room. Bonnie stood quietly, trying to figure out what had just happened.

They ate breakfast over much planning and plotting. It would be hard for Mr. Ned Bass to refuse Bonnie if they accomplished their plan.

Annie borrowed the car from Reverend Parker, and carefully and slowly, they drove to one of the beauty parlors downtown that Annie Parker had read so much about in the papers. Not only did Bonnie have her long red hair cut to shoulder length, but styled with the hair around her face, forming sleek waves. They painted her nails and lips *and* applied a bit of rouge to her already flushed cheeks.

After some time, Bonnie stood in front of the huge mirror that hung on the wall and inspected her new look.

"Land sakes, Miss Annie," Bonnie said. "The Reverend is going to commit me for sure."

Annie stood behind Bonnie with her hands on her shoulders, trying to steady her. She smiled comfortingly at the reflection in the mirror. "No, he won't, dear. You look breathtakingly beautiful. He just won't recognize you is all."

"Beautiful?" Bonnie questioned teasingly.

"Yes, dear, I just can't believe it. You look twenty-five at least."

"Twenty-five?"

"At least," Annie replied reassuringly.

Bonnie *was* beautiful. Her wheat-colored hair, parted to one side, had a distinctive wave down the other that formed an alluring curve down the side of her face. Her lips were painted a soft shade of red. Her perfect cheekbones were highlighted with just a hint of a matching shade. The powder they applied to her creamy skin hid the few freckles that stubbornly remained on Bonnie's nose. The addition made her brilliantly green eyes look like pools of cool water on a smooth, sandy beach. Annie was pleased, and so was Bonnie.

Bonnie took a deep breath. "Well, let's go."

"You're missing one thing, Bonnie, a hat! We must buy you a hat. Let's go," Annie said after they paid the attendant.

Annie pulled up to the curb of the building with the brass plate on the front that read "Bass and Bass, Attorneys-at-law." Bonnie made a mental note. She'd never noticed that before. *They must own the entire building?* she thought.

"Now, don't be nervous, Bonnie. I'm sure he's a gracious man from what he did last time you met him. He'll at least be able to tell you what to do."

"I hope so, Miss Annie," Bonnie said. She opened the door to exit the car.

"I'll be waiting, dear," Annie reassured her.

Bonnie stared up at the tall stone building that loomed in front of her. This time, Bonnie couldn't be as fierce as she'd been before. This time, Bonnie had to be humble instead of humbling someone else. It was hard for her to do, but she quickly reminded herself she would do whatever it took to get those girls. She squared her shoulders and purposefully set her chin before entering the building.

Bonnie walked over to the big, brass elevator doors and punched the button to go up. As the doors opened, the same elevator attendant smiled as she entered the box and turned to face the doors. Bonnie hoped quietly to herself that he wouldn't recognize her as the young Mr. Bass's long lost cousin.

The doors opened on the fifth floor, and Bonnie made her way down the dark hallway. This time, her little black heels clicked against the marble floor. She went in the painted door and walked over to the lady behind the big desk.

"Good afternoon. I'd like to see Mr. Ned Bass please."

"Do you have an appointment?" the lady asked.

"No, I don't, but—" Bonnie told her.

The lady behind the desk interrupted her. "I'm sorry, but if you don't have an appointment, you'll have to wait. Please take a seat." Bonnie looked over at the leather chairs against the wall that she pointed to.

"What's your name?" she asked before Bonnie turned to sit down.

"Miss Bonnie McCaverty," Bonnie informed her.

"May I ask the nature of your visit, Miss McCaverty?" the lady asked.

"No, you may not." Bonnie smiled at herself as she turned to be seated. The look on the woman's face went from being wholly uninterested to perfectly indignant in a matter of seconds. Bonnie tried not to smile as she sat on the rather stiff leather chair.

The lady behind the desk disappeared for a few minutes, then reappeared, this time on the other side of the desk.

"I'm sorry, Miss McCaverty. Mr. Bass won't be able to visit with you today. His calendar is full. If you would like to make an appointment for another day, I—" Bonnie cut her off.

"Did you even go ask him?" she asked as she stood quickly to her feet.

"Well, I—"

"Did you?" Bonnie hammered at her again.

"Miss McCaverty, you don't understand, Mr. Bass is very busy!"

"I'm a friend of his, and you're going to be in big trouble if you don't go tell him I'm here!" Bonnie threatened.

"Now, look here, Miss McCaverty," the lady began to say.

"Hey, what's going on here?" the young Mr. Bass said as he turned the corner with his hat in his hand. "I can hear you two all the way down the hall!"

Bonnie looked up at Mr. Ned Bass. She relaxed her narrowed eyes. The tightness of her lips slowly gave way to a warm smile.

"I'm sorry, Mr. Bass. I was trying to tell this young lady that your schedule was full today, and she would have to make an appointment." Ned's eyes never left Bonnie.

"Nonsense, Mrs. Cooper. I'll take care of this," he said, stepping between Bonnie and the secretary, who folded her hands and stiffly walked away.

"You'll have to excuse Mrs. Cooper. I'm afraid she's a little over-protective," Ned Bass said. He pulled his arm from under the overcoat that hung over it and offered his hand.

"I'm Ned Bass, and you are . . ."

"Don't you know who I am?" Bonnie asked curiously.

"No, I don't believe so," Ned said. He looked confused.

"Why, sure you do, Mr. Bass. I'm Bonnie McCaverty. Remember? I'm the one that drug you away from breakfast at Underwood's that morning."

"Well, well," Ned said stepping back to give Bonnie another look. "Miss McCaverty, I didn't recognize you. You were in uniform the last time we met. You, you look so different."

"Thank you, I think," Bonnie said, the two of them laughing nervously.

"What is it you came to see me about? I understand from Mr. Howell that Mrs. Sutton is all paid up as promised and they're moved."

The mention of Mrs. Sutton's name flooded Bonnie with emotion. Her throat felt constricted; her hazel eyes filled with tears.

She pulled her handkerchief out from her suit sleeve.

"Miss McCaverty?" Mr. Bass looked concerned. He led Bonnie to one of the lobby chairs. "What is it?"

"I'm sorry, it's just that, well . . . Mrs. Sutton died . . . and her two children have been sent to an orphanage, and I can't get them out." Bonnie grabbed Ned by the arm. "You have to help me. You have to!"

"Help you what?" Ned said, trying to calm her down.

"I have to get them out of there."

"Out of the orphanage?" Ned asked incredulously.

"Yes. I want the girls to live with me."

"Wait a minute. You want to take care of two children?" Ned asked, standing to his feet.

"Yes," Bonnie said as she turned her face up to him, the alluring curve of her hair against her face only making her vulnerability more attractive. Her hazel eyes blazed a beautiful green even in the dimly lit office.

"Miss McCaverty, excuse me, but aren't you a bit young to be raising two children alone?"

Bonnie stood defiantly, her green eyes now flashing brightly. "I may be, but no one could love those girls as much as I do. No one could take better care of them!"

"Okay, all right," Ned said. He made a shushing motion with his right hand. "I understand. Listen, what do you want from me?" Mr. Bass said, turning the palm of his free hand up toward the ceiling.

"Why, I want you to help me get them out."

"Oh no, I'm afraid that's not my expertise," Ned said. He put his hat on his head and began to thread his arm through his overcoat.

"You're a lawyer, aren't you?" Bonnie asked him.

He looked at the floor. "Yes."

"Then why can't you tell me what to do?"

Ned, apparently wary that someone was listening, ushered Bonnie around a corner into the hallway for privacy. Bonnie leaned against the wall in the narrow hall turning her eyes up to Ned, waiting for an answer. Suddenly, Ned became extremely nervous.

"Look, Miss McCaverty—"

"Bonnie," she interrupted. "My name is Bonnie."

He lowered his voice. "Look. Bonnie. You're still young. In a year or two, the girls would've found a good home and, well, you'll have your mind on other things."

Bonnie looked down at her gloved hands, trying to make them stop twisting and pulling at her handkerchief.

"How will you take care of them? How will you feed them?" he asked.

Never looking up, Bonnie said quietly, "If I don't get them out of there, they'll get separated and sent to different families."

Bonnie's eyes flashed at him. "I can take perfectly good care of them, Mr. Bass. If you're not going to help me, I'll simply find someone who will!" She turned and began walking toward the elevator.

Ned leaned back against the wall, pulled out a cigarette and lit it. He shook his head and went to find his hot-headed visitor.

He walked up behind Bonnie while she was still waiting for the elevator doors to open. Bonnie stood coyly hoping he hadn't noticed the light wasn't lit up on the floor indicator. She hadn't summoned the car yet.

Ned leaned over and whispered into her ear, "Don't you think you should push the button if you want to go down?"

Bonnie's lips tightened across her smooth face. Her eyes narrowed to small slits. She leaned forward and pushed the button.

Ned smiled. "Look, why don't you tell me what's happened so far and maybe I can at least tell you what you need to do next."

"I don't want your help," Bonnie replied without looking at him. "Forget that I even asked."

Ned grinned. "Cat and mouse, huh?" he asked Bonnie.

"I beg your pardon?" she answered flatly. "I don't have the faintest idea what you're talking about."

"Look, Bonnie . . ."

"Miss McCaverty to you," she snapped.

"Fine, Miss McCaverty," he said as the doors to the elevator opened, and Bonnie stepped inside. She slowly turned to face him. "I'm probably the only attorney you know. Anyone else will laugh you out of their office." He leaned forward, his head now crossing the threshold of the elevator doors. "You need my help."

The bellhop held the doors open, an uncomfortable smile on his face, while Ned awaited a response.

"Oh, all right," Bonnie said finally, stepping off the elevator. The bellhop tipped his cap at Mr. Bass as the shiny brass door closed behind Bonnie. Ned took Bonnie's arm and led her toward his office.

He yelled over his shoulder to Mrs. Cooper, "Two cups of coffee please!"

Bonnie turned around placing a hand on Mrs. Cooper's desk. "I like lots of cream and sugar," she said smartly.

Mrs. Cooper frowned at her. Nevertheless, she left her desk to retrieve the two coffees, one with extra cream and sugar.

Over their coffee, Bonnie explained the whole situation to Ned. When she was done, Ned scratched his chin thoughtfully.

"Bonnie, I have to ask you this. Exactly how old are you?"

"Nineteen," Bonnie answered sheepishly.

Ned shook his head. "I have to tell you, it would be hard to convince a judge that you could care for two young children. You don't even have a job or a place of your own to live, and I guess I don't need to tell you, you're also unmarried."

"I guess I don't need to tell you then that it's the mother does the raisin' anyway. I do have a job. I work for Reverend Parker. I keep the books at the church and play the piano. Besides, I don't need a place to live. I live with the Parkers, and they won't mind."

Ned stood and leaned against his desk in front of Bonnie. "Have you asked them that?"

Bonnie looked down at her gloved hands again. "Well no, I guess I haven't, but I could take them back to my parents' farm in Smithville. What a better way to grow up than on a farm! They're bound to think that's a good idea."

"Bonnie, I think it's swell for you to think so much of these two girls. I can tell you love them very much, but the judge isn't going to be looking at who loves the girls more. He's going to be thinking about what's in the best interests of the children in the long run. I have to tell you, it's a long shot. Maybe we could play the angle that the children wouldn't be getting split up if they went with you." He moved to take his place behind his desk.

"Does that mean you're going to help me?" Bonnie asked coyly.

Ned leaned over his desk stubbing his cigarette out in the ashtray. "I know you don't have any way to pay me."

"Well," Bonnie stammered, "not right now. But I'll find a way, I promise."

She stood and looked Ned in the eyes. "You must understand, Mr. Bass. I have to get those girls. It means more to me than anything else ever has. You see, all my life, my only concern has been with myself and, well, they've brought something to me that I didn't have before they came into my life. I couldn't bear to lose that."

Ned, uncomfortable with Bonnie's emotional display, cleared his throat. "Yes, well, we'll just have to do our best. Won't we?" He smiled nervously.

"I know you can do it, Mr. Bass. I know you're a good lawyer in this wonderful office and all. You must be very successful."

Ned stared out the window as he lit another cigarette. "I wouldn't say that. I'll do some checking, then we'll get together," he said, facing Bonnie again. "Leave your phone number and address with Mrs. Cooper."

Bonnie brightened. Her girlish enthusiasm took over, making her forget her manners again. "Thank you, Mr. Bass! Oh, thank you!" she said. She threw her arms around him and kissed his cheek. Ned blushed. She took his hand and shook it vigorously. "I promise I'll find a way to pay you. I promise."

"Let's just consider this charity work and leave it at that, okay?" Ned asked.

"Okay," Bonnie said, stepping away from him. "Mr. Bass, since you're calling me Bonnie, may I call you Ned?"

"Sure," he answered.

Bonnie walked to the door. At the last moment, she turned around, a wide smile breaking across her face. "Thanks, Ned," she said, leaving the room, softly closing the door behind her.

The cold November air forced Annie into the lobby of the Bass & Bass building to wait on Bonnie. She watched every passenger exit the elevator, anxiously awaiting the outcome of Bonnie's meeting.

When Bonnie finally emerged from the elevator, Annie rushed to meet her.

"Well?" Annie asked as she grabbed Bonnie's hands.

"He's going to help me," Bonnie whispered. "He was a tough nut to crack, but he finally agreed to help. C'mon, I'll tell you about it in the car!"

The two women drove home in the Reverend's car. Bonnie relayed the whole story to Annie. At Bonnie's pauses for breath, all Annie was able to manage on her end of the conversation was the occasional "Bonnie!" an exclamation Bonnie knew, was a confirmation of her disapproval.

When Bonnie laid her head down that night, she discovered she was happier and more hopeful than she'd been in a long while.

CHAPTER TWELVE

"I'll bet you dance as well as you do everything else."

THE DEPRESSION WORSENED, and thoughts of Christmas placed a heavy burden on most parents in Nashville, although it never affected Bonnie. She hadn't returned to her Red Cross duties but unofficially volunteered at the Protestant Orphanage. Bonnie soon came to be loved and cherished by both the children and the staff there.

She played Christmas carols on the old piano, a dusty instrument that no one had touched in years. She taught the children about the birth of the baby Jesus, the baby who was born in a manger. Much to her surprise, she found that most of the children didn't even know why Christmas was celebrated.

She taught the girls how to make paper ornaments for the Christmas tree. She taught the boys how to make paper airplanes. Bonnie brought a certain hopefulness to the orphanage, and Mrs. McCullough, the head matron, seemed particularly happy about it.

Bonnie couldn't tear herself away from the girls long enough to go home for the holidays. She wrote frequently and kept Lizzie and Jessie current with everything in her quest to become the legal guardian of the two Sutton girls.

᪥

Meanwhile, Mr. Bass turned out to be a helpful ally for Bonnie. Judge

"Ivory" Whitaker was, of course, an old friend of the family. Ned had paid him a visit. Afterward, he stopped by the orphanage to tell Bonnie the outcome of the meeting.

Ned stood in the large anteroom watching Bonnie as she sang *Silent Night* one more time before the children had to go down for their naps. He thought about the meeting that morning with the judge and how happy Bonnie would be when she learned how favorable he had been toward giving her custody of the children. That made him think about what would happen then if she did get custody. Ned knew that her plans were to take the girls back to her parents' farm and raise them there. Even though Smithville wasn't far, it was a world away as far as Ned was concerned. His daily calls and visits would come to an end after the hearing. That meant no more Bonnie. He wouldn't see her bright, smiling face or hear her voice over the telephone.

If she didn't get custody, he knew that heart of gold that beat so lovingly in Bonnie would be crushed. It was a hard place for Ned to be, and he grew increasingly uncomfortable with it with each passing day.

Bonnie finished her song. Mrs. McCullough instructed the children to their rooms for naptime. As the children poured out of the door, Ned finally caught Bonnie's attention.

"Hi, Ned!" Bonnie waved from across the room. After the last of the children had filed out, Ned made his way inside and shut the door while Bonnie moved about the room picking up toys and straightening chairs.

"What are you doing here?" she asked cheerfully.

"I came by to tell you about my meeting today with Judge Whitaker."

"You saw him today?" She picked up a stuffed bear and turned to face Ned.

"Yes, this morning."

"Well, what did he say?"

Ned smiled. "It looks good. He's a bit concerned about your age but likes the fact they'd be growing up on the farm with your parents. Oh, by the way, he'd like a written statement from your parents stating that the children are welcome to live there."

"Doesn't he believe us?" Bonnie asked incredulously.

Ned laughed at her defensiveness. "Yes, it's just a formality, Bonnie."

"Oh, okay, well, I'll write them tonight and have them send it back right away."

"Good. That'll be good."

A brief silence fell between them then. Ned fidgeted, fumbling with his hat.

"What is it?" Bonnie prompted. "Is there something you're not telling me?"

"No, no," Ned answered. "Everything is looking well."

"What's wrong then?"

"It's nothing." He paused, then decided to proceed with the question that loomed in his mind. "Bonnie, if you do get custody of the children, when will you leave?"

"As soon as we could, I guess," Bonnie answered slowly. Ned could tell she was nervous. She repeatedly squeezed and released the belly of the stuffed bear she still held in her hands.

"I guess that means we won't see each other anymore," Ned said, forcing what was in his mind to come out of his mouth.

"I guess not," Bonnie answered softly. She placed her hand on his arm. "Ned, you've done so much for me, I can't begin to thank you enough. I wish you would at least let me pay you something."

Ned smiled. "With what? You don't even have a job." He tipped the end of her nose with his finger. Bonnie blushed.

"But I'll have to get a job sooner or later. I could pay you then."

I don't want your money," he said smiling. "I think you're going to need it."

"That's true," Bonnie said. She placed the bear on a shelf.

Ned grabbed her arm before she could turn away from him. She turned halfway back around, and Ned began fumbling with his hat again.

"Bonnie, I don't want you to think I do this with all my female clients, visiting them and all," he said as he moved a bit closer to her. Bonnie only looked at the floor.

"I don't do that," Ned continued, lowering his voice. "I just enjoy your company."

The sound of her heart pumping filled Bonnie's ears. Her face flushed. "I've enjoyed yours, too," she said, finally meeting his gaze.

Ned reached out and took her hand. "Bonnie, please do me the honor of joining me for dinner tonight. Don't say no, just dinner, and maybe a movie, if you'd like, or dancing. Just one night. Then you can consider yourself paid in full!"

Bonnie grinned. "That's blackmail."

"I know," he said, glancing at her with a nervous grin.

"I've never been dancing before."

"Never?"

"Well, if you don't count square dancing."

Ned smiled at her. "I'll bet you dance as well as you do everything else."

"I'll let you decide that," she answered.

"Tonight?" Ned spoke quickly. He wasn't going to take the chance that she'd change her mind. "I'll pick you up at seven-thirty."

Bonnie saluted with two fingers. "Seven-thirty it is!

"Okay. I'll see you then," Ned said. He turned and left the room.

҉

Bonnie stood, rocking on her heels like she used to when she'd done something wrong and was trying to hide it. She bit down softly on her bottom lip, wondering if what had just happened was good or bad, then she heard Annie's voice, telling her over and over that she needed to get out and date and see people her own age. Ned wasn't exactly her own age, but he was handsome. Encouraged, she decided that it *was* the right thing to do and immediately began to wonder what she should wear.

She burst through the front door of the parsonage and ran straight upstairs to her room. Curious, Annie followed to find out what was happening.

"Bonnie, what's the matter, dear?" Annie asked as she reached the top of the stairs.

Bonnie peeked her head out from her closet.

"Ned Bass came by the orphanage today to tell me he met with the judge," Bonnie said quickly, then stuck her head back into the closet. When she surfaced again, she finished her sentence. "Ned said that the judge was pretty favorable toward letting me have the girls. Isn't that great?"

"Yes, dear, but what are you doing?"

"I'm not finished yet!" Bonnie told her excitedly. "Then, he told me that on one hand, he hoped that I would get the girls, but on the other, he didn't want me to move back home! Then, guess what?" she asked.

"What?" Annie answered. She grew more excited herself.

"He asked me to dinner tonight!"

"Bonnie!" Annie exclaimed. "That's wonderful!" Her smile then turned to puzzlement. "I think. I mean, are you sure you should do this? After all, he is your lawyer."

"I'm not paying him, though, so you could say he's not really my lawyer. Miss Annie, I wasn't sure if it was the right thing to do, then I heard you and the Reverend telling me I needed to go out more," Bonnie explained. She backed out of the closet with a wide assortment of shoes in her arms and a look of disappointment.

Annie smiled. "You're perfectly right, dear. It's fine. You'll have a wonderful time! I don't believe you've been on a date since you've been here."

"I haven't," Bonnie answered. "He said he wanted to take me dancing. I've never been dancing before. What am I going to wear? I don't have anything that fancy."

"Come with me," Annie said, grabbing Bonnie's hand, leading her toward the hallway. She unloaded the shoes on the bed and followed Annie. "I have the perfect dress!"

The two women dashed into the Parkers' bedroom. Annie opened the trunk at the foot of the bed. She began to carefully spread its contents on the bed until she found what she was looking for, then she delicately unwrapped the dress and held it up for Bonnie to see. "This will look absolutely beautiful on you. I guarantee there won't be anyone else wearing anything like this."

"What is it?" Bonnie asked, admiring the material.

"It's silk from China. I bought it when Reverend Parker and I were there on a mission trip."

Bonnie walked around it, surveying the garment from every angle. The dress was a midnight blue made of the finest silk. It had a tiny waist and a high Mandarin collar. The sleeves were long and elegant, and the train fell straight to the floor in waves of flowing silk. "It's the most beautiful dress I've ever seen! Miss Annie, I'll never get that on me. It's tiny!"

"It's supposed to be," Annie whispered to Bonnie as if she was afraid someone might hear her. "It'll fit fine. You just can't eat too much at supper!" They giggled simultaneously, like two young school girls.

Bonnie undressed. She pulled the new dress over her head, allowing it to fall softly over her body. She stepped in front of the mirror, running her hands over the smooth silk. She had to admit, it looked as if it had been made for her. It hugged the curves of her body like a glove. The high collar added a look of sophistication she would have never believed she could achieve.

"Miss Annie, I can't wear this," Bonnie exclaimed, grinning from ear to ear. "Reverend Parker won't let me out of the house!"

"You have to dress for dinner," Annie replied. "Believe me. The women will all be dressed in evening attire. You'll look breathtaking."

"I don't know about *looking* breathtaking, but breathing is certainly not something I'll be doing much of in this thing!"

Annie laughed. "You're just not used to it. Everyone will be wondering where you got that dress."

Bonnie picked through the other dresses that were still laid out on the bed. "Miss Annie, why don't you wear these anymore?" she asked.

Annie sighed. "We don't ever go dancing anymore, I guess."

Bonnie whirled around to look at Annie, who was holding one of the other dresses up to herself in front of the mirror. "You and the Reverend went dancing?" Bonnie asked.

"Yes, we used to dance quite a bit. We've been dancing in New York, Hong Kong, and Africa. Even here in Nashville."

"You went *dancing?*" Bonnie asked again. It was hard to picture Reverend and Miss Annie as a young couple.

"Bonnie, dancing's not a sin," Annie admonished. "We used to love to dance. In Africa, we used to dance under the stars. Mr. Parker would hum a song, and we'd dance in the moonlight."

Bonnie flopped down onto the bed. "That sounds so romantic!"

"It was," Annie said. There was a sad look of nostalgia in her eyes. "It's a shame that we grow old and forget about those things." She began to pack the dresses.

"But, Miss Annie, you don't have to. I've got an idea." Bonnie stood from the bed. "While I'm gone tonight, you put one of these fancy dresses on, and you and the Reverend can dance right here to the radio!"

Annie offered a shy smile. "No, I don't' think so, Bonnie," she said, shaking her head.

Bonnie picked a long red dress from the pile on the bed and held it up to Miss Annie. "Yes, you can, Miss Annie. If the Reverend comes home and sees you in this dress, well, he's liable to do just about anything!"

Bonnie reached over and slapped Bonnie on the shoulder. "Don't talk like that!" Bonnie giggled. Annie's face turned the same color as the dress Bonnie was holding up for her.

"Put it on, please!" Bonnie begged. "I want to see you in it."

Ultimately, Annie relented. She tried the red dress on and was surprised to discover that it fit the same as it had before. Against her dark hair, the red dress created a glowing effect on her face that Annie didn't remember having noticed in years. Her mind drifted back to the last time she remembered wearing the dress and dancing with Mr. Parker. Behind her, Bonnie was saying something. Her voice broke the reverie and brought Annie back to the present.

"What did you say, dear?" Annie asked.

"You didn't hear a word I said. Did you?"

Annie smiled sheepishly. "No, I guess I didn't."

"Listen, after supper, when Reverend Parker goes to the living room to smoke his pipe, you go upstairs and put the dress on. Then go back downstairs, dim the lights, and turn on the radio. He won't be able to resist."

"Oh, fiddle!" Annie said, forcing herself back to reality. She slipped out of the dress and all the memories that went with it.

"Will you do it?" Bonnie asked.

"Bonnie!"

"Miss Annie," Bonnie said sternly.

"All right," Annie promised. "I'll think about it."

"Good!" Bonnie said.

"Now, let's go get you ready." Annie grabbed Bonnie's hand and led her back to her own room.

At seven-thirty the door chime sounded. Bonnie was upstairs getting ready. Annie was in the kitchen. Reverend Parker opened the door, his evening paper in one hand and his pipe in the other. Before him stood an obviously nervous Ned Bass, looking like a kid who'd just washed his hands in the holy water.

"Mr. Bass, hello. Come in. It's nice to finally meet you," the Reverend said. He popped his pipe into his mouth and offered his free hand. Ned shook it.

Reverend Parker nodded toward the stairs. "Women," he said, grinning. "They're never ready on time."

"Bonnie! Mr. Bass is here!"

Faintly, from somewhere on the second floor, they heard, "I'll be right down."

The two men walked into the living room to wait. Reverend Parker folded his paper and laid it on his chair.

"I want to tell you that we're all thankful for the help you've given Bonnie," he said. "She really loves those girls."

"Yes, I know," Ned told him. "I met with Judge Whitaker today. It's looking favorable."

"Good, good," Reverend Parker said. "We want her to have the girls, of course, but I tell you, we sure would miss Bonnie around here. She's just like part of our family, you know."

"Yes, I'm sure she is," Ned said. There was a short, uncomfortable pause before he continued. "Reverend Parker, what happens if she doesn't get the children? Will she stay here?"

Reverend Parker shot him a curious glance. "Son, you can't think that far ahead with Bonnie. I don't know how she would take it. She's had so many disappointments and . . ."

Just then, they heard Bonnie coming down the stairs with Annie close behind. Reverend Parker turned to look, then gaped at her in surprise. Ned just smiled.

"Bonnie! You look . . . sensational!" Ned said as he walked over to greet her. The Reverend looked a bit shaky.

"Hello, Mr. Bass," Annie said, stepping out from behind Bonnie. "It's so nice to finally meet you." She turned to look at Reverend Parker. "Frank? Frank, aren't you going to say anything to Bonnie?"

"Well, I," Reverend Parker stammered. "You look lovely, dear." He walked over and kissed her forehead.

"Okay, you two. Have fun," Annie said. She kissed Bonnie, shook Ned's hand and whisked them out the front door.

Annie watched as the couple drove away for their date. She quickly returned to the living room.

"Are you okay, Frank?" she asked. The Reverend had deposited himself in a chair. He leaned backward with a pleasant smile that eventually produced a laugh.

"When Bonnie walked in wearing that dress, all I could see was you twenty years ago," he said. He stood sweeping Annie into his arms. Together, they began to slow dance around the room. "You're a beautiful woman, Annie Parker," he whispered softly, gazing into her eyes. Reverend Parker hummed in time with their steps.

Annie swallowed and found her voice. "Frank, what about supper?"

"Let it burn," he said, then he kissed his wife.

Bonnie and Ned strolled into the Grill Room at the Hermitage Hotel just as the Francis Craig Orchestra began their show. The maître d' greeted them at the door.

"Good evening, Mr. Bass. We haven't seen you in a few weeks. I hope everything is well with you?"

"Everything is fine, Robert. Just fine."

"Your regular table is open. Would that be all right?"

"That will be marvelous," Ned answered.

Bonnie held onto Ned's arm as she walked through the smoky room. Her hair shimmered in the evening light, her dress appearing to change colors from blue to black as she walked. She felt the eyes of the whole room on her, no doubt wondering who this girl was whom Ned had on his arm tonight.

"She must be from New York," one of the matronly regulars said to her husband. She stopped Ned just as he walked by the table. "Ned, dear! How are you? We haven't seen you in a while. Have you been busy?" Ned bent down and kissed the old lady on the cheek.

"Hello, Mrs. Lakeford. You look ravishing as ever," he told her, making the old woman blush. Ned leaned over the table and shook hands with her husband.

"Good evening, Mr. Lakeford."

"Good evening, Ned," the old man said. He drew a puff from his cigar. "You'd better introduce your girl before Lydia busts out of that dress she's wearing." Ned laughed, Bonnie covered her own smile, and the old lady shot her husband a look of warning.

"Yes, Ned. Introduce us to this lovely girl."

"Miss Lydia, this is Bonnie McCaverty. Bonnie, this is Lydia and William Lakeford."

"I'm pleased to meet you," Bonnie said. She shook the old lady's hand, then her husband's never taking her eyes off the dance floor.

"Tell me, dear, where are you from? New York? Boston?"

"Smithville."

"Smithville?" Lydia Lakeford asked, a bewildered expression on her face. "Smithville, Tennessee?"

"Yes, ma'am."

"Well, what family in Smithville, dear?"

"The McCavertys."

"The McCavertys," Mrs. Lakeford repeated. "Tell me, Miss McCaverty, where did you get that exquisite dress?"

"From China," Bonnie answered.

Ned swallowed against a snicker as poor Lydia Lakeford tapped her lower lip with her index finger, unsure where to take the conversation from there. Ned knew she would spend the rest of the evening trying to figure out what a girl from Smithville was doing in China.

"Our table's ready," he announced. "Nice to see you again."

Mr. Lakeford waved the pair away. "Go now, son. I see another question forming in Lydia's head."

Bonnie and Ned tried to hide their laughter as they were ushered to Ned's favorite table against the far wall away from the door.

They had a perfect view of the dance floor. Bonnie sat in the plush seat inspecting the ornate ceiling and the rich interior of the room.

"Ned, this place is awfully nice. You didn't have to bring me here."

"Of course I did. You want to dance, don't you?"

"Oh, yes!"

"Let's have some supper, then we'll dance."

The waiter approached the table and greeted Ned. "Good evening, Mr. Bass," he said, laying a bourbon on the rocks in front of him. "Are you ready to order?"

"Bonnie, may I order for you?" he asked. Bonnie was still busy surveying the room.

"Okay, fine. I eat just about anything. But, Lord, don't order too much for me or I won't be able to breathe in this dress."

The waiter smiled.

"Do you prefer fish or beef?"

"Oh, I don't care, whatever you get," Bonnie answered. She was too distracted, listening to the music and watching the dancing, to pay attention. Ned ordered, and the waiter left the table. He smiled at Bonnie, who looked like a crane with her neck stuck up so high trying to see everything.

"What?" Bonnie asked, catching his amusement.

"You think if we went out on the dance floor, you could get a better look?" Ned whispered.

"Now? Can we dance before supper?"

"We can dance whenever you want to," Ned told her.

The music stopped, and everyone applauded. Bonnie started to stand as well, but Ned pulled her down.

"C'mon," he said, gently gripping her hand. "I better get you out there before you bust!"

He guided her through the dinner tables. The orchestra began another song just as they stepped onto the dance floor. Ned faced Bonnie and took her right hand in his. He put his other hand on the small of her back. Bonnie unconsciously drew a deep breath. Ned whispered into her ear, "Are you ready?"

She nodded, smiling.

Ned guided Bonnie gently back and forth with the beat of the music. He never took his eyes off her.

"You tricked me," he said.

"What do you mean, tricked you? About what?"

"You led me to believe you'd never been dancing except for square dancing."

"No, I didn't trick you," Bonnie said unable to curb her enthusiasm. "I've never been dancing before."

"Then where did you learn to dance so well?" Ned asked.

"My living room," Bonnie said. "My mother. She told me one day I'd be glad I learned."

"Well," Ned said, grinning, "are you?"

"Very," Bonnie answered.

The song ended. They separated long enough to clap. The band launched into a swing. Ned grabbed Bonnie unaware and whirled her around. Bonnie followed right along, never missing a beat.

Ned's intuition had been correct. She danced as well as she did everything else. He'd never danced so perfectly in tune with anyone. No one had ever been able to follow his lead completely until now.

Two songs later, Ned finally talked Bonnie off the floor and back to the table.

"I'm starving!" she exclaimed when they sat down.

"I guess so after all of that," Ned replied. "You sure you've never been dancing before?"

"I'm sure. Believe me, just ask my feet!"

Ned let out a hearty laugh. He laughed at everything she said. He'd never met anyone like her. She was honest and straightforward, yet simultaneously intelligent and demanding. Ned had known every kind of woman anyone could imagine, but had never met anyone who could hold a candle to this determined redhead who had come into his life under such unusual circumstances.

After supper, Bonnie and Ned danced almost every song until ten o'clock. Afterward, Ned drove Bonnie around the city to look at the Christmas decorations. He had her home by eleven. It was the earliest date Ned had in years.

"I'm sorry I have to end the night so soon," Bonnie said as they drove up in front of the parsonage. "But I guess you just plain wore me out on that dance floor. Besides, I have to get up early and get over to the orphanage."

"It was the best two and a half hours I've spent in quite some time," Ned answered, smiling.

"I bet you say that to all of your dates," Bonnie said, returning his smile as she pulled her coat closer to her.

"C'mon, you better get inside," Ned said as he got out of the car. He ran around to her side, opened the door, and helped her out. They walked to the front door together, where Bonnie looked him directly in the eye.

"Thank you," she said. "I had a wonderful time tonight." She extended her hand toward him. "Am I considered paid in full now?"

Ned grinned. "Reluctantly," he said in a small voice, then he shook her hand. "I guess a deal's a deal."

"You're the lawyer," Bonnie said.

Ned leaned down kissing her cold cheek. "Better get inside," he said softly as he nodded toward the door.

"Yes, I guess I better. Goodnight."

"Goodnight, Bonnie," Ned said as he slowly let go of her hand and headed for his car. Bonnie waved one last time, then opened the door and went inside.

In the car, Ned glanced at his watch. It was only eleven-thirty, still early. He pulled out of Sylvan Park and took a left down West End Avenue. He decided to go down to Fourth Avenue and have a nightcap with the boys. It would seem a little unsettling to go home at such an early hour.

Bonnie leaned her back against the door reflecting on the evening. She'd had a splendid time. Ned was wonderful and handsome. Any girl in town would've traded places with her tonight, she was sure. Still, something gnawed at her, an irritating feeling that she had done something wrong by going out with him. Quite unexpectedly, the face of Calvin Wade surfaced in front of her mind.

It dawned on her that subtle memories of him had been getting in her way all night. She thought about his eyes, his hands, his face. It had been over two years, and Bonnie had refused to let herself think about those things all this time. Why tonight? Why after all of this time did his face loom in front of her eyes?

"Bonnie?" Annie called from the living room, "what are you doing standing there?"

"Nothing, Miss Annie," Bonnie said. Annie flipped on the hall light and examined her.

"What's the matter, dear? Didn't you have a good time?"

"Oh yes. It was absolutely marvelous. Ned took me to the Hermitage Hotel for supper, and we danced and danced. He's the best dancer."

"But?" Miss Annie said.

"But what?"

She reached out to help Bonnie off with her coat. "I can tell there's something else on your mind. What is it?"

Bonnie hung her coat in the closet, walked into the living room, and stood in front of the fire. "I don't know, Miss Annie," she said. "It's just that, of all nights, I started thinking about Calvin! It's been over two years! I have my first date and what do I do? Think about Calvin." She rubbed the back of her neck.

Annie smiled joining her in front of the fireplace. "It's only natural, Bonnie. You haven't been around anyone who might make you think about him. You've occupied your mind with everything you could so that you wouldn't think about him. Then, tonight you're around another man . . . it made you think of him. It'll go away, Bonnie. The feelings will eventually fade away, and it will seem like a distant memory."

"It's not so distant right now," Bonnie whispered as she stared into the fire.

"It'll all be different in the morning," Annie assured her. "You go to bed and sleep on it. When you wake up, things will look differently."

Bonnie did as she was told. Her feet were hurting, and she was glad to rid herself of those dreadful heels. After she had kissed Annie good-night, she went to her room and dropped the shoes onto the floor, then fell across the bed staring at the ceiling. Words began to fill her head. Words that she thought she'd forgotten long ago.

Calvin, I know how much you loved Rosalee. I know you loved her a great deal and it was a great loss when she died.

Calvin, I just have to tell you. I know you saved my life and know you were there for me. I just can't stand it any longer! I just have to tell you . . ."

Bonnie, stop.

But Calvin, I know I'm not Rosalee, but no one, no one could love you as much as I do. No one!

Bonnie, you've got to realize. I'm just too old for you. We're eleven years different, you and me. Why, people look at us as brother and sister. I know how you feel, but it . . . it just won't work.

Why, because you don't love me? Is that why?

Bonnie . . .

Look at me, Calvin Wade. I'm not a child anymore! You can't turn your back on me! Turn around and tell me face to face that you don't love me! Turn around and look at me! Turn around and face me!

Bonnie, stop it!

Stop? You want me to stop? I'll stop. You might not be able to admit it, Calvin

Wade. That's fine, but I know it. I don't know why, but if that's the way you want it, fine! I'm leaving, and I'll not be back again ever!

The sounds and smell of Calvin's tool shed filled her senses. Tears began to roll down the sides of her face as she relived the vivid scene in her mind. She balled her hands into fists and rubbed at her eyes, trying to fight back the tears and sounds that filled her head.

"No, no," she whispered to herself. "I won't let you do this to me, Calvin Wade. I won't."

CHAPTER THIRTEEN

*"I've never been in love before, Albert. I'm
not quite sure what it feels like."*

THE NEXT DAY was Christmas Eve. Bonnie's mind filled with
sharing her joy for the season with Polly and Cora. In her mind,
there was no question the girls would be spending the evening
with her and Reverend and Mrs. Parker. She couldn't wait to find Polly.

As Bonnie entered the large room where the children usually spent
their mornings, she found Polly sitting in the window seat staring out at
the December landscape.

"Polly?" Bonnie called softly as she walked up behind her and bent
down to look at her face to face. When she did, she saw that Polly was
crying. "Polly, honey, what's wrong?"

"Miss Bonnie, my Mommy's not here to help me open my presents.
I want my Mommy to come back from heaven. I don't like her up there.
I want her to come home!" the little girl cried. Bonnie scooped the now
five year old into her arms. They sat on the window seat together and
held each other close.

"Polly, you've got to remember that Mommy was sick when she was
here. Up in heaven, she's not sick anymore."

"I don't care!" Polly screamed with the natural selfishness of a little
girl who missed her mother. "I want her to come home!"

Bonnie realized there was no comfort for what Polly was feeling
after these months. All she could do for her was hold her and love her.

Finally, Polly cried herself to sleep. Bonnie took her up to her bed for an early nap. After that, Bonnie was more determined than ever to take them out of there if just for one night. She went to find Ida, who just happened to be leaving Mr. Jordan's office. She knew Ida had put in a good word for her.

"Well, what did he say?" Bonnie whispered.

"He said you could take Polly, but he doesn't want you to take Cora. He says it's much too cold, and she hasn't felt well anyway. He'd just rather you left her with us."

Bonnie looked confused. She knew Polly wouldn't want to leave Cora. "Well, Polly probably won't like it, but . . ."

"Oh, Bonnie," Ida said, rolling her eyes. "Cora won't know if she's here or there, but Polly will. Take the girl home and tell her you'll bring presents back for Cora. She'll understand."

Bonnie thought a moment. "You're right," she agreed. "I'll tell Polly when she wakes up.

Bonnie helped Ida wrap the presents they had managed to buy thanks to Bonnie and Mrs. McCullough's tireless efforts to raise money. All of the children would have two gifts, one of clothing and one small toy. At the end of the morning, when all the toys were out and placed under the tree, the children bristled with excitement.

Polly had come down from her nap and was just joining them. One look at the presents diminished her somber mood. Before she became completely lost in the gifts, Bonnie pulled Polly off to the side to tell her the good news.

"Polly," Bonnie said as she pulled the little girl up onto her lap, "how would you like to come home to the Parkers' with me tonight and spend Christmas Eve with us?"

Polly's eyes lit up immediately. "Really, Miss Bonnie? Can we go to your house? Really?"

Bonnie smiled and nodded.

Polly hopped out of Bonnie's lap. "I'll go and get Cora ready to go. She'll be so happy!"

Bonnie stopped her before she ran off. Now was the hard part.

"Polly, Mr. Jordan thinks it would be better if Cora stayed in tonight. It's freezing outside."

"I can't leave without my sister!" Polly proclaimed, stomping her foot.

"Polly, we'll be back first thing in the morning, I promise. We'll bring Cora's presents back with us. She won't mind. Besides, she'll probably sleep right through Santa Claus."

"If I leave Cora, Mommy will be mad at me," Polly spoke softly to Bonnie.

"What do you mean?" Bonnie asked.

"Before Mommy went to heaven, she told me to always look out for Cora, not to ever leave her. Mommy told me not to ever leave her, Miss Bonnie."

Tears filled Bonnie's eyes. She reached out and pulled Polly close. "Oh, honey, don't you worry. We won't go anywhere without Cora. I promise." She took Polly's hand and stood. "C'mon, let's go tell Mr. Jordan that we're not going anywhere without our Cora and we mean business!"

Polly giggled. She followed Bonnie to Mr. Jordan's office, stomping her feet in determination with every step, just as Bonnie did.

When they arrived, Bonnie stormed past the secretary directly into Mr. Jordan's office.

"Bonnie! Bonnie!" the secretary shouted. "I'm sorry, Mr. Jordan, she just—"

"Mr. Jordan," Bonnie interrupted her, "I'm taking Polly home with me for Christmas, and we're taking Cora with us. After all the help I've given you and all the money I've raised, which I didn't mind at all, mind you, I enjoyed every minute, you'd think you'd give just a little. Just a little! We won't take no for an answer!"

Bonnie folded her arms and began tapping her foot. Polly took her cue and followed suit. She folded her little arms in front of her, crinkled her forehead, narrowing her eyes, just like Bonnie. She began to tap her foot, both of them in silent anticipation of Mr. Jordan's reply.

Mr. Jordan rose from his desk and walked out from behind it. "Polly, if we let Cora go, do you promise to look after her?" he asked, bending down so that he was eye to eye with the child. Bonnie slowly relaxed. There was a tone in the man's voice she'd never heard before, and he smiled in a way she'd never seen.

"Yes, sir. My Mommy told me never to leave Cora, and I promised I'd take care a her," Polly told him. Mr. Jordan looked up at Bonnie and back down to Polly. He reached down, swept Polly up into his arms and stood.

"Well then, I don't guess you can go to Miss Bonnie's without Cora, now can you?"

Polly's eyes lit up. She turned and smiled at Bonnie. "You gonna let me take Cora wif us?" she asked Mr. Jordan.

"Yes, if you promise to keep her warm."

Polly hugged his neck and gave him a peck on the cheek. "Thank you, Mr. Jordan. Hey, you wanna come wif us too?"

He blushed. "No, I can't. I have to be home when Santa comes to visit my house."

"Oh yeah!" Polly said excitedly. "Santa Claus."

Mr. Jordan sat Polly on the floor. She took Bonnie's hand. "C'mon, Bonnie, let's go tell Cora!"

"Thank you," Bonnie said to Mr. Jordan.

"You all deserve to have a good Christmas. Bonnie, I do want to thank you for all of the help you've given us. This place hasn't been the same since you've been here to help us. Even Mrs. McCullough smiles every now and then! I really do want you to know how very much I appreciate it."

Bonnie blushed, remembering the harsh words she'd said when she first burst into his office. "Oh, Mr. Jordan. I'm sorry I said those things. I just . . ."

Mr. Jordan raised his hand. "No, you should have said them. Sometimes, I get so carried away with the children's physical well-being that I don't take time to consider . . . well, other things."

Bonnie walked up to Mr. Jordan and shook his hand. "Thank you again."

"You're very welcome," he said, smiling.

"Oh. And have a Merry Christmas, Mr. Jordan."

"Good night, Mr. Jordan, and thanks again," Bonnie said.

"Good night, Bonnie."

As the front door of the parsonage opened, Polly took in everything, not wanting to miss one decoration, chair, picture, or lamp. Bonnie held the baby and watched as Polly went from room to room her eyes roaming every wall, her mouth hanging wide open.

When she got to the living room, she stood in front of the fireplace putting her gloved hands out to feel the warmth.

"It's so warm," she intoned.

"What's that, Polly?" Bonnie asked. She handed the baby to the Reverend long enough for her to remove her coat.

Polly ran back to the entrance, her eyes twinkling with excitement. "Miss Bonnie, it's so big!"

Bonnie bent down to hug her. She took Polly's coat and whispered, "Go look under that tree, and I'll bet you'll find some presents."

"For me?" Polly squealed.

"For everyone, but don't open them now. We have to wait until Christmas morning!"

Polly disappeared into the living room while Bonnie and Annie removed the baby's many wrappings.

The four girls had a big day that day. Polly helped Bonnie with the cookies and pies. She even helped baste the huge turkey that was cooking in the oven. It was all so unfamiliar to Polly; the smell coming from the kitchen, the decorations, the fire burning in the fireplace, all the sights and smells of a home. Polly had no memories of the Sutton family farm kitchen. She'd never helped in the kitchen nor sat in front of the fire nor made Christmas decorations. It was all a dream come true for the little girl.

While Cora took a nap, Bonnie and Polly cuddled in Reverend Parker's big chair in front of the fire and talked. For a long time, they sat and stared into the fire, enjoying each other's company.

"Miss Bonnie, if they give me to you, is this where we'll live?" Polly asked sleepily.

"No, we'll go back to my house in another town. It's a big farm with a porch and a barn. We even have a swimming hole out in the woods!"

"I've never been swimmin'," Polly said.

"Oh, it's fun. And guess what?"

"What?" Polly said as she sat up in Bonnie's lap and turned to face her.

"I have a horse for us to ride."

"A horse? I ain't never been on a horse," Polly said.

"His name is Danny," Bonnie told her.

Polly laughed. "Danny? That's a funny name for a horse."

"Well, he's more like a person anyway. He'll love you. And then there's The Dark Forest, where I used to play when I was a little girl with my sisters and Calvin."

"Who's Calvin?" Polly asked.

Bonnie looked into the fire, her mind drifting back to her childhood days when she would play in the path that connected the two farms. "He's sort of like a brother. His mother and father died when he was a boy, then Calvin came to live with us."

"Kinda like me?" Polly asked.

Bonnie realized what she'd said and turned her attention back to the little girl. "Oh, Polly, I'm sorry, honey. No, not like you. You're special. You're going to be my little girl, and I'll sort of be like your mother."

"I'll like that," Polly said laying her head on Bonnie's shoulder. "When can we go, Bonnie? I'm tired of that ol' orfig."

Bonnie smiled through her tears. "Soon, honey. I hope very soon," Bonnie said. She wrapped her arms around Polly and began to rock her gently. Soon, Polly drifted off to a warm and safe sleep.

Christmas Eve was the best night Polly had had in a long while. Reverend Parker made a perfect horse for riding. Of course, he rode Polly around every room in the house. When he finally made it back to the corral, Reverend Parker collapsed in his chair and didn't do much else the rest of the night.

Polly was allowed to open one present that night. It turned out to be a music box that played *The Viennese Waltz*. There was a little ballerina under the lid who twirled around and around as it played. Polly set it on the table and watched her dance. When the music stopped, Polly wound her up again and again. She watched the little ballerina dance over and over.

"Miss Bonnie, she's the most beautiful ballerina I ever saw," Polly said quite seriously. "I want to be just like her when I grow up."

"You'd make a beautiful ballerina, Polly," Bonnie said, smiling. "It's late. You better go to bed so Santa can visit."

"Can I take her wiff me?" Polly asked.

"Of course you can," Bonnie said.

Bonnie put the two girls to bed. In no time at all, they were both sound asleep. It had been a big day, and everyone was tired. Bonnie went back down to join the Parkers in front of the fire. Reverend Parker lit his pipe. The aroma slowly filled the room. Bonnie sat on the couch next to Annie.

"They're precious, Bonnie," Annie said to her.

"I know. What am I going to do if something happens and I don't get them, Miss Annie? I just can't imagine it."

"Don't be thinking about that tonight. Just enjoy this night together and know that no one can take this time away from you."

"I understand that everything is going well," the Reverend stated, raising an eyebrow.

"From what Ned tells me it is," Bonnie replied. "I'm to go in for an interview with the judge after Christmas. He got the letter from Mama and Daddy, so Ned says everything looks favorable. Oh, if I could have any Christmas present in the world, it would be for him to give me custody. I just don't think I could bear it if he says no." Bonnie leaned on Annie's shoulder. Annie put her arm around her.

"Now, Bonnie, I told you we won't think about those things right now. It was a lovely evening, don't you think?"

Bonnie smiled, "Yes, the children really enjoyed it. I think it will be hard to take them back tomorrow."

"Yes, well, we better take care of Santa right now," Annie said. "I have a feeling someone will be up mighty early."

The women brought the toys and gifts out of the closet and laid them all around for Polly when she woke. It was entertaining for Reverend Parker, who hadn't left his chair since retiring from his job as a riding pony earlier that evening.

After all was done and everyone was in bed, Bonnie lay next to Polly in bed watching her sleep. Her thoughts went to her mother and how she must have watched over Bonnie and her sisters on Christmas Eve. Suddenly, Bonnie missed her mother very much.

"Albert, where's Ned?" Mrs. Bass asked her long-time butler.

"I'm not sure, mam," he answered.

"Please go and find him. It's not like him to miss the party. Besides, we're ready for him to play the piano."

"Yes, ma'am."

Albert walked outside onto the back veranda where he found the young Mr. Bass smoking a cigarette.

"Mr. Bass," he said, formal as always. "Your mother wants you to join the party."

"I'm not much in the partying mood, Albert," Ned replied. The butler turned to go indoors, and Ned stopped him. "Say, have you ever met anyone you felt like you've known all of your life?"

Albert locked his hands in front of him, the stance he always took when spoken to.

"Yes, sir, I have," he answered frankly, for Albert that is.

"You have?"

"Yes, sir. My wife, sir."

Ned dropped the cigarette from his mouth. "Your wife? Albert, I didn't know you had a wife. Where is she?"

"Gone, sir," Albert said, uncharacteristically dropping his gaze toward the ground. "She contracted influenza right after we came over, sir. She died our first week in America."

"Why did you never marry again, Albert? That had to have been quite a long time ago."

Albert's eyes misted over. He cleared his throat. "There's no room for anyone but her, sir."

Ned looked at the butler, suddenly realizing that he was a stranger. He had known Albert since he was eight years old. His first recollection of the man was his coming to live with them. Soon after, his father had built the house on Belle Meade Boulevard. They'd never had a man before that. To have known someone as long as he had and still *not* know them, it made Ned wince. It dawned on Ned that he'd spent most of his life thinking of only himself and not much else.

He'd never known Albert was married and here the man stood before him, sixty years old and still in love with his dead wife.

Ned shook his head.

"I've never been in love, Albert. I'm not sure what it feels like."

In the dimness of the evening, Albert raised his eyebrows at the young Mr. Bass. He smiled. "Oh, you'll know, sir. When it happens, I mean. There won't be any doubt about it. Your mind, it tends to wander."

"Yeah," Ned said, returning the smile.

"And you don't get much work done."

"Yeah," Ned agreed again.

"You're just generally out of sorts, sir."

"Yeah!" Ned exclaimed. He grabbed Albert's hand shaking it liberally. "Thank you, Albert. Oh, and Merry Christmas!"

"Merry Christmas to you, too, sir," Albert answered, allowing a slight grin to show.

Ned turned to make his way inside to join the festivities.

CHAPTER FOURTEEN

"Nothing that hurts this bad could be for the best, Your Honor."

THE NEXT MORNING the parsonage was full of gleeful volume, probably the most noise since their arrival two years ago. The Reverend and Miss Annie didn't mind at all. In fact, Polly and Cora received a little help making joyful sounds from Reverend Parker as they opened their gifts.

Christmas dinner was perfect. Polly met all the visitors who came by to pay their respects to the Pastor and his wife. Bonnie was wished much luck on her upcoming custody case. All in all, it was the best day either Polly or Bonnie had had in a long while.

The afternoon came, and it was time to take the girls and their presents back to the orphanage. Bonnie held off leaving them as long as she could, but rules were rules, and she couldn't stay overnight. She waited until both of the girls had fallen asleep before she dared to leave them.

Bonnie was up early the next day preparing to leave for the orphanage when she heard the phone ring downstairs. Annie answered it.

"Yes, yes, she's here. One moment please," Annie said into the receiver. Bonnie had come halfway down the stairs when Annie turned to her. "It's for you. It's Judge Whitaker's office." Bonnie closed the distance between her and the receiver at a run.

"Hello?" she said breathlessly. "This is Bonnie McCaverty." A pause. "Yes, well, yes. I'll be there as soon as possible." She hung up the phone.

"What is it, Bonnie?" Annie asked.

"They want me to come down to Judge Whitaker's office for an interview."

"Today?"

"Yes, today. His secretary said the judge was going to make a decision soon and wanted to speed this along." Bonnie's knees buckled. "Miss Annie, I'm not sure I'm ready for this. What if he says no?"

"Now, Bonnie, don't be nervous. Just be yourself. He can't help but like you," she said, smiling. "I'm sure he won't make a decision today. He just wants to meet you and talk to you. That's only normal."

"Yes, but why is he in such a hurry all of a sudden?"

"I guess he doesn't want to keep the children in the orphanage any longer than he has to."

Bonnie shook her head slowly. "Yes, I guess that's it."

"Now, you go along and get ready. I'll call Reverend Parker and have him come over and drive you downtown. Run along."

"Yes, ma'am," Bonnie said as she quietly climbed the stairs; however, she was unable to squash the eerie feeling that something was wrong. Her heart pounded in her chest.

Bonnie walked into the judge's office just a bit after ten o'clock. The reception area felt rather intimidating with its solid wood paneled walls and marble floors, much like Ned's office. She thought that Judge Ivory Whitaker must be an important man.

"Hello, I'm Bonnie McCaverty," she informed the lady behind the desk. "Someone called for me to come down for an interview today."

"Oh yes, Miss McCaverty," the woman replied sweetly. "Take a seat. The judge will be right with you." She pointed to the couch along the wall. Bonnie saw a couple sitting along the opposite wall. She made her way over and sat down.

"Hello. My name is Bonnie," she said with a smile to the couple opposite her.

"Hello," the gentleman said. "My name's John Carter and this here's Helen."

"Nice to meet you," Bonnie said. She reached out and shook their hands. Bonnie smiled warmly at the couple. There was a kindness about them she could detect immediately. They reminded her of folks back home, plain and simple.

"What are you here for?" the woman asked Bonnie.

"I'm here for an interview with the judge for custody of some children. I have to admit, I'm mighty nervous."

The lady leaned forward and lowered her voice. "We are, too. We jest got a call this mornin' and here we are!"

"Yes, me too," Bonnie answered with a knowing smile.

Just then, the big oak door opened, and all three of them looked up. The judge's secretary stood looking at the three of them. "Mr. and Mrs. Carter?"

"Yes, that's us," the gentleman said, standing.

"Right this way. The judge will see you now."

Bonnie leaned over and took the lady's hand in hers. "Good luck!" she whispered.

The lady shook her hand back, smiling gratefully.

The couple entered the judge's chambers. Meanwhile, Bonnie tried to think about something else to take her mind off her nervousness. After some time, the couple emerged from behind the big door, nodding and thanking the lady who escorted them out. They said goodbye to Bonnie and left the office. The secretary stood at the judge's door. "Miss McCaverty?"

Bonnie stood. "Yes?"

"Right this way, please."

"Thank you," Bonnie said. She stepped past the secretary into the large plush office of Judge Ivory Whittaker.

He turned around in his big chair to face Bonnie. He had white hair that hung past his collar and a white beard that made him resemble Santa Claus. That thought made Bonnie relax a bit. His cheeks were bright red, and he wore a warm smile.

"Miss McCaverty?"

"Yes," Bonnie said as she offered her hand. The judge stood.

"I'm Judge Whittaker," he said. He accepted her gloved hand and shook it. "Please, have a seat." He motioned toward one of the big leather seats in front of his desk. The leather chair squeaked as Bonnie sat down. The judge sat back down in his chair and lit his pipe.

"Miss McCaverty, I'm sorry to bother you so soon after Christmas, but I think this matter would be better settled as quickly as possible."

"Yes, sir, I agree. I'd like to get them back to Smithville as soon as I can," Bonnie said quite excitedly.

"Yes, yes, well, Bonnie. May I call you Bonnie? I feel as if I know you because Ned has told me so much about you."

"Yes, Judge. Bonnie's just fine."

"Bonnie, how old are you exactly?"

"I'm nineteen, Judge. I'll be twenty in February."

"I see. And you're not married, is that right?"

"No, sir. I'm not," Bonnie said, looking down at her hands. She knew that wasn't favorable for her and immediately began her defense. "But, Judge, my parents have a beautiful farm in Smithville for the girls to grow up on and you got their letter tellin' how much they would love to have them. They just love children. My sisters, Emma and Nettie, both have children, and they'd have so much fun together. And, Judge, the girls would go to church and be taught the Christian way, I can tell you that."

The judge grinned at her innocence.

"I'm sure they would, Bonnie. Although, I do feel two children who've gone through what they have would profit better from having a mother and father. Don't you think?"

Bonnie's face wrinkled, "But, Judge," she said, leaning forward, her gloved hands clutching her pocketbook. "I can love those girls as much as any two people could. They mean the world to me. I promise they'd always come first."

Judge Whittaker leaned over and patted Bonnie's hand. "I'm sure you would, Bonnie. I'm sure you would. May I ask you another question?"

"Yes, sir. Anything."

"What if, say in two years or so, you meet someone, fall in love, and want to get married."

"Well, we'd all get married," Bonnie answered.

"Bonnie, what if the man who fell in love with you didn't want two children coming with you? What if he just wanted you?"

Bonnie shot straight to her feet. "Why, I wouldn't love a man like that!" she shouted. "Any man who didn't want Cora and Polly sure as heck wouldn't get me! I could never love a man who was like that, Your Honor!"

The judge stood to step out from behind his desk. He put his big hands on Bonnie's shoulders. Bonnie pulled a handkerchief from her purse. "I wouldn't, Judge. I promise," she said, wiping her eyes. "There won't ever anybody love those two girls like I do. I just can't explain it. It's like they've just come into my life as something that was meant to be." Bonnie put her hands on his big arms. "Judge, no one could love those girls like me, no one," she pleaded.

"I understand, Bonnie. Sit down here," he said. He sat in the chair opposite her. "Bonnie, you're a young girl, and I'm concerned that it wouldn't be fair to you to start your life out with two children. I'm also concerned that the children would be better off with a couple, with a mother and father."

"What couple?" Bonnie asked.

"The couple who just left," the judge replied. "The Carters. They've agreed to take both girls. Before, they only wanted the baby, but they've reconsidered."

Bonnie looked devastated. The couple she had just wished good luck to were actually the two who had wanted Cora. Bonnie's face became ashen.

"Are you all right, Bonnie?" the judge asked.

"I just didn't know. That's all."

"Didn't Ned tell you?"

"No, he didn't."

"Well, I'm sorry, Bonnie. I didn't mean to spring the news on you like that."

"It's all right, Judge. I'm sorry. I was just a bit surprised is all."

"I understand, dear. Listen, I haven't made my mind up just yet. Don't worry. I've talked to little Polly, and I know how she feels about you. She loves you very much. I just want to get this moving along as quickly as possible, and I didn't think it was fair to either of you to not meet you and talk with you. I know you love those girls. I see you have a great deal of love to give them, but I have to think about the girls, too. I have to do what is in the best interest of their future."

"Yes, sir. I understand," Bonnie said. She hung her head.

"I believe we'll meet here tomorrow for an informal hearing, and I'll make a decision. My secretary will phone you with the time.

"Miss McCaverty, I've heard all about what you've done for this family, and I know of your dedication to Mrs. Sutton and her children. You're a brave girl. I salute you for what you've done. Now go home and don't worry. Everything will turn out for the best."

Bonnie offered her hand. "Thank you, Judge."

As Bonnie traversed the hallway outside the judge's office, her pace quickened. She had one thing on her mind—Ned Bass. Why had he kept the other couple a secret? She'd tell him a thing or two! She got into the car and asked Reverend Parker to drop her off at the Bass Building. She'd catch the streetcar home.

Bonnie stormed past Mrs. Cooper at the front desk, walked right down the hall and into Ned's office. Ned was leaned back in his chair with his feet on his desk and a stack of papers in his lap. When Bonnie barged in the door, he jumped. Papers flew everywhere.

"Why didn't you tell me the couple had decided to take both girls?" Bonnie said coldly, placing both hands on her hips.

"I'm sorry, Mr. Bass," Mrs. Cooper called from the door. "She went right by me again. I couldn't stop her!"

"It's okay, Mrs. Cooper. I'll handle it. Thank you," he said to the secretary. As she closed the door, his eyes went back to Bonnie's. "Bonnie, I—"

"How could you do that to me? I just came from the judge's office, and I was sitting right there with the very couple who might get Cora and Polly instead of me, and I wished them good luck!"

"Bonnie, sit down," Ned told her.

She folded her arms in front of her. "I don't want to sit down. I want to know why you didn't tell me!"

Ned walked out from behind his desk. "Sit down, Bonnie," he said, pointing at the couch. Finally, Bonnie sat, her hands clenched into fists, her back rigid. She was mad, and she wanted Ned to know it.

Ned pulled a chair closer and sat across from her.

"I'm sorry, Bonnie," he said. "I didn't know he was going to call you so early for your interview."

"Why didn't you tell me?" Bonnie asked again, this time a bit calmer.

"I didn't want to spoil your Christmas," Ned replied, looking down. "I didn't have the heart. I wanted you to have a good time with the girls, and I didn't want anything to spoil it." The hard look on Bonnie's face softened a bit. "I know how much you love them, Bonnie, and I figured if you knew about the other couple, you'd worry. I guess I was wrong not to tell you. I'm sorry. I was going to come by and tell you after court this morning."

"Well, I guess you did the right thing. I'm sorry. I didn't mean to shout at you," Bonnie whispered. "I'm just so worried." She began to cry into her handkerchief. Ned lifted her from the couch and put his arms around her. "Don't cry. It's not over. The judge hasn't made a decision yet."

"I know. But he's going to tomorrow." She pulled away from him and walked to the window, a bit embarrassed at her show of emotion and a bit nervous with Ned's arms around her. "He said the hearing would be tomorrow and that someone would call and let me know when.

"Do I have a chance, Ned?" she asked, turning back to face him. "Do I have a chance at all with a mother and father saying they'll take both girls?" Bonnie's strong, defiant nature was completely neutralized by her love for these two children.

"You never know which way a judge is going to go, Bonnie. I think we have a good chance. I'm sure he sees how much you care about them."

"Yes, I told him that. I wanted him to know that for sure!"

Ned smiled. "Then let's not worry. I'm sure you did fine," he said. He patted her shoulders. "Now, let me drive you back home."

"No, I want to go to the orphanage."

"Okay. Any objections to me driving you there?"

Bonnie smiled for the first time since she'd burst through the door. "No."

"Good. Let's go."

"Ned, I'm sorry I was cross with you," Bonnie said. "You've done so much for me, and I know you didn't tell me because you wanted me to have a good Christmas. I'm sorry."

Ned kissed her forehead. "Don't think another thing about it. You're just worried. I understand."

"Thank you," Bonnie replied. Ned opened the door and allowed Bonnie to go first. He drove her to the orphanage, where she spent the remainder of the day. While Bonnie worked, Ned paid a visit to Judge Whittaker.

Ned offered Bonnie one of the chairs that had been arranged to face Judge Whittaker's desk. The Carters sat at the other end of the room, and Mr. Jordan sat in the middle. Ned quietly explained to Bonnie that Mr. Jordan was there to execute the judge's decision as soon as it was stated.

The judge entered the room and quickly took his seat behind his desk. "Good morning. Thank you all for coming.

"As you all know, this is an informal hearing to discuss the future of . . ." The judge put his glasses on and read from his papers. "Polly and Cora Sutton." He laid the papers down on the desk and removed his glasses. "This is never an easy decision, but let me assure you that I've thoroughly interviewed everyone associated with this case. The decision that I make here today will be in the best interest of the children in this case. It's only the children's best interest I'm concerned about, not anyone else." He slid his glasses back onto his face.

"Miss McCaverty."

"Yes, sir," Bonnie answered.

"I understand that your parents back in Smithville are willing to take the two girls in at their expense."

"Yes, sir. They are. They—" Ned reached out and put his hand on Bonnie's arm to prevent her from adding anything else.

"Will you get a job when you return back home?" the judge asked.

Bonnie looked confused. She hadn't even thought that far in advance. She glanced at Ned. "Well, yes, sir. I'm sure I will eventually after the girls get used to the farm and all."

"Very well," the judge said. Bonnie glanced at Ned. The judge was acting quite differently than he had the day before.

"Mr. and Mrs. Carter, you have a farm in Nolensville, is that right?"

"Yes, Your Honor," they answered in unison.

"It's my understanding that you've agreed to take both girls in this case instead of just the younger. Is that true?"

Mr. Carter spoke up. "Yes, sir. We decided that we couldn't live with ourselves if we were the reason those two girls got separated, Your Honor. We wouldn't want the little one to blame us when she got older. Why, we'd love 'em both as much, Your Honor."

"Thank you, Mr. Carter. Do you have the means to support both girls, sir?"

"Why, yes, sir. My farm's been doin' good enough even in these hard times. I got two boys to help with the farm, but my wife, she cain't have no more kids on account of the last boy really did her in. She wants a girl real bad to keep her company and help out with the house and all. But, yes sir. We're doin' pretty good and well enough for two more."

"Miss McCaverty, your family's farm does pretty well, doesn't it?"

"Yes, sir. We've always had the luck of the Irish when it comes to our crops, sir. My daddy, he just seems to have a way with plantin'. My family has always had everything we needed."

"Very well," the judge said. He removed his glasses again. "I'd like to recess for a bit while I think some things over. If you would all wait outside, the secretary will let you know when to come back in."

Everyone stood and began walking toward the door. The judge motioned to Ned. "Ned, would you mind if I talked to your client alone?"

"No, sir. I'll be right outside, Bonnie," Ned assured her.

Bonnie sat down again.

He came out from behind his desk and sat where Ned had sat next to her. "Bonnie, I wanted to talk to you alone because I have a question for you. I want you to make up your mind all by yourself, without any help from anyone."

"Okay," Bonnie said quietly, now quite nervous.

"Bonnie, I believe that Polly would be better off with you. She loves you very much. She's at such a tender age. But I believe that Cora is better off with the Carters. She won't remember you or Polly as she grows older. It will be as if she was born into this family. I believe I owe her that kind of start in life, after all she's been through. Yet, I don't want to split these girls up. I've talked to Polly. She loves her sister very much. I believe if I gave you custody of her, she'd go with you. She loves you that much. But that's not a decision a four-year-old should have to make.

"Don't you agree?"

In an instant, Bonnie realized where the conversation was leading. "Yes, sir. I do."

"So, I'm afraid I'm going to have to ask you to make it for her. I'll let Polly go with you, but the baby must go with the Carters. It's the only right thing to do. The only thing my conscience will allow me to do, but you have to make the decision for Polly. Does she go with you and leave Cora, or does she stay with Cora and go with the other family?"

Bonnie sat staring into space, her mind reeling. The judge's words echoed in her head.

"Bonnie?" the judge said.

"Yes?"

"Do you understand?"

"Yes, I do. If I take Polly, she'll be separated from Cora. If I don't take her, she'll be able to grow up with her little sister."

"Bonnie, I'll understand no matter which decision you make. I know you'll do what's right." He patted her hand. "I'll leave you alone for a few minutes to think about it."

Bonnie only nodded.

The judge left the room.

As she sat back in her chair, Bonnie could see little Polly's face just two nights before, telling her of the promise she made her mother that she would always look after Cora. How could Bonnie ask Polly to break that promise? She couldn't. It was over. Bonnie had lost.

Bonnie's heart began to hurt. Why was this pain so familiar? Why had it come back to her again? Bonnie shook her head, trying to fight the tears that were starting to form there. She tried to stop the pain in her chest from crawling up into her head. Moments later, Bonnie heard the door open. She swallowed the lump in her throat and sat up in her chair. The judge sat across from her.

"Have you made up your mind, Bonnie?" he asked.

"There's nothing to decide," Bonnie said coldly. "I can't split them up."

"Very well," the judge said. He opened the door and summoned the others back into his chambers. After everyone had taken their seats, the judge stood to speak.

"This is never an easy task for me, so I'll be brief. I believe that, for the sake of the children, they would be better served growing up with both a mother and a father. It is the decision of the court to grant the Carters custody of both Cora and Polly Sutton."

The Carters hugged one another joyfully as Bonnie, Ned, and Mr. Jordan rose to their feet. Mr. Carter shook the judge's hand. "Thank you, sir. Thank you."

"Very good. Very good. Take good care of them."

"Yes, sir. We will. Yes, sir!" the two said. They made their way out of the room. Bonnie stood with Ned's help and turned to Mr. Jordan.

"I'm sorry, Bonnie," Mr. Jordan said.

"May I go say goodbye to them?" she asked Mr. Jordan. He looked at the judge, who nodded his approval.

"Of course," Mr. Jordan said.

"Bonnie," the judge said, stopping her as she was about to leave. She turned to face him, but couldn't look at him.

"It was a wise decision you made. You'll see. It will be for the best."

Bonnie raised her head, locking eyes with him. "Nothing that hurts this bad could be for the best, Your Honor." She turned and left the room.

Ned shook hands with the judge and ran to catch up with her. She was already in Annie's arms walking down the hall when he caught up with them.

"Bonnie! Bonnie!" he called. The three of them stopped and turned to face him. "Bonnie, I . . . I, I'm sorry. I really didn't think things would turn out this way. What did he mean by you made the right decision?"

"It doesn't matter," Bonnie mumbled. "It's over." She offered Ned her hand, which he took and shook gently. "Thank you for everything, Ned. I know you did the best you could."

Ned glanced at the Reverend and Annie. They took the hint and slowly withdrew a short distance. Ned lowered his voice. "Let me drive you home," he offered.

"No, I just want to go and see the children."

"Let me drive you there, then."

"That's all right, Ned. The Parkers can take me."

"Bonnie, I'm sorry."

"I know," she replied. "I know you tried. It was my decision. The judge wanted to give Polly to me, but it would mean splitting up the girls. I made the decision. It wasn't your fault."

"Oh," Ned replied softly. Judge Whitaker hadn't told him he was going to do that. Probably because he didn't want him warning Bonnie.

"May I call you tonight? Can I take you out and cheer you up?" Ned asked, trying to smile.

"I don't think so. I don't feel much like it, Ned. I'll see you." She turned away and walked down the hall to the where the Parkers waited. They put their arms around her. Together, the three of them walked down the long hallway and out of the courthouse.

Bonnie waited in the anteroom while Mrs. McCullough went to get the girls. She and Bonnie had a cry together. After they'd both managed to pull themselves together, Mrs. McCullough went to get the girls. Less than a minute later, Polly's arms were around Bonnie's neck.

"Oh, there's my girl!" Bonnie said, hugging her tightly.

"Bonnie, that man with the white hair came and talked to me."

"He did?"

"Yes, he looked like Santa Claus!" Polly laughed. "What's a matter, Bonnie? You sad?"

Mrs. McCullough put her hanky to her mouth and left the room to cover the sound of her sobs. Bonnie blinked back the tears.

"Polly, come over here and sit down with Cora and me," Bonnie said. Polly sat down on the couch next to Bonnie. Her solemn blue eyes wrenched at Bonnie's heart. "You know, your mother would be proud of you, Polly, the way you've taken care of Cora. You should be proud of that."

"She's my sister," Polly said, her voice cracking. She knew something was wrong. "What's a matter, Miss Bonnie?"

"Come here and look at me," Bonnie said. She sat Cora down on the couch next to her. "You have to make a promise to me that you will always look after Cora. Don't ever let anything happen to her."

"I won't, Miss Bonnie. You'll be wiff us on your farm, won't you?"

Bonnie swallowed hard. "No, Polly," she said. "I'm afraid the judge decided that you and Cora should go with Mr. and Mrs. Carter to their farm."

Polly shot to her feet. "No! I won't go! They can't make me go!" she shouted. Bonnie grabbed her by her hands and pulled her close. Polly kicked and screamed, but was soon too overcome with emotion to fight. She pulled away and looked at Bonnie, her little eyes nearly swollen shut from crying. "Don't let them take us. Please, don't let them take us!"

Bonnie's heart broke. Tears rolled down her cheeks and onto her skirt. "Oh, Polly, I can't stop them, but you'll be happy. I promise. They're good people. You have to promise me that you'll be good so they won't take you away from Cora. Promise me!"

"No, I want to go with you," the little girl screamed, clinging to Bonnie.

"Oh, Polly, please promise me you'll be good! You have to make a promise to me that you'll be good so that they'll let you stay with Cora, okay? Polly, promise me!"

Cora began to cry. Bonnie picked her up and held the two of them close.

Mrs. McCullough called to them from the other room. "Bonnie, the Carters are here for the girls."

"Okay, we'll be right out."

"No, no, no!" Polly cried. Bonnie gripped her by each arm and forced her to look into her eyes. "Polly, listen to me. Listen to me! You have to promise me, honey. Please promise me you'll be good."

"I love you, Miss Bonnie! I love you!" Polly screamed. Mrs. McCullough came up behind her and put her hands on the girl's shoulders, trying to gently pull her away from Bonnie. "No, no, I want to go with Bonnie!" Polly screamed, "I want to go with Bonnie!" She stomped her feet. Bonnie looked up at Mrs. McCullough and motioned for her to take her out of the room. Mrs. McCullough picked Polly up, wrapping her arms around the sobbing girl. The child clung to her, crying into the old lady's soft shoulder. Bonnie pulled Cora to her and cried as Polly left the room. She pulled the baby away and looked at her.

"You won't remember me when you grow up, but I love you very much. Grow up to be healthy and strong and know that someone will always be praying for you no matter where you are."

Just then, Mr. Jordan came through the door.

"I'm sorry, Bonnie, but they're waiting for the children so they can get back to their farm before nightfall." Bonnie kissed the baby on the cheek. Cora smiled at her. Bonnie smiled back. "Godspeed, little one," she said as she handed the baby to Mr. Jordan. When he was gone, she stood and took a deep breath.

Bonnie ran for the door but managed to stop herself. If she fell apart, it would only be harder for Polly. Instead, she leaned against the doorway and cried. Just then, the door opened. Annie Parker stepped inside the room. Bonnie fell into her arms, all self-control lost.

The phone rang at the parsonage. Annie answered.

"Hello."

"Mrs. Parker, how is Bonnie?"

"She's asleep, Ned. It's all been quite a shock. I don't think it ever occurred to her that she might not get the girls."

"I know. I was afraid this might happen. At the last minute, the Carters changed their mind about Polly."

"Yes, we understand that's what happened."

"May I come by and see her, Mrs. Parker?"

"Oh, Ned, I don't think so. I think she needs some time. Let her rest a bit."

"Mrs. Parker, will you let me know if anything happens?"

"Yes Ned, I'll phone. You're very sweet to care."

"I do care, Mrs. Parker. Very much so."

"I understand. Well, good day, Mr. Bass."

"Good day, Mrs. Parker."

The next morning, Bonnie rose early. She was packing her trunk when Mrs. Parker heard her rustling around and came to check on her.

"Bonnie? Dear, what are you doing?"

"I'm packing, Miss Annie. I want to go home for a while."

"So soon? We could drive you if you—"

"Miss Annie," Bonnie interrupted. "I've called Doc Morgan. He's going to pick me up at the train station in McMinnville. He's going to be there later today anyway, and he said he'd wait for me. I've got to go home, if just for a while."

Annie put her arms around Bonnie. "I understand, dear. I thought you'd probably want to go home for a bit, but so soon? Are you going to stay or come back? You know you're welcome to come back anytime you want."

"I don't know," Bonnie said. She sat on the bed. "I feel so tired, Miss Annie. I'm almost twenty years old and look at me. I don't have a job or a family. I don't seem to fit anywhere. What am I going to do?"

"Oh, dear, don't worry. Everything will fall into place. You'll see. The Lord has His hand on you, Bonnie. He knows where you're going."

"Well," Bonnie replied angrily, "I wish He'd let me in on it."

"Bonnie!"

"I'm sorry, Miss Annie. I don't mean no disrespect. I just feel all out of sorts."

"Well, I know one person who doesn't want you to leave."

"Who?"

"Ned Bass," Annie said, grinning. "He called last night asking if he could come see you. I really think he cares a great deal for you, Bonnie."

"Ned? I don't think so, Miss Annie. He's one of the most eligible men in town. He could have any girl he wanted. What would he want with me?"

Annie shot her a reproachful look. "Don't go talking like that, Bonnie McCaverty. That's just not like you."

"Oh, I'm sorry. I just . . . I can't feel anything for anyone right now. First Calvin, now this. It takes too much work to love. I think I'm just not going to do it for a while."

"Well, I think you ought to give Mr. Bass a chance."

Bonnie shook her head. "I can't. There's too much in the way; too much from the past still inside me. When I can forget all of that, then maybe. I guess that's one reason why I want to go home. I want to make sure there's nothing for me there. You understand, don't you, Miss Annie?"

"Yes, I do," she said, reaching over to kiss Bonnie's forehead. "I'll go break the news to Reverend Parker."

"Thank you," Bonnie said. "Thank you for everything."

"We love you, Bonnie. We want what's best for you. You know that."

"Yes, ma'am."

Some time later, Bonnie heard the front bell ring. She waited in her room, hoping someone else would answer it. When no one did, Bonnie walked slowly down the stairs to see who was there. Through the sheer curtains, she could see that it was a man. She cracked the curtains and peeked out. There on the front porch stood Ned Bass.

Bonnie sighed and opened the door.

"Bonnie!" He looked surprised to see her. "I'm sorry to stop by so early, but I have to talk to you."

"Ned, I really have things I need to do."

"It's important. I promise not to take up much of your time."

"Fine," she said. She opened the door, not looking at him. "Please come in."

"Thank you," Ned said, following her into the living room. Bonnie took a spot in front of the fireplace, her back to Ned. She stared into the fire, not speaking. Ned twirled his hat in his hands for a moment before breaking the silence.

"Bonnie, I have something to say to you, and I want you to hear me out," he said. "I know you're thinking about going back home. Well, I don't want you to." Bonnie turned around to face him. "I mean, I know your heart is broken, but I want a chance to make it better. I want a chance for us, Bonnie."

"For *us*?"

Ned smiled. "Yes, us. Look, I know we haven't known each other long, but I've never met anyone like you, Bonnie. I want you to stay and give me a chance to get to know you."

Bonnie turned around and stared into the fireplace again, steadying herself against the mantle with both hands. Ned placed his hand on hers standing behind her. He spoke softly over her shoulder. "Please, Bonnie. Don't leave. It won't do any good. You'll feel just as bad there as you'll feel here. Only here, I'll do my best to try to make you feel better."

Bonnie snatched her hand out from under his. Tears began streaming down her face. "I don't want to feel better!" she shouted at him. "Why does everyone think this is just going to go away? Like I'm just not going to see their little faces anymore or think about them anymore or know I'll never see them anymore. How could you know? You didn't love them!"

"Bonnie . . ."

"Did you? Do you know how much it hurts? How can you just ask me to stay here and act like nothing happened?"

"I'm not asking you to do that," Ned replied soothingly. "I just want a chance. Bonnie, I have a feeling when you came to Nashville you were running from something back in Smithville. What makes you think it will be any different than running from here to go back there? Don't run away, Bonnie. Stay."

"How can you know? How do you know? You don't even know me!" Bonnie shouted at him.

"Maybe I don't," Ned replied, "but I want to. Why don't you give that a chance? Maybe something would work out for you for a change."

Bonnie slapped Ned across the face.

His head rocked back on his neck. When he straightened, he raised a hand to the stinging, glowing mark on his left cheek, testing the tenderness. For a second, Bonnie saw anger flash in his eyes, before he wrapped his arms around her and kissed her square on the lips. She struggled briefly against him, pushing at his chest and shoulders, but then gave in to the comfort and security she felt in the strength of his arms. His lips pressed against hers tenderly, firm but not forced.

Bonnie thought her knees were melting.

Ned gently released her, steadying her with both arms, looking in her eyes. Half-lidded, they fluttered open and gazed back at him.

"I don't want you to leave, Bonnie," he said. "Take that or leave it, but I couldn't let you go without telling you that." He let her go, grabbed his hat from the chair, and showed himself out of the front door.

Bonnie ran upstairs and shut the door behind her. Her head was spinning. She was angry with Ned, but now reluctant to leave him and Nashville behind.

"How dare he kiss me like that! How dare he!" she said. She wiped her lips with the back of her hand. She ran to the window and looked out unsure of what she was suddenly feeling.

He was already gone.

CHAPTER FIFTEEN

"How can anybody think that what their heart is telling them is so true, and it be so awfully wrong?"

I T WAS TOO early for visitors and bitterly cold that January morning, but that didn't stop Jessie from calling on Calvin Wade. Buttermilk was taking out the leftovers from breakfast when he saw Jessie coming up the drive from the road.

Calvin walked out onto the porch to smoke a cigarette just as Jessie reached the front steps. "Morning, Jessie," he said. "Kind of early. Everything all right with Lizzie?" Calvin asked.

"Morning," Jessie replied, offering Calvin his hand. "Lizzie's fine. She's not what I came to talk to you about, son."

Calvin flipped his cigarette into the dirt and opened the front door. The two men sat in front of the fire. Jessie rubbed his hands together, which made a noise of two pieces of sandpaper rubbing against one another. He held them up to the radiant warmth.

"Well, what is it?" Calvin asked.

"Bonnie's home."

Calvin stood and faced the fire. "That so?"

"Yes, she didn't get custody of the girls. We suspected that might happen."

"I'm sorry. I know that really meant a lot to her."

"It did." He paused. "Something's wrong with her, Calvin. She's been home for a couple of days and, well, she's just not the same. She sits up at the window and stares out. She don't even talk much any-more. You know Bonnie's never had trouble with talkin', even when she's mad or upset. I don't like it, Calvin. We're worried. She's had so many disappointments."

Calvin turned to look at Jessie. "You still blamin' me for her going to Nashville, then?"

Jessie ignored him. "I want you to come see her, Calvin," he replied. "You've got to cheer her up. We've tried everything. She won't even ride Danny, for heaven's sake! She's just so young, and it's like all the life has been drained out of her."

"I don't think seein' me is going to help her any. I imagine it'll only make things worse."

Jessie stood. "I don't think you understand, Calvin. I'm not ask-ing you. Son, I remember a time when the two of you were insepa-rable. Remember when you lost Rosalee? Bonnie didn't run from help-ing you. If it weren't for her patience, you might have died a drunken fool!" Jessie's voice rose, the veins in his neck bulging. Calvin knew he meant business.

He was right. Calvin remembered Bonnie standing in the kitchen night after night, cooking the suppers that he never ate, the coffee that burnt on the stove that he never drank. He remembered that last night he got drunk, the night he opened the door and threw Bonnie onto the ground. He thought about those nights often, but not in a con-scious way. They crept into his mind when his guard was down, when his mind wandered, bumping into the past, activating stored thoughts and smells he tried so hard to forget.

He remembered the feel of the stinging cold as tears fell down his face that morning he ran from his house when he found out that his mother was dead. He remembered the rain that poured from the brim of his hat, the mud that covered his body, stifling his breath when he lifted Rosalee from the muddy road and walked her limp body home.

As it always did, the smell that filled the tool shed when Bonnie found him there that morning, determined to tell him how she felt about him would return. Calvin drank in that scent for as long as he could before he turned to face her.

None of that, however, compared to the memory of how she looked standing there in her mother's skirt and vest, her hair piled up on her head, her eyes twinkling, her skin glowing. Calvin held onto that memory, as brief as it was, as long and hard as he could, trying not to let it slip from his mind as the faces of his mother and father and Rosalee had.

"Calvin!" Jessie's voice brought him back from his ghosts.

He blinked, clearing away the visions from the past. "Okay, Jessie. I'll come to see her. I'll do my best to cheer her up."

"That's all I ask of you, son," Jessie said, quietly picking up his hat and making his way out the front door. Calvin watched him go, thinking how old Jessie looked.

Calvin wasn't looking forward to the task. Bonnie had been away for almost two years now. The last time he'd seen her was when she'd left the tool shed that day, vowing never to return. Calvin had relived that day over and over in his mind often wondering what he could have done differently. Thinking about how things might have been different had he been honest with her. In the end, he always came to the same conclusion—she was better off in Nashville away from him and this curse of death that befell everyone he loved. He could love her, but only in his mind and heart. Telling her how he felt could only mean disaster.

※

Reverend Parker had just finished his coffee and stood from the table when the phone rang.

"I'll get it, Annie," he yelled to his wife, who was clearing the breakfast dishes. It was their third morning without the constant chatter from Bonnie that they had grown accustomed to. Both were already missing her.

"Hello?" Reverend Parker said into the receiver.

"Reverend Parker?" came the voice from the other end. "It's Ned Bass, sir."

Reverend Parker smiled. "Oh yes, Ned. How are you, son?"

"I'm fine, sir. I'm sorry for calling so early in the morning, but I, well, I wanted to find out if Bonnie was there, well, today I mean," the young man stammered. "I guess I'm wondering if she went back home, sir."

Reverend Parker paused for a moment chewing on what to say. Ultimately, he couldn't come up with a way to soften the news, so he just said it. "No, Ned. Bonnie's gone home."

There was a long moment of silence from the other end of the call. Finally, Ned spoke up.

"I see," he said solemnly.

"I'm sorry, son. Mrs. Parker and I were sad to see her go."

"Yes, sir. Has she gone home for good or will she be back?"

"I'm not sure, Ned. I really don't think Bonnie knows either. She's confused. She needs time with her family. It's been awhile since she's spent any time with them. She needs to get her mind off Polly and Cora. I just don't believe she could do it here. You understand."

"I guess," came the reply. "I was just hoping . . . well, anyway. She's gone. I just wanted to see what she had decided. I'm sorry for calling so early. Please excuse me."

"Oh, it's quite all right, Ned. You call or come by anytime. We'll tell Bonnie you asked about her."

"Reverend, that won't be necessary. Please, don't tell her I called."

"Well, son, you know if she asked me . . ."

Ned laughed out loud. "Right, yes, sir. I know. You can't lie."

Reverend Parker laughed. "That's right, son."

"It was very nice meeting you and Mrs. Parker," the young man said.

"We were glad to meet you, Mr. Bass. Please, do come and visit."

"Thank you. Goodbye."

"Goodbye, Ned," Reverend Parker said. Slowly he put the receiver back onto its hook.

"Who was that?" Annie said. She was carrying his coat and held it open for him to slip his arms inside.

"That was Ned Bass," he said, threading his arms through the sleeves. "He was quite disappointed that our Bonnie has gone home. What a shame. I think he was really taken with her."

"Oh, he was. I could tell."

"You could. Could you?"

"Yes. Women can tell these things."

"Well, can you tell me why Bonnie left then?" Reverend Parker asked.

"Frank," Annie scolded. "You know why Bonnie went back home. It's Calvin. It'll always be Calvin. People come along and occupy Bonnie's mind for a while, but when the emptiness creeps back in, and there he is again. She'll always go back to Calvin. I only wish that boy knew how much she loves him."

"Well, don't you think time will have made any difference when Bonnie gets home?"

"I really don't know," Annie said. "Neither does Lizzie. Of course, we've discussed these things."

"Of course."

"Lizzie says he never goes out with anyone. Never goes to the dances. Rarely even goes to church."

"You don't say! I wasn't aware of that."

"You know how Lizzie is about church. If she doesn't have any control over him, no one does."

"He's not back to drinkin' is he?"

"No, no. He just stays on that farm with his two hired hands. Never does much of anything, Lizzie says. I just wonder . . ."

"What?"

"I just pray that maybe he's missed Bonnie enough to put those old superstitions of his aside. Lordy be, it's the thirties. You'd think someone would have enough sense not to believe something so outrageous."

"Annie, when you're as young as Calvin was when he lost his folks *and* his fiancée, superstitions like that can sink deep roots. It's a hard thing to quit."

"I know. I just wish the both of them could find some happiness. They've both been through so much."

"I know, dear," Reverend Parker said. He pulled his wife to him, holding her close for an extra moment. "All we can do is pray. God will see them through."

Calvin saddled Buck and rode out into the morning light. Shorty caught him from the front porch.

"Where you goin', Mr. Calvin?" Shorty asked.

"Ridin' over to Jessie's. I'll be back in a bit," Calvin said.

Shorty's eyes lit up. "You goin' to see Miss Bonnie? Mr. Jessie done told us she back."

"Yes, Shorty. I'm going to pay my respects."

"Mr. Calvin, when you goin' to ask that girl to marry you?"

"Shorty . . ."

"Aw, Mr. Calvin, I don't mean no disrespect. We know how you feel about that girl. It don't seem right you livin' on this big ole farm with two old goats like me 'n Buttermilk instead a that pretty Miss Bonnie."

Calvin reined his horse away from the house toward the trail that led to the McCavertys. "I'll be back for supper."

Shorty waved him away, mumbling, "Shore seemed like a waste to me. Ought'a have a bunch a chillen runnin' round this house sted a me 'n ole Buttermilk. Ain't no kind a life for no young man. Sho ain't."

Buttermilk opened the door just then. "What you out here talkin' to yourself about? Get in here and help me!"

Shorty jumped to attention. "I was just tellin' Mr. Calvin how he oughta go over there and bring Miss Bonnie back here 's all."

"What you doin' meddlin' in Mr. Calvin's affairs? Don't you know better? Get in here and help me!" Buttermilk shouted.

Shorty ducked as Buttermilk's hat came down on his head. "Just seemed like somebody oughta say sumpn'."

"Well, it sho ain't you! Get into that house!"

Calvin could hear the two old men continuing to bicker on their way into the house. He smiled and snapped Buck's reins, urging him onward.

When he reached the top of the hill, Calvin noticed a figure sitting on the rock at the top of the bluff overlooking his farm. A few steps closer and he recognized her. It was Bonnie. His heart missed a whole beat. The next one was hard enough to make up for it. Calvin was sure everyone in the county, including Bonnie, had heard it.

Buck made his way straight to where Danny stood tearing leaves off the trees. The horses nuzzled each other.

Bonnie didn't look at him. She looked so different, so grown up. Her long hair was gone, cut clean up to her chin, but that only seemed to have enhanced her face. The clothes she wore looked familiar. The pants, the coat, the boots, even the gloves she wore were all the same, although the person wearing them didn't. She barely looked familiar at all.

Calvin dismounted and approached her. "Hello, Bonnie," he said. "I was just coming to see you."

"I see Buttermilk and Shorty are still fighting," she said without looking at him.

Calvin's heart skipped another beat. She'd overheard them as well. She must've been watching all this time. "Of course," he replied, laughing nervously. "They never stop."

Bonnie still hadn't turned to look at him. She sat on the rock with her legs pulled up to her chest gazing over the valley. "Everything looks the same, but different."

"We've made a few changes," Calvin said, twisting Buck's reins between his fingers.

"How can everything look the same 'cept different?" Bonnie asked. She seemed to be talking to herself more than to him.

"I don't think everything else changes," he replied. "I believe that we do."

She finally turned to look at him, smiling sweetly. He had the same blue eyes, the same face, the same coal-black hair.

"Have we changed?" she asked him.

"You certainly have. Look at you! You're all grown up!" Calvin said. "I see you've even cut your hair." Calvin's heart made loop-the-loops inside his chest.

"Yes, I guess I have changed from where you're sitting, but I haven't. Nothing has changed for me." She sighed, returning her gaze to the valley. A moment later, she stood and walked to the edge of the cliff. "You know, I made so many plans from up here, dreamed so many dreams. I never doubted that they would come true."

Calvin shifted uncomfortably.

"Now, I don't even dream anymore," Bonnie continued, looking down at the ground.

Calvin's heart ached for her. He wanted to take Bonnie into his arms and tell her he'd take care of her for the rest of her life, that he'd never leave her and never let anything ever hurt her again, but he couldn't. As much as she was hurting, at least she was alive. If he gave in for his own happiness, she'd pay in the long run. As long as she was with him, she was in danger. Everyone he'd ever loved and had loved him back was gone, and any happiness Calvin wanted for himself could never outweigh the threat of something happening to Bonnie.

"Bonnie," he answered softly, "you can't quit dreaming. Everyone has to have dreams."

She looked up at him. "Why? Why should I dream and wish for things that never come true? It'd be easier to never have dreamed them in the first place. Seems to me it'd be a lot easier that way."

"Things might seem hopeless now," he assured her, "but they won't always be that way. Look at the bright side."

Bonnie glowered. "What bright side?" she snapped back at him. "There is no bright side, Calvin. Polly and Cora are gone! I'll never see them again." She held her hands out in front of her. "Everything I ever want seems to just keep slippin' through my hands." Slowly she raised her hands to her face and cried. Her whole body shook with each heaving sob.

Calvin stood awkwardly behind her, not knowing what to do.

"Bonnie," he said, placing his hands on her shoulders. She instinctively buried her head in his chest wrapping her arms around him. Calvin wrapped his arms around her slowly, closing his eyes. Her smell was so familiar, like coming home. Her hair still had the same soft touch.

"The bright side is you're back home where you belong."

Bonnie looked up at him with those beautiful green eyes. "Where

I belong? What do you mean, where I belong?" Bonnie asked. Calvin dropped his hands to his side.

"Bonnie, Jessie and Lizzie are so glad your back."

"And?" Bonnie asked. Her eyes pleaded with him. Calvin turned and looked out over the valley.

"We're all glad you're back."

Bonnie sighed, dropping her hands to her side as if she'd lost another great battle the weight of her arms too heavy to bear.

"You're not going to say it, are you?" she said. She walked over to her horse and tossed Danny's reins over his neck.

"Say what?" Calvin asked.

Bonnie stuck her foot into the stirrup and launched herself onto Danny. "It wouldn't matter how long I was gone and came back. You'll never say it, will you?" She rolled her eyes. "I'm tired of playing games with you and wasting my time."

Calvin walked over and put his hand on Danny's neck. "Bonnie, why are you angry? Everyone's so happy you're back. This is where you belong."

"You've not changed your mind. Have you?"

"Bonnie," Calvin murmured, looking down at his feet.

"I came back to see if there was anything here for me," Bonnie said coldly. "I don't know why I thought anything would be any different. I guess I hoped that time might have made a difference. Obviously, it hasn't."

"Bonnie," Calvin pleaded again. "I . . . You're right," he said, surrendering. "I guess nothing's changed."

"How can anybody think what their heart is telling them is so true and it be so awfully wrong?" Bonnie said, mostly to herself. "Well, goodbye again, Calvin. I'm sure that I'll never come back this time."

"Bonnie! Why?" he asked. Danny instinctively turned toward the McCaverty farm. Bonnie reined him around again to face Calvin.

"Why should I?" she said plainly. "Why should I stay here and be constantly reminded of the dreams that didn't come true and never will? Why should I stay here so you can treat me like a perfect stranger? I told you last time I'd never come back and I did." Her face wasn't flush, and there was no anger in her eyes. There was only distant, cold reason. "Something on the inside of me hoped that you might have changed, but just like with everything else, I was a fool to think it would. I'm leaving, and this time I promise I won't ever be back."

She kicked Danny, who galloped down the path through the forest. Calvin stood behind, not sure what to do. Bonnie meant what she said. He could sense that. She was no longer a child with an innocence that allowed her to show her emotions at will. She was all grown up now and still felt the same way. Now, the hurt was deeper, and she was stronger. Calvin realized that he would never see her again this time unless he stopped her.

He mounted Buck, still uncertain whether to give chase. If he went after her, he would never be able to go back to the way things were. He would have to be honest with her, and he couldn't risk that.

"Damn it," he whispered. Meanwhile, Buck pranced around the overlook.

"I'm sorry, Bonnie," Calvin said.

He turned Buck toward home.

CHAPTER SIXTEEN

*"Am I real? Well, what kind of question is that to ask
someone who's come all this way to see you?"*

B ONNIE WALKED UP the steps from the train shed at Union
Station around eleven Saturday morning, stopping only at the
phone booth to call Reverend Parker and let him know she
was there.

After she had hung up the phone, she noticed a rather loud group
of well-dressed people making their way through the lobby. The man
leading the pack was dressed to the nines complete with a slick black
walking cane he was using to chase everyone out of his path.

"Boy, take our luggage over there," the man shouted, then he
leaned near the girl who was with him. "We'll be taking the noon train
to West Palm. I need to get out of here for a while."

As the group made its way to the ticketing counter, Bonnie found
an exit and backed through it, keeping a wary eye on them. The exit
turned out to be an entrance into the Lunch Room.

She backed against the wall of the diner away from double doors
as if she were hiding from someone. Nell, the counter waitress, had
been watching her. Finally, she couldn't stand it any longer. She made
her way over to the young girl, who was now peering back through the
doors of the Lunch Room.

"Can I help you?" the waitress asked. Bonnie started only just becoming aware that she was in a room full of people and most eyes were on her.

"Oh. No. I'm sorry, I just stepped in here to a . . ."

"Hide," the waitress whispered.

Bonnie smiled. "Yeah, I guess I was," she said, a bit red-faced.

Nell looked out the Lunch Room doors scanning the lobby.

"Who are you hiding from?"

Bonnie laid her grip down on the floor and straightened her hat. "He's gone."

"Gone?"

"Yeah, he was boarding."

"Where was he going?"

"Well, it looked to me as if he was going for a long stay with someone in some place called West Palm, wherever in the world that is," Bonnie said.

"Well, I guess you won't be bothered with him anymore, huh?" Nell replied, swishing her hands together as if dusting dirt off her hands. It took a moment for Bonnie to realize her intention.

"No, I guess I won't," Bonnie said, smiling at the waitress.

"So you should celebrate! How 'bout a cup of coffee on the house?"

"No, thank you. I've called the Reverend to let him know I'm here."

"The Reverend? Well, best not keep *him* waitin'."

"Yes, but thanks for your offer."

"Anytime, honey. The name's Nell. What's yours?"

"Bonnie, Bonnie McCaverty," she replied, offering her hand. "Thanks for a place to hide."

"C'mon back anytime," Nell said. She pushed the door open to help Bonnie through with her bags.

"It's for you, Bonnie," Reverend Parker called to Bonnie. She had hardly been aware that the phone had rung. "It's Mr. Jordan from the orphanage."

Bonnie looked alarmed. "Mr. Jordan? Why would he be calling?"

"Talk to him. He'll tell you all about it."

"Mr. Jordan?" Bonnie spoke into the phone.

"Miss McCaverty, thank God you're back. I have to talk to you right away."

"What's the matter? Has something happened to the girls?" Bonnie asked, feeling her chest tighten.

"No, not exactly."

"What do you mean, 'not exactly'?"

"The Carters are having some problems with Polly. It seems she's decided not to eat again."

"Oh, my Lord! Why hasn't someone called me?"

"The Carters tried their best to handle the situation, but they can't seem to console her. Bonnie, I know it's not fair to ask this of you, but would you consider going out to see her and talk to her to try to make her understand that this is how it has to be?"

"My poor Polly! When should I be ready?"

"As soon as possible, Bonnie. They live pretty far out. I'll come by, pick you up and drive you out there."

"I'll be ready," Bonnie told him.

Bonnie placed the receiver onto its cradle and turned to Annie who, as always, offered an arm to hold her up. "Polly won't eat again. She's so upset! Poor dear. This isn't fair!" Bonnie stomped her foot. "Why can't they just see she doesn't want to be there and let me have them? Why can't they do what the children want? I don't understand!"

"It's a hard thing to do, Bonnie, but you're going to have to make her understand," the Reverend spoke up.

She glared at him, surprised. "What do you mean, Reverend?"

Reverend Parker put his big hands on her shoulders and looked her squarely in the eyes. "Bonnie, listen to me. Polly is a scared, frightened little girl right now. What she needs from you is love. The Carters will love her, but they haven't had the chance to prove that to her. You have. She trusts you. You're the only person in the world she probably does trust.

"Now, it's up to you to pass that trust on to the Carters. Polly can sense what you feel. She knows what you're going through, and it's tearing at her heart. She doesn't know she can trust these people, but you have to get her to understand that." He lifted her face to look at him. Her chin quivered against his fingers. "You have to let her go. The court has made its decision, and you have to let her go. Give her the chance to start new again.

"Bonnie, she won't be able to do move on until you let her go and until she knows you've let her go. I know it's hard for you, but think of the girls. Think of their lives and how they need to forget the past."

Tears rolled down Bonnie's face as the Reverend pulled her to him. "There, there, dear. Don't cry. You're a brave girl, Bonnie McCaverty. I know you can do it."

Bonnie pulled away, wiping her face with Annie's hanky, then nodded. "Okay, I'll do my best." She turned to go up the stairs. Halfway up, she looked back. "I'll make her think I've let go, but I'll never let her go. Never! I'll love her till the day I die no matter what anyone says!"

She ran the rest of the way up the stairs.

∾

Mr. Jordan came to the parsonage and picked up Bonnie. Together, they drove to the Carter farm in Nolensville a short distance to the south of Nashville.

After they had turned off the twisting, dusty lane onto the drive that led back to the Carters' farm, Bonnie looked out over the land. There were wide-open fields and low rolling hills, quite different from the hilly area she'd grown up in, with its dark, cool hollows and deep green valleys.

The pasture where her family grazed their cattle was pretty much the side of a steep hill. Calvin often teased Bonnie when she was young and told her the cattle they raised were 'hill cows.' He told her that one set of their legs was shorter than the other so they could stand straight on the hill. He told her when they got to one end of the field they would have to back up and start over again because if they turned around, their shorter legs would cause them to roll down the hill.

Calvin . . . Bonnie's heart leapt at the memory just like it did when she left Smithville the first time. Now she wished she had never gone back home even for such a short time. She wished she had never seen Calvin again. Now, these familiar pains stabbed at her heart again.

One again, Bonnie swallowed the knot in her throat. She looked forward to the time when she would feel nothing whenever she thought about him, when her heart wouldn't nearly burst from her chest because it beat so hard, when the pain would go away. The best thing for her to do now was to stay busy and keep her mind on other things.

Bonnie was jarred from her thoughts when Mr. Jordan pulled up in front of the farmhouse. Mr. Carter and two young men greeted them from the front porch. Mr. Jordan walked up the planked steps to the porch of the simple farmhouse and shook hands with Mr. Carter.

"Good day, Mr. Jordan," he said as he shook the hand Mr. Carter offered.

"Good mornin', Mr. Jordan. Mornin', Miss McCaverty," he said. He nodded at Bonnie and removed his hat. "We sure do look kindly on you doin' this for us. I knowd how much you love them girls, Miss McCaverty and, well, we just didn't know who else to turn to."

Bonnie walked up the stairs and offered her hand to Mr. Carter. "Call me Bonnie," she told him.

"Why sure, thank you, Miss Bonnie," he replied with a pleasant smile.

"These here's my boys, Billy and Sam. Shake hands, boys." The two young men, still dressed in their work clothes, looked at Bonnie warily as if she was a snake come to swallow them. The older one blushed, shyly offered his hand, mumbling something underneath his breath. The younger one just stared all bug-eyed like he'd never seen a girl before. Bonnie tried to hide her amusement.

"Let's go inside, Mrs. Carter's waitin'," Mr. Carter said.

The older boy flew to the door and pulled it open. The younger one tried to fight him for it.

"I got it!"

"No, I got it," the older boy said through clenched teeth.

"Boys!" Mr. Carter snapped. They immediately dropped their hands to their sides. "Since you can't act like civilized folk, I'll get the door." He pulled it open as Bonnie stepped into the house.

The Carters' house reminded Bonnie much of her own home in Smithville. She could smell fresh baked bread coming from the kitchen. There were pictures of family on the walls. A warm fire crackled and spit in the fireplace. Mrs. Carter walked into the sitting room just as Mr. Carter showed Bonnie to a chair by the fire.

"Hi there, Miss McCaverty," Mrs. Carter said, her hand extended. Her other arm was wrapped around Cora, whom she held in her arms.

Bonnie stood and slowly extended her own hand to Mrs. Carter, but her eyes were on Cora. "You wanna hold her for a while?" Mrs. Carter prompted.

"Oh yes, please," Bonnie answered. Mrs. Carter handed over the little girl who instantly went to Bonnie with a smile.

"I think she knows who you are," Mrs. Carter said.

"I'm sure she does," Mr. Carter added. "Please, Miss Bonnie, have a seat." He showed her to Cora's favorite rocking chair. Everyone else, including the boys, found their own places to sit.

"Miss McCaverty," Mrs. Carter began, "Polly's upstairs sleepin'. I thought maybe we could talk to you for a few minutes before you go up to see her. Well, she's been mighty upset as of late, and now she's took to not eatin'. She just sits and looks out the window and don't never talk much. We're real worried. We didn't want this to happen. We just wanted both of them to have a good home and good God-fearin' people to care for them. I do love them both so."

Mrs. Carter pulled out her handkerchief and put it to her face, trying to stifle her emotion. "I just want her to be happy, Miss McCaverty and, well, if that means her going with you and Cora staying with us, then we'll understand. We've just decided that if losing her means her being happy with you, then we'll give her up to you no matter what the court said."

Bonnie's heart leapt. Her eyes met Mr. Jordan's. He regarded her with a hard stare, then Reverend Parker's words from earlier that morning came flooding back to her memory.

"Miss Bonnie," Mr. Carter said, "we don't want these two children to be split up, but we can't get little Polly to eat or even try to be happy. I guess she's just too old to adjust to new folks. She's been through an awful lot in her short life, and well, I guess we just can't ask any more from her."

Bonnie stood and handed Cora over to Mrs. Carter. "May I see her?"

"Well, sure. She's just upstairs asleep," Mr. Carter said, standing.

"I'll see what I can do about getting her to eat," Bonnie said. Mr. Carter led Bonnie up the stairs to Polly's room.

Mrs. Carter watched as they ascended the stairs. Bonnie hadn't reacted to anything she had said. She turned away in tears and went to the kitchen with the baby. The two boys were left there sitting with Mr. Jordan.

The older boy spoke up. "We're sorry 'bout Ma, Mister. She cries a lot lately. Anytime they even talk about Polly going away."

The other boy joined in. "Yeah, we don't want her to go. I was just building her a treehouse out near the edge of the woods, and Pa said we could teach her to ride soon." The young man looked down at the floor. "We ain't never had no sisters before."

"Well, I certainly hope you keep this one," Mr. Jordan said, shaking his head as he looked up toward the second floor. He hoped Bonnie would do the right thing.

Mr. Carter opened the door to the girls' room. Bonnie walked softly into the room. Mr. Carter closed the door behind her. She stood there in the quiet looking about the place where Polly now lived. It was a bright room with yellow and white gingham curtains. There was also a quilt with matching swatches of cloth intertwined in its design. There was a hand-made toy box at the foot of the bed. It had been painted white and contained modest dolls that looked as if they'd been handed down quite a few times. They were well taken care of, propped up against the foot of the bed in a neat little row. They looked as if they hadn't been disturbed in a long while.

The bookshelves in the corner were full of trinkets. Among them was the music box Bonnie had given Polly. Bonnie lovingly traced the gilding of the box, remembering that Christmas. On the far wall of the room was a dressing table with a mirrored tray. Atop that mirror sat Bonnie's grandmother's silver hairbrush. Bonnie's hands went to her face. She choked back the emotions that grabbed at her throat.

That was it. Just at that moment, Bonnie knew what she must do. She couldn't take Polly away from Cora. Even if Polly decided to go, she would always remember that she left Cora. Eventually, she would blame Bonnie. The Carter family was a good, kind family who seemed to love the girls very much. They were just like everything Bonnie had when she was growing up and, after all, that was all she had ever wanted for the girls. She felt selfish for having believed that she was the only one who could have provided the girls with that kind of loving home.

Polly began to stir.

Bonnie walked to the side of the bed and watched her. She looked so troubled, even in her sleep. How unfair life had been to this child. Bonnie sat on the edge of the bed. Polly slowly opened her big blue eyes. She pushed her hair away from her eyes with the back of her hand and sat up, staring at Bonnie without saying a word. Her eyes grew wide.

"Are you real?" Polly asked.

"Am I real? Well, what kind of question is that to ask someone who's come all this way to see you?"

"Miss Bonnie! It is you! I thought I was dreamin' again!" Polly said. She jumped into Bonnie's lap and wrapped her arms around her neck, kissing her face.

"Whoa, slow down, you're going to knock me off the bed!"

"I was having a dream you were here. I wudn't sure it was you!" the little girl said as Bonnie pulled her away to look at her.

"It's me, all right. I've come out here to talk to you, little missy," Bonnie said in a stern tone. "I hear you haven't been eating."

"I don't wanna eat here, Miss Bonnie. I wanna go home wiff you."

Bonnie slid to her knees on the floor so that she was face to face with the little girl sitting on the bed. "Polly, don't you like this place?"

"It's all right, but I miss you," Polly replied with a whimper.

"I miss you, too. You know, I think about you all the time. You're with me everywhere I go. Did you know that?"

"No, I'm not. I'm here," Polly said. "How can I be with you?"

"Because you're here in my heart," Bonnie said. "You'll always be with me. I carry you around right here." She pointed to her chest. "That way, I'm never lonely."

"I'm lonely. I want to be with you," the little girl said with a whimper.

"How could you be lonely with all these people around? You've even got two brothers! They're good for all sorts of things. They can teach how to ride a horse and fish. Did you know I even had a tree house?"

"You did?"

"Yes, it was the best tree house in the world. Calvin built it for me."

"Was Calvin your brother?"

"Well, sort of, remember? His parents died when he was sixteen, and he came to live with us. Kind of like you coming to live with the Carters. He taught me how to ride a horse, how to fish, and how to shoot a gun . . ." She trailed off.

"You shot a gun?"

"Well, sure. You have to learn how to shoot a gun if you live on a farm."

"You do?"

"Oh, yeah. If you're going to go hunting and fishing, you'll have to learn those things. That's why older brothers are so great."

"I have two older brothers now!" she remarked gleefully.

"I know!"

"You think they'd teach me how to ride a horse?"

"I bet they would."

"There's some horses here. Look," Polly said as she scrambled to the window, pulling the curtains back to show Bonnie her view of the farm. "Look over there, behind that barn. See?

"Polly, they're beautiful. I wonder what their names are. "Remember Danny?"

"*Danny,*" Polly said, laughing. "That's not a horsey name."

"Well, yes it is. If it's an Irish horse!" The two of them laughed together. Polly raised her arms for Bonnie to pick her up. Bonnie swept the girl up into her arms and began to walk around the room.

"This is a nice room," she said. "I've never seen so many dolls. I never had this many dolls."

"You didn't?" Polly scrambled from Bonnie's arms and picked up one of the dolls on the toy chest. "This one is my favorite."

"She's beautiful. She has red hair like me," Bonnie said.

"I named her Bonnie," Polly said with a long face. Bonnie sat on the bed and pulled Polly over to her, wrapping her arms around her.

"Polly, honey, you have to eat. I don't want you to get sick. What would Cora do if she didn't have you to look after her?"

"I don't want to leave Cora."

"Well, you have to take care of yourself, then. That means eating. Polly, the Carters care a great deal for you. They want you and Cora to be happy here. Why, you'll have so much fun, riding horses and playing cowboys and Indians with your brothers. When Cora gets old enough, you can teach her those things."

"I like Billy and Sam. They're funny!" Polly smiled. "They're always fightin' and hittin' on each other, but they don't really mean it," she said, wrinkling her nose as she shook her head.

"Will you promise me you'll take care of yourself now and help Mrs. Carter take care of Cora? She has a lot to do with such a big family now. She's going to need your help.

"She's a nice lady. I just missed you, Bonnie. I wanted to see you."

Bonnie whisked Polly into her arms and sat her on her lap.

"You have to be good, Little Bit. Do you promise me?" Bonnie fought tears but to no avail. They managed to make their way down her face.

"Don't cry, Miss Bonnie," Polly said, wiping her face with her little hands. "I promise I'll be good."

"I love you, Polly. You have to be good. You promise me."

"I promise," the little girl said with a smile. They sat on the bed for a while just holding onto each other. It was as if they both knew they would never see each other again. Except that this time, it was Polly letting go of Bonnie. It was as if she needed Bonnie's approval to like the Carters and start enjoying her life again.

"Let's go downstairs and see Cora," Polly said with great excitement.

"Okay," Bonnie said. "You go on. I'll be right behind you." Polly scrambled down and ran downstairs, hollering for Billy and Sam. She was gone. The Reverend was right. All she had needed was Bonnie's approval. All she had needed was to get rid of the guilt she felt, then Bonnie knew she would get on with her life.

Later, Bonnie and Mr. Jordan drove quietly back to Nashville. The sun was beginning to set on that cold, February afternoon, casting a red-gold shimmer on the countryside. Bonnie sat staring forward, numb and tired. The performance she had just given was the hardest she'd ever put on, and it had drained the life right out of her.

"You did the right thing, you know," Mr. Jordan said, breaking the silence between them. "I think she just wanted to know if it was okay with you that she be happy. You should be happy for her, Bonnie. She actually has a better life than she would have had if her parents were still alive."

"I am happy. For them," Bonnie answered.

They drove the rest of the way in silence. It was quite late when Mr. Jordan dropped Bonnie off at the parsonage. Bonnie stood in front of the house, looking at it from the sidewalk, finding it difficult to put one foot in front of the other. The strain of the last few weeks had finally caught up with her.

Reverend Parker stepped into the cold and helped her inside.

CHAPTER SEVENTEEN

*"Great, you have John D. Rockefeller nipping at
your heels, and you run home to Alvin York!"*

B ONNIE SAT AT the Lunch Room counter eating a grilled
cheese sandwich and reading the newspaper while Nell walked
the length of the counter, filling coffee cups in her usual
manner. When she got to Bonnie, she put the pot down, her eyes drawn
to the back page of the section Bonnie was holding in front of her.

"Well, well. It looks like Mr. Bass has gotten himself on the society
page again," she said to Bonnie, who had become her best friend over
the last few years.

"Where?" Bonnie asked.

"Here, on the back page. Who's that with him?" Nell said, craning
her neck to get a better look at the picture. "What a dreamboat. Ned
Bass is the most handsome bachelor in town. You know, he dropped out
of the limelight back two or three years ago. Word is someone broke his
heart." She leaned over the counter and propped her chin in her hand.
"Imagine that, someone breaking that heart of steel."

"Heart of steel? Why do you say that?" Bonnie asked.

"Why, he's the biggest playboy in town!"

"I don't believe that," Bonnie said.

"Don't believe it? Honey, he's had more peroxide on his arm than
all the hospitals in Nashville could use in a year!"

Bonnie giggled. She'd never known anyone like Nell, who seemed to have something to say about everything and everybody. She'd been working in the Lunch Room of the Union Station for four or five years now. Anybody who was anybody came through the station, and Nell knew everything there was to know about most of them. Most of them except Ned Bass, it seemed. There was a piece of his story missing that Nell knew nothing about.

Bonnie looked back at the picture. "Well, I don't believe what you say about him. I bet deep inside he's a decent, caring man."

"It's just like you to say that. Always got to see the bright side of everything." She paused and eyed Bonnie suspiciously. "Or do you know something I don't know?"

"Whatever do you mean?" Bonnie asked. She straightened her dress, pulled her gloves on, pressing her purse into the crook of her arm.

"You sure were looking at that picture awfully funny. Do you know him or something?" Nell asked.

Bonnie grinned.

"Maybe," she chided her roommate.

"Come on! Spill it," Nell whispered.

"Okay, I had one date with him," Bonnie confessed. Nell came out from behind the counter, quickly ushering Bonnie to the side of the busy room.

"Bonnie McCaverty, I've known you for three years now. Since that day you wandered in here trying to avoid . . ." Nell's face lit up. "It was him," she whispered.

Bonnie smiled.

"I remember now!" Nell exclaimed. "Why haven't you ever told me about him?"

"Now Nell, there was nothing to tell. He was the lawyer who tried to help me get custody of Polly and Cora. We had one date."

"One date! Honey, half the girls in Nashville would like to say that. Just half, though. The other half would be right up there in the 'one date' category with you."

"That's exactly why I didn't bring it up. I didn't know what a scoundrel he was when I went out with him. Actually, I'm quite embarrassed at having been seen with him."

"Stop!" Nell said. "Listen, little-miss-country-girl-come-to-the-city, don't tell me you went out with Ned Bass and didn't have a good time."

"I won't," Bonnie quickly added. "It was a lovely time. Probably one of the best times I've ever had." A melancholy overcame her as she leaned against the wall remembering.

"Then what happened?" Nell asked rather impatiently.

A gentleman at the counter leaned back on his stool and shouted, "Hey, Nell. I need some more coffee!"

"Keep your shirt on. I'll be there in a minute," Nell snapped back.

"Do we have to talk about this now? I've got to get back to the store!"

"Oh no, you are *not* leaving here until you tell me what happened," Nell said, shaking her finger at Bonnie.

"It's very simple. He was my lawyer. We spent a lot of time together. We went on one date. I felt so bad when I didn't get custody of the girls that I wanted to go back to Smithville. He asked me to stay and give our relationship a try. I went home like an idiot thinking that things might be different there."

"Calvin?" Nell asked.

"Yes, Calvin."

"Great, you have Nelson Rockefeller nipping at your heels, and you run home to Alvin York!"

"Nell!"

"Well, Bonnie, it's true. He's still ruining your life. I've known you for quite a while now, and you haven't done anything but work at that store day and night and sit in this train station for God only knows why and help at the Red Cross. You won't go out with anybody."

"Bonnie," she pleaded, "when are you going to forget him?"

"I have forgotten him. I just . . ." Bonnie fiddled with her purse.

"Just what?" Nell said, tapping her foot.

"Nell! How 'bout some coffee?" the man from the counter yelled again.

"All right, all right, I'm coming."

Bonnie relented. "I wanted to come back to Nashville and see Ned and put Calvin behind me once and for all. Then I walked into the station and who do I see? Mr. Ned Bass boarding a train for West Palm Beach with someone dressed from head to toe in pearls and mink. Well, it just hit me that I . . . I just wasn't meant to have a life like that. I didn't work out with Calvin, and I messed things up with Ned. Oh Nell, can't you see? I'm just never going to have that kind of life. I know that, and I just have to live with it."

"Bonnie, honey, that's not true," Nell said, softening her tone. "You should have told him you were back."

"He obviously didn't take too long to forget about me," Bonnie said.

"Well, like I said. The rumor was someone broke his heart about three or four years ago. Really, Bonnie, he literally dropped out of sight for a while. He's never married. He just goes from one girl to the other. I see him all the time. I can't believe you haven't run into him. His office is just down the street you know."

"I know. I almost ran smack dab into him one day on the street."

"Bonnie, let him know you're in town," Nell pleaded.

"No!" Bonnie straightened up. "No, I like my life just the way it is and don't you go getting any ideas either," she warned, wagging a gloved finger at her friend. "If he was serious about me, he would have waited to find out if I was coming back."

"Oh yeah, just like you thought Calvin was going to welcome you back with open arms whenever you decided to come home. Maybe he was hurt."

"Well, hurt or not, I wouldn't be caught dead with a man like him. He's a disgrace!" Bonnie added.

"Honey," Nell said, placing a free hand on her hip, "disgrace or not, I'd take him any way I could get him."

"No, you wouldn't. Now I have to go. I'm late. I'll see you tonight." Bonnie rushed from the Lunch Room and hurried out of Union Station, leaving Nell to fume over her customers and their coffees.

She made her way down Broadway, turned at Fifth, and walked from the corner of Union Street to Loveman, Berger, and Teitelbaum's Department Store, where she was now late for work. She hurried in the side entrance and tried to get to the elevator before Mr. Bowman saw her.

"Bonnie, you're late," Mr. Bowman's stern voice sounded from behind her.

"I know," she replied, facing him. "I'm sorry. Is Mr. Berger in?"

"No," Mr. Bowman said, smiling. He was never able to maintain that harsh tone in his voice. "He went a bit early to Satsuma for lunch. He said he hadn't had much breakfast."

"Lucky for me!" Bonnie whispered as she unbuttoned her gloves and hurriedly pulled her hat off her head.

Mr. Bowman had been in Mr. Berger's employ for many years now. He walked the floor, greeted customers at Loveman's, and generally kept tabs on everything. He helped Bonnie get her job there three years earlier when she had come wandering in begging for work even though they were right in the middle of a depression. The young girl was so insistent that he finally mentioned her to Mr. Berger, telling him that the girl insisted she was good with numbers and, after all, he and Mr. Teitlebaum did need help with the bookkeeping. The problem was she was only twenty-two. Everyone who worked there was much older and more experienced. Still, Mr. Berger had been gracious enough to give Bonnie a chance to prove herself. Now, after almost four years, she was one of their many loyal employees.

The store had become part of Bonnie's life. She knew all the customers by name even though she didn't work on the floor all of the time. She was a great help to Mr. Berger. Bonnie would often slip down the stairs to deal with customers Mr. Berger had a difficult time remembering. She'd greet them sweetly, call them by name, then disappear, leaving Mr. Berger with the full assurance he was calling his customer by the correct name.

Even when Bonnie wasn't busy with the books, she would help Mr. Berger and Mr. Bowman with customers, or assist the ladies in the different departments. Often, she could be found with Miss Mamie Brennen in the glove department. Like some people who preferred to buy hats or an overabundance of shoes, Bonnie had a weakness for gloves. She had a pair for every outfit she wore. She'd never had much of an occasion to wear anything but work gloves on the farm. Now she was making up for every occasion she had missed out on that luxury.

Every day at six o'clock, Bonnie would leave Loveman's and walk from there to the Red Cross office on Fourth Avenue, where she helped pack boxes for the needy or helped with office work. She never went out into the field anymore. The ordeal with the Sutton children had demonstrated to both Bonnie and Mrs. Greenfield that Bonnie tended to get too emotionally involved for the rigors of fieldwork.

Bonnie's days were long, just as she preferred. She had promised herself that when she found a job and began working, she would keep herself so busy that she wouldn't have time to think about Calvin, or Ned, or Polly and Cora.

That is just what she had managed to do for quite some time.

"Charlie, hold the fort. I gotta make a call," Nell told the cook.

"Hurry up, Nell. We gotta get this mess cleaned up."

"I know. I know. Just give me a minute." Nell drew some coins from her apron and went out to the lobby to use the telephone. She stepped into the booth and closed the door behind her. She sat down pulling the city directory into her lap, opened it to the "Bs," and scrolled her finger down the lists until she found the number she was looking for.

"Bart, Barton . . . here it is. Bass and Bass, Attorneys at Law," Nell said. "Forgive me, Bonnie. I know you don't want me to do this, but you'll thank me one day."

She dialed the number. A lady answered on the other end. "Bass and Bass."

"Yes," Nell stammered nervously. "I need to speak with Ned Bass please."

"Your name?"

"He won't know me. My name is Nell."

"One moment please," the operator answered. She rang the younger Mr. Bass' office. "Mr. Bass, there's a young lady on the line says you don't know her. Her name is Nell. She'd like to speak with you."

"Well, I would never turn down the chance to talk to a girl I don't know, now would I, Marie?"

"No, sir," the operator answered.

"Put her on," Ned told her. There was a tiny click in the earpiece. "Hello. This is Ned Bass."

"Hello," Nell said, "listen, you don't know me, but I'm a friend of Miss Bonnie McCaverty."

Ned shot straight up in his chair at the mention of Bonnie's name. "Okay," he said.

"You know who I'm talking about, don't you?"

"Sure, who is this?"

"Never mind, just listen. Bonnie is a friend of mine, see, and if she knew I was calling you, she'd be mighty upset with me. But just today I learned that she, well, she knew you at one time, and I just thought you might like to know she's in town."

"How long has she been back?" Ned asked soberly.

"Since right after she left the first time. See, that's the beauty of it all. She came right back to town after she visited home."

"She's been in town all this time?"

Ned stood at this desk looking out the window. He didn't say anything for a moment. "Listen, I don't know who you are, but she didn't let me know she had returned, so she obviously must not want to see me."

"Mr. Bass, listen. Bonnie saw you at the train station with another girl on your way out of town the day she came back. She figured the same thing. Listen, I have to go now. I just thought you might care to know she's here. She works up at Loveman's. If you arrange to run into her, I'm sure she'd be glad to see you."

Ned smiled. "Thanks, I sure do owe you one . . . what did you say your name was?"

"Gotta go," Nell said. She set the receiver on its hook, grinned to herself, and went back to work.

"Bonnie, would you be a dear and help me out for a few minutes? I need to take a quick break. I have to telephone Wilbur and see how he is. He wasn't well this morning."

Bonnie stood from behind the big counter in the Loveman's main office. "Oh sure, Margaret. I'd be glad to."

"Thank you. I promise I won't be but a minute."

"That's okay. Take your time." Bonnie closed the office door and headed to the elevator. As the doors opened onto the first floor, she discovered Mr. Bowman standing there, looking desperately for Mrs. Price.

"Bonnie, where is Margaret? She has a customer."

"I'm watching for her," Bonnie explained. "She's gone upstairs to call her husband. He was ill this morning. Don't worry. I'll take care of it for her."

Mr. Bowman pointed to the young man standing in the midst of the corsages.

Bonnie followed the course of his finger, then froze in her tracks. It was Ned!

"Nell!" Bonnie whispered vehemently.

Mr. Bowman appeared to notice that something was wrong. "You know Mr. Bass?" he asked.

"Oh, yes, I know him," Bonnie said. Her mind raced for a way to quietly plead her way out of waiting on the young Mr. Bass.

"Bonnie? Bonnie, is that you?" Ned asked.

He had seen them. Ned walked closer to where the two of them stood talking. Bonnie's palms felt sweaty, and her knees became weak. For once in her life, she felt at a loss for words. Slowly, she turned to look at him.

"Bonnie! It is you! I can't believe it. You're here! I'm so glad to see you," he said. He bent down and kissed her cheek. Mr. Bowman made a slow exit from the conversation, conveniently finding another customer with which to speak.

Bonnie stood there blushing both from the kiss and the embarrassment of everyone in the store looking at her. The women who worked on the first floor craned their necks to get a look at Bonnie and the young, sophisticated bachelor who seemed to know her.

"Bonnie McCaverty. Imagine seeing you here. I thought you were still back in Smithville."

"No, I . . . came back."

"Well, obviously. How long have you been working here?" Ned asked.

Bonnie, knowing Nell must have tipped him off, wasn't sure how much he knew and decided she'd better take control of the situation.

"For a while now," she said casually. "I've been reading a great deal about you in the paper. Why just today I saw your picture on the society page."

Just then, Mr. Berger got off the elevator. He saw Bonnie and Ned talking and walked over.

"Ned, my boy. How are you, son?"

"Mr. Berger, I'm fine, sir. How are you?"

"Well! I'm doing well, thank you. How are your mother and father faring in these trying times?"

"Father stays busy, as usual. Mother has her duties she attends to. She still plays bridge at the Club quite a bit. How is your family, sir?"

"They're fine, just fine. I see you've met our Miss McCaverty."

"Yes," he answered, looking coyly at Bonnie. "I have."

"Well, fine. You're in good hands, so I'll leave you to her. Good day."

"Good day, Mr. Berger."

"Say hello to your mother and father for me. Won't you?"

Ned smiled at the man, then cast his glance back to Bonnie.

"Am I in good hands?" he teased.

That charming smile tore through her defenses. Bonnie relaxed. "Oh, stop it, Ned," she said, trying her best not to smile.

"Stop what?" he asked.

"You know what I mean. Nell called you, didn't she?"

"Now who is Nell? I was just stopping in to buy my mother some new handkerchiefs and maybe some flowers."

"Don't tease me. I've been here all this time, and you've never set foot in this place. Now all of a sudden here you are."

Ned burst into laughter. Bonnie glanced around. Everyone in the store seemed to be watching the mysterious conversation unfold. They weren't accustomed to Bonnie speaking with any young men, much less the infamous Ned Bass.

"Bonnie, I'm so glad to see you!" Ned exclaimed. He threw his arms around her and whirled her off the floor.

"Put me down!" Bonnie said through clenched teeth as she felt her high heels leave the floor. "Ned!" Bonnie whispered, "Have you lost your mind?"

"Let's go somewhere and talk, okay?"

"No, I'm not going anywhere with you. I'm working."

"Let me pick you up when you get off tonight. Please. You do owe me that much, considering you've been in town for four years and I'm just now hearing about it."

Bonnie's face flushed again.

"That rat Nell. She did call you."

Ned threw his head back, laughing heartily. "Well, I'm glad she did. Now, c'mon, let me pick you up for supper tonight."

"Ned Bass, I'm not going anywhere with you. Why you . . ."

"What?"

"You're a disgrace, the way you act."

He looked hurt. "How is that?"

"Why, the way you run all over town with every kind of girl imaginable. It's just disgraceful, and I won't be seen with you." She folded her arms.

Four years had come between them. Ned almost didn't recognize Bonnie. Her shapely frame filled out the green wool dress she wore. Her red hair had grown long again and was pulled back in a tight ball at the nape of her neck. Unlike the girls she worked with, Bonnie didn't hide her creamy complexion behind layers of powder. Her skin needed no help. Those few freckles on her nose still captivated him even after all these years.

Ned looked down at his hat, which he twisted in his hands, his face turning more somber. "It's all your fault, you know."

"My fault?"

"If you'll remember, I asked you not to leave. I thought you were gone for good."

"It didn't take you long to forget about me."

"I never forgot about you, Bonnie. But I've been trying hard to."

That stung her.

"I'm sorry I didn't let you know I came back. It's just that, well, when I came back I saw you leaving town with—"

Ned interrupted. "Bonnie, I've got an idea. Let's forget all about that and start over again. That was a hard time for you. I know it was. It wasn't too grand a time for me either after you left. So, what do you say? Let's just forget about the last four years and start over. Friends, okay?"

Bonnie smiled. "Okay, friends," she said as she offered her hand to him.

He reached out for her hand, then quickly pulled it to his mouth and kissed it. "I'm so glad to see you again, Bonnie McCaverty," he said. "May I call you?"

"Well," Bonnie said, flustered, "I go the Red Cross when I leave here, then there's church on Sunday. I don't have a great deal of free time."

"How about Saturday? I'll pick you up, and we'll go for a ride in the country."

"Ned, I don't know. It's the only day I have free, and I usually have so many errands to run."

"Nonsense. From what I hear, all you do is work. Now, I insist on some fresh country air for you."

Bonnie thought about the country air. The idea of getting away from the busy city and all of the smoke did sound inviting. "Oh, okay. But I can't stay away long."

"Swell! Where do you live?"

"In The Vauxhall. Just tell me what time, and I'll meet you in the lobby."

"I'll meet you there at say eight o'clock. A.M. that is," he went on to say. "Let's make a day of it."

"Okay, eight o'clock," Bonnie said, smiling.

Ned smiled back. "I swear, if we weren't standing in the middle of this store, Bonnie McCaverty, I'd kiss you square on the lips."

"Ned!" Bonnie whispered, hoping no one had overheard what he had said to her.

"See you Saturday," he said as he turned to go. Just before he walked out the door, Ned turned around and addressed all the ladies who had been peeking around displays and cabinets to watch all that had transpired between him and Bonnie by tipping his hat to all of them. Bonnie gasped, looking around, quite embarrassed. Giggles seemed to bubble up from every corridor of the trademark store.

By eight o'clock Saturday morning, Bonnie was waiting patiently in the lobby of her apartment house. At 8:03, a shiny, red Roadster pulled up to the front of the entrance, and a casually dressed Ned Bass stepped out. He walked into the lobby, his eyes lighting up when he noticed Bonnie standing there.

"Good morning," he said.

"I see you're only a few minutes late," Bonnie replied sarcastically.

"A mere few, don't you think?" he said, smiling. "If you only knew, this is early for me, even on a Saturday."

A smile crossed Bonnie's own lips. "Very forgivable."

"Good!" Ned exclaimed jubilantly. "I have a day of days arranged for us that you, my dear, are going to absolutely love."

"Well, I certainly hope I'm not underdressed for the occasion," Bonnie said, looking down at her slacks.

"You look perfect," Ned replied. "Let's go. The car's waiting on the street."

He ushered Bonnie outside and opened the passenger door to his convertible. It was a lovely day, and the top was down. Bonnie pulled her scarf from around her neck and carefully arranged it over her hair. Ned pulled away from the curb, gliding into traffic.

First on Ned's agenda was a tour. He showed Bonnie every part of Nashville he thought she might not have previously seen, including all the fine homes one can't see from the streetcars. They also went to the stables at Percy Warner Park, where they rode for hours, ending at the highest point in the park. Ned spread a blanket under a huge tree at the

top of a hill with a fantastic view. There they enjoyed a spectacular picnic lunch made especially for them by the cook at the Bass house. They
ate cold fried chicken and biscuits until Bonnie felt she would pop, then
came the Bass' cook's secret recipe, homemade apple turnovers.

"No, no!" Bonnie cried, holding her hands up in front of her. "I
can't take any more! I haven't eaten like that since I lived with the
Parkers. I haven't had turnovers that good since home." The latter produced a faraway look in her eyes.

Ned lay back against the tree looking out over the park. "You miss
home, don't you?"

"Yes," Bonnie admitted. She couldn't hide it. "My mother and
father are both getting on in years. I guess I should go home more."

"But," Ned started. Bonnie interrupted him.

"Well, I just don't feel the same as before, you know. Like when
you're a kid and everything looks so big, then you grow up and realize
that it wudn't that everything was so big, you were just tiny compared
to it all." She looked down at her hands. "I haven't been back but twice
a year since I moved here for good. I only go back for Easter and then
for Thanksgiving and Christmas. I'm usually home by the New Year so
I can spend it with Nell. Or rather, Nell and whatever beau she happens to have at the time."

"Just the three of you. How cozy," Ned teased.

Bonnie blushed. Ned was obviously fishing for information on her
dating habits. "Don't be silly. Every year they fix me up with some kinda
guy." She laughed as she rolled over onto her stomach and propped her
chin in her hands. "One year, they fixed me up with this traveling brush
salesman. You know, the kind who goes door-to-door selling brushes.
Well, it was awful, just awful!" She cackled. "He was six inches shorter
than me and blind as a bat! Well, now you can just picture how dancing with a fella that don't near come up to your neck and can't see, so
he's talking to your neckline the entire night thinking he's staring right
into your lovely green eyes. Somebody must'a told him I had green eyes
cause he sure never looked square into them the whole night!"

Ned sat entranced. He watched her face as she talked, how it
changed expressions with every emotion. She was even more beautiful

than he remembered; whenever he tried to remember, that is. More than once Ned Bass had made a conscious effort to push that pouty little face out of his mind, but not once did his memory of her genuinely dim. Not once could he erase the look on her face when Judge Whittaker told her that the Sutton children were going to the Carters. Not once could he forget the softness of her lips that day at the parsonage when he asked her to stay. Now here she was, smiling back at him, rattling on about Christmas and New Years and who cared what else. All that mattered was here she was, and Ned knew he would never be the same again.

When she was done with her story, he stood and helped her to her feet. "C'mon, I have one more thing I want to show you."

"But, Ned, it's late . . ."

"No arguments on this one now. We have to go before it gets dark."

Bonnie looked at him inquisitively as they repacked the lunch basket and folded the blanket. "What have you got up your sleeve anyway?"

Ned smiled. "I think you'll like it. No clues. You'll just have to wait."

After the horses had been delivered back to the stables, they loaded the car and headed out of the park, back to West End Avenue. Ned started back toward downtown.

"Is that the joke? Are you taking me home?" Bonnie asked.

"Relax, you'll see."

He could tell Bonnie's curiosity was getting the better of her.

Ned turned east and made his way over to Gay Street, then turned right. As they drove along, Bonnie became quiet. The energy of the ride had changed somehow. She wasn't sure she liked the way things were going.

When they reached an intersection that wasn't far from where the tenement house stood where Ned and Bonnie first met, Ned stopped the car.

"I want you to close your eyes," he said.

"Ned, I haven't been down here in a long time. I—" Bonnie tried to speak, but Ned interrupted.

"Close your eyes," he said softly to her. "I promise. It won't hurt."

Bonnie sighed impatiently, closing her eyes. Ned pulled the car around the corner and down a block or two and stopped the car.

"Okay. Open your eyes," he instructed. Bonnie heard him open his door and slide out of the car.

When she opened her eyes, Bonnie was looking at the same house in which she had volunteered so many years ago, the building where so many parts of her life had come together. Her heart leapt with waves of nostalgia, but it wasn't the same. She stepped out of the car and joined Ned in the yard.

"How do you like it?" he asked nervously.

"Ned, it's so different," Bonnie said. "It's, it's . . ."

"Decent," Ned said, hopefully putting word to her thought.

"Well, yes. When did this happen?"

"After you left. It was the only thing I could do to make myself feel any better for losing the case over the Sutton girls. I know it doesn't seem like much, but I knew you would approve. If you knew . . ." Ned trailed off, looking away.

Bonnie moved slowly around in front of Ned and met his eyes. "It was a wonderful thing to do . . . for whatever reason."

"You were the reason," Ned said, gazing into her innocent face. "You swept through my life, then you were gone. I was so lonesome. I didn't know what to do. I know some of the things I did weren't right, but I wanted to show you that some of them were."

"It's wonderful, Ned. You should be proud of yourself." She smiled broadly. "I'll bet your father had a cow!"

Ned laughed. "You have no idea! He was so mad when I told him I was going to fix this place up. I thought he'd bust a gut!"

"I'm so proud of you."

"I guess that matters more to me than anything in this world," Ned said, smiling. She turned to take another look at the apartment house. Although it was different, some things were still the same. Bonnie could almost see Polly sitting on the steps, waiting for her visit. She could almost hear her voice.

Ned caught the memory in her eyes. He could tell it was time to go.

"C'mon, you've seen enough of this. Let's go," he said. He turned Bonnie and put his arm around her shoulder to walk her to the car.

"Miss Bonnie McCaverty," he added, "would you do me the honor of having supper with me tonight? We'll go back to The Hermitage Hotel, order champagne and dance the night away. What do you say?"

"Ned, thank you, but you've worn me out. Besides, I have church in the morning. I can't dance the night away."

"All right then. I'll take you home. But it's against my better judgment."

"Well, my judgment is that I have to have my beauty sleep."

"By all means then, let's get you home."

CHAPTER EIGHTEEN

*"Don't you ever interfere with his life again or
I personally will make you pay for it."*

A FTER THAT SATURDAY, Ned refused to let Bonnie have
one minute of spare time. Over the next two years, her
visits to the Red Cross became less frequent, but even Mrs.
Greenfield was happy that she was actually trying to live the life of a
twenty-eight-year-old.

Ned took Bonnie to every social event in town. There wasn't a
dance or show happening in Nashville that they didn't make. Ned's
new love was quite the talk of the town, and every bit of it made
Bonnie uncomfortable.

One Sunday, she was particularly upset when she found her name
on the society page in the Sunday paper.

"Well, kid, you've made the papers," Nell informed Bonnie as she
handed over the newspaper.

"What do you mean?" Bonnie asked, afraid of what Nell had
just read.

"Look, there you are. Nice picture."

"Oh, rats, what does it say?"

"Right there, look," Nell said, pointing to the far right column.

Bonnie read it aloud. "Who is the girl seen on the arm of the eligible Ned Bass every time he steps out? Her name is Bonnie McCaverty,
daughter of a farm family from Smithville, who works at Loveman,

Berger, and Teitelbaum's as a bookkeeper and volunteers for the Red Cross. Could the young Mr. Bass be off limits to the debutantes of high society? I guess we'll just wait and see!"

"Oh, how awful!" Bonnie said.

"Why is it awful?" Nell asked, astounded. "There's plenty of girls who would give anything to be written up in the Sunday society page."

"Nell, you know what I mean. His parents already don't approve of me. In the paper, they are practically saying I'm a nobody. It'll just make it harder on Ned."

"Honey, I don't think Ned minds. They've talked about him before, they're talking about him now. He's been seen with worse than the likes of you."

"Maybe, but not at all the right places, at least that's what I've heard."

Nell sat next to Bonnie on the sofa. "Don't you think you're making more of it than it is, Bonnie? You're just different, honey. They don't have anything in common with you. That doesn't make you less of a person."

Bonnie stood and began to pace the living room of their apartment. "I just feel so out of place. You know what I mean? We go to the country club out there where his parents live, and he tries to teach me how to play tennis. Then they're all of these girls standing around in their fancy outfits and, well, I just feel so underdressed and awkward every time he makes me go to these places."

Nell laughed.

"What's so funny?"

"Oh, to have that dilemma! Look, Bonnie, Ned loves you for who you are. He had his chance with every girl in town, and you're the one who turned his head. Don't let those pea brains make you feel inferior. They're just jealous, you can bet on that."

"Jealous? What makes you say that?"

"Bonnie, I love ya, honey, but you need some help. Come sit down here and let me give you some lessons about high society."

Bonnie sat back down on the sofa. "I don't care what you say. It's not going to make me feel any better."

Nell rolled her eyes. "Listen, you have to go into this with your chin up," she said, using the back of her hand under her chin to raise her head high. "Show 'em some of that McCaverty green blood. Don't ever let them catch you looking down or looking away when they make eye contact with you. You be proud to be on his arm. Swirl into the room, knowing that they'd do anything to trade places with you." Nell stood, pretending to pick up the flow of an evening dress and waltzed around the room.

It worked, too. Bonnie laughed. "Nell, you're so funny. What would I do without you?"

"I hope you never have to find out, kid. Now get going. Your date awaits you."

"Oh my, I didn't realize the time. Ned's probably already wait-ing!" Bonnie grabbed her bag and her Bible and hurried out the door. Bonnie had been everywhere Ned had ever asked her to go. This time, it was his turn. He was going to the morning church service with her.

"Well, Claudia, have you seen the paper this morning?" the elder Mr. Bass said as he entered the breakfast room.

"Yes, I have. Did I miss something?"

"Well, you did if you missed the society page. Did you see your son in there?"

"What's unusual about seeing Ned in the papers? He's always in there for something or other," Mrs. Bass answered as she poured a cup of coffee.

"You know what I mean. Did you hear what they said about the McCaverty girl?"

"Her name is Bonnie."

"I just don't know what he sees in her," the old man said. He slapped the paper down and picked up his coffee. "All the girls he's been out with, and he decides to get serious with this farm girl from Smithville. Why can't he get serious with one of the Lakeford girls or that girl from New York? What's her name? Iris?"

"Why not Della? There doesn't seem to be any problem with him seeing her," Mrs. Bass said as she left the room. She knew the mention of that name would stop the subject cold in its tracks . . . and it did.

Mr. Bass said nothing more.

Della worked at a rather less-than-desirable establishment on Fourth Avenue. Ned met her on one of his many trips to the saloon his father had frequented for many years. The young Mr. Bass had infinitely filled his father's shoes when it came to drinking and women, and Mrs. Bass knew it. It was something she had lived with for years during her marriage, and now the blame fell on Mr. Bass' shoulders anytime Ned's unethical behavior came up between the two of them.

Mrs. Bass had retreated to the kitchen to talk to the cook about the day's lunch. Ned was bringing Bonnie home to have lunch with them, and she wanted to make sure everything was ready.

Ned and Bonnie got to the Bass house in Belle Meade shortly after one o'clock that afternoon. Albert showed them directly to the dining room where his parents were waiting.

"I'm sorry we're late, Mother," Ned said as he kissed his mother's cheek. He then pulled out a chair for Bonnie.

"Reverend Parker went over with his preaching today. I think he was trying to impress Ned," Bonnie replied, quite nervously.

"Yes, I believe he was," Ned agreed uncomfortably.

"Well, did you see the paper this morning, son?" his father asked, forgoing any semblance of propriety.

"Yes, sir. I did," Ned answered. He knew where this was headed. "It was an excellent picture of us don't you think?"

"Yes, I guess so."

"It *was* a good picture," Mrs. Bass broke in. She addressed Bonnie. "You looked charming, dear."

"Thank you," Bonnie replied. "Those cameras just make me so nervous. I feel like I have pepper between my front teeth or something."

Albert chuckled from the corner of the room. Ned joined him. Bonnie looked at Ned for some indication of what she said that was so funny.

"They are rather nerve-wracking, aren't they, Carlton?" Mrs. Bass said to her husband. "Here you are trying to have a good time and along comes this dreaded flash in your face."

The elder Mr. Bass ignored her. "Ned, listen. You have to get on the telephone to the councilmen first thing in the morning about this public housing. We've got to act fast if we're going to try to put a stop to this!"

Ned's father, once a towering man who commanded attention the moment he entered a room or a conversation, had now withered quite a bit. His tall frame stooped somewhat, his skin wrinkled from years of stress and long nights and way too much drinking. His hair, or what was left of it, was completely gray and slicked back against his scalp.

"Now Carlton, you promised we would not talk about business during lunch."

"What public housing?" Bonnie asked Ned.

"I'll tell you what public housing thing," Ned's father said. "The Council wants to use five million dollars of federal money for public housing in Nashville. Free housing for the poor! All of our apartments will be empty."

Bonnie looked confused. "But wouldn't that make it easier for the people who are out of jobs right now to feed their families and get back on their feet?"

"The best way for them to get back on their feet is to get a job."

"Father," Ned said quickly, "let's talk about it tomorrow."

"Mr. Bass, a lot of people can't find jobs right now," Bonnie said, continuing the conversation. "They can't feed their families because of it."

"Oh yes, I forgot. You work with the Red Cross people."

"Yes, sir. I do," Bonnie said defensively. "There are a lot of people who would love to work, but they can't find any."

"Well, that's a problem, but why should we go footing the bill to put these people in free housing? It doesn't make sense."

"I'm sure it would if you were out of a job," Bonnie said. Mrs. Bass looked up abruptly at Bonnie.

"Now see here, girl."

"Father, I think maybe we should change the subject," Ned said, looking at Bonnie, who had, by this time, stopped eating and placed her hands on her lap.

"Very well, we'll talk about something else. You have a job. Don't you, Miss McCaverty? At Loveman's, correct? What do you do there?" the old man asked. Mrs. Bass knew there was a point to his questioning.

"I keep the books for Mr. Berger and help on the floor when they need me."

"See? An honest job. Why can't these other people find jobs? You found one. You're doing a job that is traditionally always been a man's job. See here, if you were married, maybe some hard working man could have that job."

"Carlton!" Mrs. Bass said.

"Father, that's enough!" Ned warned.

Bonnie looked up from her meal staring coolly into the uncaring eyes of Mr. Carlton Bass. "Yes, Mr. Bass. I do have a job, an honest job making an honest living. I had to beg for that job, and I might add I'm very good at it, but there are others who aren't as fortunate as I am. If you ever left your soft, cushy office and went down to some of those pigs sties you call apartment houses, you might see some of them!"

By now she was standing. She set her napkin in the chair behind her and looked at Mrs. Bass.

"Mrs. Bass, thank you for lunch, but I have to be going now. I have to get ready to go back to church this evening. Ned, would you take me home?" She and her little black heels clicked across the polished floor and out of the room.

"Yes, I think it's time to leave," Ned said, standing himself. "Are you proud of yourself?"

Ned left the room and joined Bonnie, who was already outside.

Mrs. Bass peered out the window. Ned was consoling Bonnie as he helped her into the car. Mrs. Bass turned around to face her husband, who was sitting there with his mouth open wide.

"Now don't you start on me, too," he said to his wife. "Albert! Bring a sherry to my study."

"I just don't understand Ned," the old man said, pitching his napkin onto the table. "Since he helped this girl out, to help her try to get custody of two children, which is odd indeed, he's been distant and unhappy. He never used to question my authority before. Now he talks to me like he just did there. You heard him. What's the matter with him is that girl. She's under his skin."

He got up to go to his study.

"Hold on just a minute," Mrs. Bass said. "I have something to say to you," she said as she moved to stand directly across from where he stood at the head of the long dining room table.

"Carlton, I've sat back all these years and kept quiet about the things that, how do you say, don't concern me. I've held my peace about so many things over the years, but the way you just treated that girl was beyond anything I thought you were capable of. What has happened to you, Carlton? When did you get this way? How could you do this to your son, who has finally found happiness in his life, no thanks to you? Bonnie may not be born into a wealthy family, but she's a good girl, and Ned loves her. I'm warning you now. Don't you ever interfere with his life again, or I will personally make you pay for it."

With that, Mrs. Bass disposed of her napkin, dropping it right in the middle of her lunch plate, and left the old man standing there agape with his half-eaten lunch.

Bonnie sat all the way against the passenger door of the car with her arms folded. She refused to speak. Ned started the engine, but didn't move.

"Bonnie, I'm sorry," he pleaded. "My father just has a narrow way of thinking. He's invested lots of money into real estate around here and, with times as they've been lately, he's under a great deal of strain. So many people can't make their rent. He didn't mean anything personally. He just doesn't know how to relate to other people sometimes."

"You mean he doesn't understand the hardships of other people," Bonnie said without looking at Ned.

Ned smiled. "Yes, I guess that's one way to put it," he said as he stopped the car at the end of the driveway. He put the car into park and turned toward Bonnie.

"Bonnie, look at me," he said as he took her reluctant arm. "I don't care what my father thinks. Haven't I proved that to you? Listen to me." He took her other arm and forced her to look at him. "Bonnie, I love you. I've loved you since the first time I saw you in the house on Gay Street. Remember? The day you ripped your stockings?

"I've done plenty of things I'm not proud of, Bonnie, but my life was pretty meaningless until you came along. For a long time, I thought I'd never see you again. Then, there you were standing there in Loveman's looking so clever. I swore to myself I'd never let anything get in the way of making you my wife."

Bonnie's eyes flew open wide. She covered her mouth with her hands as if *she'd* said something she wasn't supposed to say. "Wife?" she exclaimed.

"Yes. I guess now is not the most romantic nor the best time in the world, considering my father's actions, but yes. I want to marry you. I want you to know that. I want the world to know that!"

Bonnie sat staring at Ned, a horrified look on her face. She wiggled her arms free from his grasp, opened the door to the car and took off walking at a hastened clip across the plush lawn. Ned turned off the car, following her.

"Bonnie! Bonnie!" he cried. He caught up with her and turned her around to face him. As he did, he realized she was crying.

"What is it? What did I say?"

Bonnie was completely speechless. She knew Ned would eventually ask her that question, but hadn't expected it so soon. She was totally unprepared. Her mind buzzed as she tried to concentrate on what he was saying. The only thing she could focus on was the day she stood in the tool shed with Calvin, the day she finally told him how she felt about him and the total surprise she felt when he refused to say how he felt.

"Wait!" Bonnie said as she raised her hand to Ned. "Wait." She walked away from him and seated herself on a bench under a massive oak tree pulling her coat closer to her body. Ned followed. He handed her his handkerchief. Bonnie dabbed tears from her face. She sat with the handkerchief in her lap staring forward as she watched the events of her young life flash before her eyes.

Bonnie saw Calvin, Polly, and Cora. She remembered the day she woke up from being shot. She remembered the way she felt when Calvin turned away from her, the way she felt when she lost the chance to get the children. It all flashed before her in an instant. Bonnie turned and looked at the house that stood behind them. Ned turned his gaze in the same direction. He knew what she was thinking before she even said it.

"We're so different, Ned. You've grown up in this enormous house, a part of a life I never knew even existed before I met you. I guess I thought you might ask me to marry you one day, but I never thought I could be what you wanted."

"Bonnie," Ned said. He slid off the bench onto his knees in front of her. "I've never wanted anything so badly in my life as I want you. I can go into a court of law or do business and the words I need to say come so naturally to me, but when I'm with you, I can't even begin to say what's on my mind. I want to tell you how I feel sometimes, but I'm so scared of losing you again. I just can't ever seem to find the words. I know how uncomfortable you are some of the time when we go to places, and you don't feel like you belong." He took her hand. "But I just don't see it that way.

When I walk into a room with you on my arm there's no one else in the room who matters to me only you. I don't want you to fit into my life, I want you to *be* my life. I want to shower you with all the love you so deserve and need and want. Bonnie, we could move if you don't like it here. We'll go somewhere else. I'll start my own practice. I'll leave this town if it means having you."

Bonnie watched Ned's face as he spoke. She saw something there she had never seen in anyone else's. She saw in Ned the same love she had felt for Calvin, the same unconditional, uncontrollable, unexplainable love. She knew that feeling all too well.

Bonnie closed her eyes and laid her forehead against his, clasping her fingers around the back of his neck. She had often thought about her feelings for Ned. Inevitably, she compared them with her feelings for Calvin. She knew it wasn't the same. She knew she would never love anyone as she had loved Calvin, but she had also grown up enough to know that life wasn't the same fairy tale she thought it to be when she was young and full of dreams. She had resigned herself to a life without those dreams before Ned came back into the picture. Maybe this was her chance? Maybe this was her dream the way it was meant to be? She did love Ned after all.

Bonnie slowly raised her head to look at Ned. She placed her hands on either side of his face. "It's an insane idea altogether," she said. "Are you a good lawyer?"

"I'm an excellent lawyer," Ned said, smiling. "As a matter of fact," he whispered, "I'm a much better lawyer than Dad."

"Shhh . . ." Bonnie covered his mouth. "Don't say that too loud. He might hear you."

"Well, we better leave then," Ned said, helping Bonnie to her feet. "What do you say? Will you?"

"Will I what?" Bonnie teased.

"Will you marry me?"

They walked along in silence toward the car.

"Yes, I believe I might."

"No kidding? You will?"

Bonnie nodded vigorously. "Yes, I do believe I will. Oh, and we're not going anywhere. We'll stay right here."

"Well now, that's the Bonnie I know and love." Ned looked up at the house. "Do you want to go back in and tell them now? It'll sure light a fire under Dad."

Bonnie looked over her shoulder at the house. She knew she had made the right decision, but facing that part of it was another thing altogether.

"No, I think maybe we should wait awhile for that. Let us get used to it first."

Ned picked Bonnie up off her feet and carried her back to the car.

Upstairs, from her bedroom window, Claudia Bass watched her son and Bonnie on the lawn. She wiped a tear that slowly fell down her cheek. Claudia had seen the look on Bonnie's face before. It was the look of a woman who had just received a marriage proposal. She also knew it wouldn't be easy for them. Mr. Bass was completely against Ned's relationship with Bonnie.

She knew her son would have to be strong.

She prayed that Ned had made the right decision.

Chapter Nineteen

"I'm happy for you, Bonnie Girl. You sure do deserve to be happy."

B ONNIE WALKED INTO the Lunch Room in Union Station at exactly noon. Nell put her order in with the cook as soon as she saw her roommate walk through the door.

"Hey, Charlie, throw on a grilled cheese, will ya? Bonnie's here." Bonnie took her place on a stool as Nell walked over with her Coca-Cola and set it in front of her.

"There she is, the future Mrs. Ned Bass. Charlie, come here and look at this rock, would ya?"

"Hey, look at that," Charlie said. He drew in a breath and let it out in a long admiring whistle. "I bet that cost my whole year's wages."

"Oh, Charlie, don't be silly," Bonnie said. She held her hand up for everyone to see her new engagement ring.

"I tell you what, let's us just see. You go hock it, and you and me, we'll run away down to Cuba or somewhere. We'll see just how far we can get."

"Ah, get back to work!" Nell said. She slapped the cook on the chest with the back of her hand. "Really, it's beautiful, hun. I'm just so happy for you."

"Nell, you're not going to cry again, are you?"

"No," Nell replied, pulling her handkerchief out of her apron to wipe her eyes. "I promised I wouldn't."

Bonnie picked up her Coca-Cola and drew a sip from her straw as

Nell made a quick round about the room refilling coffee cups. Just then, a lone diner walked through the double doors. He stood at the door, surveying the room.

"Well, hello there," Nell said as she looked up from the last refill. "C'mon in and have a seat."

"No, I'm not here for lunch," the man told her. He twirled his hat nervously in his hands. "I'm looking for someone."

"Well, you came to the right place, honey," Nell quipped. "Say, you look familiar. Do I know you?" Nell asked offering her hand. The man she spoke to was dressed differently than the folks who usually ate there, except for the farmers who sometimes came through the station. They either had their one Sunday suit on or their Sunday afternoon sitting clothes. His neat dungarees and freshly ironed shirt didn't give him away as a farmer, but the toughness of his hand when he took hers to shake it, was the unmistakable sign of a man who works the land for a living.

"Grilled cheese is up," Charlie yelled. Bonnie turned to see what Nell was doing as she took another pull from the straw in her Coke. As if time stood still, the glass that she was holding made its way out of her hand, shattering onto the floor below.

"I found her, thanks," Calvin Wade said to Nell with a smile as he made his way through the lunch crowd and over to the counter where Bonnie sat with her hand in the air holding a make-believe glass. Her mouth hung open wide.

"Hello, Bonnie," Calvin said.

"Calvin?" she asked, standing amid the broken glass. "What are you doing here?"

Calvin instinctively placed his hands on her shoulders and moved her out of the remnants of her soda glass as she continued to stare in disbelief.

Nell walked up slowly behind Calvin with her coffee pot still in her hand.

"That's it. You're Calvin! I recognize you from your picture!"

Bonnie made a face at Nell as Calvin turned toward her.

"Oh, Calvin, this is Nell, my roommate."

"How are you?" Calvin asked offering his hand. Nell quickly switched the coffee pot to her left hand and extended her right to Calvin.

"I'm so pleased to meet you," she said. "How about that! Calvin! Bonnie, it's Calvin," she said, winking.

Bonnie rolled her eyes. "Yes, thank you, Nell. Can you help me with this glass?" she asked and nodded at Nell to go away.

"Oh, yeah, sure. Let me get something to clean that up."

"What are you doing here?" Bonnie asked Calvin.

"Well, Lizzie told me where you was working, they sent me here. Said you had lunch here every day, so I thought I'd come over and see you 'fore I went home."

"How long you been here?" Bonnie asked, her dialect from home automatically taking over her speech.

"I came down early this morning. I had to get some parts for my tractor."

"You have a tractor? I didn't know that," Bonnie said. She turned to look around the Lunch Room. Every ear seemed to be honed in on their conversation. "C'mon, let's step out into the lobby so we can talk." She led Calvin out of the Lunch Room and back into the huge Union Station lobby.

"Nice to meet you, Miss Nell. Maybe I'll see you again sometimes," Calvin called over his shoulder as Nell stepped up with a broom and pan to clean up the broken glass.

"You're not leaving are you?" she called back. "Bonnie, you're not going to let him go, are you? He just got here?"

"He has to get back to Smithville, Nell."

"Well, surely he can stay one night for supper, don't you think?"

Calvin stopped walking away and closed the distance back to her. "Oh no, Miss Nell. I just came on business, but I'm through now, and I have to be gettin' on back."

"Yes, well, okay. It was nice to meet you," Nell said as she stuck the broom under her arm and extended her hand to Calvin.

Calvin shook her hand and tipped his hat to her, then turned to follow Bonnie.

"Very nice indeed," Nell said. She watched Calvin walk out of the room.

Bonnie's heart was beating so hard, she could barely think. Calvin. There he was, walking right behind her. What would she say when she turned around? Would she tell him about Ned? She took a seat on one of the benches close to the fireplace and motioned for Calvin to join her.

"What are you doing here?" she asked him again.

"Well, I had to have some parts for my tractor right away. I couldn't get them from Lebanon without having to wait, so they sent me here and told me where to buy what I needed," he explained. He crossed his legs, propped his hat on his knee, and began to roll a cigarette.

Bonnie examined his face. It had been quite some time since she had seen him, she thought. She smiled when she noticed a few gray streaks in his hair next to his temples. Calvin licked his cigarette paper and finished his rolling job in between the words he spoke.

"I promised Lizzie I'd come and make sure you're safe and sound, as she put it. I told her you been taking care of yourself for a long while now, but you know Lizzie."

Bonnie forced herself to concentrate on what Calvin was saying. "Yes, she writes me once a week and calls Annie all the time just to make sure what I'm telling her is true." They laughed together knowingly. Calvin lit his cigarette.

"It sure is good to see you, Bonnie. Doc Morgan says to say 'Hi,' and Emma, Nettie, and the kids. Frank and Nettie just bought them a car. Sure wouldn't surprise me if they come to see you."

"Frank bought a car?" Bonnie asked. "You don't mean it."

"He did, but what's funnier than that is watching him drive it. Won't be long, he'll have to replace them tires the way he squeals around town!"

They laughed again. Bonnie smiled and sat back on the bench. The nervousness she felt began to slip away, replaced by that familiarity you get when you see someone you've known for a long time. Bonnie knew Calvin all too well. She had been in Nashville for almost ten years, and he had never come to see her, not even the times when Bonnie had found out from Lizzie that he had been right there in town.

"You didn't come all the way just to see me. What's wrong?"

Calvin smiled. "I never could hide much from you. Could I?"

"No, you never could," Bonnie said.

"Bonnie, Jessie is getting on in years. I don't know. How old do you think he is anyway?"

"Well, how old he is and how old he says he is are two different figures altogether," Bonnie said, laughing.

"He's just too old to work that farm anymore, Bonnie. We've all tried to tell him. He's just so stubborn. He won't buy a tractor. He insists on using his mules. You know how he is. He don't like for me to help with anything, but he just can't do it anymore. We've all tried to talk to him, but you know, you're the only one he'll listen to.

"Lizzie asked me to come, Bonnie. We want him to give up the farm, and him and Lizzie come live with me at my place, but he just won't hear of it. Lizzie wants you to come and talk to him. Says you're the only one who can get him to do it."

"That stubborn ole coot!" Bonnie balled her fist and struck her lap with it. "You'll never get him off that farm. I don't care who tries to talk him into it." She stood and began to pace back and forth in front of Calvin.

"Well, someone's got to. He's really not doing good, Bonnie. I know he wouldn't want me tellin' you, but he's not good."

"Is he sick?"

"Well, nothing Doc Morgan can put his finger on, and you know Jessie, he ain't a going to no other doctor. He's just aging so."

"Well, he's not a young man, Calvin. He's got to be at least 78 or 80, reckon?"

"At least," Calvin agreed. "Are you going to come and talk to him?"

"I better or Mama might come to Nashville with a hickory," Bonnie said, smiling as she faced Calvin. He stood and picked up his hat.

"Well, I better get going. I gotta get back 'fore nightfall. You know Buttermilk and Shorty. They might kill each other if I don't get back."

"How are they, Calvin? And how's Pippin?" Bonnie asked, placing her hands on his forearms. A powerful flood of memories came back to her with the sensation of touching him.

"'Bout the same," Calvin said, breaking Bonnie's hold. He scratched his chin uncomfortably. "Always fighting and feuding over something. Pippin, she's 'bout the same still coming by to try to take care of us three."

"I miss them so. Seems like a different world I lived in when I think about Mama and Daddy."

"It ain't changed much, Bonnie. You're just livin' here in the big city now and us country folk do seem like we live in another world."

"Nashville's not so big. It *is* a different world, though."

Calvin began twirling his hat in his hands again as he looked down. "I noticed you have a new ring on your finger there," he said as matter-of-factly as possible.

Bonnie's face went ashen. She had forgotten all about her engagement ring. She suddenly felt like disguising behind her back the hand she had been waving in front of everyone minutes earlier at the Lunch Room counter.

"Oh yes! My ring," she said, looking down at it.

"You gettin' married, Bonnie?" Calvin asked slowly.

A lump formed in Bonnie's throat. Some part of her wanted to scream. She suddenly wanted to rip the ring from her hand. She had been so sure of herself that her engagement to Ned was the right thing to do, and now, here Calvin was, asking if she was getting married. Bonnie swallowed hard, forcing herself to answer.

"Yes, Calvin. Ned Bass asked me to marry him."

Calvin took on a serious tone. "I take it you said yes."

Bonnie nodded, unable to speak.

Calvin kept twirling his hat. "I'm happy for you, Bonnie Girl. You sure do deserve to be happy."

Bonnie stood looking up at the one man in her life who meant more to her than anyone else. Slowly, the lump in her throat subsided. She managed to fight back tears before they crept out of the corners of her eyes.

It was over.

Her dream of marrying Calvin was never going to happen. She had been away too long. There was too much between them. Bonnie knew she was going to have to let go for good.

"I'm going to be happy," she said, quietly trying to convince herself more than Calvin.

"I'm sure you will," he replied. "I know Lizzie will be."

Bonnie grabbed Calvin by both arms. "Oh, don't tell Mama, Calvin. She doesn't know yet. I was going to come home and tell her!"

He smiled. "Okay, I promise."

"I mean it, Calvin Wade. You better not tell her."

He laughed, watching her green eyes light up and narrow into those fiery slits in her face, just like they used to when Calvin would annoy her on purpose.

"I promise. I've never told any of your secrets."

"Well, who knows for sure," Bonnie added.

"You be sure to tell this Ned Bass that I said he better be good to you," Calvin said. There didn't seem to be a need to say much of anything else.

"I will," Bonnie answered.

"I gotta go now," Calvin said. "I guess you can talk to Jessie after you tell him the good news."

"I'm not sure if it will be good news to Daddy. I believe that, in the back of his mind, he's always thought I would come back home. When I tell him I'm getting married, he's gonna realize I'm really not coming back. I'm not sure he'll be happy for me."

"Well, he loves you so much, Bonnie. He's never realized you're not his little girl anymore. I don't think he ever wanted you to grow up."

"He didn't. He'd be happy as a lark if I was ten years old again fishin' the Caney Fork with him whenever there wasn't plantin' or plowin' or something to do."

"Well, the plantin' and plowin' and things to do still haven't changed. Even if you're not ten years old anymore," Calvin said.

"Can't ever go back there," Bonnie replied sadly, "but it sure was fun."

"Yes, it was," Calvin said. There followed a pause while they both allowed the memories they had pushed to the back of their minds to play up front just for a moment.

"Well, I'll write Mama and let her know when I'm coming, but you have to promise to keep my secret."

"I promise," Calvin agreed again. He bent over and kissed Bonnie on the forehead. "Take care of yourself."

"I always have."

He smiled and put his hat on his head, then stuck his hands into his pockets just as he had always done even as a little boy.

The lump came back to Bonnie's throat when he said his goodbyes. She barely heard what he said. She just watched his lips move as she studied his familiar face one more time before he left.

"Bonnie?" Calvin said, trying to get her attention again.

"Oh yes, well, I have to get back to work now."

"Okay, I'll be seeing you."

"Okay, Calvin," Bonnie said. By then she just wanted him to leave. The battle in her mind had already been fought, and it hadn't been easy. She didn't want to fight it again. "Goodbye."

"Goodbye," Calvin said one last time. He tipped his hat and turned to exit the station. Bonnie stood totally oblivious to the busy sounds of the station at lunchtime and watched as he walked away. She watched him walk through the doorway. Inside, she fought the urge, but gave in, running to the entrance to watch as he got into his truck and pulled away.

Numb and confused, she went back inside, sat on the nearest bench, and stared at the floor.

"Hello," a familiar voice said. Bonnie looked up to see Carlton Bass staring down at her. She stood to face him.

"What are you doing sitting here looking so despondent?" he asked, a mischievous smile on his face.

"Oh, I just said goodbye to an old friend from home," Bonnie told him. She silently worried about how much he had seen.

"Well, I'm glad I ran into you. It saves me from making an appointment," the old man said to her.

"An appointment?" Bonnie asked, puzzled.

"Yes," Mr. Bass said gruffly. It was his *attorney-at-law* voice. "Miss McCaverty, it has been made apparent to me that I've been a bit hasty in my conclusion of your personage. I have been ill-mannered toward you, and I just want to take this opportunity to apologize for my harshness. Ned has informed me of your engagement, and I just want to say how happy I am for the both of you." The coat that was draped over his arm never budged the entire time he was speaking. He held his small overnight bag clenched in his right hand. It was apparent he was there to catch a train.

The elder Mr. Bass looked away from those bright green eyes he was addressing for a moment and continued. "Bonnie, I fear I've become a product of my own ambition. The past few years haven't been easy for me even though I believe you think they have. We've all been affected by the times, and I don't believe anyone has been immune to its effects. In the course of business, I lost sight of my feelings. I do apologize again for any unhappiness I caused you and Ned. I hope you'll both be very happy."

Bonnie smiled at the old man. She placed her hands on both of his arms, stood on her tiptoes, and kissed the old man on the cheek. She realized how hard that had been for him. Even as stubborn as she was, Bonnie had a soft spot in her heart for folks who could admit when they were wrong.

"Yes, well," Mr. Bass stammered. "I have a train to catch. Goodbye, my dear."

"Goodbye," Bonnie replied, knowing there wasn't anything else either of them needed to say about the matter.

Mr. Bass turned and walked toward the ticket counter. Bonnie glanced at the big clock on the wall.

"Oh dear! I'm so late!" she exclaimed. She hurried back to the Lunch Room. Nell had her lunch packed and waiting beside her bag on the counter.

"What happened?" Nell quizzed her.

"There's no time! I'm so late. Mr. Bowman will have my head! I'll talk to you tonight," she yelled over her shoulder as she scurried for the door.

Nell and Charlie laughed together as they watched her trying to hurry in her little high heels. Bonnie was always a source of entertainment around the Lunch Room with her many predicaments, and today had been no exception.

She managed to sneak into the offices at Loveman's before Mr. Bowman realized she was late. She sat down just as the phone rang.

"Loveman, Berger, and Teitelbaum's," Bonnie answered, trying to wedge the heavy receiver between her neck and shoulder so she could pull off her gloves.

"Bonnie," a familiar voice said on the other end. "I've got some good news."

"Ned, I can't talk right now," she whispered. "I was late getting back from lunch, and I snuck in before Mr. Bowman saw me. I need to get to work."

"Just listen, then. I told Mother and Father about our engagement. Dad was actually pleasant. Mother must have really lit a fire under him. Although she looked about as puzzled about his reaction as I was. Anyway, they want to throw us an engagement party at the Club. Mother wants us to get together and come up with a date so she can plan the timing on this."

"Ned, I . . . I really can't talk right now," Bonnie said, a bit aggravated. All the circumstances of the day had put her in a confused state of mind. A party at Belle Meade Country Club wasn't something she wanted to think about right now. "I don't mean to be harsh. Ned. I just need a bit of time to get used to all of this."

Ned laughed. "Honey, you'll be just fine. I know the Club isn't one of your favorite places, but just relax and let Mother handle everything. Believe me, she's a pro at it."

"Ned, I have to go now. Could we talk about this some other time?"

"How about tonight? I'll pick you up at seven, and we'll go out to the house. Dad's out of town tonight so we can have a nice time with Mother."

"Yes, I ran into your father at the station."

"You saw Dad?"

"Yes, in the lobby."

"Well, how was he?"

"Very apologetic," Bonnie said. "Actually, he was sweet. Ned, I will have to tell you about it later."

"What about tonight?"

"I can't tonight, Ned. I promised Mrs. Greenfield that I would help with the packages they're sending to England for the war effort. I have to be there."

"Bonnie, when are you going to stop with all of that? You do too much as it is."

Her fist clenched tight around the handset. Bonnie was getting aggravated. Her day had started out strangely, and it wasn't getting much better.

"I'm not going to stop. The supplies we're sending overseas are important. You know there *is* a war going on over there."

"All right, Bonnie. I'm sorry," Ned said kindly. "I know how important to you that work is. I'll call you tomorrow."

"I'm sorry, Ned. I've just had a strange day, and I really have to get back to work now."

"I'm sorry, too. I was just so excited about Dad's reaction. I'll call you tomorrow."

"Okay," Bonnie said. "Uh oh, here comes Mr. Bowman. I gotta go!" She laid the receiver down on its hook. Just then, Mr. Bowman opened the door to the office.

"Hello, Bonnie, did you have a nice lunch?"

"Yes, Mr. Bowman, I did. I saw an old friend from home at the station."

"I guess this old friend didn't realize he was detaining you from your job."

"I didn't think you noticed," Bonnie said apologetically.

"You forget, dear, it's my business to notice."

"I'm sorry, Mr. Bowman. I just haven't seen this person in so . . ."

Mr. Bowman raised his hand. "I know, I know, you didn't mean to do it, and it will never happen again," Mr. Bowman said with a smile.

Bonnie grinned. "That *is* what I was going to say."

Mr. Bowman rolled his eyes at her, reached for the door to the office, and opened it. "Bonnie, you must try harder."

"Okay," she agreed sheepishly. She smiled as Mr. Bowman shut the door behind him. "Shoo, that was close!" She wiped her forehead with the back of her hand.

She sat back in her chair and thought about all the events of the morning. It had been a busy one; first Calvin, then Mr. Bass, then Ned. For the first time since she had said yes to Ned, Bonnie was confused. She knew she wanted to marry Ned, and she knew there was no hope for Calvin any longer, but why did he want to rush her into this?

She needed time, and she was just going to have to demand it. Besides, there was the visit to Smithville she'd been putting off long enough. Bonnie knew there was no way she could get married without Ned doing the proper thing, asking Jessie McCaverty for her hand.

CHAPTER TWENTY

"Soon, she'd become the new Mrs. Ned Bass."

N ED AND BONNIE pulled up to the McCaverty house at approximately eleven on Saturday morning. The three and a half hour drive was something Bonnie had become accustomed to, but Ned, in his new 1940 Lincoln was more used to the civilized roads of Nashville. The roads of DeKalb County astounded him. After Highway 56, the road to the Wade and McCaverty farm was barely passable. Ned had little experience with country roads and wasn't particularly pleased with the look of his car when they got to the McCaverty farm.

"Look, there's Mama and Daddy," Bonnie said as they pulled to the front of the house. She leaned out the window and waved. "There's Tom and Nettie and Sam and Emma and the kids. Oh, Ned, everybody's here to meet you!"

"Bonnie, it sure is good to see you, girl," Lizzie said as she embraced her daughter.

"Mama, oh . . ." Bonnie replied, hugging her tightly. "I've missed you so much! Tom, Nettie, Sam, Emma, oh I'm so glad to see you all." She hugged all of them one by one, then she took Ned's arm. He had been standing on the outskirts of the crowd holding his hat in his hand. "Everyone, this is Ned Bass."

The crowd of McCavertys descended upon Ned with hugs, hand-shakes, and kisses from the women, while Lizzie and Bonnie held onto each other watching excitedly. Bonnie turned to the front porch, where Jessie sat waiting for them to come to him. Bonnie grabbed Ned's hand and pulled him up the front steps to the porch. Jessie slowly got to his feet.

"Hi, Daddy," Bonnie said, kissing her father on the cheek. "I'd like you to meet Ned Bass from Nashville. He's a lawyer, Daddy."

Jessie reluctantly put his hand out to shake Ned's.

"It's nice to meet you," Ned said nervously. Jessie sized Ned up from head to toe as they shook hands.

"That's a fancy car you got there, boy," he said, motioning to the Lincoln with his pipe. "Must a cost a fortune."

"Well, not quite a fortune, but it is a nice car."

"Why would somebody want to spend so much money on a car?" Jessie asked.

"Now, Daddy, be nice. He lives in the city. He needs a nice car."

"I do lots of driving, sir."

"How'd ya get that thing down them roads?" he said, motioning toward the drive with his pipe.

"Well, that wasn't an easy task."

"Calvin drives that darned ole' truck over, and he can barely get it down here. That car of yours sits so low to the ground, how'd you git it over them potholes?"

"Now, Daddy, come on and sit down. Let's talk about something besides the car. How's the farm doing?" Bonnie asked as everyone found a seat.

"It's doing just fine, just fine. Y'all stayin' the night?"

"Yes, Daddy, we're going home after church tomorrow."

"Where's *he* going to sleep? We only got two bedrooms."

"Jessie, I told you, he's going to sleep on the cot where Calvin used to sleep," Lizzie said. "Quit askin' so many questions. C'mon, Bonnie. Girls, let's get in here and get some lunch made."

Bonnie stood at her mother's request and left Ned to visit with Jessie, Tom, and Sam. As soon as the girls got into the house, they began giggling together just as they had when they were young.

"Bonnie, he's so handsome," Nettie said.

"I bet he's rich, too. Id'n he?" Emma asked.

"Now, girls, don't be prodding your sister like that. I'm sure she's going to tell you exactly what she wants you to know."

"He is rich!" Bonnie said as they all walked to the kitchen. "He and his father are lawyers. They have their very own business."

"How did you meet him?" Nettie asked.

"That's a long story, but the first time we met was at the building where I was volunteering for the Red Cross."

"Do ya hear anything about the girls, Bonnie?" Lizzie asked.

"Yes, every now and again I'll get a letter from Mrs. Carter, and she'll tell me about them. They sound happy. They're both in school now."

"You don't say?" Lizzie exclaimed.

"Yes, can you believe it? It doesn't seem like that long ago, yet it seems like another lifetime altogether." A melancholy crept into her voice.

"Well," Emma interrupted, "has he asked you to marry him yet?"

Bonnie looked over at her mother and smiled. "As a matter of fact, he has," Bonnie said cautiously.

Her sisters went wild with joy. "Oh, Bonnie, what did you say?"

"I said yes!" She looked at her mother.

Lizzie wiped her wet hands on her apron. "Well, girl, I guess we're going to be havin' us a wedding," she said, wrapping her arms around her daughter.

Bonnie pulled away looking her mother in the eyes. "What do you think Daddy will say, Mama? Ned is going to ask him. I'm just so worried what he'll say."

Lizzie turned back to the sink. "That's another thing altogether, Bonnie. You know your father. He keeps thinking you'll come home one day. When you tell him you're gettin' married, I believe he'll know for sure you're not coming home. He won't like it very much."

"Well, I just can't do it without his blessing," Bonnie said quietly. "It's been ten years, Mama. Why does he keep thinkin' I'm coming back?"

"He's an old man, Bonnie. He misses you."

"Well, I can't come back here. I wish he'd just realize that."

"I don't think he's going to have a choice anymore. Now is he?" Lizzie asked her daughter.

Emma piped up. "Bonnie, you're just going to have to be strong. Besides, he always does what you want him to. He always has."

"That's for sure," Nettie agreed.

"I take it you're going to talk to him about moving to Calvin's farm while you're here, aren't you?" Emma asked. "Mama said Calvin went to Nashville and told you about it. Why's he so stubborn, Bonnie?"

"Hold on a minute," Lizzie said. "Let's not put all this on Bonnie when she's got something as important as marriage on her mind."

"I'm going to talk to him before I go, Mama. I promise."

"Calvin comes over here all the time and does half of the work, just so it won't be so hard on Mama. I don't know why Daddy won't just move to Calvin's.

"Because, girls, he's been here a long time. This is his home. This is where we were married, where his mama died, where you girls were born. It's not an easy thing for him. Seeing all the others who had their land bought up by the government, it's just made him a bit more hard about staying here."

"Why haven't they offered to buy this farm? Or Calvin's? It's right on the Caney."

"It's more upstream where they're buying up most of the land, north toward Temperance. Seems like 'cause of our bluffs out by the river, it'll rise down here, but won't flood us. We never had much trouble with flooding here anyways, but a lot of people will lose the farms they've been on for generations. They're having a bit of trouble with old man Sawyer though," Lizzie said.

"They say they're gonna have to run him off with a shotgun if he won't get off his land," Nettie told her.

"Otis Sawyer?" Bonnie asked.

"Yes, mild-mannered old Mr. Sawyer, the one who used to hand candy sticks out at Webb's Drug Store. He's saying they'll have to kill him first!"

"My goodness," Bonnie said. "I didn't know all this was going on 'round here."

"Calvin's been right in the middle of it. He's been going to all the meetings. You know Calvin, the peacekeeper. He don't like to see nobody fighting," Emma said.

"How is Calvin?" Bonnie asked her mother as she sat down to snap some beans.

"He's okay. Working too hard. Trying to help with this place. We've just got to talk your father into going to his place, or it'll kill Calvin, Tom, and Sam. They've been doing their jobs and coming and helping with this place, too. I don't think we can go through another spring like last year. It was just too much for everybody."

"Well, he's just gonna have to do what's best," Bonnie said. "Why can't he quit the farmin' and just stay in the house?"

"He ain't going to quit farming this land," Lizzie said. "It's like an itch he can't scratch. He couldn't just sit here at springtime and not be out planting. If he'd go on over to Calvin's, he could do all the planting with him. There's plenty for him to do there, but he just can't see it. Says neither the government nor us are going to run him off his farm."

Just then, the screen door slammed shut, and Jessie came to the kitchen.

"Well, girl, I understand you're getting married. Is that right?" he demanded.

Bonnie stood. "Yes, sir. That is, if you give me your blessing."

Jessie took a draw from his pipe. "I guess there ain't no chance you'd change your mind and come home?" Jessie asked.

"No, sir, there's not. I love Nashville, Daddy. I have friends there."

"You love this Ned fella?" Jessie asked point blank. Bonnie glanced at her mother, then back at Jessie.

"Yes, sir."

"You'll never fit in, Bonnie. The kind of life you'll have with this Ned character. You'll never fit in, mark my words. But, if it means you trying to be happy, then I guess I give you my blessing." Jessie shook his pipe and tapped it against the wall of the kitchen, then relit it. Bonnie walked over and put her arms around his neck.

"I love you, Daddy. Don't you worry. I'll fit in just fine."

"Well, I hope so, girl. I hope so," Jessie said as he walked through the kitchen and out the back door.

"Where's he going?" Emma asked.

Lizzie smiled. "He's had a hard blow. Let him go think on it. He'll come back around shortly. Kind of reminds me of when you wanted to move to Nashville. Seems to me he acted the same way."

Bonnie wrapped her arm around her mother's waist. "Seems to me he came around then, too," she said. Together they looked out the window and watched the old man walk to the barn.

"Oh my, I better go check on Ned. He must be shook up after talking to Daddy!"

"I'm sure he is," Lizzie agreed. "C'mon, girls, let's get lunch made."

The rest of the day passed uneventfully. Bonnie showed Ned the barn and her tree house. They walked through The Dark Forest, down to the bluff overlooking the Caney Fork River. On the way back, Bonnie showed Ned the spot where she had been shot.

"It was right along there somewhere. I fell off Danny here at this tree. That's where Calvin found me."

Ned knelt and surveyed the spot where Bonnie told him she had landed. "It must've been awful," he told her.

"Doc Morgan still says it was a miracle I lived."

"Well, I'm glad you did," Ned said. He slid his arms around her waist.

Bonnie smiled. "Mr. Bass! Mind your manners. There's squirrels present."

Ned laughed. "They won't mind if I kiss you, will they?"

"No," Bonnie said, smiling.

As Ned bent down to kiss Bonnie, they heard the sound of something rustling through the leaves on the trail. They looked up to see Calvin, who was leading his horse through the Dark Forest, rolling a cigarette.

He looked up from his rolling and stopped dead in his tracks, a surprised look on his face. "Well, hello, Bonnie."

"Calvin," Bonnie stammered, "where are you going?"

Calvin laughed. "I'm going to your house. I heard you were coming today. I wanted to be there when you talked to Jessie." He glanced at Ned. "Hi, I'm Calvin Wade. Nice to meet you." He offered his hand.

"Ned Bass, nice to meet you."

"I'm sorry, Calvin, this is Ned from Nashville. I brought him to meet Mama and Daddy."

"Yes, I heard you were getting married. Congratulations."

"My, word spreads fast around here," Ned said.

"Well, Calvin knew awhile back," Bonnie informed him.

"He did?"

"Yes, he visited Nashville not long ago and saw my ring. I swore him to secrecy, so I could tell Mama and Daddy first."

"And you didn't tell anyone?" Ned said.

"Not a soul," Calvin answered.

A sense of illusion crept into Bonnie's belly as the two men stood together, talking with her in The Dark Forest. It was almost as if Calvin had taken offense when he looked up and saw them on the trail, almost as if they had trespassed on something sacred. *Surely he couldn't feel that way*, she thought, not after he brought Rosalee here so long ago. Of course, that was before she was shot and he went up after the McCallister boys to avenge her. She tried to force the thoughts away. They were going down a path she didn't want to follow.

"Well, let's head toward the house," Bonnie said. The three of them started down the trail toward the McCaverty farm.

"So, what business are you in, Ned?" Calvin asked.

"I'm a lawyer. My father and I own property in Nashville. A great deal of rental property."

"A lot of people are going to lose their property around here."

"Yes, so I understand. It's for a dam or something, right?"

"They're going to build a series of dams to control the flooding in this area. Upstream from here, most all of the valley will be flooded. The government will be buying up all the farms in the area, and the river will eventually rise and cover thousands of acres."

"Emma said they're having a hard time with old man Sawyer," Bonnie said, laughing a little.

Calvin smiled. "Yeah, they are. He's told them they'll have to kill him before they get him off his land. Who would've thought mild old Mr. Sawyer would be the one to be so stubborn? I tell ya, the claws came out when they told him he'd eventually have to sell. It's been a lot of heartache for a buncha folks. They just don't see that it's for a reason. We'll be getting electricity down here soon. Last year they came right up to the Bates farm and stopped. I thought we'd get it then. Now we will for sure."

"Electricity? Did you ever think you'd see electricity at your farm, Calvin?" Bonnie asked.

"Well, I was pure shocked when they put in telephones. Course, you can hardly ever get on it 'cause it's a party line, and there's always a party on the thing."

Bonnie laughed. "I can't never get through to Mama and Daddy. She says that Mrs. Foster or Mrs. Dean's always on it gabbin' about something or somebody."

"Yeah, you know those ladies had to be some kinda pleased when they realized they didn't have to leave their house to spread the latest."

Bonnie laughed. She suddenly realized Ned was trailing a pace behind her and Calvin.

"Well, don't let us bore you with home talk, Ned," Calvin said. "It would take a couple days to tell all that's happened in the county as of late. So tell me, when's the big day?"

Ned spoke up. "That we don't know. Seems like I'm having a hard time getting Bonnie to give me a date."

"That so? Now, Bonnie, don't you be hard on the man. You better be giving him a date. A man's gotta know these things."

"Well, it's a woman's right to take her own sweet time," Bonnie replied.

"I guess it is," Calvin said. "Here we are." He threw his cigarette onto the ground and stomped it out with his boot. "Look here. There's my girls!" Nettie and Emma's girls came running up to Calvin and swarmed him. The boys came up behind them.

"Hey, Uncle Calvin! Let's go fishin'," one of the older boys said.

The girls chimed in. "No, he's going to play house with us in the loft."

"He don't want to play no house with you girls."

"Yes, he does."

"No, he don't."

Calvin interrupted the conversation. "Hold it now, hold it. Let's be neighborly. We have company today. We'll have to save the fishin' and house playin' till some other time."

The kids let out a community sigh.

"Can I ride the mare?" Emma's boy asked.

"I wanta ride her," the oldest girl said.

"Well, Dumplin looks like you got your work cut out for you today," he said as he handed the reins over to Ellis, who was Nettie's boy and the oldest. "Be sure everyone gets a turn," Calvin said as the adults walked away from the frenzy.

"Those children are going to ride that big horse?" Ned asked.

Calvin laughed. "Old Dumplin? She wouldn't hurt a flea."

"Calvin, where's Buck?" Bonnie asked.

Calvin looked down at the ground. "I had to put him under last year," he told her.

Bonnie gaped at him. "What happened?"

"Well, it was rainin' real hard, cats and dogs, and we were coming down through the pass at Fall Creek comin' from Shiney Rock. Just as we came through the creek and got up on the embankment, he lost his footin' and slid down the hill. Broke his leg. Almost broke mine. I had to put him down right there."

"Calvin, I'm so sorry. I know how much you loved Buck."

"I can remember when I tried to kill him and Jessie stopped me. The last time I'd aimed a gun at Buck's head, it was for different reasons." Bonnie winced at the memory of Rosalee's death. "Sure was hard," Calvin finished.

Saturday evening was enjoyable for everyone. Even Ned began to loosen up a bit and join in with the games and conversation.

By sundown, they were all gathered around Lizzie's new battery radio to listen to the Grand Ole Opry.

The next morning, Jessie and Lizzie rode to church in Ned's new car. He pulled right up to the front door and let the women out. Lizzie wanted everyone to see them get out of it.

After the drive back to the McCaverty farm, Ned and Bonnie had to make their slow way back to Nashville before dark.

They had accomplished what they'd set out to do. Jessie had given his blessing. All that had to be decided now was the date. Bonnie knew Ned would now be even more eager. Soon, she'd have to comply. Soon, she'd become the new Mrs. Ned Bass.

PART III

World War II

CHAPTER TWENTY-ONE

"Does this mean we're at war?"

B ONNIE STOOD OVER the sink, washing the lunch dishes Annie handed to her as she cleared the table after Sunday dinner. A quiet day with the Parkers was just what she needed after all the hullabaloo over her engagement to Ned. For over a year now, Bonnie had been dragged from one party to another as the social circle that presided over this engagement finished its course.

It began with an extravagant engagement party at the Belle Meade Country Club, followed by numerous private parties at the homes of those who considered themselves friends of Carlton and Claudia Bass, not only in Nashville, but also in West Palm Beach, New Orleans, and even Atlanta. There were long train rides, sleepless nights, presents, and plenty of names and faces to remember.

Of course, there were the parties just for the ladies. Parties centered around talk of dresses and honeymoons and the inevitable subject of children and babies.

The parties the men attended were a bit more somber. There, the talk was of war. The debate raged on dividing them even at a celebration for an upcoming marriage. Many of those whose ancestry originated in the warring countries wanted to join the Allied forces and fight. They were outraged that the United States hadn't joined the fight already. Others supported neutrality, continuing to fuel the effort with supplies and ammunition instead of the country's young men. After all, they were just beginning to dig their way out of the depression of the previous ten years.

Finally, the parties were over and the wedding date, February 14, 1942, was fast approaching. But today, Bonnie was happy to be right where she was, at home with the Parkers on a cold December afternoon.

As the ladies began to clear the table, Reverend Parker retreated to his favorite chair to read the Sunday paper and listen to the New York Philharmonic on the radio. He didn't have much time before his Sunday evening service. The newspaper, the radio, his pipe, and a warm fire, especially on such a cold day, was a welcome break.

As Reverend Parker unfolded the first section of the paper, the soothing music from the radio came to an abrupt stop. The crackling sound of a live microphone took its place followed by a breathless, urgent voice:

From the NBC newsroom in New York; the President said in a statement today that the Japanese have attacked Pearl Harbor, Hawaii from the air! Once again, the President says that the Japanese have attacked Pearl Harbor in Hawaii from the air! This bulletin brought to your from the NBC Newsroom in New York.

Reverend Parker sat erect on the edge of his chair as the urgent words made their way to his mind. The newspaper he held in his hands drifted slowly to the floor in front of him. The embers in his pipe burned out as the realization of what he had just heard on the radio sank in. He knew what this meant. After all the speculation, America was at war. All the young men who had signed up for the draft in an instant became active servicemen. The Reverend himself had lived through World War I as a chaplain for the Army. He watched many men die, and it had been tragic, but this was different. This would be a war in two theaters, against two enemies as he knew that going to war with Japan would surely mean war with Hitler.

He set his pipe down in its holder, slowly pulled himself out of his chair, then fell to his knees there in the living room and began to pray.

He prayed for all of the men he knew were being assembled at that very moment to travel long distances to foreign lands to once again fight for their freedom. He also prayed that wisdom would prevail for those in authority who would make the decisions which would shape the future of the world.

"Reverend Frank?" Bonnie called as she entered the dining room from the kitchen. "Are you ready for some coffee?" She stopped dead when she saw him on his knees. It hadn't been the first time Bonnie walked in on him praying.

"Bonnie, go and get Annie," she heard him say in a low, meaningful voice. She poked her head around the corner and saw he had returned to his chair, his head cradled in his hands. She ran to his side.

"Are you okay? What's the matter?" she asked, her heart beginning to pound in her chest.

"Go get Annie," the Reverend replied. "The two of you come sit down." He turned the radio up a bit.

Bonnie streaked through the house and grabbed Annie away from the sink. "Annie, come quick! I don't know what's wrong, but Reverend Parker says come in here and sit down. He looks like he's upset!"

"Oh dear," Annie said as she pulled her apron off and began to wipe her hands. Together they ran to the living room.

"What is it, Frank? What's the matter?" she asked as she felt his head.

"I'm fine, dear," he said as he turned down the volume on the radio. "Sit down."

Bonnie and Annie sat on the sofa across from Reverend Parker's chair on the other side of the fireplace, holding on to each other's hands.

"I was listening to the radio, and I've just heard some disturbing news," he began to say. "According to the reports that are coming in, it seems as if Pearl Harbor has been bombed by the Japanese."

"Pearl Harbor! Oh, Frank, we have friends there," Annie cried.

"Where's Pearl Harbor?" Bonnie asked. "What is it?"

"It's the United States Navy base on the island of Oahu in Hawaii. I'm afraid it's where most of our Pacific fleet is based, and it seems like a great deal of them may have been in the harbor. There are no reports yet of how many ships were sunk."

Irate and confused, Bonnie stood. "What's a Pacific fleet? What's happening, Reverend Frank? I don't understand!"

"Bonnie, sit down," Annie said soothingly.

Reverend Parker began to explain. "The Pacific fleet is the majority of the Navy's ships that are stationed on the West Coast to patrol the Pacific Ocean. They're basically our biggest defense against the Japanese. A great many of those ships were in the harbor at the time. It seems as though most, if not all of them, were damaged."

"Does this mean we're at war?"

"Yes, we are. I'm sure President Roosevelt will have to go before Congress and make it official, but yes. I'm certain we will be at war with Japan."

Bonnie stood again and began to pace the room. "This means all those boys who have signed up for the draft will actually have to go, right?"

"Yes, dear, they will," Reverend Parker answered.

Bonnie sat back slowly on the sofa. "Ned says if the war ever began, he would have to go as a pilot. He knows how to fly," she said numbly.

Annie came to her side and put her arm around her. "Now, Bonnie, you don't know for sure. He's an only child."

"I do know. Ned said he would sign up as soon as we were officially at war. When do you think he would have to leave?"

"I don't know, dear," Annie answered.

"He would probably enter training as soon as possible," Reverend Parker said.

"I have to go find him," Bonnie said, picking up the telephone handset. She tried to dial the Bass' exchange, but it was busy. She tried Nell. That line was busy, too. All the lines in Nashville were busy. Probably all the lines across the country were busy. It was a peaceful Sunday afternoon in America, but after a few crackling seconds of a radio broadcast, America was suddenly at war.

Reverend Parker drove Bonnie back to her apartment building on Broadway. As soon as she entered her apartment, she saw that Nell was on the telephone.

"Oh, here she is now," Nell said as she placed her hand over the mouthpiece. "Bonnie," she whispered, "it's Mrs. Greenfield. She's been looking everywhere for you."

Bonnie took the receiver from Nell. "Mrs. Greenfield, it's Bonnie. It's so awful. I was at the parsonage when we heard the radio broadcast."

Mrs. Greenfield interrupted her. "Bonnie, I need you at the station. Mrs. Noel has been contacted to set up in the lobby of the station as soon as possible. There will be troops coming through from Camp Forrest tonight. Can you help?"

"Of course," Bonnie replied, "but I have to find Ned, Mrs. Greenfield. He said he would be joining up as soon as we were at war!"

"Bonnie, there's plenty of time for you to talk to Ned before he leaves. You have to help us with the men that are being moved now. The Red Cross needs every volunteer we have."

"Yes, ma'am, I'll be right there." She hung up the receiver. "Mrs. Greenfield wants me at the station as soon as possible. It seems as if we're moving troops out now."

"Bonnie, this is just horrible! Did you ever think this would happen? The United States being bombed! I just can't believe it."

"I can't either, Nell. Ned said he would join up as a pilot if we ever went to war and here it is! I have to find him, Nell, but Mrs. Greenfield says she needs me right away." She gazed at her roommate with pleading eyes. "Can you try to find him for me?"

Just then, the telephone in the apartment rang. Bonnie grabbed the receiver. "Hello?"

"Bonnie?"

"Ned! Oh, Ned, I've heard on the radio. It's just awful! What will happen?"

"Well, we're at war with the Empire of Japan. Dad says President Roosevelt will probably make an official announcement tomorrow. Bonnie, I have to see you."

"I can't, Ned. Mrs. Greenfield called and wants me down at Union

Station. They're trying to arrange to set up a Red Cross station. She says they'll be moving troops through as early as tonight."

"Headed west for the harbors," Ned said absently. "I guess they're wasting no time."

"Ned, what will happen to us? Are you joining up?"

"Sure I am, Honey," Ned said. She could almost hear the proud smile on his face. "I told you I would. Bonnie, look, I'll come by the station and see you, okay?"

"Okay," Bonnie said reluctantly. "I have to go now."

"All right, darling. I'll see you soon. Bonnie? Don't worry."

"Okay, Ned. I'll try not to."

At the Bass house, Mr. Bass was entering the room just as Ned placed the receiver on its cradle.

"Well, your mother is quite upset."

"I know, Dad, but you know what I have to do. I'm already a trained pilot. I have to help fight those Japs!"

Mr. Bass put his hand on his son's shoulder. "I understand, son. I know you have to do what you must."

"Would you want me to do anything else?"

Mr. Bass smiled. "No, son. I wouldn't. I'd do the same thing if I were you."

"Thanks, Dad. I knew you'd understand. Mother will, too, after she gets over the shock of it all. Just think, Dad, all those men dead, and not even a moment's notice."

"I just don't understand how it could happen, sneaking up on a place like Pearl Harbor. Why, the Japs had to have planned this for months sneaking a fleet of ships that far across the Pacific." The old man looked exasperated. He took his seat in front of the fireplace in the study. "They had no intention of accepting the proposal from Secretary Hull. It was all a scam to lull us into complacency while they made their plans. How is it we knew nothing about it?"

Ned poured them both a drink. He handed a glass to his father and sat across from him.

"I don't know, but we have no choice now. We have to fight not only with Japan but also with Germany. I'm sure they have it all planned out. Bonnie said she's headed for Union Station to help the Red Cross. It seems they're moving troops tonight. I just hate that we waited to be forced into this. Why didn't we get into the fight long ago?"

"Too much division on the matter. I guess we'll hear an official declaration of war soon. Ned, turn on that radio. Let's see if we can find out more."

The bulletins continued to pour out over the airwaves, reports of heavy casualties and destruction. As the day wore on, they were to learn that not only had Pearl Harbor been hit, but also that the Japanese had bombed the American base at Manila and other locations. The whole country was numb. The unthinkable had finally happened.

Behind the scenes, the war machine began to rev its engines. All the plans that had been made in preparation for the worst now sprang from paper into living, breathing action. The United States of America would soon become more united than ever.

As Bonnie walked up Broadway toward Union Station from The Vauxhall, she watched people who normally would be home on a Sunday afternoon pouring out onto the street. They were standing around in groups, talking to one another. Some were crying, some were ranting and raving over our hesitation about entering the war sooner.

Forcing her way through the crowds, Bonnie finally found Mrs. Greenfield in front of the big fireplace.

"Mrs. Greenfield," Bonnie said as she approached the group of women standing around her.

"Oh, Bonnie, dear, I'm glad you made it. You've met Mrs. Noel."

"Yes. Mrs. Noel, how are you?" she said politely. It wasn't that often that Bonnie ever spoke with Jeannette Acklen Noel, the head of the Red Cross.

"Bonnie, we'll be putting up a table here in front of the fireplace until we get a more permanent station. For now, we just need to be here to lend a hand. From what little we've been told, there will be a great deal of soldiers coming through here late tonight. We have to be ready. We've ordered supplies of coffee and notepads, pencils, envelopes, anything they might need as they come through. It seems a lot of the boys are coming straight from their camps with no chance to see their families before they leave. We're sure they'll want to get messages out and, of course, they will all be scared. You understand what to do, Bonnie," Mrs. Greenfield said seriously.

Bonnie listened intently to the instructions. "Yes, ma'am," she quietly answered.

Mrs. Noel spoke up, laying a comforting hand on Bonnie's arm. "Make them feel special, Bonnie. These boys are going off to strange places to fight for our freedom. We must make them know how proud we are."

Bonnie only nodded in agreement.

"I've contacted a few of the other girls, and they'll be down to help us out. I want you to be in charge of them. You're so good at those kinds of things," Mrs. Greenfield instructed. "Tell them what I've told you. Here." She handed Bonnie a handful of Red Cross armbands. "We'll wear these around our arms or on our heads for now. I believe we'll be easier to spot that way. This place will be busy soon. I have to go back to the office with Mrs. Noel. Bonnie, are you okay?"

"Yes," Bonnie answered. "Everything feels so odd. It's like I'm walking in a dream or something."

"I believe it's more like a nightmare," Mrs. Noel added.

"Yes, an awful nightmare," Bonnie said, staring numbly at the arm badges.

"All right then, we're going to pick up the coffee urns and some food. We'll return as soon as possible."

"Yes, ma'am, we'll be ready."

The two women strode toward a group of people who stood next to the ticket counter. Bonnie recognized a few of them as officers of the Nashville Chapter of the American Red Cross. One of the men was Maclin Davis, the chairman himself. Just as everything else, preparation had been made for this moment, and just as everything else, those plans were now in motion.

CHAPTER TWENTY-TWO

"How 'bout a cup of Joe?"

E ARLY MONDAY MORNING, December 8, as most of the
trains made their way west in preparation to defend the Pacific
coast, Bonnie rested on a bench in the lobby of Union Station.

"How 'bout a cup of Joe?" Nell said as she sat down beside her, a
steaming mug of coffee in her hand.

Bonnie rubbed the back of her neck as she pulled the Red Cross
armband from her arm. "No more coffee for me. I've had enough to
keep all of Nashville awake for a month."

"C'mon, honey, let's go home. I've got to get some rest before the
lunch crowd hits. This place will be hoppin' again in no time."

"I can't go anywhere just yet. I've got to help get some of this mess
cleaned up. Poor Mrs. Greenfield hasn't stopped."

"Bonnie, the reserves are here," Nell admonished her. "Look. See?
The conventional wisdom of the ladies of the Red Cross actually knows
that you can't handle all of this single-handedly. Now, you're coming
with me." She helped Bonnie up from the bench.

"I see you two are finally going to get some rest," Mrs. Greenfield
said as she walked over to where the two young women were trying to
stabilize each other through their exhaustion.

"Yes, ma'am," Nell said. "I was just telling your little volunteer here
that there are other people here who can handle the job for a while.
Don't you agree?"

"I certainly do. I'm going home for a bit of a rest myself. You girls get home and get some well-deserved rest. I have a feeling there will be plenty of time for all of us to do our duty."

"Are you sure? I could stay a bit longer if you'd like," Bonnie tried to argue. "I've called Mr. Bowman to let him know I won't be in today,"

"Bonnie, the station will still be here when you return. We've only seen the beginning of this," Mrs. Greenfield said with a dreadful weariness. "Both of you get some rest. I don't want to see you back here until after work tomorrow."

"I'll try to be back this afternoon."

"Okay, I'm too tired to argue with you," Mrs. Greenfield said. She strode back to the Red Cross table to hand out more orders.

Bonnie and Nell walked arm in arm out the side entrance of the station and into the cold December morning. Bonnie reached under her coat for her scarf. She wrapped it around her head, tucking it inside her coat. She spread a hand across her forehead, shielding her eyes as she looked up at the gray sky.

"Everything has changed, Nell. Hasn't it?" she said as they walked the sidewalk toward their apartment, their arms interlocked with one another.

"I'm afraid it has, honey. I don't think anything will ever be the same again."

"What must it feel like, Nell? All those boys knowing they're going off to some strange land to fight, knowing they may never return. They all looked so lonesome."

"We can't know, Bonnie. I don't think they know. They just know it's something they have to do. Just like we know what we have to do."

"Ned is going over there, Nell," Bonnie said, coming to a stop. "He's going to be gone soon. Just like that. He told me last night that he's been signed up to go for quite some time. He just never told anybody. His poor mother is so upset. You know he's an only son."

"Well, I think it's something that Ned feels like he has to do. It's one of the most honorable things he's ever done, next to falling in love with you, that is." She managed a sympathetic smile as she urged Bonnie to continue walking.

"We were going to be married in a couple of months. He wants to go ahead and get married before he leaves. I'm just so confused about it. I don't want to get married under these conditions. What if . . ."

"What if he doesn't come back?" Nell interjected, never looking at her roommate.

"I just can't think about that now. How can I think about that when there's so much to do?"

Nell pushed open the door to the lobby of their apartment building as the two women peeled their scarves from their heads. The lobby was unusually busy this morning with people standing around talking, all asking each other the same questions. Bonnie and Nell quietly made their way to the stairs.

"You have to decide that for yourself, honey. Just think about how Ned feels. It must be hard on him to leave his family and you behind. I'm sure he's confused, too."

"Not Ned. No, he knows exactly what he wants. He wants to fly airplanes and kill the enemy. He wants to get married. Now. How do some people know exactly what they want? Not questioning anything. How can they be so sure?"

"How can you ask so many questions even when you're so tired?" Nell said as she unlocked the door to their apartment. "I'm going to lie down for a while. You do the same and try not to think about it anymore, okay?" Nell pulled her coat off and threw it across a chair. "I'm beat."

"Me, too. I'll go in a minute. I just want to sit here for a few moments."

"Okay, just promise me you'll get some rest."

"I will," Bonnie said. She reached down to pluck her shoes from her swollen feet. Pulling her feet up onto the sofa, Bonnie curled against the arm not even bothering to remove her coat. That was all she knew until she woke up shortly before noon to the sound of the telephone ringing. She struggled to get her bearings as she finally found the receiver.

"Hello?" Bonnie said tiredly.

"Hello there, Sleeping Beauty," came Ned's voice from the other side.

"Ned! What time is it?"

"Well, it's almost noon. I called Loveman's and Mr. Berger said you had taken the day off because you had been at the station all night. I thought you might be sleeping, so I haven't called until now."

Bonnie sat up and noticed she still had her coat on. She struggled to pull it off as she balanced the receiver under her chin.

"Bonnie, I have to see you. I'll pick you up around six o'clock and we'll get some dinner."

"Ned, I promised Mrs. Greenfield I'd be back at the station this afternoon. I have to help her . . ."

"Bonnie, I'm leaving soon," Ned told her solemnly. "I've already been through classification, and I'll be leaving in the morning for training. We have to talk."

Bonnie stood slowly as her coat slid to the floor. "When?" she asked.

"Tonight."

"Ned . . ."

"Bonnie, I'll be by to get you at six," Ned said firmly.

"I'll be ready," Bonnie said. "Goodbye." She put the receiver back down onto its cradle.

She stood, her head spinning from all that had happened in the last twenty-four hours. Her feet were still numb from running back and forth from troop train to troop train, handing out coffee and doughnuts to the soldiers on board. She shivered. The wind whipping through the train shed the night before had chilled her to the bone, much like the faces of those boys staring out of the windows of those trains wondering where they were going and what was going to happen to them.

She knew what Ned wanted to talk about—marriage. He wanted to get married now, and Bonnie was frightened. The decision to marry Ned hadn't come easily to her. It had taken quite a while to grow accustomed to the idea. She had almost two more months to think about it, until now. The confusion she felt was most unsettling. She didn't know what was causing it. Bonnie loved Ned. Why couldn't she just say yes and marry him before he left? She knew many other couples would be doing exactly the same but, for some reason, Bonnie felt like they should wait.

She walked to the window and looked down on the street. She folded her arms rubbing her hands up and down the length of them trying to warm up. It would be hard to convince Ned to wait until after the war was over. After all, they didn't have any idea how long he'd be gone. Bonnie shook her head trying to clear it, then turned to get ready to go back to the station.

"Hey, hey!" Charlie yelled above the din of the lunch crowd. "Listen, it's the President . . ."

Yesterday, December 7, 1941—a date which will live in infamy—the United States of America was suddenly and deliberately attacked by naval and air forces of the Empire of Japan.

The United States was at peace with that nation and, at the solicitation of Japan, was still in conversation with its government and its emperor looking toward the maintenance of peace in the Pacific.

Indeed, one hour after Japanese air squadrons had commenced bombing in the American island of Oahu, the Japanese ambassador to the United States and his colleague delivered to our secretary of state a formal reply to a recent American message. And, while this reply stated that it seemed useless to continue the existing diplomatic negotiations, it contained no threat nor hint of war or armed attack.

It will be recorded that the distance of Hawaii from Japan makes it obvious that the attack was deliberately planned many days or even weeks ago. During the intervening time, the Japanese government had deliberately sought to deceive the United States by false statements and expressions of hope for continued peace.

The attack yesterday on the Hawaiian Islands has caused severe damage to American naval and military forces. I regret to tell you that very many American lives have been lost. In addition, American ships have been reported torpedoed on the high seas between San Francisco and Honolulu.

Yesterday the Japanese government also launched an attack against Malaya.

Last night, Japanese forces attacked Hong Kong.

Last night, Japanese forces attacked Guam.

Last night, Japanese forces attacked the Philippine Islands.

Last night, the Japanese attacked Wake Island.

And this morning, the Japanese attacked Midway Island.

Japan has, therefore, undertaken a surprise offensive extending throughout the Pacific area. The facts of yesterday and today speak for themselves. The people of the United States have already formed their opinions and well understand the implications to the very life and safety of our nation.

As Commander in Chief of the Army and Navy, I have directed that all measures be taken for our defense. But always will our whole nation remember the character of the onslaught against us.

No matter how long it may take us to overcome this premeditated invasion, the American people in their righteous might will win through to absolute victory.

I believe that I interpret the will of the Congress and of the people when I assert that we will not only defend ourselves to the uttermost, but will make very certain that this form of treachery shall never again endanger us.

Hostilities exist. There is no blinking at the fact that our people, our territory, and our interests are in grave danger.

With confidence in our armed forces, with the unabounding determination of our people, we will gain the inevitable triumph—so help us God.

I ask that the Congress declare that since the unprovoked and dastardly attack by Japan on Sunday, December 7, 1941, a state of war has existed between the United States and the Japanese Empire.

At the Lunch Room in Union Station, even the busy lunch guests were quiet as Nell, Bonnie and Charlie gathered around the radio to listen as the President spoke. Most of the men stood and applauded. The women sat in silence. Some already knew the price of war. The rest knew they soon would.

Ned and his father sat in Mr. Bass senior's office, listening to the message from the President. Mr. Bass stood with his hands clasped behind his back, staring out at the city.

"Well, Ned. I'm sure Congress can't argue with that," he said as he turned the volume down on the radio.

"No sir," Ned answered.

Mr. Bass sat behind his huge desk. "What are your plans, boy?"

"I've already been through classification, Dad. I'll be leaving in the morning for training. Then, I don't know."

"Yes, I guess we won't know for a while. What are your plans for you and Bonnie at this point?"

Ned stood, this time, shaking his head. "It seems as if the future Mrs. Ned Bass, Jr. doesn't quite understand the nature of war. I made plans with Judge Whitaker to marry us tomorrow morning."

"And?"

"I don't know. I'm going to see her tonight. I hope to change her mind."

"Yes, well," the old man said as he cleared his throat. "There's an awful lot of rash young people out there who I'm sure are doing the exact same thing. I think your Miss McCaverty is acting wisely. I think you should wait."

"Dad, let's not talk about it right now. We're still going to get married."

"I know that, son," Carlton Bass said as his tone softened a bit. "I believe if your Mother didn't have the privilege of having a wedding for you on top of your leaving for war, I'm not sure she could handle it."

"Well, it seems as if the ladies have won," Ned said with a bite. "I can only hope to change her mind. I'm going to try."

"You have to understand, Ned. They don't know what happens. I only hope for a quick victory, at least with the Japanese. It may be that we have to fight in Europe, too. Who knows how long we can let that madman Hitler go unchecked? No, son, I have a feeling this won't be over soon."

CHAPTER TWENTY-THREE

"Will anything ever be the same?"

N ED PULLED UP to the apartment building at exactly six
o'clock that evening. Bonnie hurried from the lobby where
she'd been waiting as Ned opened the car door for her.

"Hi there, beautiful. Been waiting long?" Ned asked, kissing her on
the cheek.

"Not long," Bonnie answered as she quickly slid into the warm car.

Ned put the car into gear and drove west on Broadway.

"I thought maybe we would go to the house so that we could talk."

"That'll be fine," Bonnie said without any tone.

Ned looked at Bonnie, who was staring straight ahead. "Bonnie,
are you all right?"

Bonnie smiled. "Yes, I'm fine. It was just all those boys last night.
They looked so scared. I just can't get it out of my mind."

"I'm sure they are. We all are. With the bombing and all, it's just
so overwhelming."

"Yes, that's the word all right. Overwhelming," Bonnie remarked,
all the while trying to hold her mind in one place. She felt more out of
sorts than she had since the day she visited Calvin after she was shot.

Ned steered the car through town and headed west. They both sat
quietly, neither saying much until Ned pulled up to the house.

When they walked inside, Ned showed Bonnie into the library. A roaring fire illuminated the darkened wood-paneled room with a cozy glow. Ned poured himself a drink from the bar.

"Mom and Dad are out tonight. I thought, since we had the house to ourselves, we could talk a bit more privately than over dinner somewhere."

Bonnie stood in front of the fireplace staring into the dancing flames. Ned walked up behind her, turning her around to face him.

"I don't know what I'm going to do, not being able to see you or touch you," he said as he ran his hands up and down her arms. The odor of alcohol wafted to her nostrils.

"You've been drinking."

"Just a bit. I met some of the boys I ran into at the Classification Center at the Club, and we had a few."

"Ned, you know how I feel about you drinking too much."

"Bonnie, who cares?" Ned said. He grabbed her around the waist pulling her closer. "I'm going away, Bonnie. Far away. I may never see you again."

Bonnie pulled away from his hold and looked at him. "Don't say that! Don't talk that way!"

Ned grabbed her arms, forcing her to look at him. "Bonnie, we have to face it. I'm going away to fight. I don't know if or when I'll be coming back. You can't just turn away and pretend it isn't going to happen."

"I know, I know," Bonnie said. "It's just so hard to think about it. Why does this have to happen, Ned? You don't have to leave."

Ned turned away from her this time and walked over to where he had left his drink. He turned it up, finishing it off, swallowing audibly. "I do have to go. I'm a flyer, Bonnie. I have to. I can't just sit around while other people go off and fight. I wish you would try to understand that."

"I do understand, Ned. I'm just so confused." He faced her. She laid her head against his chest.

"Please don't cry. It'll all be over soon," Ned said as he sat her down on the sofa. "Look at me." He turned her face up to his, the glow from the fire illuminating her wet green eyes. "I love you. I want you to be my wife. I want to get married before I go over there. I want to know you're waiting here for me."

"You know I'll wait for you, Ned," Bonnie said. A tear spilled from her left eye and ran down her cheek.

"I know. I just want you to be my wife before I leave," he said tenderly.

Bonnie pushed away from him and stood. "I can't, Ned. I just can't. I don't want to get married that way. I want to have a wedding and a honeymoon and . . ."

"You don't want to take the chance of becoming a widow," Ned said, finishing the thought.

Bonnie sat next to him. "Oh, Ned, that's not it at all. I've just waited so long. I want it to be perfect. Can't you understand that?"

Ned ran his hand through his hair. "No, I don't. I love you. It doesn't matter to me if we have a wedding or a honeymoon or any of that. I just want you to be Mrs. Ned Bass. I want to know I have a family to come home to." He put his arms around Bonnie and pulled her close. "I want you, Bonnie. The thought of going away and never feeling you next to me, never having you as my wife; I just don't think I could stand it."

"Bonnie," he whispered, "I love you. I want you to be my wife." He ran his hands down the back of her dress kissing her again, this time pulling her closer than ever.

"Ned." Bonnie tried to stop him. "Ned . . ."

He filled her mouth with his, cutting off her protests.

Bonnie felt a warmth spread over her she'd never felt before. Ned's breath swept over her neck and shoulders as he kissed her over and over. She felt like she would faint.

"Bonnie, I want you more than anything I've ever wanted in my life. I promise I'll come back. How could I not, knowing you're here waiting for me?" He kissed her again. "I want to see your beautiful body so that I can remember it," he said. His fingers pulled clumsily at the fasteners on her dress.

Bonnie pulled away abruptly. "What do you mean?" She looked at him. "You mean before we're married?"

Ned moved toward her. "No one is going to be home tonight, Bonnie. We have the house all to ourselves. It's just you and me." He tried to kiss her again, but she pulled away.

"You mean, tonight?"

Ned put his hands on her again. "Bonnie, we can get married tomorrow. I've got it all arranged with Judge Whitaker. I'm leaving for training in the morning."

"Just like that?" Bonnie shouted. "You have it all arranged? You want us to become man and wife here in your family's home before we're even married? How could you even ask such a thing? I want it to be right, Ned. I want it to be special. How could you even expect that from me?"

Ned sat down placing his head in his hands. "I don't know what I expect," he said as he looked back up at her. "I can go fight, Bonnie. I can go over there without even a bit of hesitation, but leaving you . . . it will be the hardest thing I've ever done. All my life I've been waiting for you, and now I have to leave you." There was a hitch in his voice as he choked back his emotion. "I just . . ."

"Oh, Ned," Bonnie said as she knelt at his feet beside the sofa, "I love you. I want to get married, but it has to be right. It has to start off right," she said as she turned his face up to hers. "I'll wait, and it will be right, and you won't regret it." She leaned up to kiss him.

Ned pulled her to him and held her tight. "I'm sorry, Bonnie. I don't know what came over me. I guess I'm just used to having everything my way. I wanted it to be the way I wanted it to be. I know that's not the way you want it. I'm sorry."

Bonnie sat next to him on the sofa. He put his arms around her as they lay back on the couch and watched the fire burning, listening to the crackle it made in the quiet room. They sat in silence.

Ned continued to drink. Neither ate. Neither felt like it. Around eleven o'clock, he dropped Bonnie off at the lobby of her apartments and walked her to the door.

"Ned," Bonnie said as she turned to say goodnight to him, "please be careful. You nearly scared me to death on the drive."

He eyed her somberly. "I'm all right," he said, kissing her square on the lips. "Goodnight, my little Irish lass." He pulled his hat off and bowed low, wobbling a bit on the dip. Bonnie caught him by the arm.

"Ned, let me get someone to drive you home."

Ned gestured with open arms. "Drive me home. Who's going home?" He turned to exit the lobby door, then turned back and tipped his hat as he headed for the car.

Bonnie watched him drive off. "Oh, Ned, please be careful," she said after him. She watched through the lobby door as he sped into the night.

Ned continued down Broadway, making his way to Fourth Avenue, telling himself that he would just have one more drink before returning to Belle Meade. He parked in his usual spot and, moments later, found himself inside The Stable, a popular nightspot where many other young men sat having their last drink before they left Nashville.

Ned strolled to the far end of the bar and picked up the drink that was already waiting on him by the time he got there. As he turned the glass up, he swaggered a bit and fell into another fellow sitting at the bar. The bartender came out from behind the bar quickly, ushering Ned into a chair before anything broke out between the two. Since Sunday, the bar had been full of men coming and going off to distant places to fight a war. Tensions were high. It was a full-time job just to keep many of them from going to jail before they had a chance to get on the train.

"Where is she, Mike?"

"She's taking a break, Ned. She's upstairs. She'll be back down in a bit," the bartender said.

"I can't wait. I'm going up to find her," Ned said. He slid off his chair and headed for the doorway at the back of the bar that led upstairs.

"Ned? Ned!" Mike pleaded. He motioned to one of the men charged with keeping peace in the club.

"Mr. Bass, where do you think you're going?" the voice at the bottom of the stairs shouted up at him.

302 | Lisa Kaye Presley

"I'm going to find Della. Where is she?"

"Mr. Bass, you know I can't let you up there. C'mon down now," the big man said, knowing Ned wouldn't get any farther than the locked door.

Ned turned on the stairs, looking down at the huge man who stood at the foot of them. "The door's locked," he slurred. "Why is the door locked?"

"That door is always locked, Mr. Bass. You know that."

Ned laughed. "Yes, I guess I did," he said as he slid down to sit on the top step. The big man made his way up to where Ned sat.

"Mr. Bass, come on downstairs now. If Della comes out and finds you sitting at this door, she's going to be hoppin' mad."

"Della knows how to get mad, doesn't she?" Ned laughed again. "Jack, why do you think Della gets mad so much?"

"Because I'm always having to put up with guys like you," a voice said as the door at the top of the steps swung open wide and the manager of the saloon with her hands mounted on her hips eyed Ned with a scolding glare.

"Sorry, Della, I was trying to get him to come downstairs. He wouldn't listen."

"What are you doing, Ned?" Della asked.

Ned grabbed the railing pulling himself up to look at her face to face. Her beautiful deep brown eyes, which mostly hid any emotion or pain from the rest of the world, became soft and misty whenever they met Ned's.

"I came to see you. Why are you hiding up here?" Ned asked. He began to sway back and forth on the top step. Della put a quick arm around his waist, pulling him away from the stairwell before he fell backward.

"It's okay, Jack. I'll take care of him."

"Yes, ma'am. Call me if you need any help."

"Oh, I won't. He won't give me any trouble."

She kicked the door shut behind her and led him down the hallway to her room.

"Okay, big boy, come on in here and behave yourself."

"I didn't come here to behave," Ned said, pouring himself out onto Della's bed.

"Oh, really? And just why did you come here?"

"I came here to see you," Ned told her. He clumsily hoisted himself up on one elbow.

"Is that right? What about your little fiancé? Did you forget about her?"

Ned looked somberly at the bed, then tried to sit up. Della reached out, grabbed his feet, guiding them to the floor to help.

"My fiancé? Della, did you know I'm leaving in the morning?"

"Where are you going this time?" Della asked rather sarcastically.

"To war," Ned whispered.

Della's face fell. She sat on the bed next to Ned. "What do you mean, to war? Tell me you didn't enlist."

Ned laughed. "Yes, ma'am, I sure did."

Della looked at Ned, studying his face, his hair. She looked at his rumpled suit. She reached over pushing his hair back out of his face.

"Oh, Ned, why'd you go and do something like that?"

"I wanted to, Della," Ned said as he reached out for her hand. "I'm a flyer." He laid back on the big bed again and closed his eyes.

The Ned Della knew was wild and impetuous, but she also knew his quiet, reflective side, the one who was always trying to get out from under his daddy's shadow. She knew that he signed up to be Ned Bass, not Ned Bass, Junior. She knew instantly that Ned had done this to be his own man. He had always been under the shadow of his father and now, here was an honorable task to prove himself as his own man. She understood. Della always understood.

Della had been born in one of the upstairs rooms at the Southern Turf Saloon, which was right down the street where her mother had worked. Her father was a steamboat captain who regularly came to see her mother whenever he made his way up the Cumberland River to deliver goods to Nashville. Della still had a picture of him. He was dashing in his captain's uniform.

The talk back in those days was that most river men were riff raff, usually drifters and heavy drinkers. The men on Captain Bennett's boat were different. The captain himself was a gentleman, and he expected the same from his men. Anyone who got into trouble while on shore and didn't make it back to the boat got left behind. The word was, too, that Della's mother and Captain Bennett were terribly in love, but he was from up North, and she from the South. He traveled constantly. She knew he would never get off the river, and she knew she'd never get out of the life she had lived for so long.

One night, in the back room behind a heavily locked oak door on the second floor where all of the card playing took place, Captain Bennett won a large amount of money from a wealthy man who lived in Nashville. It was old money he won, and lots of it. The captain and the gentleman from Nashville almost came to a duel over the amount of money, but the captain, being the gentleman that he was and the man, who had lost to him being who he was, knew that a duel in the streets of Nashville would surely slander the family name much more than merely losing lots of money would. That could be hidden for the most part anyway. A duel would surely be the end of the moral, social standing of this particular long line of Nashville blue blood.

After that, Captain Bennett proceeded to buy one steamboat after another until he owned what was called The Bennett Line. Well, of course, along with his new wealth came a new wife from an upstanding family in Louisville, Kentucky. By the time Della was born, Captain Bennett didn't come around anymore, although he did send money.

Her mother named her daughter Della after her best friend who died when they were children. Her last name was Houston, same as her mother's because that was where Della's mother was from, Houston, Texas. Della was sent off to boarding schools with the money from Captain Bennett and grew up educated, unlike her mother. Every time she came home from school, Della would help out at the saloon, cleaning and cooking. She loved that place. It was home. All the people who worked there were her family. Now, it was the newspaper office. Her mother died there. Captain Bennett never came to the funeral. Della never met her father.

Now here she was in love with a man whom she knew she could never marry. She had been satisfied all these years to see him when he decided to come by. She never allowed herself to think about him. She learned long ago not to dream too big. It was a real world for her. So real it sometimes was unbearable, but she had managed. Now, Ned was leaving for war. How would she manage that? He had always been there for her, always been there when she needed him.

They understood one another, Ned and Della, like an old married couple who didn't need to have a conversation to trade thoughts. They could always pick up right where they left off. Sometimes Della wouldn't see Ned for weeks if he was traveling or busy, then when she'd see him again, it would be like she had just seen him the day before. They were friends. They had been friends for a long time. Nothing would change that.

Or, so she had thought.

Now that he was engaged she seldom saw him. When she did, he was sullen or deep in thought over something.

At first, she'd been happy for Ned. He had finally found someone who would make him happy and fit into the lifestyle he lived. He'd been in good spirits most of the time. His well-behaved side seemed to be showing more than not, then as time went by, he grew impatient and unsure of himself.

The ringing of the telephone shook Della out of her thoughts. She walked across the room and picked up the receiver.

"Yes?" Della asked. Albert was on the other end of the connection.

"Miss Houston, this is Albert. I'm looking for Mr. Bass. Junior. Would he happen to be there?"

Della turned to look at Ned lying across his bed.

"Yes, he's here, Albert. I'm afraid he's sleeping like a baby."

"Oh, dear. Well, I'll have to come and pick him up. His train leaves in the morning."

The seriousness of Ned's news began to hit home. "Sure, well, you know where we are. I'll try to get some coffee down him before you get here."

"That would be fine, Miss Houston. I'll be there as soon as possible."

Della hung up the phone and walked over to the bed. "Ned, you silly boy," she said as she sat down, leaning over him and studying his face again. He looked so peaceful. Like a baby. "Why did you have to go and sign up? Here you are with all the advantages anyone can have, and you go and sign up."

She delicately stroked the side of his face with one finger, then knelt by the bed and glared at him sleeping. "You fool. Always trying to make Daddy proud. Why can't you just stop and be Ned? I love you just the way you are." Ned's hand reached up and stroked her face.

"Della," he said weakly, trying to sit up. Della stood and helped him sit. "I have to leave for a while, but I'll be back."

"You better," Della said, trying to manage a smile. "I'm not sure if life around here would ever be the same."

"I'm serious, Della. If I don't come back, I just wanted you to know I've left some things for you to have. I want you to take them if that time ever comes." He rubbed his head as the effects of the liquor began to fade.

"Stop it now. I won't listen to that," she replied, turning away from him. She reached into the bosom of her dress, pulling out a handkerchief to dry her eyes before facing him again. Ned reached for her hand and curled her fingers around his.

"Della, I want you to realize I know I've not been fair to you. You've always been such a good friend, and you're always there for me. I just want you to know how much you mean to me." He pulled at her arm, forcing her to sit next to him. Now, she couldn't contain the tears that flowed from her eyes. She laid her head on his shoulder.

Ned pulled her closer finding his way to her lips. It had been a long time since they had shared a kiss and, fiancé or not, Della wasn't about to pull away.

Morning arrived all too soon for Ned Bass. As he came downstairs for breakfast, he found his father standing in front of the huge windows that looked out on the lawn of their beautiful Belle Meade home.

"Morning, Dad," Ned stated in a rather flat tone.

"Oh, good morning, son," Mr. Bass said, a forced grin on his face.
"Where's Mother?" Ned asked.

"She's still in her room," he said, his grin faltering. "I'm afraid she didn't sleep much last night."

"I guess that makes two of us," Ned replied.

Albert walked in the dining room with Ned's breakfast.

"Good morning, Albert."

"Good morning, Mr. Bass," he replied. The weight of what the day would bring could be heard in his voice as well.

Ned looked at the plate in front of him. On it was all of his favorites; two eggs over easy, biscuits with red-eye gravy, and a generous slice of country ham. Ned smiled. "What's this? I'm getting a Sunday morning breakfast on Wednesday?"

"I, well, Mrs. Bass gave the instructions for your breakfast, sir."

"Mothers. What would we do without them, Albert?"

"I don't know, sir. I'm sure," Albert said. He poured the coffee and quietly left the room.

"Do you think everyone is going to be like that today, Dad?" Ned asked nodding toward the door Albert just closed behind him.

"Oh, don't let it bother you, son," the old man said as he sat in his seat at the end of the table. "It's not every day that a man goes off to war."

Ned made an attempt to eat the breakfast that sat in front of him. After a few attempts, he pushed his plate away and settled for coffee.

"Ned, there's a few things I do want to say to you before everyone gets about this morning." Ned drew a quiet breath

"Ned, we've had our differences over the years as any father and son would have, of course, but I've been thinking. I've been rather amiss in my old age, son. It seems as if I've been so busy trying to make a name for this family, something you could carry on with, well, I believe that there are some things I've not quite been able to say to you. Sometimes, I think I was trying, but they just didn't come out the way I wanted them to." He refilled his coffee, then stepped back to the window with his cup and saucer in hand.

Ned thought his father looked a bit older today, a bit wearier. The old man had probably been up all night, too.

"I want you to know, son, that all I've done, all that we have, all I've tried to do in my life has all been for you and your mother. I realize I've gone about it in the wrong sort of way sometimes. Ned, I don't want you to think ill of me."

"Dad . . ."

"No, let me finish. I've gone about many things in the wrong way so that you could have the things that I didn't have. We weren't born into this community. We had to earn our way into it. It was important to me that you grow up with all the social amenities that life had to offer. Even in these hard times lately, we've managed better than some, maybe because I made different business decisions than others made; maybe hard work. I'm not sure at this point, but I want you to know there were many people I didn't collect rent from when I should have, as was the case of that family Bonnie asked for help on with their rent—"

"Dad . . ." Ned attempted again.

"No, let me finish," Mr. Bass said. He was still staring out of the window. "I . . . I just don't want you going away thinking of me in a certain way. I never knew how to be any other way, son. The way I am is the way my father was, and I want you to understand I'm not as hard as I pretend to be."

Ned stood from the breakfast table and walked over to his father. The cup and saucer shook in the old man's hands. His father's eyes were fixed on the floor.

"Dad," Ned said as he took the saucer from his father. "I'm the one who should be apologizing to you. You're a wonderful father, and here I am running around carousing most of the time. I've not been much help to you and, for that, I'm sorry. Dad, don't for one moment think that I'm not as proud of you as any son could be of their father."

The old man lifted his head and met his son's eyes. "And I you, son. And I you."

The platform under and around the train shed bustled with people.

There were mothers, fathers, babies, wives, uncles, aunts, and cousins. Anyone who was related to someone who was leaving for the war crowded the areas around the departing trains trying to get one last look at those in their families they knew they may never see again. The same eerie thought lurked in the back of everyone's mind. *Will this be the last time?*

Mothers cried. Fathers and sons shook hands. Everyone was hugging someone. Those too young to understand looked bewildered at the mixture of excitement and sadness. Bonnie and Mrs. Bass held onto each other tightly in the claustrophobic pressure of the crowd as they all said their last goodbyes to Ned.

"Mr. Bass? Your bag, sir," Albert said to Ned as they made their way toward the doorway of the train car.

"Thanks, Albert," Ned said, shooting the butler a serious look knowing Albert would know the thanks wasn't meant for the handling of his luggage.

"You're welcome, Mr. Bass," Albert answered, swallowing his emotion. Albert had lived with Ned all of his life. He had done many things for him throughout the years, including as he'd done the night before collecting and getting him home safely, but Albert never thought he'd be here saying goodbye to Ned as he left for war.

"I'm going to miss you, Albert," Ned said as he offered his hand. "I know you'll take care of everything just as you always do." He pulled the older man aside, dropping his voice to a whisper. "There's an envelope in the top drawer of my bureau at home. If anything should happen to me, please see that Miss Houston gets the contents of it."

"Yes, sir. That you can be assured of, sir."

Ned nodded and turned away from Albert, who was pulling a handkerchief from his suit coat. "Dad, I guess it's time for me to get on."

"Ned, son . . ." the senior Mr. Bass began.

"Dad, it's not necessary. I'll be back." The two men shook hands stiffly, then embraced. Mrs. Bass was in tears before Ned ever reached her. Mr. Bass joined her at her side for support.

"Now, Mother. I'll be fine. You've got to understand."

"Well, I don't," his mother said, as resolutely as she could, still staunch in her opposition to his choice.

"I know. But you have to try," Ned said as he put his arms around his mother. "I love you."

"Oh, Ned, please don't go, please," Mrs. Bass whispered as she held on to her son.

"I have to, Mother. You'll understand one day."

"The only thing I understand is that you are my only child. That's all I can think about."

"Yes, and your only child is doing something he has to do. Don't make this harder than it already is."

"I'm sorry, son. I love you. You take care of yourself. Promise me," his mother said as her bottom lip began to quiver. Ned knew it was time for him to end this conversation. Ned's mother had made a lifetime of being strong. No matter what Ned's father managed to do, Mrs. Bass always kept her head high and her dignity intact. Ned knew this was way too much for her. He glanced at his father, who immediately put his hands on his wife's thin shoulders, pulling her gently toward him.

Ned turned to Bonnie, who was standing with her hands clasped in front of her face, looking horrified at the scene unfolding in front of her eyes. Tears pooled in her eyes and rolled down her face. Ned pulled his handkerchief from his pocket. He gently pulled her hands away from her face and dabbed at the tears.

"Okay, kitten, you promised you wouldn't cry, for Mother's sake. Remember?" Ned said quietly.

Bonnie threw her arms around his neck. "I'm sorry. I can't seem to stop them," she whispered to Ned as she held on tightly.

Ned smiled. "It's all right. I don't suppose I'd want someone who wants to be my wife not to cry for me."

Bonnie pulled away slowly. Ned seeing the obvious shock on her face.

Regret immediately clawed its way into Ned's heart. He felt badly enough about last night, which of course neither Bonnie nor Ned's parents knew anything about. As usual, Albert's discreet qualities increased his already incalculable worth in Ned's eyes.

"Ned, I . . ." Bonnie began.

"Shhhhh. It's okay. Everything will be okay," Ned tried to assure her as he studied her face, stroked her coppery hair, gazing into her cool green eyes, taking in as much as he could.

"Will it be okay, Ned? Will anything ever be the same?" Bonnie asked, pensively. Ned knew she was speaking both for their relationship and for the whole of the country.

"I hope so. That's why I'm going." Ned looked around the platform at the sea of people all having the same conversation. "That's why we're all going," he said, trying to smile.

Bonnie leaned against his chest and drew in a long, shaky breath. She smelled the familiar smell of him. She was so used to it by now. Could it be she just took it for granted? Suddenly, Bonnie wasn't sure the decision she made last night was the right one.

"Ned, I love you. I know you're not really sure of that—"

"Bonnie," Ned stopped her. "I understand. Really, I do. I know you want everything to be just right," he said quietly to her as he wrapped his arms around her waist. "I love you. I want you to be happy. If waiting until this is all over will make you happy, then that's what I want, too."

Bonnie dropped her head to his shoulder again as tears continued to drip down her face. Ned slowly lifted her chin to look at him.

"I'll be back, and you will be Mrs. Ned Bass. Is that understood?"

"Aye aye, Captain," Bonnie said, trying to manage a smile. Ned tried to not to look directly into her eyes, but couldn't help it. A knot formed in his throat.

"I love you, Bonnie," he said, kissing her on the mouth just as he had the night before. This time, Bonnie kissed him back. He slowly pulled away from her as he heard the conductor call for his train to load.

Ned held her hand as long as he could before he turned to his mother, whose face was buried in her husband's coat. Ned leaned down and kissed her cheek as he shook his father's hand.

"Goodbye, son," Carlton Bass said as a tear made its way down the worn flesh of the old man's cheek.

"Goodbye, Dad," Ned said. He started for the train, then turned slowly and put his arms around both his mother and father.

As he pulled away, he put his arms around Albert and patted him solidly on the back. "Take care of Mother and Father, Albert. And yourself," he said.

"Of course, sir. You take care of yourself," Albert sniffled as the hug turned to a hearty handshake. Ned turned once again and looked at Bonnie. He knew they had no time for another embrace. He blew her a kiss.

"Bye, Sweet Face. I love you."

Bonnie blew him a kiss back and mouthed *I love you* back to him.

Ned jumped onto the train as the conductor removed the step and, within minutes, he was on his way to training camp.

Nell came up behind Bonnie just as the train pulled away. She waved to Ned, who was leaning out of the window to get one last look.

"Oh, honey, I'm sorry I'm late. I wanted to say goodbye. The Lunch Room is packed," Nell said, wrapping an arm around Bonnie's waist. Bonnie stood like stone with her hands clasped together again pressed against her face with her eyes closed.

"Oh, Bonnie. I'm sorry, honey. It's okay." Nell pulled Bonnie to her. "He'll be back. You just wait and see. He'll be back."

The small band of this family, like all of the others who stood on the platform as the train made its way out of sight, stood numb and dumbstruck, the same thought running through every mind, *What do we do now?* Slowly, one by one, they began to depart putting one foot in front of the other doing the only they knew to do; going on about the business of their day.

"C'mon, doll, you need to just go on home for a while," Nell said to Bonnie.

"No, I can't. I have to go to work," Bonnie said as she put her handkerchief to her eyes and face. She said her goodbyes to Ned's family and informed them she had to go to work at Loveman's today.

Mr. Bass cleared his throat. "If you would like, I could call Mr.

Berger and ask if he could see to give you the day off considering the weight of your burden."

"No, thank you, Mr. Bass. I'll be better off working. I can't just sit and think about it but thank you. I should go to work."

"As you will. Come now, let's get on with the day," he said as cheerfully as he could muster to his wife.

"I better get back to the counter before Charlie sends out a search party for me," Nell said. She grabbed Bonnie's hand, pulling her up the stairs and inside the Lunch Room . Together, they watched the Basses walk by, making their way slowly through the lobby of the station to their car.

"Bonnie," Nell said when they were gone, "are you sure you want to go to work? Don't you think you need to stay home? Go spend the day with Miss Annie. I think you need to."

"No, I can't," Bonnie said. She blew her nose. "I'm fine. I really need to work. I'll go crazy if I sit at home and think about it."

"All right. Well, I'll see you later, I guess."

"I probably won't be back down for lunch, Nell. I'll see you tonight."

"Keep your chin up. You hear?" Nell hugged her.

"Thanks, Nell, I'll try," Bonnie said as she opened the door to the Lunch Room to make her way up to Loveman's.

As the door swung shut, she heard Charlie yelling for Nell.

"Keep your pants on. I'm comin'!" Nell screamed back at him.

Bonnie smiled. At least some things would never change.

Ned sat back on the bench on the train full of recruits, all of them headed to different places and all for the same reason. No one spoke. The incessant click and clack of the train's movement against the tracks comfortably filled the silence. All of them were reflecting, thinking, doing their best to remember every detail, every smell of home. Most of them knew it might be a long time before they ever saw it again. Some craned to look out the window for one last look. Some just sat, feeling awkward and unsure of their destiny.

Finally, one by one, they lit cigarettes and slowly began to talk among themselves. Ned didn't feel like talking. His head hurt, and he felt terrible. He thought about the night before. He remembered Della. He remembered enough to make him feel like a perfect heel. He had avoided going to see Della for that very reason. It wasn't fair to her. Here he was engaged to be married, going off to war, and what did he do but run straight over there the night before he was to leave.

"Ahhhhh," he said disgustingly to himself as he flipped his cigarette out the window of the moving train. "You big dope. What have you done?"

Meanwhile, the train rocked, swayed, and clicked as it began to pick up speed.

Above The Stables in her room, Della looked out of her window on the alley below and thought about going to the train station. She would just watch from a spot where she couldn't be noticed and see if she could find him. She wanted just one more look but knew she couldn't do that.

Della opened her dresser and took out the picture she had put away some time back. She promised herself she'd never take it out again. It was from years ago, on the beach in Florida. That was the last trip they ever took together. Della smiled nostalgically. She and Ned always had fun together, but that wasn't what counted when it came to spending his life with someone. In Ned's position, some judged you by who you were married to, not whether you were happy. She knew that even if he were unhappily married, it would never make it right for him to marry someone like her, even if she was the only woman who understood him.

Della set the picture on the top of her dresser. She knew she could no longer act as if she didn't love him, as if he wasn't the most important person in her life. No longer would she pretend for the sake of others. From this point on, she decided, she wasn't going to hide it for anyone's sake.

On Thursday, December 11, Hitler declared war on the United States.

America was now at war on two fronts.

CHAPTER TWENTY-FOUR

"I can't wait to see you!"

B ONNIE KNEW THAT from this point on, she wouldn't be working much at Loveman's. With the war effort at full steam, Bonnie would be spending most of her time at the station. She knew it was time for her to move back in with the Parkers, but didn't think it would be so soon after Ned's departure.

"Nell, you could stay at the Parkers', too. They won't mind. We can ride the bus down to the station."

"Oh no, I don't think so. Me and the Reverend? I mean, I don't know," Nell said nervously.

Charlie, listening to them from his position over the grill shouted, "Reckon he'd have to meet your dates before you could go out with them, Nell!"

"Yeah, yeah," Nell quipped over her shoulder. "Go ahead and laugh."

"Mrs. Greenfield has been bugging me that she needs me down here full time," Bonnie said thoughtfully. "Maybe if I went to live with the Reverend and Miss Annie I could afford to volunteer full time until the war is over, of course. I'm sure they wouldn't mind if we stayed with them."

"Hey, look, sweetie. I know the Parkers are like family to you and all, but I don't think I could make that kind of change. Look, if you need to go back and live with them for a while so that you can be down here full time for the guys and all, it's okay with me. Listen, I can find a place, no problem. We'd probably get to see each other more than we do now. At least you'd be here during the day to keep me company. With you working during the day and at night, I hardly get to see you anymore."

"Hey Nell, grilled cheese is up!" Charlie yelled.

"Oh, there's your lunch. We'll figure something out, honey. Don't worry. Everything will be all right."

Nell retrieved Bonnie's lunch and set the plate down in front of her.

"I retrieved something else while I was home," Nell said. She pulled an envelope out of her apron and handed it to Bonnie. "It's a letter from Ned."

"A letter! Nell, why didn't you tell me?"

"I wanted to surprise you."

"That's why you had me rush down here," Bonnie said as she carefully opened the worn envelope.

"So where do you think he is?" Nell asked inquisitively.

"I don't know, but it's postmarked England." Bonnie quickly began to read the letter aloud.

"*Dearest Bonnie*," she began with a smile. "*It's dark and rainy. That's about all I can say as far as what it's like here. We went out today and lost a few men.*" Bonnie looked up sadly at Nell. "That must be just horrible for them, Nell."

"Hey, Nell, got some lunches up. Are we working today or not?"

"You read your letter. Looks like I've got some hungry mouths to feed."

Bonnie continued to read in silence.

This place is beginning to look more like hell every day, Bonnie. I miss you terribly. The reason I'm writing to you is to tell you that I'll be coming home soon.

"Nell! Ned says he's coming home!" Bonnie shouted across the Lunch Room.

It's just for a visit. Seems like after so many runs, we get a reprieve. I need it. I need to see you. I need to wrap my arms around you and feel you next to me. I want you to think about something. What we talked about the day before I left. Being away from you makes me realize even more that we should have gotten married before I left. I know I've said it before in my previous letters, but I can't stand it, Bonnie. I need to know that you want to be my wife. I want to get married when I come home.

It won't be an extended stay, I'm afraid, but we can manage. I know you want to wait, but I can't. I think about your face all of the time. Your smile, your laugh, the way you walk, your voice. It echoes in my mind. Through all of the noise over here, all of the death, I can only think about you.

I've written to Mother and Father and asked for them to make arrangements with Judge Whitaker. You can move into the house with them until all of this is over, and when I come home, we'll get a house, and we'll be so happy. I realize you want it to be a big ceremony and all, but Bonnie, this is not going to be an easy war. It's been a year already. The fighting goes on and on and, well, a lot of men never make it back. I couldn't go back without knowing, without having you as my wife.

Well, lights out, my darling. I hope this letter finds you well and not working too hard with your Red Cross duties. You know to let Mother and Father know if you need anything at all. They wrote and told me you came for dinner and that you are keeping in touch when you can. I love you, Bonnie. Please give it some thought, and we'll talk when I get there. I'm leaving the second of December, and should be there by Christmas. I can't wait to see you. What a wonderful Christmas it will be!

With all of my heart, Ned.

"When's he coming in?" Nell asked as she whizzed by with a coffeepot in hand.

"He'll be here by Christmas," Bonnie murmured.

"What's the matter? Anything wrong? Looks like something took the wind clear out of your sails," Nell asked.

"He wants to get married when he comes home for Christmas."

"Oh," Nell said somberly. "Look, honey, he's got to be some kinda scared over there. We can't know what it's like for him. He's probably scared and wants to hurry up and get it over with. But look, if you don't want to get married yet, well, you do what your heart tells you to do. You're good at that."

"Nell, I don't know what to do. He wants me to get married, and he wants me to live with his folks until the war is over! I can't do that. I can barely visit, I'm so uncomfortable there. How can I live there? He's been away for over a year. We have to get to know each other again. I feel like everything in my life would change so drastically. How can he rush me into this?"

"Because, honey, he's a man with little time. I've seen them when they come back. It's like they've walked through a door into another world. When they get back, they try to stuff as much as they can into the short time they're here. You can't blame them. It must be awful what they see and what they have to do, losing friends one after another."

"I know. I don't mean to be selfish; it's just . . . I'm just not sure."

"Look, like I said, follow your heart. You always do. That's the only thing you can do, right?"

"I guess," Bonnie said as she lowered the letter into her lap and sat back on her stool at the counter. "He'll never forgive me if I say no this time."

"He'll have to if he wants to keep you, won't he?" Nell said, trying to cheer her up. "Look, he's coming home! He'll be here in less than a week. That's good news. Cross that other bridge when you come to it, okay?"

"Always trying to cheer me up, aren't you?"

"Somebody's gotta have that job. I'm glad it's me," Nell said, patting Bonnie's hand.

"Thanks, Nell," Bonnie said with a smile. "Wrap this up for me, and I'll take it back to work. I'll be down here after work."

"All right. See you later."

Bonnie gathered her bag and gloves and headed back up to Loveman's to finish the day before returning to her Red Cross duties for the night. Mrs. Greenfield saw her in the lobby.

"Bonnie? Bonnie!" Mrs. Greenfield called as she hurried over. "Bonnie, dear. I'm glad I ran into you. We have an enormous amount of men coming through here tonight. Do you have any idea if Mr. Berger would let you get down early? I hate to ask, but Marilyn is at home and not feeling well. Could you?"

"I'll try, Mrs. Greenfield."

"Thank you, dear. See you later," she said, hurrying off to meet her tasks.

Bonnie lumbered slowly back to Loveman's.

Her mind wandered back to the last night that she had spent with Ned. How intense he'd been, how much he'd drank. She thought about the next day, the day she said goodbye at the train station. Had he been sarcastic or sincere? She'd thought about him all the time over the year wondering, worrying, writing as often as possible, waiting for his letters, but the thought of getting married in such a hurry—why was she so opposed to that? Why? After all, she was in love with him. She had to face the fact that when he went back, he may never come home, then she would be a widow at thirty, or, if she didn't marry him, she might end up an old maid. Why couldn't she make up her mind? Why did it have to be such a big deal?

She thought about Ned's parents. They had been so kind since Ned left for the war. Even Ned's father had gone out of his way to be considerate. He would stop by the store or come by the station to check on her, always talking about the last letter he'd received and comparing information with Ned's last letter trying to figure out what he was doing, but she couldn't live with them. How could she? Bonnie's mind drifted to her Mother. She smiled. Lizzie McCaverty, a woman of few words, but always wise.

Bonnie remembered when she'd tried to stop her from going to see

Calvin after she had recovered from the gunshot wounds, the day she wanted to tell him how she felt about him. Lizzie had known it was the wrong thing for Bonnie to do. She had known Bonnie would get hurt, but how had she known? Had Calvin confided in her?

Calvin . . . why did her mind always drift back to Calvin when she was alone? He couldn't have anything to do with why she wouldn't marry Ned right away. After all, she had agreed to marry Ned. It was just a matter of wanting to do it the right way. Bonnie had witnessed so many disappointments. She decided to call Lizzie. She would know whether it was the right thing for her to do just by the tone in Lizzie's voice.

Ned leaned against the chalkboard in the command room, lit a cigarette, and waited for his commanding officer to join him. It had been a long flight, and he was dead tired. The raid on Schweinfurt had taken two planes in his group and over sixty out of a total of 376 bombers. Now, he was waiting to tell his captain his version of what had happened. He stood at attention as Commander Walker entered the room.

"At ease, Captain Bass. Sit down. Let's have a look at your report," the commander said as he pulled a chair to the desk at the front of the room.

"From the looks of this report, it seems like everyone has the same story. Lieutenants Brackard and Smiley took a bad hit."

"Yes, sir. We had finished the mission, sir, and were preparing to turn home when they started shooting at us from nowhere. We didn't think there was anything left down there to shoot at us. I would never have thought those factories would have been so heavily guarded. They got Brackard and Smiley on the right flank of the formation. The rest of us got out of range fast enough." Ned hung his head. "They were the last in and the last to release their load. It just came out of nowhere. We didn't even know those guns were there, sir."

"I understand. Reconnaissance didn't uncover that location if they came from where you pinpointed them."

"It's the only point they could have come from, sir. It's like they knew we were coming this time. Fighters were coming from all directions."

"We made a mistake, Lieutenant. Maybe they had moved in some new artillery since our last report before the mission. I don't know," the commander said, rubbing his eyes. "We've lost over sixty planes." He leaned back in his chair. "Thank you. That's all. I just wanted to get everyone's report while it was fresh on your minds."

Ned stood, saluted the commander, and turned to leave the room.

"You're getting ready for some R & R after this mission, aren't you?" the commander called from behind him. Ned felt his shoulders relax a bit.

"Yes, sir. I'm looking forward to it, sir. Thirty days. I haven't been home since I joined up right after Pearl. With all the training and straight over here, I never had time. It's been over a year now."

"I hear you're hoping to get married while back home."

"Yes, sir. That is, I hope so. She wants to wait until all of this is over. Needless to say, I don't want to. I wanted to marry her before I left, but she was adamant that we wait. By the time I get there, I'll have about a week to change her mind and get back."

"Well, good luck, son. You deserve some time off. You pilots who joined up when this started sure saved us quite a bit of time getting new pilots in the air. You deserve a break. How many missions have you flown?"

"Since I got here, twenty-six, sir."

"I would think you would rotate back to the States for a training assignment."

"No, sir. As long as they'll let me fly, I'll fight."

"Don't get me wrong. I need you here. We've had so many losses here lately. Do you have any idea why?"

"Speaking openly, sir?"

"Of course."

"If you ask me, I believe I'm not the only one who's tired. We're all tired. The bombing runs seem to be getting longer and longer. It's taking more out of the pilots, sir. The night raids were particularly difficult, as I'm sure you're aware. I know this isn't going to be a hasty war, but my squadron has been at it straight since we got here. The mechanics, the crews, the pilots, we all need a break. I'm not complaining, sir. I know we have it better than some do, but mistakes are made unwillingly when men are as tired as they are. Just a little time off would help."

The commander smiled. "Thanks. You're right," he said as he stood from the little desk and walked to his office. "I'm tired myself. I'll recommend it."

"The men will be grateful. I'm sure."

"Thanks for your honesty. You tell that girl she's getting a smart captain. She better act now."

"Thank you, sir. I'll tell her. I only hope she agrees."

"Goodnight," the commander said as he closed the door to his office.

"Goodnight, sir."

Ned looked around the room. He'd been there with Brackard and Smiley just this morning. He tipped the chairs, where the two men ritually sat, against the chairs in front of them.

He didn't have to.

No one else would sit there until someone had been sent to take their place.

B ONNIE WALKED OUT to the little Red Cross hut with her coat wrapped tightly around her. The wind had picked up, and it was fiercely cold outside. She quickly opened the door and shut it behind her. At the sound, Mrs. Greenfield looked up from her work.

"Bonnie," she said, "you look so tired. I'm sorry we couldn't do without you tonight. I just got word we've got a couple of troop trains coming through. Quite a few servicemen on Christmas leave it seems, on their way home. At least that's better than seeing them off."

"Yes, ma'am. It is," Bonnie agreed.

"I've got to get home and get some rest. Marilyn will be here soon to help you. I just got a fresh load of pies here, and there's fresh coffee on. I'll send someone to relieve you as soon as I can. When is Ned getting here?"

"It should be tomorrow sometime."

"I'm sure you're so excited. Now, while he's here, you're not to worry about this place. We'll get someone in to help out. You enjoy your Mr. Bass while you can."

"You never know when you'll ever see them again," Bonnie said out loud, seeming to finish Mrs. Greenfield's thoughts. "I'm sorry, Mrs. Greenfield. I know you didn't mean it that way. I guess it's just seeing all these . . . all this death returning to us. It just came out. I'm sorry."

"No need to apologize, dear. We all feel that way of course. It's just better if we don't say it out loud."

"Yes, ma'am," Bonnie said, regretful she had said what she was thinking. She wondered if she would ever come to the place where her brain engaged before her mouth did.

"Well, I'm off now. You girls call if you need anything."

"We'll be fine. You go get some rest now," Bonnie said. Mrs. Greenfield quickly left the small hut that stood outside by the tracks and made her way to the station.

"Brother, why do I always stick my foot in my mouth?" Bonnie asked herself as she readied the cups for coffee on a tray and began to cut the pies. She'd been extremely irritable today. She was excited that Ned would be here soon, but also nervous. It had been so long. Had he changed much? Did he still look the same? Bonnie tried to shrug off her thoughts and get on with her duties. The timing of the troop trains was never revealed to them, so they always had to be ready.

Marilyn hurried in around seven o'clock and told Bonnie she thought there was a troop train on the tracks. The men down the track always tried to send word best they could when they knew that an oncoming train was full of soldiers. Before long, Bonnie and Marilyn were out on the tracks, passing out pie and coffee for those who would remain on the trains to farther destinations.

Soon, the trains were on their way again. Bonnie went inside the station lobby to help with some of the incoming soldiers. The minute she walked in, she noticed there were two men on crutches looking for a phone.

"Can I help you, Sergeant?" Bonnie asked.

"Well, yes, you can. We need to get to a phone. Can you help us?" the Sergeant said, as a pleasant grin began forming on his face. "My, you're the prettiest thing I've seen in a year!"

"Now, now, Sergeant. I'm just the first girl you've seen in a year. There's plenty more where I came from. Besides, I'm taken."

"Drat. Day late and a dollar short. The story of my life," the sergeant joked.

"The phone's right over here. Would you like for me to make the connection for you?"

"Naw, I can manage. Just help my friend here while I make the call."

"Sure, I'll be glad to," Bonnie said as she helped the other man over to the bench to sit down.

"I sure would like a cigarette," the private intimated. "I haven't had a cigarette the whole train ride. Think you could roust me up one, ma'am?"

"Sure, you sit there. I'll be right back," Bonnie said as she walked up to the USO room at the front of the station to borrow a cigarette from one of the girls in there.

As she walked back across the floor of the lobby, the sergeant joined his friend on the bench. He sat down, and they both gladly accepted a cigarette from the pack she offered.

"A cigarette and a pretty girl. Now I know I'm home!"

"Not quite. I wouldn't call Union Station home," Bonnie said as she looked around the lobby. "Where are you boys headed?"

"I'm headed for Cookeville," the sergeant replied, "and he's headed for Springfield. We met up on the train on the way down here. Found out we was both from Tennessee and sparked up a conversation."

"Did you get your party on the line?" Bonnie asked.

"Yes, ma'am. I got a friend here in town, and he's going to come by and pick us up. We're going to have some fun before the ride home!"

"Well, you boys just be careful. Don't let things get out of hand."

"Yes, ma'am, we'll be real good." The two men laughed.

"Yeah, well. Don't have *too much* fun. Now, you two just yell if you need anything. I've got to see to some of the other men," Bonnie said as she got ready to head back to the train shed.

She walked through the door that led outside and began to make her way down the steps to the tracks and the little hut. She pulled her coat closer as the wind whipped around the side of the building.

"Why does it have to be so cold?" she said to herself, pulling her collar around her neck and looking down to see where she was stepping. As she did, she noticed a man in uniform standing in the shadows on the landing outside the entrance.

"May I help you?" she asked him.

"You can if you promise to marry me," he said, stepping out into the light.

"Ned . . ." Bonnie said, steading herself on the railing of the steps. Ned ran to catch her.

"Ned! Ned!" Bonnie leapt into his arms.

"Bonnie," Ned whispered as he held her for the first time in over a year. "I . . . I couldn't wait to see you again. I missed you more than you could know."

Bonnie tried to pull away to get a better look at him. Ned pulled her back to him, his face still buried in her neck.

"No, don't pull away. Just let me hold you. Oh, that smell, that wonderful smell," he whispered.

"Ned . . ."

Bonnie finally pulled him away and held his face in her hands. "You're home. Look at you," she said as she studied his face. "Oh, Ned, you're home," she said as she fell back into his arms.

"Let me look at you."

"Oh, you're so bad. I didn't think you were coming in until tomorrow. Look at me," she said wiping tears from her face with the back of her hand. "I look just awful!"

"Never," he said. "You're the best-looking thing I've seen in a year," he said, as he pulled her close again.

The wind picked up again, forcing them to move closer to the door entering the lobby. Ned pulled her close. He kissed her mouth, her face, her eyes, her neck.

"Ned," Bonnie said as she tried to pull away. "They're going to lock you up before you even get home if you keep that up."

"I don't care," he said, kissing her again.

"C'mon, let's get in out of this cold," Bonnie urged as she pulled him up the stairs and into the lobby. As soon as they were in the door, Ned wrapped his arms around her and kissed her again. He was like a hungry man who hadn't had a meal in a long time.

When he stopped for breath, Bonnie took the opportunity to speak. "How long have you been here?"

"I got off the last train. I thought you might be working, so I snuck around so I could watch you for a while."

Bonnie slapped him against his lapel. "You bad boy!"

"You're even more beautiful than I remember," Ned said as he looked directly into her eyes. "I've missed you so much, Bonnie."

"I've missed you, too," she said with a warm smile. Bonnie began to relax. The surprise of seeing him without warning had actually put off her nervousness about seeing him again. Now here he was, the same old Ned. He hadn't changed, and she was glad to see him.

"Have you thought about what I said in the letter?" he asked quickly, hoping to get the answer he wanted right off the bat.

"Ned, we have time to talk later. Have you let your parents know you're here?"

Bonnie hoped Ned hadn't noticed how quickly she tried to change the subject.

"No, I haven't called them yet. I wanted to see you first," Ned said pulling a cigarette out and lighting it.

"They'll be so surprised! Let me go and tell Marilyn you're here. I don't know if I could leave right now, Ned. We have quite a few troop trains coming through tonight. There's lots of men coming in for Christmas. It's been so busy since the first of December."

"I know. I shouldn't have surprised you like that, I guess. I just couldn't wait."

Bonnie stood on her tiptoes and softly kissed Ned's lips. "I'm just glad you're here."

The tradition in the Bass house was to have a quiet family dinner together the night before Christmas Eve. The next night would be a constant trail of people in and out of the Bass home during their annual Christmas Eve party.

It was early, and Ned had already had too much to drink.

"Ned, dear, have you and Bonnie decided on another date yet?" Mrs. Bass asked. She observed Bonnie as she winced.

"I'm glad you asked that, Mother. I'd like to make a toast," Ned said as he raised his glass and stood at his place at the table.

"I'd like to make a toast to my beautiful fiancée, the ever loyal, ever dedicated Bonnie McCaverty. She assures me that she'll wait for me forever if that's what it takes. Forever, for I may be overseas forever, if this war ever ends . . ." Ned ranted. Mr. Bass stood.

"Ned . . ." he tried to interrupt.

"No, Dad, let me finish!" Ned said abruptly. "She'll wait. We'll wait. No, we won't be getting married while I'm here at home. She'll wait. She's assured me. Let's drink to my fiancé, Bonnie."

Bonnie gritted her teeth through the rest of Ned's soliloquy. She knew that his speech stemmed from the last words they had before he dropped her off the night before. She had tried her best to convince him again of her insistence on waiting until the war was over to marry, but Ned wasn't accepting her arguments. She had done everything to try to make him see her point of view, but to no avail. Now, he was making sure everyone at the table knew how he felt about it.

When he finished speaking, Ned hung his head, clumsily placing his glass on the table, turned, and walked out of the room. Albert immediately entered the room to begin his duties, removing plates from the table. Mr. Bass followed Ned to the library. Bonnie and Mrs. Bass sat at the table, alone.

"Bonnie," Mrs. Bass said soothingly, "now don't let Ned upset you, dear. He's just tired."

Bonnie stood, unable to contain herself any longer. She threw her napkin onto the table. "I just can't make him understand! I tried. He just won't accept it.

"I just want it to be right. I don't want to get married in the middle of this horrible war. I see it every day; mothers and fathers coming to fetch the bodies of their sons, wives sitting in the station, broken-hearted, knowing their husbands are never coming home. Why can't I make him understand that?"

"Bonnie, come with me, dear. Let's have a talk," Mrs. Bass said as she stood and motioned for Bonnie to follow. The two of them walked to the front of the house into the large living room. Mrs. Bass motioned for Bonnie to sit. Albert, with his usual promptness, entered behind them.

"May I get you ladies anything?" he politely asked, as if it were any other normal day in the Bass household.

"No. We're fine, Albert. Thank you."

"Bonnie," Mrs. Bass continued after Albert slid the big oak doors shut behind him, "I believe I need to say something here. You have to understand something about Ned. He's our only son; therefore, he's used to having his way. All of his life, Ned has gone about as if the world were his. When he saw something he wanted, he simply went after it. Just like his father, he usually got it.

"Don't misunderstand me, dear. Ned is a good man. You know that and so do I, but I'm afraid he's a little spoiled. It's our fault, I guess," Mrs. Bass said as she pulled the sheers back to look out on the lawn of their spacious home. "We just wanted him to have the best. Now, I'm afraid with the seriousness of the war and his love for you, he only sees what he wants, to be married to you. Please try to be patient with him, Bonnie. Ned is a wonderful man, and I believe the war has changed him quite a bit. We'll never know what those men go through. I was selfish at first myself. I didn't want him to go, but now I understand. I see it in his eyes. He's proud of what he's done and rightly so. But I believe Ned feels like he won't be complete until he has married you.

"Try not to be angry with him," she finished with a smile as she sat next to Bonnie on the sofa. "He's just a desperate man right now."

"I'm sorry, Mrs. Bass. I'm not trying to hurt Ned. I do love him."

"Oh I'm sure you do, Bonnie," Mrs. Bass said as she patted Bonnie's hands, "I'm sure you do. We just have to be patient with him while he's with us. Now, I think what we need is a brandy."

"Brandy?" Bonnie asked, rather confused. "Oh, Mrs. Bass, I don't drink."

"I understand, Bonnie, but in times like these us women need a little something for the nerves, too," she said as she strode to the side table and poured a dark brown liquid into two glasses, then delivered one to Bonnie.

"Here we go, my dear. Just take a little sip and try not to think about all that's happened tonight. Maybe we can all get back to dinner."

Just then, Mr. Bass pulled the heavy door back and entered the room without pulling it shut behind him. "Oh, here you two are. Well, Ned has just left us. He said he needed to be alone."

"Alone?" Bonnie said as she bolted to her feet. "Where did he go?"

"He said he was going out. Look, you understand, Bonnie. He's been away for a long time. He just needs to blow off some steam. Don't worry, I'll have Albert drive you home," he said as he poured himself a brandy.

"Mr. Bass, I hope you're not upset with me," Bonnie said, once again feeling the need to defend herself.

"No, Bonnie, I think Ned just needs some time alone. He'll be fine. Albert!"

Albert appeared.

"Please drive Miss McCaverty to her residence. I'm afraid we won't be finishing supper tonight."

Ned drove the streets of Nashville, stopping here and there for a drink, trying his best to resist the urge to stop by The Stables. His last visit with Della had only served to make a mess of things, and he didn't want to give in to his desire to see her.

Della had always been the one who Ned ran to when he needed to talk. She was always there and, as always, understood him better than anyone ever had. He could say anything to her. If there was anyone in the world who knew Ned Bass, it was Della, which is exactly what Ned wanted at the moment; someone to listen, someone who understood him better than he understood himself.

Around midnight, Ned found himself walking into The Stables against his better judgment. Although the liquor had dulled his senses, Ned's heart still raced in his chest as he made his way through the doorway and into the crowded bar.

Della stood at the far end of the bar minding the business of a packed bar complete with crowds of thirsty servicemen on leave. The minute Ned walked through the doorway her eyes fell on him. It was almost as if she knew he would be walking through any moment, her eyes landed singularly on him. She watched as Ned pulled his hat from his head, his eyes scanning the crowd absently. As his eyes passed over the bar, his gaze ultimately landed on her. The look in her eyes caused Ned's heart to pierce.

They stood there smiling at one another for what seemed like an eternity. Neither moved from where they stood. Finally, almost at the exact same moment, they began to move toward one another, their eyes fixed. In the middle of the crowd, they met. Della's arms wrapped around his neck and his around her waist. Their lips met without hesitation. At that moment, there was no one else in the busy barroom—no one but the two of them.

Moments later, upstairs in Della's room, she poured a drink. Neither spoke. Della held Ned's drink while he removed the jacket of his uniform, loosening his tie. He took the drink she offered him, setting it on the table next to the bed. He cupped Della's face in his hands. Tears welled in her eyes. She tried to turn from him. Instead, Ned pulled her back to him.

"You shouldn't be here," Della whispered as Ned's mouth found her lips and began to kiss her softly.

Ned looked into her eyes. "I tried to stay away."

"I'm glad you couldn't."

The next day was Christmas Eve. Bonnie woke not knowing quite what to do with herself. She had been excused from her duties at the station for the time that Ned was on leave, and she and Ned had made plans for the day; however, as of noon, she hadn't heard from him.

Ned pulled into the driveway at his parents' home around that time, his head slowly clearing from the night before. Memories of the previous night were flooding back to him. He sat in the car, wishing he didn't have to face his parents, but knew he might as well get it over with. He needed to check in with Bonnie, too. He had some reparations to make, and it wasn't going to be enjoyable.

"Have you heard from Ned yet?" Nell asked when Bonnie answered the phone at the parsonage. She was still busy with lunch even though it was after two o'clock in the afternoon.

"No, I haven't. I'm about to give up," Bonnie replied.

"Oh honey, don't be angry. He was just out blowing off steam. They all do it when they're home trying to pack in as much as they can in as short a time as possible."

"Blowing off steam; that's what everyone keeps saying. I just know Ned's not acting like himself. I've never seen him so moody. I think it's not very gentlemanly of him to keep me waiting like this without even a phone call."

"I know, sweetie, but he'll show. Give him some time. Okay, I gotta go. Man alive, we're really cookin' today. I think everybody's trying to get somewhere before Christmas Eve. Listen, if you get bored, c'mon down, and we'll try to spread some cheer around here."

"All right. If he doesn't call soon, I'll be down."

"Bonnie, was that Ned?" Annie asked as Bonnie placed the receiver back onto the cradle.

"No, ma'am." She sighed. "I just don't understand, Miss Annie. Why does he have to be so angry with me? All I'm asking is to wait until we can have a right church wedding. I want Daddy to give me away. I want Mama and Emma and Nettie all to come. Of course, I want Reverend Frank to marry us. What's so wrong with wanting everything to be just right?"

"Nothing, dear. Our wedding day is a special thing for us girls. I understand Ned's feelings, but you have yours, too. If that's the way you feel, he'll just have to understand. I'm sure he will. He knows deep inside why you feel like you do. I believe his mother was right when she said he's used to having his way. He'll come around."

"I think he will, too. I'm just tired of waiting. He's going to be leaving after Christmas. He's been here almost two weeks, and he seems to just be getting madder and madder.

"Well, I'm not going to sit here any longer," she fumed. "When and if Mr. Bass calls, I'll be down at the station." Bonnie went to the closet for her coat and hat.

"Let me drive you down there, Bonnie. I need to pick up a few things for tomorrow's dinner."

Just as they reached the car, the phone rang inside the parsonage.

By five o'clock, Nell was finished cleaning from a busy day. She decided to join Bonnie at the front of the station in the USO lounge. By the time she got there, a large crowd had gathered around the piano. Bonnie was seated on the bench with Maryanne. The crowd sang Christmas carols as some waited for trains, some waited for their rides, and others waited for nothing more than the refreshing sound of the girls' voices.

Nell smiled as she looked at her little friend. Bonnie always seemed her happiest when she was in the station. She spent all of her days there and some of her nights on weekends. Nell never quite understood her dedication, but there she sat, smiling happily. Bonnie was at her best when she was trying to make someone else happy. Making herself happy was another thing altogether.

"I hope I'm not too late to hear my favorite song," Nell said leaning over the piano.

"No, you're not," Bonnie replied, positioning her fingers on the keys. "I waited just for you so that you could help me."

Nell made her way over to Bonnie. Maryanne stood next to her. They took their places, as they had so many times during the past month and every Christmas since 1941. There had been a lot of men coming home on leave, but more were being shipped out. The pace had quickened the last few months and only seemed to grow worse as the buildup of men and machinery made its way to Europe.

As Bonnie began to play, the crowd grew silent. The regulars had heard the song many times over, but they never seemed to grow tired of it.

Bonnie began to sing. Nell and Maryanne followed her cue singing the words to *White Christmas*; their voices resounding through the cavernous station.

Many in the station stopped what they were doing to listen as the girls sang. The song resounded through the cavernous station. Even those in the offices upstairs stepped out onto the balcony to listen. A few hurried to the front room just to watch. As they filed into the room, Ned made his way in, unnoticed.

The girls sang the last line in perfect sweet harmony. Many in the room dabbed their eyes, finding a comforting hand to hold. There was an unspoken silence as everyone thought about the men and women they knew who were overseas. As usual, someone began clapping, and everyone joined in another chorus as the girls sang it one more time.

When it was over and people began to go about their business, Ned made his way to the piano. "Hi, there, Sweet Face," he said to Bonnie.

"Hello," she answered indifferently as she made her way from behind the piano. Maryanne moved to the bench and began to play.

"I thought I would find you here."

"I've been here for a while. We like to sing when we can find the time."

"That was beautiful, Bonnie. Look, I'm sorry about last night. I'm afraid I slept a good deal of the morning away. Can you forgive me?" Ned asked bashfully.

"Well, probably. That is, if you promise not to do that again."

"I promise," Ned said as he moved closer to Bonnie and put his arms around her. "I don't know what's wrong with me, Bonnie," he added. "I guess I, well . . ."

"Never mind. Let's forget about it, okay?" Bonnie said, realizing how hard it must be for him, knowing he had to leave again.

"Can we try it again? Mother is all ready for Christmas Eve, and I've promised to not be a heel. She's excited and wants the both of us there."

"Okay. Could you take me back to the parsonage and let me change clothes?"

"Sure."

"Just let me say goodbye to Nell."

"All right. I'll get the car."

"Nell? Nell!" Bonnie said as she motioned her away from the piano. "We're going to the house. I just wanted to wish you a Merry Christmas."

"Thank you, doll," Nell said with a big smile. "You have a good time with Ned.

"Obviously, prince charming is back."

"Yes. I think he feels bad enough without me adding to it. We're going to his parents' for supper. There's going to be a big crowd there tonight to see Ned. It should be fun."

"Well, you have a Merry Christmas, too. I'll see you soon. Let me know when Ned's leaving. I want to see him off."

"I will," she said, hugging her best friend. "Bye!"

When they stopped by the parsonage, Ned talked to the Reverend and Mrs. Parker as Bonnie ran upstairs to change. She had made a green velvet dress just for the occasion and wanted to surprise Ned. As she entered the living room, Ned stopped talking, his words lost before they left his lips. Bonnie's golden red hair was swept up on her head. Her dress draped over the edges of her shoulders, exposing her long neck and shoulders. She had borrowed the perfect necklace from Annie. It contained one teardrop pearl that centered itself in the middle of her chest; from her ears hung matching earrings. Ned's heart leapt in his chest.

"My goodness, you look like you just stepped off the pages of *Harper's Bazaar*! Wow!"

"I made it. Just for tonight," Bonnie said proudly as she twirled around one time for his benefit. The dress clung tightly to Bonnie's curves and flared a bit just below the knees. Her shoes and bag were exactly the same shade of green.

"You're absolutely the best-looking thing this soldier has ever seen," Ned said as he kissed her cheek. Bonnie's hazel eyes blazed a bright green.

"Thank you, sir," she said with a curtsy.

"Well, we better be going," he said. "It was nice to see the both of you again."

"Nice to see you, too, son," Reverend Parker said, shaking his hand. "Ned, we want you to know our prayers are with you."

"Yes, Ned," Mrs. Parker added.

Ned shifted uncomfortably. "Thank you" was all he could manage. "Thank you both."

The Bass home bustled all through the night. People were coming and going. Well-wishers stopped by to see Ned and say hello. Some stayed. Some were off in no time to other parties around the city. The war had been going on for over a year now, and many people had been touched by it, one way or another. War contracts and increased employment had resulted in increasing prosperity, and many were enjoying it this Christmas season.

Ned insisted Bonnie sing *White Christmas* as he played the piano. Everyone in the room seemed charmed by the country girl from Smithville. She had become quite a beautiful woman and was surrounded the entire night by eligible young men. Ned noticed she was being cornered by the son of one of Belle Meade's finest when he decided he'd better rescue her.

"Now, you can't believe a thing this man says about me," Ned said, interrupting the man's conversation.

"Ned, man, where have you been? I've been having to keep your fiancé company. I was just telling her about some of our adventures."

"Rollins, don't you know that's in bad to taste to talk about a man's past to his soon-to-be wife?"

"Not in bad taste, man, I was trying to steal her away from you."

"Fat chance," he said, the three of them laughing. "I'm afraid I have to take you away from all of this tale bearing, dear. I have some people I'd like you to meet." Bonnie was moving to his side away from her corner as soon as Ned motioned for her.

"Thanks," she whispered as they walked away.

"I thought you looked a little bored," he said, smiling. "Come with me. I have a surprise for you."

"A surprise?" Bonnie whispered.

"Yes, this way. Maybe no one will see us."

Ned showed Bonnie into the library, pulling the doors closed behind him. He walked over to the bar and poured himself a drink. Bonnie lay back on the overstuffed couch.

"Quiet. This is nice," she said.

Ned took his place beside her.

"Bonnie, I haven't truly apologized for last night. I'm sorry for what I said. You should tell me to go away and never look back."

"I couldn't do that," she said, pushing his hair away out of his face and resting her hand on his cheek.

He lifted the hand that wore his engagement ring and kissed it. "I want to make up for it. I got you a present," he said, pulling a jewelry box from his jacket pocket. Bonnie sat up.

"Ned! You didn't have to—"

"It's your Christmas present. I wanted you to have something special." Bonnie slowly opened the box to reveal a diamond and emerald brooch. "I saw it in a shop in London. It reminded me of you."

"Oh, Ned, it's beautiful!" she said, wrapping her arms around his neck. "But you know the only thing I want is for you to come home safe and sound."

"I know. I know you don't care about this stuff, but I knew it would match your eyes. I couldn't resist."

"Thank you," Bonnie said as she held his face in her hands. Ned couldn't stand the way she looked at him with such trust. Never failing; never second-guessed him; never questioned him. Looking into her eyes made him feel even worse about the night before. He'd thought long and hard about what he was about to say, but he knew now was the time. He stood and walked over to the fireplace.

"Ned, what's wrong?"

"Bonnie, I have something I want to say to you. I just want you to listen to me."

Bonnie sat with her hands folded in her lap.

"Bonnie, the war in Europe is just getting started. We're having a hard time of it with Hitler and, well, I don't think I'll be coming back home anytime soon."

"Ned," Bonnie tried to speak up.

"No, hear me out. I just want you to know if someone else should come along . . . I mean, if . . . well, if anything happens to me . . . well, you know all I want is for you to be happy," Ned said, continuing to stare into the fire. "It's hard to explain to you, Bonnie. It's so different over there. There's so much killing and, well, I've realized that life is short and . . ."

Ned turned around to see Bonnie's face buried in her hands. "Bonnie, I don't want to upset you tonight. Please don't cry," he said as he sat beside her, pulling her to him. She laid her head on his chest. "I'm sorry for what I've done to you. I've spoiled our time together by being selfish, and now I have to leave again. Please, Bonnie, promise that no matter what happens, if I don't come back, you'll move on."

Bonnie sprang to her feet. "I won't listen to this anymore!" she screamed. "Stop talking like that. Stop it!"

Ned stood. "All right. All right. I'm sorry. I just . . ." He stopped as he heard his own voice begin to crackle. "I miss you already."

Bonnie wrapped her arms around him. They held onto one another for some time before a knock came on the library door. "Mr. Bass, are you in there? Your mother is looking for you, sir."

"We better get back. Mother has sent out the search party," Ned said, trying to make Bonnie smile. He reached into his jacket and handed her his handkerchief. "Here, dry your eyes. Let's go back in there and have a merry Christmas. What do you say?"

"Okay," Bonnie replied.

Ned wrapped his arms around her one more time. This time, he found her lips. "I love you, Bonnie McCaverty. You're the best thing that ever happened to me. Don't ever forget that."

The last day of Ned's leave came early. He was summoned back to England before his leave was up and, once again, those who knew and loved him were standing at Union Station, saying goodbye only a few days after Christmas.

"Well, here we are again," Ned said to Bonnie. "I'm sorry it wasn't longer, darling."

Bonnie threw her arms around his neck wondering, once again, if she hadn't made a mistake by not marrying him. Since that supper at the Bass house, Ned had been distant and somber. Even so, he'd been particularly thoughtful and had spent every minute of leave he could with her.

"Please take care of yourself," she whispered into his ear, her body already beginning to shake.

"You know I will. The next time I come back, this will be all over, and we'll have that big wedding. I promise."

Ned pulled away to face his parents. Bonnie held on to Nell for strength.

As Ned said his goodbyes to his parents, Bonnie noticed a look of surprise pass across his face. She looked toward where he was looking and saw a well-dressed woman standing not far from them by the stairway. She was looking directly at them. Bonnie watched as the woman turned and hurried up the stairs toward the lobby. She looked at Ned to see if he was still watching her. Ned was making his way over to say goodbye to Nell.

"Well, it was fun. Take care a my girl, will ya?"

"You bet," Nell said as she hugged him and kissed his cheek.

"Well, doll face," he said to Bonnie. "I guess I better get on board. I'll write every chance I get."

"You better," she said, barely above a whisper.

It seemed like he'd only been there a few days, and now he was leaving again. This time, Mrs. Bass hadn't even been able to come to the station. She had said her goodbyes at home.

"Well, goodbye, son," Mr. Bass said. "We'll be here waiting for you. I've got plenty of work for you when you get home. So, make it quick, will you?" the old man said. Ned knew he was trying to make light of the situation.

"I will, Dad. We'll get Hitler out of the way in no time at all. In the meantime, don't give away my office."

"Never," his father assured him as the two men exchanged a hearty handshake and embraced.

"Well, Albert, here we are again. I know you'll take care of everyone just like you always have."

"Yes sir, I will," Albert said. Ned wondered if Albert had noticed Della.

"Is there anything you'd like me to do for you, sir?" he asked.

"The same thing you've always done, Albert. You've always known what to do for me even before I knew what to ask." Ned pulled Albert aside for a moment. "Albert, I do want you to remember the envelope in my room. Please take care of that should anything happen."

"I'm sure it won't be necessary, sir," the dutiful butler answered.

"You always know the right thing to say, don't you, Albert?"

"Not in this situation, sir," Albert answered. Ned's chest tightened as he watched his old friend trying not to show emotion.

Once again the conductor called Ned's train and, once again, Bonnie watched him board and wave goodbye. This time, there was no shock, only sadness. Bonnie hid her face in Nell's embrace, unable to watch the train pull away. As she pulled away from Nell, she noticed the woman she'd seen before standing on the landing above the tracks. That woman was also crying.

"Nell, who's that woman standing there? Do you know her?"

Nell turned to see where Bonnie was looking. "That's Della Houston. She works down at The Stables. Best poker player in town, they say. She must have someone here who's leaving, too. You've never seen her in the station before?"

"No, I don't think so. Well, she does look familiar." Where have I seen her before? Bonnie thought. She pushed the question to the back of her mind as Ned's train made its way down the track and out of Nashville.

"Well, Albert," Mr. Bass said, "we better get home to Mrs. Bass. I'm sure she needs us. Bonnie, can we give you ride?"

"No, thank you, Mr. Bass. I'm going to stay and work. I think it would do me better working than sitting around and thinking. It'll help keep my mind off of things."

"Sure enough. Sure enough. Well, here we go, Albert." Mr. Bass said as he motioned for Albert to join him on the stairway.

"Goodbye, Miss McCaverty. Call if you need anything," Albert said.

Bonnie hugged Albert. "Thank you, Albert," she said as she kissed the old man's cheek. She knew Albert felt like a father to Ned, and it wasn't easy for him to say goodbye either.

As the two men made their way to the lobby, Bonnie stood still, her mind wandering, recalling memories stored away, names and faces. She knew she'd seen that woman somewhere.

"Nell!" Bonnie said, grabbing Nell's arm. The blood drained from her face. "That's it. I know where I've seen her before!"

"Who?"

"The woman standing up there, Della Houston."

"Where?"

"That's who was with Ned the day I came back from Smithville! He was leaving on a trip somewhere. Remember? That's the day we met. The day I hid in the Lunch Room. Remember?"

"Sure, honey," Nell said, with a confused look.

"She was with Ned."

Suddenly, the pieces of the puzzle began to fall into place in Nell's mind, as it had Bonnie's.

"Now, Bonnie, you don't know why she was here. There are a lot of people leaving today," she warned.

"She was here to say goodbye to Ned. I know it!"

"Now how do you know that?" Nell asked.

"I just do," Bonnie answered with a knowing that was impossible to explain, but easy to defend. Her knees were weak. Her mind began to visit places she didn't want it to.

Albert and Mr. Bass made their way onto Broadway and headed west, back to the Bass home. Mr. Bass didn't want Mrs. Bass to be alone today.

Albert looked at the elderly Mr. Bass in the rear view mirror as he sat quietly. Mr. Bass wondered if he was thinking the same thing as he was.

"Albert," Mr. Bass spoke up.

"Yes, sir?"

"Was that Miss Houston I saw at the station?"

"I believe it was, sir."

"What was she doing there?"

"I'm not quite sure, sir."

"That wasn't a wise thing for her to do."

"No, sir. She was probably sad Mr. Bass was leaving, sir. They've been friends for quite a long time."

"Yes. I know, Albert. I know."

CHAPTER TWENTY-SIX

"Gather `round, boys. Place your bets!"

TWO MONTHS HAD passed since Ned's visit home. The station was constantly full of new recruits. From what Bonnie and Nell could gather from their conversations with the soldiers coming through there, many were going to Europe. Maneuvers were being held all around Nashville and parts of Tennessee. Lizzie had written Bonnie telling her that they were being conducted everywhere at home back in Smithville. The soldiers explained that the terrain there was much like the terrain where they would be fighting. The worst part was that the recruits all seemed to be getting younger and younger looking.

"Bonnie, look over there. Looks like there might be another fight in the lobby," Ruth pointed out.

"Oh, dear, I'll help with this one," Bonnie answered as she rushed into the crowd, hoping to stop the disturbance before any of the officers noticed.

"Hey . . . hey!" Bonnie shouted as she squeezed through the crowd of uniformed soldiers. Suddenly, she was at the forefront of the battle. She placed her hands on her hips looking around. The soldiers standing nearby stopped everything they were doing, as most did when Bonnie commanded their attention.

"Okay, boys. What's going on here?" Bonnie asked. They all started talking at once like children wanting to plead their case before punishment. Bonnie held her hands up, motioning for them to stop talking.

"One at a time! I can't hear all of you at once!" she said. She put her arms up as if holding two forces away from one another.

One of the young soldiers spoke up. "He's trying to steal my girl! That's what's going on," he said as he tried to lunge toward the other. Bonnie placed herself between the two boys, pushing them away from each other. Each boy was holding his wallet in one hand, the photo compartment open to the image of a girl, who was smiling prettily.

"Am not!" the other boy shouted. "She was mine first."

"How do you know that?" the other asked.

"I just do!"

"Okay, okay, what's going on here?" a sergeant standing nearby asked as he pushed his way through the crowd. As he reached where Bonnie and the boys stood, Bonnie had both wallets in her hands, admiring the same picture of the same girl in both wallets.

"Oh nothing, Sergeant," Bonnie assured him. "I think there's some misunderstanding as to who is the prettiest. Nothing urgent."

"Well, hold it down and quit making such a ruckus," he said as he looked at the floor. "We have a long trip in front of us."

The group of men surrounding the two combatants began to quiet down.

"Okay, how did this happen?" Bonnie asked as she shook both wallets in their faces.

One of the boys spoke up. "Well, we've been in training together and realized our girls have the same first name. Then, we got here, and I decided to show Roy here Carol's picture when—

"When I realized he had a picture of my girl in his wallet!" the other boy interrupted. Bonnie began to laugh.

"Well, boys, I believe you've both been had! Believe you me, Carol's probably got her picture in a dozen other wallets as we speak!" The other men who were milling about began to laugh, too. The two boys fumed. Obviously, they didn't think it was funny. Bonnie realized their pride was hurting. She had to put an end to this before they got on that train.

"Let me tell you something. Carol will probably be here and probably be with someone else while the two of you will be over there with each other. Now listen," Bonnie said as she pulled the two boys closer. "You have to be together for a while and, well, Carol isn't going to be over there with you. So, I want you to end this before you get on that train.

"I tell you what. We'll Indian wrestle for her. The man who wins gets to deal with Carol, which I'm not so sure is winning. The other has to take her picture out and promise never to bring it up again, okay? Do you both agree with that?" The boys eyed each other and nodded simultaneously.

"Okay! It's a deal. Gather 'round, boys. Get that table over there. Okay, here we go. You sit down there and you . . . sit down here," she said as she pointed to their seats. The crowd in Union Station was beginning to turn their eyes to the commotion in the middle of the lobby.

"Gather 'round, boys. Place your bets!" shouting like a barker at a carnival. "Which one will it be, boys? Which one will it be? Which one gets to keep the pretty lady?" Bonnie called out to the crowd. Behind her, money began to change hands as the soldiers picked their favorite. She leaned over the boys, grabbing their hands, which they had clasped together on top of the table. She looked at them both square in the eyes. "What's your name?" she asked one.

"Bill," he answered.

"What's your name?" she asked the other.

"Roy," he replied.

She spoke low so that the others around her couldn't hear her. "Listen to me. Where you're going, you're going to need each other. Now after this, you promise that you'll leave this right here. Deal?"

Roy and Bill looked at each other and smiled, nodding in agreement.

"Okay, here we go," she said as she cupped her hands around their entwined fists. "On the count of three. Ready?" They nodded again. "One, two, THREE!" Bonnie yelled as she released their fists.

The two boys engaged in a good old-fashioned game of Indian wrestling. The men gathered about them shouting for their favorite.

After some time of back and forth, Roy ultimately forced Bill's arm to the table. Roy rose to his feet, hoisting his hands in victory. Bill stood slowly, defeated. Bonnie watched with her hands resting on her hips.

"Okay, shake hands, guys," she instructed. The two boys shook hands. Bill reached for his wallet and tore up Carol's picture. Roy took his out and began to rip his in half, too. Bonnie joined the crowd of young soldiers in a raucous laugh.

As the crowd began to clear, Bonnie talked with the boys, trying to find out where they were headed. Two young soldiers leaning against a railing across the lobby watched Bonnie through the whole event. One reached over and slapped his sergeant, who had been attempting to roll a cigarette, on the shoulder.

"How about her, Sarge? Is that a looker or what?" one of them asked.

"Look at that red hair. Boy, I'll bet she has a mean temper!" the other said. "What I wouldn't give for something like that to be waitin' for me to come home."

"Yeah," the other soldier agreed as they watched Bonnie through the crowd of soldiers.

Bonnie was looking around, trying to talk to them all and put them at ease, when she looked up. Her eyes met the sergeant's, who was still staring at her. He looked away quickly and lit his cigarette. Puzzled, Bonnie started toward where the three of them were standing.

"She's coming this way!" one of them said. The sergeant grabbed his bag and started to relocate, but it was too late. Bonnie tapped him on the back.

"Excuse me," she said to the sergeant. "Don't I . . ." she said as he turned around slowly to face her. The two young soldiers stood by and watched.

"Calvin?" Bonnie whispered.

"You know her?" the two boys asked in unison. Neither Bonnie nor Calvin paid them any attention.

"Calvin!" Bonnie shouted as she jumped up, hugged him around the neck, kissing him on the lips. The two soldiers stood with their mouths hanging open, continuing to watch in disbelief.

"Calvin, what are you doing in that uniform?" Bonnie said with a smile. "Is this a joke? Did you come here to pull a joke on me?" Bonnie asked, the full impact of what she was seeing still not registering with her.

"Bonnie, honey. It's no joke," Calvin said apologetically.

"Honey?" the two soldiers said simultaneously.

"I joined the army, Bonnie . . . I, well, I . . ."

"What do you mean, you've joined the army?" Bonnie asked. "You can't join the army! Why, you're too old, Calvin Wade. You can't go over there!" she babbled, now panicked. The blood drained from her face. She grew pale.

"Can we go somewhere and talk?" Calvin asked.

Bonnie could only point toward the stairs to the shed where the trains loaded and unloaded. Calvin grabbed his bag and Bonnie's arm pulling her toward the stairs. Still holding one arm, he dragged her down the stairs and down one of the ramps to a secluded spot. He dropped his bag onto the floor. Bonnie was fully hysterical by that time.

"I don't understand, Calvin. Why didn't you tell me? Why hasn't Mama told me?" she asked, stomping her right foot in anger against the concrete.

Calvin reached out for her other arm and turned her to face him. "I asked her not to, Bonnie."

Tears began to roll down Bonnie's face. "Why, Calvin? Why?" she asked quietly. Calvin turned and walked a few steps from her, then turned back, his eyes meeting hers.

"Because, Bonnie. I got tired of all of the boys in the county coming home in caskets. I got tired of going to funerals." Calvin's voice began to rise. "They're all dead, Bonnie. The McCallister boys, the Fletcher boys, even Rosalee's brother Jimmy. He's dead, too! I just couldn't stand by and watch no more." He pulled his hat off twisting it in his hand. "Here I am with no family, no kids, no ma, no pa, and they don't ask me to go. So, I volunteered. I lied about my age. Told them I was thirty-four. They believed me. I been here in Nashville training."

Bonnie started to say something. Calvin put his hand up to stop her. "I didn't want to see you, Bonnie. I didn't know you was here at the station. Lizzie didn't tell me. I'm beginning to understand why now."

Bonnie put her hands on Calvin's big arms. "You can't do this. Please, Calvin. Not you. I've seen all kinds of things happen here. I've had to see a lot of wives and mothers let their sons and husbands go only to see them come back dead! You can't go, Calvin! You can't!" she screamed hysterically. Tears flowed freely down her face now.

Calvin drew his little friend to him. She looked deep into his blue eyes. Having seen it first hand too many times, Bonnie knew she might never have the chance to look into them again. She buried her face in his big chest. He wrapped his hand around her head, stroking her familiar red hair. He breathed her scent in deep. "I have to go, Bonnie. I have to."

The two of them stood, holding onto each other for what seemed like only a few short minutes when they heard the conductor call for his train.

"All aboard . . . Main 1455."

Bonnie wrapped her arms around him tightly and closed her eyes. "No. You can't go. I'll tell them you're too old. I'll . . ." Calvin put his hand to her mouth and smiled.

"Do you think that fiancé of yours would mind if you gave a soldier a goodbye kiss?" he asked her.

They stood there face to face. The years between them vanished as Calvin bent down to kiss her. The passion between the two of them, hidden for so many years, came rushing to the surface. Bonnie kissed him back, not as the young girl who had confronted him so many years ago, but as the woman who realized in an instant that he was still the only man she ever really loved. Calvin lifted Bonnie off her feet; she wrapped her arms around his neck as they held onto each other for perhaps the last time.

Calvin whispered into Bonnie's ear, "I'm sorry I forgot the dance I promised you. I'm so sorry for hurting you. I'm so sorry I forced you away. Please forgive me, Bonnie. Please forgive me." Bonnie pulled away and held his face in her hands. He looked into those beautiful green eyes. He looked at the stubborn freckles perched on her nose. He drank in every part of her face he could.

"I love you, Bonnie McCaverty," he said solemnly. "I've always loved you. Since you was a little girl sent home from school for punchin' Josh McCallister. I knew it when you was lying there on the trail when you got shot."

The young soldiers who had been standing with Calvin came tearing down the stairs. They peered down the landing and motioned to him.

"Hey, Sarge! C'mon, you're going to miss the train," they yelled as the crowd came pouring down the stairs to get on their appropriate trains.

Calvin looked at her. He'd done it. All this time had passed, and she had forgotten him. All this time and now there he was, about to leave for war, he saw her and what did he do? He told her he loves her! Calvin pushed it out of his mind. All he cared about at that moment was making sure Bonnie knew he never meant to hurt her.

"Bonnie, I . . . I couldn't tell you how I felt when you told me you loved me. I couldn't. Everyone I've ever loved has died, Bonnie. Everyone. My Ma and Pa, then Rosalee, but none of them meant as much to me as you do. I couldn't stand it if something happened to you like it did them. I thought if maybe I stayed away from you, nothing would happen."

Bonnie pushed his dark hair away from his face. "You silly fool. I knew you loved me. Remember? I told you I knew it, Calvin. You can't leave me now. Please stay. Tell them you lied. We'll go back home and everything can be like it should have been before. Please, Calvin," Bonnie begged desperately.

The two young soldiers stood close by, watching their train load, waiting until the last minute before they came to get Calvin.

"C'mon, Sarge!" one of them yelled. "The train's about to leave! C'mon!"

Bonnie turned to look at the soldiers, then turned back to Calvin.

"I can't, Bonnie. I have to go."

Bonnie pushed him away and stomped her foot. "No, you don't!

You don't have to go!" Calvin stepped up to her as she covered her face with her hands and began to cry. "You can't leave me . . . not now! Please!" Bonnie cried.

Calvin wrapped his big arms around her. "I have to go, Bonnie Girl." She looked up at him, her face wet with emotion, stifling the cries that came from her. Calvin smiled. "I'll be back for you. I promise."

Bonnie saw that look on his face. The look she had seen on so many other soldiers' faces as they said goodbye to the people they loved. It was a look of pride, a look of courage. It was a look of devotion that couldn't match a mother's love or the loyalty of a wife. It was a duty that men understood and took on willingly. To Bonnie, it was mysterious because many of them knew they would never come home. It was a force that pushed them to fight for the freedom of those mothers, sisters, and wives. A job they knew they had to do to keep it safe and free for those they left behind.

Bonnie stepped aside as the young soldiers ran up, grabbed Calvin and his bag, and rushed him away to his train. She stepped over to the cold stone wall of the station, burying her face in her hands. Her head was spinning. She felt faint. Nell grabbed her just as she felt her knees give way and walked her over to a bench.

"Bonnie! What's wrong? Bonnie! Is it Ned? Oh God, what's happened, Bonnie?" Nell questioned her frantically. Nell sat and pulled Bonnie to her shoulder as she continued to sob uncontrollably, rocking her gently.

Nell pulled her away so that she could see her face. "Bonnie, what is it? Tell me!"

Bonnie straightened up on the bench and took the handkerchief Nell offered. "It's Calvin, Nell. He's gone. He joined up, and no one told me. He's been here in training, and I didn't even know!"

"Oh, dear. Oh, Bonnie, I'm sorry," Nell said. She knew Calvin was special. Bonnie had told Nell all about Calvin and why she moved to Nashville in the first place, but she never told her that she was still in love with him. She never told her that Calvin's picture was still the last thing she looked at every night before she went to bed.

Bonnie sat straight on the bench, grabbing Nell's arms. "He told me he loves me, Nell. He apologized for hurting me. He said it was because everyone he'd ever loved had died and if anything happened to me, he wouldn't have been able to stand it, so he just pretended not to love me so he could run me off!" She stood and began to pace back and forth. "I knew it, Nell," she said, smiling through her tears. "I knew he loved me. All this time and I still felt it. That's why I haven't been able to marry Ned. I just knew he loved me . . ." She stopped and put her hands to her face again. "Now he's gone . . . he's gone, Nell!"

Nell stood and wrapped her arms around Bonnie again. "Oh, honey. I wish I could take it away for you," she said. "What are you going to do about Ned?"

Bonnie looked up at Nell. "Ned? Oh my goodness, Ned!"

"You know, your fiancé," Nell pointed out.

"Ohhhh . . . I don't care right now. I don't know," Bonnie said as she continued to pace back and forth.

"C'mon, Bonnie, you've got to pull yourself together. I came down here to find you because Mrs. Greenfield is looking everywhere for you. Let's get out of this cold and get you straightened up," she said. She led Bonnie back up the steps into the station lobby.

Bonnie entered the parsonage that night numb from the day. It was nearly midnight before she left the station and could barely put one foot in front of the other to get inside. She went straight to the living room and sat in front of what was left of the evening fire. Annie heard her and came downstairs.

"Bonnie, you must be exhausted," she said. She found the switch to the lamp beside the Reverend's chair and clicked it on. "Would you like something to eat, dear?"

Bonnie hadn't even bothered to remove her coat. She just sat staring into the fire. Annie stoked the fire and added another log.

"Bonnie, what's wrong? Has something happened?" Annie asked as she sat on the sofa next to her. The glow from the fire illuminated a single tear that traced its way down the young woman's cheek.

"He's gone, Miss Annie."

"Who's gone, Bonnie? Is it Ned? Oh, dear, what's happened?" she cried.

"No, it's not Ned. It's Calvin."

"Calvin? What's happened, Bonnie? Please tell me."

"I saw Calvin at the station today."

Annie's eyebrows shot up quizzically. "What was he doing there?

"He was going off to war," Bonnie answered numbly, never changing her expression.

"Off to war? Calvin? Why he's—"

"Too old?" Bonnie said finishing for her. "Yes. He lied. He told them he was younger, and now he's gone. I saw him standing there, Miss Annie, in a uniform. I thought maybe he was playing a joke on me." Bonnie buried her head in her hands. "Now, he's gone."

"Does Lizzie know?"

"He made her promise not to tell me. Why hasn't someone told me?" she asked, standing from the sofa.

"Here, let me take your coat, dear. You're in shock. Now, sit down and tell me what happened.

"I saw him standing there, and I asked what he was doing in that uniform. I begged him not go. I begged him, Miss Annie. It hit me all at once. I can't make no sense of it. It just hit me."

"What, Bonnie?"

"That I still love him. I love him, Miss Annie," Bonnie cried, turning her face to her. "That's why I couldn't marry Ned. There he was, standing there in front of me. He said he was sorry for hurting me. He was sorry he forgot our dance at the picnic. He said he knew he loved me since the night he found me lying on the path when I'd been shot. He thought that if he ran me off, I would stay safe. He thought that since everyone he's ever loved was dead, that if he loved me, too . . . oh Miss Annie, what am I going to do? After all of this time, he finally tells me he loves me, and now he's gone."

Annie stood and held Bonnie as she cried. "It's not fair! It's just not fair!"

"I know," Annie said consolingly. "I know, dear. But look at the bright side. Now you know. Now you finally know how he feels."

"What am I going to do about Ned? What about Ned? I knew there was a reason I couldn't marry him. Something just kept pushing at me and pushing at me," Bonnie said, pacing the room. "I knew I loved him, but it just wasn't the same as with Calvin. All this time, I thought it had gone away and just the thought that I might never see him again, and I just knew."

"You've had a long day. Come on and let me get you in bed. Tomorrow things will look differently. You won't be so tired, and you'll be able to think clearly."

"Tomorrow won't be any different than today, Miss Annie. Today's no different than yesterday or last year or the year before that. I've always loved Calvin, and I knew he loved me."

"Well, you're going to be good to no one if you don't get some sleep. Come on now. Let's go upstairs. We'll talk about it in the morning," Annie said as she turned off the lamp and helped Bonnie up the stairs.

CHAPTER TWENTY-SEVEN

"This is the day we've all been waiting for."

THE DECK OF the *Argentina* pitched up and down in the rough sea as Calvin flipped his cigarette over the side. The sun was setting on their ninth day at sea, and he was trying to get a breath of fresh air before he bunked down for the night, his least favorite part of this strange journey.

Every night, it was the same. So many men huddled into such a small area, bunks stacked three high, some even hanging from the ceiling. By now, many of the men had overcome their seasickness, something Calvin had never had a problem with. It was the lack of space he hated most. He was used to wide open fields, standing on his porch having a smoke before bed and looking out at the night sky. The deck of the ship wasn't his porch, but at least he could see the sky.

Calvin looked out at the blanket of stars, said goodnight to Bonnie, then decided to make his way down to his bunk to attempt another letter that he hoped he could eventually mail to her. He'd tried many times and, as always, he would crumble it up and throw it away. The battle would rage on as he tried to write version after version.

He knew he should tell her that he shouldn't have said those things to her at the station. She was to be married to someone else, and he had no right, then he remembered the look in her eyes, the taste of her tears, the smell of her hair and her kiss.

Calvin would tear the up letter and start over with another version, one in which he'd tell her through all the years he had loved her. How he wished it could have been different. How he wished he hadn't been so stubborn. He would apologize again for hurting her. He would think about Ned and how it wasn't fair to him for Calvin to cause problems for him. He thought about writing to Ned and explaining. That would be the gentlemanly thing to do. He would decide that he had loved Bonnie all of his life. She didn't belong to anyone else but him. Finally, as always, he would tell himself that he was being selfish, then he would start all over again, trying to apologize for the things he said to her.

This battle had gone on for almost a month. Calvin knew he'd be in England soon, and he might not have a chance to mail a letter, so tonight was the night. As he made his way off the deck, he looked once more at the evening sky. Just as he did, he caught a glimpse of a shooting star burning across the black night.

Calvin made up his mind.

Tonight, he would finish his letter.

As the ship slowly made its way to the dock in Liverpool, Calvin stood at the bow, gazing at the shoreline of England, his first look at foreign soil. The soldiers quickly disembarked from the ship and made their way to the trains that would take them to what would become their new home, at least for a while. Already, he was getting his first taste of wartime. The sun had set, and the trains were ordered blacked-out because of a German air raid.

Calvin was a member of the 117th Infantry Regiment, part of the 30th Infantry Division under Major General Leland S. Hobbs. Because of his expertise with guns and partly because he was quite a bit older than anyone in his regiment, Calvin was put in charge of a rifle squad of nine men. They were the infantry, the ground forces—the backbone of the army. These were the men who marched to the front with rifle and bayonet.

By March of 1944, the men of the 30th were seeing a great buildup of men and machinery around London. Invasion was on everyone's lips. The men were tired of training day after day. Just like the rest of his division, Calvin was itching to fight.

On June 6, 1944, the day was at hand. They woke to a sky that buzzed from horizon to horizon with bombers. Not the heavy bombers they were used to seeing deployed to bomb strategic sites, but light twin-engine attack bombers headed for the shores of France. They appeared and disappeared between the intermittent clouds as if playing a game of hide and seek.

"Would you look at that, Sarge? It's finally here. Maybe we're going over now," one of the soldiers in Calvin's platoon said. He was a young man from Indiana who had already lost part of his family to Hitler's forces. Johnny Duke was his name. Calvin worried about his impatience. The only thing he talked about was killing Krauts.

"Maybe so, but if we don't get to the chow line, we'll go hungry," Calvin answered as he moved his men toward the tent.

"Why don't you see if you can find out what's going on, Sarge?" Benny Long asked. He was one of the soldiers who had stood with Calvin when he met up with Bonnie in the station back in Nashville.

"I'm sure we'll find out soon enough," Calvin said to the men. "Let's go."

As Calvin passed the adjutant general's office, he dropped his letter into the mail. A few other men followed him in like fashion. They'd all heard the same speech. You never knew when you might have another chance to write.

Calvin's division had been on alert. They were packed and ready to go. Just like all of the men packed on ships at sea, waiting, all the pilots were on hold. They all knew they were part of something big. This war had raged on for over five years, and now, all hoped this invasion would put an end to Hilter's reign. The past few days they were moved, unit by unit, to the staging areas near the docks and finally, to Southampton, where they were loaded onto transports that would cross the English Channel to meet other troops on Omaha Beach. They would continue to wait. The 117th would be one of the last troops to hit Omaha Beach.

On June sixth, at one-thirty in the morning, Ned and his fellow pilots strode into the briefing room with extreme anticipation. Four o'clock was the usual roust for a briefing before a mission, so this one was unusually early. Everyone knew something was at hand.

As they entered the room, they all stared at the draped map of Europe hanging on the wall, holding its secret for the pilots. If the target was deep into Germany, they knew this meant heavy opposition from German fighters and heavy flak. The men waited quietly, some smoking, some whispering, some just waiting for the commanding officer to enter the room.

"Ten-hut!" came the command from the front of the room. The pilots stood at attention. The door was locked behind Colonel Walker as he took his place in front of the pilots.

"At ease, men," he commanded somberly as the men quietly took their seats. The colonel motioned for the map to be uncovered. The pilots were confronted with the coast of France.

"This is it, men. This is the day we've all been waiting for," Colonel Walker announced.

As the news began to sink in, the pilots began to whoop and holler. Some threw their hats into the air. The days of waiting were over. The rumors of invasion were true. The colonel began to explain their targets.

Ned's heart slowed as the seriousness of the news sank in. Troops would be making their way to the coast as they were being briefed. It would be a massive undertaking. Finally, after all the bombing of German cities, all the bombing of strategic sites, railroads, factories, oil refineries; finally, they were laying the groundwork for a major offensive. This would pave the way for the troops to penetrate the coast of France and push the Germans back across Europe. Everyone had been waiting for this day and, finally, it was here. Now maybe it would end. Now maybe there was an end in sight.

"I have a message to you from General Doolittle," Colonel Walker said as he pulled a paper from his jacket.

The Eighth Air Force is currently charged with a most solemn obligation in support of the most vital operation ever undertaken by our armed forces. It will be necessary during certain stages to attack with tremendous intensity the area immediately in front of our advancing troops . . .

Ned thought about Bonnie.

It had been six months since his visit at Christmas, six months since that night with Della. Ned felt caught somewhere between guilt, anger, and confusion. Guilt for seeing Della before he left, anger toward Bonnie for not marrying him while he was home, and confusion over his feelings for both. Since he saw Della standing at the end of the bar that night looking up at him, since he wrapped his arms around her, no words needed between the two of them, he was confused about how he felt about her.

Ned had always considered Della his best friend. He just assumed after he and Bonnie were married, he would have to stay away from her, maybe seeing her for an occasional drink or so, but now, as the casualness of life was gone and the harsh reality of war was a day-to-day occurrence for him, he thought about her often.

He wrote to her from time to time, trying to keep his words as vague as possible. No more mention of Bonnie or their impending marriage. Ned knew Della too well. That wouldn't be fair. He hoped that maybe she had found someone. Maybe she wasn't thinking about him as much as he was thinking about her, but, deep down, he knew that wasn't the case.

On the other hand, there were his letters to Bonnie, his wife-to-be. Bonnie was everything Ned had always wanted; innocent, unwise about his past, totally trusting; not like the debutantes he'd been accustomed to. As much as he regretted it, their life together would begin with a secret.

The colonel finished reading the statement from General Doolittle as Ned pulled himself from his private thoughts.

. . . The necessary hazards have been accepted. They can be minimized

only through exalted performance on the part of our air leaders and bom-
bardiers. I have every confidence in you.

"That's it, men," the colonel finished. "I don't have to give you all a speech. You understand the seriousness of your actions today. Through all of these months we've spent luring the Luftwaffe into the air with continuous strategic bombing, I'm sure you all knew this day was coming. You've given the men on the ground a tremendous amount of backup, relieving the Germans of precious supplies. We've thrown a wrench into Hitler's precious Reich! Now the troops on the ground are ready. It's our job to clear the way for them.

"We'll sink or swim based on what happens here today, men.

"God Bless you all, and good flying."

After the briefing, the pilots were escorted out to the canvas-covered trucks that would take them to their bombers. No one spoke. The ground crews went through their usual checks as the bomber crews took their positions. Ned made his way to the pilot's seat and went about his usual pre-flight when he realized he'd forgotten one thing, a picture of Bonnie he typically carried in his flight jacket, his good luck charm. He retrieved it, said good morning to her, stowing the picture away. In minutes, the pilots were in line waiting for takeoff. Slowly, Ned's bomber lifted into the gray skies at 3:30 a.m., June 6, 1944.

The long formation assembled together in the skies above England. Intermittent clouds lingered below them in the early morning light as the droning of the engines carried them closer to the coast of France.

"Geez! Captain Bass, look below," the co-pilot said as Ned looked out the window through a break in the clouds. Below, in the choppy English Channel, thousands of ships dotted the water, crafts of all sizes, some with barrage balloons looming over them. The ocean teemed with what seemed like the entire Allied fleet, all headed in the same direction. Ned knew they would be opening the way for the troops below. He focused intensely on the mission before them. The bombardier gave instructions for the bombs to be activated.

As they neared the shores of Omaha Beach, the signal plane

released a smoke bomb, indicating that it was time for the aircraft to release their bombs.

"Bombs away," the bombardier said matter-of-factly into his microphone. With those two simple words, one hundred tons of explosive-laced metal slowly made their way to the ground.

The transport pitched and yawned in the busy ocean off the northern coast of France. The area was anchored with ships and landing craft busy transporting men and machinery onto landing boats to be taken ashore.

Calvin tried to focus on the cliffs ahead as their boat pitched up and down. He saw a C-47 taking off from a makeshift landing strip. He supposed it was full of wounded going back to England. Above the beachhead and the cliffs, puffs of smoke filled the sky as the sound of heavy explosions reverberated in his ears. The sea around him was littered with boats lying on their sides. Huge open wounds gaped where the German guns had ripped back their armor. They drifted in the sea like drowned livestock after a flash flood.

Once the massive door on the landing craft dropped open into the water, Calvin and his men could see the beach, which was teeming with activity. There were makeshift command centers and medical posts, tanks, jeeps, rows and rows of tangled wire, and bodies, hundreds of bodies. Some would eventually make their way home, some would not. A steady stream of men and machinery made its way onto the shores of France.

As they reached the beach, the toll paid by the men who had made the initial landing at Omaha became painfully clear. The smell was the first thing that Calvin noticed, a mixture of gunpowder, metal, smoke— and death. It was overpowering. The percussive blasts continued in the air just above their heads. Confusion reigned, making it hard to keep men and machinery moving.

A thin front had been established just past the beach since June 6th, and division headquarters had set up just south of the town of Insigny, farther inland. For the next two weeks, Calvin's regiment moved intermittently by night through the fields and hedgerows as the 30th gathered for their first full-scale attack.

They had driven the enemy backward, past the Vire River, and now their crossing was vital. The road that linked the two American beachheads together had to be conquered to prevent the Carentan Peninsula and the port of Cherbourg from being completely neutralized by the Germans.

By the time they made it to the assembly area on the east side of the canal, the 117th had become accustomed to the fighting. Moving forward at night, being pinned down most of the day by machine gun fire and withstanding the strangely acute mortar shells had become routine.

Now, after a month of preparation, the Vire River crossing loomed in front of the men of the 30th Infantry Division. Calvin's regiment, who demonstrated river crossings at Fort Benning, would be the first to cross. At 4:20 a.m., July 7, the first wave began the crossing.

Calvin's platoon, part of the Second Battalion, F Company, were some of the first among thirty-two boats that began the seventy-yard trek across the river. Calvin, Johnny Duke, "Cookie" Bennett, Benny Long, and Sam Henry lowered their rubber boat down the muddy embankment, slipping into the dark water as they made their way unnoticed to the other side. Once at the opposite end of the river, scaling ladders were erected, and the men began the slippery ascent up the six-foot bank in the dark drizzle of early morning.

The first part of the company crawled off ladders and scrambled to the first hedgerow on the west side of the river as the boats made their way back for the second wave. Just as Calvin and his men found cover behind a hedgerow, enemy artillery and mortar fire began to rain down on the men in the small boats.

Eighty-eight-millimeter guns dropped their deadly mortars on the engineers as they hurriedly placed the preassembled footbridge bays into the water. Working to connect the bays to form the much-needed bridge, the soldiers remained under constant fire. A direct shot hit a team carrying one of the bays to the water, killing four men. Simultaneously, another hit destroyed the six bays already in the water.

Sprays from the impact of each mortar shell nearly toppled the boats carrying men and artillery to the other side.

By 5:30 that afternoon, the construction, reconstruction, then repairs had been made, and the bridge was ready for use.

The men already on the other side had begun their artillery barrage. They moved forward, taking a hundred yards from the enemy every five minutes. It was a good feeling. Calvin, his men, and the remainder of the 30th Division were taking back foot by foot, yard by yard, what the enemy had stolen.

As they approached the small town of St. Fromond, Lieutenant George Seaforth, in charge of the three platoons of F Company, motioned for Sergeant Wade.

"Sergeant, I need four volunteers to take out that machine gun. My guess is it's one of those buildings facing east. We're not going to be able to move another inch until we get rid of that fire. We've already lost six men."

"I'll take care of it, sir," Calvin assured him as he backed away down the hedgerow back to his men.

"Duke! Cookie!" Calvin yelled over the blast of mortars and the non-stop machine gun fire. "Make your way over to Benny and Sam and tell them to get over here. The lieutenant wants four volunteers to take out that machine gun," he said as he pointed toward the buildings where the shots were originating.

"Right, Sarge," the private said.

The four soldiers made their way into the town of St. Fromond slowly, picking their way through the shell-torn town. They located the position from which the deadly fire was coming, then made their way into the building and up the stairs to find the gunners.

Just as they reached the fifth floor, a German burst through a closed door and opened up on the squad. Calvin riddled the doorway with holes as it closed again. The German soldier fell face forward onto the landing. Two more floors to go.

Calvin motioned silently for Benny and Sam to move to the other side of the hallway, outside the door of the room where the machine gun sat facing west, cutting down the men of his battalion. Calvin and Johnny laid flat against the wall on the other side.

As Sergeant Wade gave instruction to the others, two Germans ran up the stairs toward them, trying to shout a warning to the soldiers inside the room. They hadn't heard Calvin's men making their way up the stairs. Calvin instinctively leaned over the railing and extinguished their voices. Quickly, he lay back flat against the wall and gave the signal that he was about to put his foot through the rickety door, not taking the chance that the soldiers inside had heard the warning.

As the four soldiers rushed the room, three Germans turned their weapons toward the door, but not fast enough. Sergeant Wade and Privates Duke, Henry, and Bennett unloaded their Brownings into the bodies of the Germans as they one-by-one fell to the floor.

"That's how it's done! Need a German killed, just call Johnny Duke!"

"Johnny," Sergeant Wade said firmly, "let the lieutenant know the machine gun is out," he instructed, trying to keep Johnny's exuberance intact.

"Yes, sir."

"Benny, Sam, let's get this gun broken down and packed up," Calvin instructed as he crept over to the door to watch the stairway. As soon as the men packed the gun, Calvin gave the order to move out.

The 117th's main objective, at this point, was to secure the crossroads of the two main highways that ran north to south and east to west. As they worked their way south from St. Fromond to secure the intersections of the roads, they met with the enemy's first heavy counterattack.

The 2nd SS Panzer and Artillery Division had moved up from its position near St. Lo and were pounding the 117th and the 120th with fifteen tanks and an ongoing barrage of artillery. Nothing short of panic ensued, and both battalions began to fall back. This was the type of fighting these men hadn't witnessed since they hit the beach at Omaha. Losing ground, men, tanks, and equipment quickly began to take its toll. The commanders knew they had to quickly regain control of their troops. Some men were accidentally shot by friendly fire or desecrated by mortar shells being constantly expelled from the tanks and artillery of the German division.

Lieutenant Seaforth and his company of men were part of the forward line and were suffering the worst of casualties.

"Lieutenant!" Corporal Williams, who had made his way back to Command from part of F Company, yelled over the percussions of the mortar hits, "Lieutenant, my sergeant is dead, and I've got men who refuse to fight! I don't know what to do. Our advance has come to a standstill. Do I join the others or fall back?"

"You're in charge now—Sergeant," the lieutenant yelled back. He left his position long enough to follow the newly promoted sergeant down the front line to determine their status.

"All right, men," the lieutenant shouted above the shots. "Corporal Williams is now Sergeant Williams, and he's in charge. We're retreating only long enough for the division artillery to get here. We'll gain back the ground we've lost in no time."

"Sergeant, where are the men who refused to fight?" he asked.

"Down the line there, sir." Williams pointed down the line.

"Let's have a word with them."

"Yes, sir," Sergeant Williams said as he picked his way over to the hedgerow where the two men were. They were cowering from sheer fright behind the wall of ground, and neither man would move an inch.

"Privates!" the lieutenant shouted as bullets and shells continued to assault the line.

Hearing the commanding voice of Lieutenant Seaforth dislodged them both from their grip on the earthen wall, continuing to stay low, refusing to stand. The lieutenant bent low to speak with them.

"Privates, what's the problem? Get up, get your guns, point them over that wall, and shoot. That's an order!" the lieutenant barked angrily.

"But, Lieutenant, it's no use. We're all gonna die! I don't have nothin' against them Germans. They ain't done nothin' to me! Why I got to come over here and die?" one of them ranted hysterically.

"Get up from there, Soldier, or I'll have you court-martialed as soon as this is over!" the lieutenant screamed, his disgust apparent in his voice.

As the two privates slowly rose to their feet, a tank mortar blasted a hole in the wall of the hedgerow right where the newly appointed sergeant and the lieutenant stood. The two men, who only moments ago stood side by side, were now gone. The two privates who hadn't even fired a shot were riddled with shrapnel; one was missing an arm.

Word spread fast down the line that the lieutenant was dead. As soon as Sergeant Wade heard, he made his way to their position not a hundred yards to the east of where he had been to assess the situation. He began to question the men lined up against the wall of the hedgerow.

"Who's in charge? Who's in charge?" he asked as he made his way from one cluster of men to the next. The men stared blankly back at him. Calvin quickly raised his head over the earthen to wall check the enemy. In the distance, he could see a lone Panzer tank making its way unfettered across the open field, headed straight for the hole the mortar had created in the hedgerow. Quickly, he barked orders for the men to move west, back to the square his men were desperately defending.

Sergeant Wade waited on the far side of the break in the hedgerow until all three platoons were safely on the other side, then he scuttled across. By now, his men had made their way to where he was and met him there.

"Sarge, what's going on?" Johnny asked.

"Lieutenant Seaforth is dead. Johnny, Sam, you got any grenades left?

"Sure, Sarge. Why?"

"Get the men to pass down as many grenades as possible. We've got to take this tank out. He's headed straight for this hole."

"You got it, Sarge!" Johnny smiled as he instructed the men to pass down their grenades. Calvin and Johnny Duke gathered as many as they could crossing to the other side of the hole. Benny, Sam and Cookie waited on the other side for Calvin's signal. Calvin peered over the wall to determine the tank's position. In a matter of minutes, the tank would plow through the hole, leaving them totally unprotected. They had one chance to do it right.

Calvin counted silently, then signaled to the men on the other side of the hole. While the two men closest to the opening on either side lobbed grenade after grenade into the tank's path when it got close enough, the others laid grenades just in front of the hole as it made its way through the opening in the hedgerow.

Right on time, the grenades began detonating and were just enough to stop the tank's onslaught. A track rolled off, causing the tank to spin and jump without one of its tracks making the giant metal goliath ground to a halt. The men left standing against that hedgerow made their way to the tank just as it lost momentum. Slowly, the soldiers in the tank made their way out with their hands raised. One was immediately shot down by enemy fire, the other two scrambled to the wall for safety.

Johnny Duke rammed the butt of his gun into the belly of the first soldier and was going for the head of the other as Calvin stopped him.

"Johnny!" Calvin yelled as the boy raised his gun at the German, "not now, Johnny. This is not the time."

Johnny Duke wiped his face on the back of his sleeve. He turned, walked away, and sat against the earthen wall. Calvin looked around, trying to figure out what to do, and realized he had three platoons, maybe four, that he needed to get out of the way of this attack.

"Cookie, Sam, you've got the prisoners. Let's get out of here while we can." Just at that time, a corpsman scrambled over to Calvin.

"Sir? Sir, we've been instructed to stay in place. Division artillery is setting up to fire, and we have to stay put."

"What'll we do with the tank, sir?" Private Willie Payne asked.

Calvin looked around, dumbfounded thinking maybe they should just wait until he could ask someone what to do. As he took another look at the two Germans standing there with their hands on the heads, he changed his mind.

"Blow it up."

"Yes, sir!" the private answered as he and some of the other men tossed grenades inside the tank, causing the ammunition and gasoline to ignite. The explosion sent a stream of fire into the sky above the hedgerow.

"Corpsman, relay coordinates to division. Tell them to hit just east of that explosion."

As the Corpsman gave the coordinates, artillery rained down on the other side of the small shelter of ground.

The men of the F Company, along with the remnants of other companies who now followed Calvin, cheered.

CHAPTER TWENTY-EIGHT

"I hope your fiancé makes it home okay."

"JOEY . . ." NELL WHISPERED, lowering the letter she held in her hands, her mind languishing in the past.

"Joey? Who's Joey?" Bonnie replied. "And what ya got there?" She indicated, nodding toward the letter Nell was reading.

"Just a letter from an old pal in St. Louis. Seems like one of my old flames has been drafted. Joe Delrina. Old Joey," Nell said somberly. "He'll make a hell of a sailor."

"Nell, who's Joey?" Bonnie asked again.

"Just an old beau from home. I haven't seen him in years. My girlfriend up there writes me every now and then and fills me in on what's going on."

"Why did you come here from St. Louis? Why do you never talk about it?"

"Nothin' to talk about. My parents are gone. I got a few friends left there; no one to write home about."

"Why did you come to Nashville?" Bonnie pressed.

"Oh, c'mon, you don't want to hear that story," Nell said, struggling to remain her unmovable self.

"Yes, I do," Bonnie argued softly.

Nell sighed reluctantly, but finally opened up.

"I worked at the station in St. Louis. Things were going along pretty well and, I don't know, *things* happened. I asked them for a transfer, and here I am." She smiled, but it was forced, as if she were saying *See? I'm fine.*

"Nell, you can tell me. I'm your friend, remember?"

"I know, honey. It's just . . . well, I left it behind. I don't even think about it much anymore. Now, this letter comes. I don't know." She leaned across the counter, resting her head in her hands. "I just wish she wouldn't have written me about him. It's been so many years ago."

Bonnie urged her on. "You've always been there for me. If you want to tell me about it, I just want you to know I'm here."

"Thanks, sweetie. It just seems like so long ago."

"Well, I know, but sometimes those things we've tried to run from come back and eventually catch up with us. Look at Calvin and me. I tried to run as hard and fast as I could from that, then he shows up ten years later, and I realize I'm still in love with him."

"It's not quite that simple, kid," Nell said, a distant look glazing over her eyes as if she were looking into a mirror to the past. "Joey Delrina was everything. We had known each other since we were kids. He taught me how to play stickball, how to drive a car. He taught me how to do a lot of things. I loved him so much. He was my hero."

"What happened?" Bonnie squealed, barely able to contain her curiosity.

"We were going to get married, Joey and me. We were so in love. Then, Joey fell in with this tough guy crowd, you know? We were all just getting by back then. Well, these guys talked Joey into knocking over a little grocery stand not far from the neighborhood. The problem was, they got caught. Joey went to jail. My parents died one after another that same year. I was working at the train station in St. Louis then, so I transferred, and here I am."

"Did he ever get out?"

"Oh, yeah. He didn't spend that much time down. He was only in jail for less than a year. Seems like he didn't have anything to do with the actual robbery. He was just on the lookout, and a reluctant one at that. He's been out for a long time."

"Did he ever come looking for you?"

Nell smiled wanly, bittersweet. "No, he didn't. My girlfriend back home says he kind of disappeared. He pops into town every now and then. He's asked about me, she says, but I made her promise not to tell him where I went to."

"Why, Nell? Maybe he wants to find you. Did he ever get married?"

"Why so many questions?"

"He might still be in love with you, Nell. You might still be in love with him."

"Oh, I don't think so. He's just a funny memory. You know, I can barely remember his face anymore. Isn't that funny?"

"Nell . . ."

"C'mon, little matchmaker, I have to get back to work. Time for another round of coffee," she said as she turned around, picking up the nearest coffee pot.

"Well, I think you should let him know where you are," Bonnie said, finishing her lunch.

"I can't now even if I wanted to, which I *don't*," Nell said. The emphasis on the last word indicated to Bonnie that the conversation was over although, Bonnie couldn't resist getting in the last word.

"You never know what might happen is what I say," she quipped as she gathered her things to head for the Red Cross hut by the tracks.

"Is that so?" Nell said as she set the coffee pot down on the counter in front of Bonnie. "I've never heard so much as a peep more about Calvin Wade all these years, and now he shows up and you say, 'You never know what might happen.' Don't give me that, little miss 'I'm going to marry the richest man in town until my childhood sweetheart shows up and decides he wants me back.' You had no idea how Calvin felt until he got here."

Bonnie stared at Nell in disbelief. She'd never heard Nell speak that way to her before. Nell, perhaps realizing she had gone too far, grew flush in her cheeks. Bonnie stood quietly and paid for her meal.

"Bonnie, honey . . ."

Bonnie leaned over the counter so as not to yell. "At least I tried to do the right thing," she whispered. "At least I haven't given up." She turned and made her way outside the busy lunchroom.

Nell, remorseful, was way too busy with customers to go after her.

Annie Parker rushed into the Lunch Room, looking for Nell, who was just cleaning up after the lunch crowd. She popped up from behind the counter.

"Nell, where's Bonnie?"

"I don't know. She was in here for lunch. Is anything wrong?" Nell asked, noting the excited look on Annie's face.

"I don't know. I have a letter for her. It's from Calvin. I knew she would want it right away."

Nell smiled. "Oh, I hope it's good news," she said as she came around the counter, removing her apron.

"So do I," Annie said. The two women faced each other, hands clasped together as if they were saying an unspoken prayer for Bonnie. It had been a long haul for Bonnie since she had left Smithville. Both women knew where her heart had always been, and both hoped that her dreams would finally come true.

"C'mon, let's go find her," Nell said.

Nell and Mrs. Parker picked their way across the railroad tracks to the Red Cross shack. They could see Bonnie through the open door. She was digging through some boxes. June was upon them. The days had grown longer, and the temperature had begun to rise. Bonnie's electric fan buzzed in the corner of the dreary shack.

"Miss Annie, what are you doing here?" Bonnie asked. She kissed her on the cheek. "Is anything wrong?"

"Bonnie, I have something for you," she said excitedly.

"What is it?" Bonnie asked suspiciously.

Annie reached into her purse and pulled out an envelope. "It's from Calvin, Bonnie."

"Go ahead, Honey. Open it," Nell urged.

Bonnie reached out with shaking hands to take the envelope from Annie's hand. She knew that what was inside could change her life. Had he changed his mind? Did he still want her to wait?

As she reached for the letter, Bonnie felt a flash of anger at Calvin, or at herself because he still held such a great deal of power over her emotions. For a split second, she wanted to rip the letter to shreds.

Slowly, Bonnie opened the envelope and began to read. Her two best friends held onto one another not knowing whether they'd have to mop Bonnie off the floor or pull her down from the ceiling. They were prepared for either.

Bonnie began to read:

Dearest Bonnie Girl,

I am lying here in my bunk on the ship. It's almost lights out. I made a promise to myself that tonight I would finish this letter to you.

We're headed for England now. Finally, it seems as if I will get my chance to fight.

Seeing you at the station was probably the worst timing I ever had. I have to admit, I been around Nashville on maneuvers for quite some time, and I had avoided going into town for that very reason. I was scared what happened at the train station might happen. Sure enough, it did. Now I'm glad I saw you.

I guess I sure need to apologize for what happened, you being an engaged woman and all. I don't know what come over me, Bonnie. I hope that, because of me, your reputation has not suffered. You were just such a sight all my feelings just came out from inside of me like they was controlling me. The thought I might never see you again has crossed my mind before, like when you was lying in that bed near your death. I guess I just never thought I'd feel that way ever again.

I realize I had no right to ask the thing that I did of you, to wait for me. I realize you are already waiting for someone else, and I am truly ashamed of asking such a thing of you. I know you are going to marry Ned, and I have no right, especially after what I have done, to ask such a thing. But there are some things I just have to get off my chest, Bonnie, before I help to finish this war that has taken away so many friends and people we know and love.

Bonnie, I've made a lot of mistakes. Seems like every decision I have made has had some awful ending that I was never able to turn around. Like with Rosalee. I can't change what happened to Rosalee, and eventually, I knew I'd have to learn to live with it. With your help, I did. But the night I saw you lying on that path, pale white with the life draining out of you, I knew there was something I could do. I've always known how you felt about me, Bonnie. Even before you told me. But 'til that day, I didn't know how much I loved you. I knew from that point on, I would have to forget the way I felt and never, ever risk your life with this terrible curse I had on my life, no matter what it meant to me.

I made a promise to God that I would never, ever let you into my life if he would just spare yours. It was the hardest thing I'd ever done to turn you away that day you came to visit me after you got better, but I knew it would have to be that way, to keep you safe. When I looked into your eyes that day in the train station, I knew I had made a terrible mistake.

Here I am, practically an old man, and I realized I have never lived my life. I've just gone through the moves, never allowing what's in my heart to come out. All my life, it's only been you. As guilty as I feel about it, even when I was to marry Rosalee, I knew it wasn't love that I felt for her, not the kind of love I've carried around in my heart for you. All of these years I never regretted my decision. Even when I knew you were to be married. The day I came to talk to you about Jessie and I saw that ring on your finger, I wanted to tell you right there in the station how I felt and ask you not to marry Ned. To tell you I wanted you to come home with me. But I felt in my heart I had done the right thing.

I know I can't ask you to wait for me. I know you are to marry

Ned. He's a lucky man. But I love you, Bonnie, with all of my life I love you. You have to know that and know that I am truly sorry for all of the pain I caused for you. I want to mail this to you and maybe I will. I hope for once in my life I have the courage to tell you the truth.

I won't write anymore except for this letter. Whatever you decide to do is up to you. I can face going over there now, knowing I have finally told you how I really feel. I'll remember your face looking up at me the day I left for the rest of my life, and that's enough for me. But I will be back. And if fate sees its way for us to be together, I'll live the rest of my life trying to make up for these past years we've missed.

Well, I guess that's most of what I wanted to say.

By the way, Roy and Bill have become fast friends thanks to you. They are in my regiment and are loaded up on this ship with me. They are inseparable.

Jessie and Lizzie are awfully worried about you, Bonnie. Go visit. Give them my love. Tell Buttermilk and Shorty to keep that farm running straight 'til I get back.

With all my love,

Calvin

Bonnie leaned backward and slid into the chair against the wall. She buried her face in her hands.

Annie put her arms around Bonnie. "Well, what did it say, Bonnie?"

Bonnie handed the letter to Nell, who began to read it out loud so that Annie could hear.

"I'm so happy, Bonnie. I know that's what you wanted."

Bonnie pushed her hair back away from her face. "I don't understand. Does he want me to wait or not?"

The oldest of the three women laughed out loud.

"I don't think it's so funny," Bonnie said, trying not to laugh through her tears.

"Don't you see, honey? You have to read between the lines. He did ask you to wait, but he asked you in the most gentlemanly way he could so as not to ruin your honor."

"My honor? What's that got to do with anything?"

Annie tried to explain. "You see, Bonnie. Calvin is a gentleman, and gentlemen don't steal other men's fiancés. So, Calvin has to let you make the decision. He could never feel in the future that it was any other way. The choice has to be yours."

"In the meantime, he sure let you know which way he wants it to turn out. Didn't he, kid?" Nell added.

Bonnie smiled. "Yes . . . he did." She stood, hugged Nell, then turned to hug Annie.

"See? I told you everything would be all right," Annie said.

"I know, and you're always right!"

"I have to get back to the parsonage. We'll talk more tonight, dear," Annie added as she kissed Bonnie goodbye.

"Goodbye, Miss Annie. I'll see you tonight."

Nell and Bonnie stood in the doorway of the little shack, waving goodbye to Miss Annie as she crossed the tracks and headed back up the stairs to the lobby of the station.

Nell took the opportunity to make up for what she'd said earlier.

"Bonnie, about what I said at lunch; I'm sorry. I shouldn't have spoken to you like that."

"No, Nell. You should've. Who am I to give advice to anyone? I've been so mixed up about Calvin, then Ned, and now Calvin and Ned. No, you were right. I just want you to know you're my best friend in the whole world, and you can tell me anything, okay?"

"The truth is . . . I do still think about Joey. All the time. I see someone walk in the Lunch Room who walks like him or looks like him, and I think about him. Or I brush up against someone at a table serving coffee who smells like him, but it's been so long ago. Oh, I don't know. Maybe I'll write my girlfriend back and tell her to give him my address if she hears from him."

"Oh Nell, that would be swell. You never know. He just might walk right into that Lunch Room one day."

"All right. Let's not get carried away!"

"Thanks, Nell."

"I'm happy for you, Bonnie. You would've never been happy with Ned. You would have never been able to be yourself. That's a world you practically have to be born into."

"Oh, Nell, what am I going to do about Ned? I do care about him deeply. What am I going to do?"

"Honey, I think you'll see that he'll take it better than you think. He knows deep inside how hard it would have been on you. We'll figure it out, okay? Now, I have to get back before Charlie sends out the dogs."

"Okay, bye," Bonnie said as she hugged her friend. Bonnie sat back on the chair and read the letter again and again.

"Hey, can a guy get a cup of coffee around here?" a soldier asked from the doorway. Startled, Bonnie leapt to her feet.

"Oh, I'm sorry, I just got a letter from my fiancé," she said as she poured a cup of coffee. Bonnie smiled at herself at referring to Calvin as her fiancé. She handed the coffee to the soldier.

"Thanks, I hope your fiancé makes it home okay."

"He will," Bonnie said as the soldier turned to walk back to the station.

The days at the station had become slower than usual. It seemed as if they shipped everybody out all at once right after Christmas. Every day people read the papers hoping to find out more about what was happening over there.

Bonnie continued to receive letters from Ned, who was stationed somewhere in England. She knew he had been flying a great deal and, by way of his letters, he seemed to grow more and more depressed about the situation. She knew she couldn't tell him about Calvin while he was fighting and had made the decision to wait until he was home to get it straightened out.

Bonnie took Calvin's advice and decided to go home and visit. She had told Lizzie about seeing Calvin in the station before he left, but she hadn't said more than that. She wanted to be able to see her face when she told her. Bonnie knew that if Lizzie disapproved, she would have a hard time of it.

July in Smithville revived Bonnie as nothing else could. She carried a peace about her now; a peace she hadn't felt in a long time. She walked the path through The Dark Forest toward the Wade home smiling when she passed the spot where Calvin found her on the trail that evening. It had always been a painful memory, but now she thought about it fondly knowing that it was that point in time that turned her whole life around. She felt closer to Calvin just thinking about it.

Summer was in full steam on the Cumberland Plateau. As Bonnie walked along the path, a breeze danced through the trees, making the most welcoming sound as the leaves rustled together. Bonnie leaned on a small sugar maple closing her eyes, letting the sound rush through her mind. Nowhere on earth did Bonnie feel like herself more than right here, walking barefoot through the path she had played on so many years before.

Bonnie found her seat on top of the rock on the bluff overlooking the Wade farm. She pulled her legs to her chest, wrapping her arms around them, propping her chin on her knees. As she looked down on the little valley, she could imagine Calvin on the front porch shielding his eyes from the bright sun the day he decided to rejoin them after Rosalee's death. She saw him on his old mule, riding out of the field as Bonnie walked beside him after school. Bonnie's eyes made their way to the tool shed, where Calvin had spent so much of his time. Bonnie closed her eyes, remembering the day she confronted Calvin there. She felt the pain again in her heart as she remembered the words he had said to her.

"You were lying to me," she whispered to herself. "You were lying. I knew you loved me. I knew it. Why didn't you tell me the truth?" Bonnie said to herself as she put her forehead on her knees and squeezed tears from her eyes. The lump in her throat swelled painfully.

"God, please bring him back home to me. Please watch over him and keep him safe. Please."

The sound of voices shook Bonnie out of her thoughts. Below, Buttermilk and Shorty stepped outside their little house arguing, as usual, about who was going to do which chore. She even saw Pippin yelling at them from the house. Bonnie jumped to her feet.

"Buttermilk! Shorty!" she yelled from her perch as she waved to them below.

"Who dat be?" Buttermilk asked Shorty.

"I dunno," Shorty said as he squinted in the noon sun to get a better look. "Why, Lordy be. It's Miss Bonnie!"

"It sho is. Lookee there, Shorty. It's Miss Bonnie!" Buttermilk said as they both made their way down the front porch steps.

Bonnie was down the path and standing in front of them in seconds flat. "Buttermilk, Shorty," she said as she hugged them both. "I'm so glad to see you."

"Why, Miss Bonnie," Buttermilk said. "You sho done growed up."

"You sho have," Shorty agreed with a smile. Bonnie noticed his smile quickly disappeared.

"What's the matter, Shorty?" Bonnie asked. Shorty reached up and pulled his hat off his head.

"Miss Bonnie, Mr. Calvin not here. He done gone and joined the war!"

"I know, Shorty," Bonnie said solemnly as she put her hand on his. "I saw him at the train station in Nashville. He tried to sneak out of town without me seeing him, but the Lord put him right in my path to make sure I didn't miss him," she said with a smile. Buttermilk and Shorty's smiles reappeared.

"You saw him?" Buttermilk asked. "How he look? We ain't seen him in months. He wrote us letters through Miss Lizzie, and she brings them over and reads to us, but we hadn't heard from him since he went and joined up to go overseas."

"I know, Buttermilk. I don't know where they sent him. I've gotten one letter from him. I'm sure he'll be fine," Bonnie said, trying to assure them and herself. "I'm so glad to see both of you," she said as she hugged them both again. "Let's go inside and visit with Pippin for a while."

"Well, we got some chores to do right away, Miss Bonnie. We promised Mr. Calvin wouldn't let one thing go undone whiles he was gone," Shorty told her.

"Oh, I don't think he'll mind if you take a few minutes to visit. Come on, let's have some coffee," she said, locking her arms in theirs heading for the house.

That night after supper, Bonnie, Lizzie, and Jessie sat out in the evening air on the front porch.

"Tell me again how he looked when you saw him," Jessie urged.

"Jessie, she's told you over and over again already," Lizzie said. She turned to Bonnie. "He just misses him so much."

"He's a strong boy. He'll go over there and whup them Krauts and be back in no time," Jessie added. Bonnie smiled as she stood at the railing looking at the night sky. She was wondering which of her parents was trying to comfort the other the most.

"He made me mad standing there in that uniform," Bonnie told her father again. "I still can't believe no one told me."

"Now let's not go into that again. I told you, Bonnie. He made me promise," Lizzie said once again.

"You say you got a letter from him?" her father asked.

"Yes," Bonnie said as she turned to sit with her parents. "That's one reason I came home. I wanted to tell you about his letter."

"What's wrong?" Lizzie asked, laying her mending down in her lap and sitting up a bit straighter as if she was steadying herself for bad news.

"Nothing's wrong, Mama," Bonnie assured her as she reached over and put her hand on top of hers. Lizzie cocked her head to the side a bit and took a closer look at her daughter.

"What is it, girl? You've got something on your mind. Out with it," her mother said.

Bonnie began with the news Jessie and Lizzie had been waiting years to hear. Calvin had finally come to terms with his demons.

Chapter Twenty-Nine

"Mr. Bass, this is Colonel Appleby from Washington calling."

───────────◆═══◆═══◆───────────

THE WINTER SEEMED to drag on interminably. Calvin's men had fought across the European countryside through the heat, the rain, few rations, and a steady stream of reinforcements. Sam, Cookie, and Duke were the only soldiers left from Calvin's original Company. Now the worst winter Europe had experienced in years plagued the battle against the Germans.

The troops fought through Belgium's Ardennes Forest. Now they were experiencing a drive from the Germans that pushed them back almost sixty miles. Three days after a cold, wet Christmas, they were gearing up to squeeze the enemy back and regain the costly ground they had lost.

Calvin opened his eyes and began shifting slowly under the newly fallen snow, leaning back against the wall of the foxhole. He had managed a few hours' sleep while Johnny Duke took the watch. He instinctively began to move his feet around, trying to get his circulation back. He rubbed his hands together, blowing breath into them so that it would back up onto the exposed skin on his face to help to thaw it a bit. It was no use. He couldn't feel it.

Dawn was breaking, and they'd had a long night of German stragglers trying to make it by their position. He and Johnny were dog tired.

"Have you heard anything?" Calvin asked the private.

"No, sir. A few stray shots every now and then. Man, it's cold!"

he said as he laid his rifle down, rubbing his hands together. Calvin instinctively grabbed his rifle, shoving it over the edge of the foxhole, to give Johnny a few minutes to warm up. Just then, Cookie slid down the edge of the foxhole crouching to relay a message to Calvin.

"Sergeant Wade, the lieutenant says we're going to move today," he said excitedly. "He wants to see you right away."

"All right. Stay here with Johnny until I get back."

"Okay, Sarge."

Calvin picked his way back to the foxhole the lieutenant occupied and got his orders. They were going to move in less than an hour. Three platoons were going to move to the right flank of the Germans and try to box them in. Air support would accompany them after coordinates were given for the Germans' location. That would be Calvin's job. They'd be the first to move.

Calvin made his way back to his foxhole and relayed the orders to his men. They all sat quietly, waiting for the signal. Calvin pulled Bonnie's tattered picture from his pocket, wiping the snow from it for one more look before they moved again.

"Hey, Sarge, you gonna marry that girl when you get back?"

"I hope so, Cookie," he said as he placed the picture back into his pocket. "That is if she's not already taken. There's the signal. Let's move."

"Lieutenant Bass, proceed to your bombing location," Ned heard over the radio as he led the squadron east toward their destination. Their bomber began to drop altitude as they got closer to the front. The Germans recently regained the ground they had lost in part because the Allied bombers had been grounded during snowstorms and gray skies.

Ned was excited. This bomb run would be different. It wasn't a city where women and children and old people lived and were trying to survive. This was a German camp. Information had been provided that this location held a secret supply of gasoline, a precious commodity for the German Panzer and the Luftwaffe.

As they crossed the front, the navigator informed him they had just passed the line of the American troops below. The bombers humming overhead signaled to the forces on the ground below the push had begun. Ned gave the bombing order. The cumbersome bombers tipped their wings to the troops below. It was time for his good-luck charm. He retrieved his worn picture of Bonnie one more time. "See you soon, Sweet Face," he whispered as he tucked it back into his jacket.

"Hey, Sarge, did you see that? The bombers tipped their wings at us!" Calvin looked upward. "They know where we are."

"Hey guys, bomb the hell out of 'em!" Duke yelled, precarious as usual.

Calvin handed the phone back to the corpsman.

"All right, men. Let's go!" Sergeant Wade said as he gave the signal to proceed.

The Germans fought feverishly to defend the ground they had taken, giving every resource they had to hold their position. Behind them, Berlin lay like a prisoner waiting to meet his executioner. With the Russians pushing at the eastern front and the Allies advancing on the west, its destiny held precariously in the balance, the Germans pulled out all the stops trying to hold their ground.

As Ned's squadron neared their destination, anti-aircraft guns began blasting artillery into the air. Two bombers immediately went down. An onslaught of Luftwaffe planes appeared out of nowhere.

"Eight o'clock! Eight o'clock!" the gunner screamed into the microphone. The navigator shouted corrections to avoid their steady stream of fire. Ned pulled hard on the controls as the nose of the aircraft rose swiftly. The waist gunner unloaded as the fighter planes flew under and emerged on the other side.

"They're turning around! They're turning around!" the co-pilot yelled. The two German fighters had managed to separate Ned from the squadron.

"Give me a correction to our target," Ned ordered the navigator.

"But, sir!"

"Give me the coordinates!" he insisted.

"The squadron is taking a beating, sir," the radioman informed him. "Eight down!"

"We're taking our target. Anyone with any objections should get off here," Ned shouted into his mike.

The crew of *My Bonnie Lass* sat silent as the German fighters made another approach. The gunner from the back of the plane spoke up. "We're with you, sir," then screamed, "Two o'clock! Two o'clock!"

The gunner stared down the sight of his gun. The stream of bullets raked across the window of the fighter. Immediately it began to dive to its grave.

"I got one, sir! I got one!" the gunner yelled. The second fighter closed in and aimed directly at him. Bullets raked across the bomber, ripping through the fuselage. The plane dove quickly to avoid colliding with the bomber. The gunner regained control of the machine gun as the fighter dove underneath them. He let go of a round aimed at the tail of the plane, but missed. The rear gunner picked up fire shooting feverishly into the air. The tail of the fighter blew, and the plane exploded into a fireball. The percussion of the explosion rocked the heavy plane. The crew applauded as the bomber settled.

"Jimmy! Coordinates!" Ned demanded as he corrected his course. The directive was right before them. The sluggish bomber slowly descended. Flak from below began to rock the ship as they got closer. Ned's mouth grew dry. The bombardier plotted his release. The bombs dropped one after another as the ground below gave up its prize. The last two bombs were a direct hit. The secondary explosion from the gasoline dump climbed higher and higher behind them. The crew was exuberant, if only for a short while.

Ned climbed as high as the wounded plane would allow. A fire broke out in the second engine. They watched as it spitted and sputtered to a stop. They lost altitude quickly. The cold carpet of the Ardennes Forest lay before them. Ned gave the order to bail out.

Ned clung to the controls as the plane began to shake violently and his men began to empty from the plane.

"Come on, Captain. Come on!" the co-pilot shouted.

"Jump, Ted! That's an order. I'm right behind you!"

The co-pilot made his way to the jump door and spilled out into the cold December air.

As Ned let go of the controls, the plane pulled hard to the left. Ned fought against the gravity of the pull to make his way to exit the plane. He jumped just as the nose of the plane dipped sharply. Slowly, *My Bonnie Lass* turned on its side and crashed into the thick carpet of trees below.

"Hey, that was close," Sam said to Cookie, watching as the plume of fire and smoke rose to the sky where the bomber downed.

"Yeah, too close."

Calvin's regiment was pushing hard against the Germans. They had lost a great deal of men. The Germans seemed to be coming out of nowhere. Dressed in white, they could barely be seen against the stark white snow that covered the surrounding landscape. That is, until they moved. By then, it was usually too late.

Mortar shells began to hit all around them, sending snow, frozen ground, and tree splinters in all directions. It made it hard to use the trees for cover. Not far away was a clearing. Calvin was to have some of his men circle around and come in on the right flank of the Germans' position. As they trekked through the deep snow, circling wide to come around to the edge of the clearing, Duke saw something in a tree ahead. Slowly, they moved closer. It was an American pilot hanging from the tree still in his parachute harness. The cold breeze that blew through the trees as the concussions from the explosions that filled the air caused the body to sway back and forth in unison with the trees. He hung lifeless above them as they watched.

"Probably broke his neck in the fall," Calvin said as he inched closer. Suddenly, stray fire ricocheted through the trees. The men dove into the snow.

"C'mon, we've got to get out of here, Sarge," Johnny insisted.

"Cut him down," Calvin ordered.

"But, Sarge!" Cookie argued.

Calvin pulled a knife from his pants leg, stuck it in his mouth as he quickly climbed through the tree limbs and cut the harness from the dead pilot. The men below stood long enough to catch the falling body and lay it softly in the snow.

"C'mon, let's get moving," Calvin said, staring at the body of the pilot. His mask was frozen to his face. There wasn't anything else they could do for him.

"Sarge, look, he's got something in his hand," Johnny said as he tried to pry his fingers open. Stray fire from across the clearing ricocheted through the trees again. Johnny dove for cover.

"C'mon, there's no time, we've got to move," Calvin ordered.

As they neared the clearing, they saw a band of German soldiers gathering at the far end of the clearing. They were pouring over a map and appeared to be arguing. Soon, they seemed as if they had settled their matter and began to move into the forest to join the line pushing toward Calvin's platoon. Calvin and company followed them along the edge of the forest, remaining behind them. Calvin gave the order to open fire. Once the volley had ended, only Calvin's group remained alive. Before moving on, they double checked to ensure that all the Germans were dead.

That was Duke's favorite job.

He didn't like to take prisoners.

The small band of men from Company F moved forward, hoping to sneak up behind more of the enemy trying to regain ground. Calvin sent word that his plan was working and gave the order for more troops to join him. Just as he transmitted his coordinates, mortar fire rained down all around them.

They'd been spotted.

A shell hit directly in front of them, taking two of Calvin's men with it. The radioman was down, too. Calvin crawled to the radio.

"This is Sergeant Wade. Ignore the last coordinates. Heavy mortar fire. I repeat . . ." he shouted. Another mortar dropped behind them. The receiver fell from his hand and into the blood-soaked snow. Calvin opened his eyes to see tall evergreens pointing toward the clear blue sky. As he lay on his back looking up, he struggled to reach into his coat. He pulled out his picture of Bonnie and painfully brought it to his lips. He looked up at the trees again. They began to spin in a dark circle as he fought to keep his eyes open. He blinked slowly, fighting against his heavy lids. Finally, his eyelids won. Calvin's eyes closed against his will.

"Bonnie . . ."

The German soldier in charge reminded his men to follow the order that had come down to strip the dead American soldiers of everything they could as quickly as they could. All papers, personal effects of any kind, warm clothing, boots; anything that the Germans could use to find out anything they could about the Americans; and to keep warm. The clothing was to be put to future use by the Germans but also so that the Americans, couldn't put it to their own use, just in case the ground where the dead soldiers lay on was ever recaptured.

This small patch of forest, including the few farmhouses and barns, which had been taken by the Americans, then lost again to the Germans, teemed with activity. They didn't want to take any chances if the Americans came back to reclaim this ground.

Most of the excitement was centered around the downed bomber. The search proceeded for the other men that had parachuted out as it was going down.

A young soldier cleaned up the outskirts of the battle, making sure they didn't miss any strays. He poked at the dead body with his rifle, making sure the American was dead. The commander came to his side and put his hand to his arm, reminding him to use caution. More than one careless German had had his throat slit by an American waiting with a knife tucked underneath him.

He pointed to the soldier's hand that obviously held something in its grip. Slowly, the young German unfolded the hand. He looked back up at his commander, showing him a picture of a stunning redhead. He tossed the picture back to the snow and proceeded with his search.

"Mr. Bass," the operator said to Carlton Bass over the speaker.

"Yes, what is it, Miss Cooper?"

"Mr. Bass, you have a call from Washington on the line. Would you like for me to put it through?"

"Washington?" Carlton Bass repeated to himself as he stood at his desk. "Yes, girl. Yes, put it through."

It rang once as Mr. Bass hesitantly picked up the receiver.

"Mr. Bass, this is Colonel Appleby in Washington."

"Oh yes, Colonel. How are you?"

"I'm just fine, thank you. A bit busy as of late, you know."

"I'm sure, I'm sure. Listen, I've wanted to thank you for your help with Ned's appointment overseas. I've never had the chance to thank you properly," Mr. Bass said, nervously avoiding what he feared would come next.

"Ned has done a splendid job with the Eighth Air Corp, Mr. Bass. I would have thought after his initial twenty-five missions, he would have been happy to come home to a training job, but not Ned. He . . . is a fine pilot," the colonel said with hesitancy.

"Yes, we're proud of him.

"Carlton, I'm afraid I have a bit of news. Not bad news, but not good news either," the colonel continued. Carlton Bass swallowed hard as he tried to find his voice. "I'm afraid that Ned's plane has gone down in the Ardennes Forest in Belgium. We were getting a good fight in Carlton, regaining ground from the Germans hour by hour that we lost in this blasted winter snow. The planes had been grounded for days on end, then finally we got a break in the weather and sent our bombers out to make some headway for the troops on the ground.

"The Germans were ready for us, and we lost a number of planes. In fact, Ned was the only one to make it to his target and accomplish his mission. Unfortunately, the plane was badly hit, and all of the men bailed out before it crashed; all, that is, except Ned. The co-pilot reported that Ned held the plane together while his crew jumped. He doesn't know if Ned got out of the plane before it crashed into the forest."

Carlton Bass closed his eyes, rubbing his forehead slowly as the colonel told his story, trying to comprehend the words Colonel Appleby was saying. They seemed to all be running together. The sound of his voice was distant, as if he was listening to a story on the radio or reading it in the newspaper, but it was Ned he was talking about. It was Ned who made his bombing target. It was Ned who may have gone down with his plane. In his mind, Mr. Bass pictured the bomber going down in the snow-covered forest. The sound of an explosion in his mind jolted him so hard his body actually jerked in its chair.

"Carlton? Carlton, I'm sorry to have to call you with this news. We lost that bit of ground back to the Germans. It was a tough battle. I'm afraid we won't be able to look for his . . . we won't be able to look for him until we claim that sector back. The weather's gone bad on us again and . . ."

"Yes, yes. I understand," Carlton Bass uttered weakly.

"Carlton, the minute I hear something . . ."

"Yes, Colonel Appleby, I know . . . I mean . . . I understand."

"I'm sorry to call with this news, but I didn't want you to hear it by any other means."

Mr. Bass managed to pull himself together enough to thank the colonel.

"Colonel Appleby, yes. Thank you. I mean, thank you for taking the time to call me. I know you have much on your mind."

"As I'm sure you do, Carlton. It was no trouble. I only hope when we speak again, I have better news."

"Yes, as do I, sir. As do I." He hung up the phone.

Carlton Bass stood and looked out his window onto the street below. In an instant, he saw Ned in the many phases through which he had seen him approach the building as he had grown. He saw him as a young boy, dashing up to see his father who was too busy to play ball. He saw him as a teenager, reluctantly reporting to work. He saw him after college, in his pressed linen suit and hat, lingering as long as he could on the street, talking to the ladies who passed by before entering to show up for the day. More recently, he saw him arm-in-arm with Bonnie, smiling. Mr. Bass reached into his coat pocket, removing his handkerchief as he sat back down on the thick, leather chair.

Mrs. Cooper had gotten the word that Mr. Bass had received a call from Washington. She knocked lightly.

"Yes?" Mr. Bass answered the knock.

Mrs. Cooper opened the door slowly, not knowing quite what to do next. "Mr. Bass, is everything all right?" she asked as he remained with his back to the door facing the window.

Mr. Bass tried to clear the lump in his throat before he spoke. He answered with an exhausted sigh. "Mrs. Cooper, please cancel my appointments this afternoon and have Albert come down early. I . . ."

Suspecting the worst, Mrs. Cooper threw her hands to her face to stifle her cry. "Is everything . . . okay, sir?"

"Seems as if Ned's plane has gone down. They're not able to look for him as of yet. I guess you could say he's missing," Mr. Bass said as he turned to face his secretary.

Mrs. Cooper had been with Carlton Bass for over twenty years. She had witnessed the young Mr. Bass grow up and knew and loved him probably as much as his own mother did.

"It's okay, Mrs. Cooper," Mr. Bass said, coming out from behind his desk to try to comfort her. "It's okay." He placed his hands on her shoulders. "He's missing; he's not dead. That's what we have to say. We have to say he's missing because that's all we know.

"Now, pull yourself together. We mustn't think the worst."

"I'm sorry, Mr. Bass. I just thought . . . he just must be all right. He has to be."

"Yes, he does," Mr. Bass agreed. "Now, get Albert here early. I have to break this news to Mrs. Bass."

"Yes, sir," Mrs. Cooper answered as she turned to exit the office.

"Mrs. Cooper," Mr. Bass called after her as she dried her face on her scarf. "Thank you for your concern." Mrs. Cooper tried to smile, although it never quite made it to her face. She shut the door behind her.

Mr. Bass sat in his chair turning to face the window. For maybe the second time in his life, Carlton Bass prayed.

"Mr. Bass?" the intercom screeched.

"Yes?" he answered.

"Albert is here. Shall I send him back?" Mrs. Cooper asked.

"No, that's fine," Mr. Bass spoke as he slowly got up from his chair. "I'll come on out."

Carlton Bass gathered his things for the ride home. Mrs. Cooper came in to help.

"Are you all right, Mr. Bass?"

"Yes. Yes. I'll be fine. If I get any calls from Washington, please send them home, will you?"

"Yes, Mr. Bass."

"I don't know if I had any appointments, Mrs. Cooper. Can you . . ."

"Don't worry about them," she said, laying a comforting hand on his. "I'll take care of it." She handed him his briefcase. Suddenly, Mr. Carlton Bass, the obstinate, single-minded land baron and one of the brightest lawyers in the country, seemed extremely old. His walk was no longer swift and purposeful, but slow and cumbersome.

As he made his way to the elevator, he spoke to no one and answered no one as they told him goodbye. He didn't hear them. All he could think about was Ned.

Albert slid into the driver's seat after helping Mr. Bass into the car. Mrs. Cooper had already filled him in on the news, and he waited patiently, as always, for Mr. Bass to bring it up.

"Ned is missing," Carlton informed his butler. He rubbed the late-afternoon stubble on his chin.

"Yes, sir. Do we know where the plane went down?" Albert said, looking into his rear view mirror.

"Somewhere in Belgium, they believe in that dreadful fight in the forest over there. They had pushed the Germans back, it seems, when Ned's plane went down. Then they lost the ground again. So we can't go back in to look for him."

"Sir, Ned is a resourceful boy and a damn good pilot," Albert said.

Mr. Bass looked up briefly at him. Albert didn't typically use profanity, at least not in Mr. Bass' presence. He smiled.

"Yes, he is. They said he held the plane steady for his crew to bail out. The co-pilot was the last to go. He just didn't see Ned make it out of the plane before it went down. We'll just have to wait."

After some silence, Carlton spoke again. "How will I tell Claudia? How? This will . . ."

"Sir, maybe it's better if she doesn't know just yet. After all, he's only missing. It could be a cause for a lot of unnecessary worrying on the Miss's part."

"You could be right, Albert. Then there's Miss McCaverty. With all of her Red Cross work, maybe it wouldn't be right to tell her such news until we know something."

"I agree, sir."

"That's a good decision, Albert. We'll wait. Wait until we know something more. I'll have to inform Mrs. Cooper that Claudia doesn't know."

"I'll phone her and let her know, sir."

"Thank you, Albert. Thank you."

Chapter Thirty

"Will you marry me, baby?"

"HEY, BONNIE. WHEN am I gonna get some more of those good pickles from home?" Henry asked as he took a seat in the Red Cross hut after bringing in a load of food.

"Mama don't part with her pickles here at the end of winter, Henry. You out already?"

"Been out. They go real good with a cold beer."

"Henry, Mama wouldn't even send them to you if she knew that. You'll have to wait until the spring batch I'm afraid."

"Henry?" the trainmaster said as he stuck his head in the door of the hut. "I got a train of coffins comin' in, and I'm short on the shift. Reckon you could give those guys a hand for me?"

"Sure, just what I want to do on a cold afternoon."

"Sorry, Miss Bonnie," the trainmaster said. The women particularly avoided the tracks when they knew the coffins were arriving. It made the reality of war much too hard to bear.

Bonnie just nodded to him. The knot in her throat was too big for her to speak. He shut the door as he left.

"You okay, Bonnie?" Henry asked as he stood to go help the guys on the track.

"Yeah, I'm fine," she managed to get out.

"I don't think he meant to bring it out so blatant in front of you."

"It's okay, Henry. I understand. You go on now, and I'll have coffee waiting."

As Henry left the little hut, Bonnie sat down hard, wrapping her arms as close around herself as she could. The image of the stacks and stacks of coffins that she had accidentally seen once had horrified her. It was a stark reality. Men were dead. Boys were dead. Some women had even died. Hundreds, thousands were dying daily. Bonnie's body shook hard. She decided to go up to the lobby and help out there for a while. It always helped to be around people.

She pulled the collar of her coat up around her neck as she stepped into the cold. It was the end of February and winter was still holding on as best she could. Bonnie made her way to the lobby and popped her head in to see Nell.

"Hey, you look like you've just seen a ghost. What's the matter with you?" Nell asked as she took a seat at the counter.

"They're bringing in a load of coffins. Mr. Nelms just asked Henry to help unload. I just can't get that picture out of my head."

"Now, Bonnie, try not to think about it. Stay in here, and you won't see it again. You paid for your curiosity last time you had to see what was going on."

"Oh, I don't want to ever see that again."

"Well, help out in here for a while."

"Let me make my rounds through the lobby first, she said turning to exit the Lunch Room.

Bonnie walked into the crowded lobby of the station and looked around to see if there was anyone who needed help. Just then, she saw a family enter the side entrance, a man, a woman, and two little girls with lost looks on their faces. They looked like the folks back home. Bonnie smiled. She decided she had better give them some directions.

As she approached, she realized she knew them; it was the Carters! The two little girls were Polly and Cora.

"Polly!" Bonnie yelled across the lobby. "Polly!" she yelled again as she got closer.

"Miss Bonnie!" Polly said, recognition dawning in her eyes.

"Look, Mama. It's Miss Bonnie," the little girl said as she pointed toward Bonnie.

Bonnie wrapped her arms around the little girl, holding her tight. "Look at you! My goodness, you've clear grown up."

"And look here," Bonnie said as she bent down again. "This must be little Miss Cora." Cora hid her face in Mrs. Carter's dress.

"I'm afraid she's a bit shy," Mrs. Carter said.

"Oh, it's so good to see you," Bonnie said as she extended her hand to both the Carters.

"We're awfully glad to see you, Miss . . ." Mr. Carter stammered.

"Miss McCaverty," Bonnie reminded him.

"Miss McCaverty, yes. It's good to see you. Are you here to pick someone up, too?"

"Oh, no, I work here. Still volunteering for the Red Cross. I help with feeding the soldiers when they come through. That kind of thing."

Mrs. Carter hung her head and pulled out her handkerchief.

"My brothers are soldiers, Miss Bonnie. 'Cept Billy. He's dead. We come to git his body and take him home and bury him."

"Polly," Mr. Carter said as he gave a stern look to his daughter. Mrs. Carter began to cry. Bonnie put her arms around her and walked her to a bench. Mr. Carter took the hands of the two girls and led them over to where the women sat.

"Mrs. Carter, I'm so sorry," Bonnie began in her comforting words as she had so many times before.

"He made it through the landing at Omaha Beach and fought all the way through France. He killed a bunch a Germans," Mr. Carter said.

"I'm sure he did his part. All the boys who have died did their part," she said as she tried to comfort Mrs. Carter. It didn't seem to be working. The woman was overcome with grief. Mr. Carter had to calm her down.

"Now, honey. I shoulda left you girls at home. I knew this was too much for you."

"I'll be okay. I'll be okay. I wanna spend as much time with him as I can."

Bonnie turned to the two little girls as Mr. Carter tried to comfort his wife.

"Well, look at you two. You've just grown up so much."

"Cora, she don't remember you, Miss Bonnie."

"I know," Bonnie replied. "She was just a baby, but I remember her." She touched her finger to the end of Cora's nose. Cora smiled.

"You don't remember, Cora, but Miss Bonnie helped us when our first mama got sick. She got us a place to live. She was almost gonna be our mama, but we came to where we are now," Polly said, trying to sound as grown up as possible.

"That's my mama," Cora said to Polly as she pointed to Mrs. Carter.

Bonnie decided she better step in before little Cora really became confused. "Yes, she is, and she's a good mama. Do you have any dolls, Cora?"

"Yes, ma'am. I have one doll. Polly has two."

"I'm bigger. That's why."

"My brother is dead," Polly told Bonnie as her little lip began to quiver and a tear made its way down her pudgy cheek.

"Oh, I know, honey, but he's up in heaven with Jesus now."

"I sure hope Sam comes home and don't die too."

"Miss Bonnie," Mr. Carter spoke up, "I need to go do my business. Reckon the women could stay here till I get everything ready to go?"

"Of course, Mr. Carter. We'll go into the Lunch Room there and get some coffee."

"That'd be fine. Thank you. Where do I find the stationmaster?"

"Just go down the stairs, and as you go down the last set of stairs, there's an office just down there. They'll help you."

"Thank you."

"Come on, girls. I have someone I'd like you to meet," Bonnie said as she took the two girls' hands and led them to the Lunch Room to meet Nell.

As they entered the Lunch Room, Bonnie yelled to Nell, "Look, Nell! I have some girls I'd like you to meet."

"Well," Nell said as she wiped her hands on a towel and came out from behind the counter. "Who are these pretty girls?"

"This is Polly and Cora Carter. This is Mrs. Carter."

"Polly," Nell said thoughtfully. "Oh, *Polly*! So, *you* are Polly. I've heard a lot about you, Polly. Is this your little sister?"

"Yes, ma'am. This is my little sister. Do you know Miss Bonnie?"

Nell smiled up at Bonnie, suddenly aware of why the girls had had such an effect on her. "Yes, Bonnie is my best friend in the whole wide world."

"She must be your sister then 'cause my sister is my best friend."

"Well, you could say that. We're practically sisters." Nell answered. Bonnie hoped Nell realized that the family hadn't come to town just for a friendly visit.

"I'm pleased to meet you, Mrs. Carter," Nell said, offering her hand.

"Pleased to meet you," Mrs. Carter managed to return.

"Well, girls," Nell said, "you sit here, and I'll get you a Coca-Cola with a big straw if that's okay with your mother."

"Yes, that'll be fine."

"Would you like a cup of coffee, Mrs. Carter?" Bonnie asked.

"Yes, that would be good of you," she said, taking a seat at the table.

"Miss Bonnie, guess what I got?" Polly announced.

"What?"

"I got a pony."

"A pony!"

"Yes, ma'am, and guess what I called him?"

Bonnie thought she knew, but decided to let Polly spring the surprise. "Well, I'm sure I couldn't guess."

"I call him Danny. You know, like you called your horse."

Bonnie tried her best to hold back the tears that were welling in her eyes. *She remembered.*

Mrs. Carter spoke up. "Don't think for a minute that this child forgot you, Miss Bonnie. She talks about you all the time. She tells the boys what you used to do on your farm. They built her a tree house because of it. She's always thinking 'bout you."

"Thank you," Bonnie said quietly, knowing Mrs. Carter was now trying to console her.

"We ain't been in touch because, well . . . we just thought it would be better if'n the girls growed up some first. Got used to us."

"I understand. You've done a splendid job. They're good girls."

"My daddy says I'm the apple of his eye," Polly said as she took the cola Nell set in front of her.

The three ladies snickered at the young girl's openness, causing them to relax a bit.

"May I get you something to eat?" Nell offered to Mrs. Carter.

"No, no. I'm fine. I don't think we'll be here long."

Nell retreated back to her duties. "It was nice meeting you, Mrs. Carter, and you too, Polly. Goodbye, Cora. I hope to see you again someday."

"I hope to see you, too!" the four-year-old answered between draws on her straw.

"I'd like for you to come see the girls if'n you'd like, Miss McCaverty."

"Thank you. That would be lovely."

"It might be a good thing for Polly. Her 'n Billy was real close."

"I'd love to."

Just then, Mr. Carter came through the Lunch Room doors looking for the girls. His eyes were now swollen as well.

"Looks like we better be gettin' back home now," he said.

Mrs. Carter shot out of her chair and gathered the girls. "Come on, girls. We got a long ride home. Everything all right, John?"

"We've done what we came for," he answered solemnly.

Bonnie knelt so that she was face to face with Polly. "Would you like for me to come visit sometime?"

"Miss Bonnie, could you?"

"I'd love to. I miss you so," she said wrapping her arms tightly around the little girl.

"I miss you, too," Polly said with a pout.

"It's been a long day, girls," Mrs. Carter said. "Let's get on home."

"Bye, Miss Bonnie," Polly said over her shoulder. "I love you."

"I love you, too. Be a good girl, and I'll come and see you soon!"

Quickly, Mr. Carter herded the girls out of the Lunch Room into the lobby and out to the truck that waited. Bonnie decided not to follow them. She had seen that before, and she didn't want to see it again.

"You all right?" Nell said as she came up behind Bonnie, placing her arm around her shoulders.

"I'm okay. I just hate that they're having to deal with another death. Poor Polly."

"She seems like she's doing okay. She's a strong little girl. You going to go see them sometime?"

"Maybe. Mrs. Carter said it would be good for Polly. She and her brother were close." She realized Nell knew nothing of the Carter boy's death. "Oh, Nell, they came to get their son's body. How awful for them!" Bonnie cried, putting her hands to her face. "I'm so tired of this war. When is it going to end? When? I just can't stand it anymore!"

"Take it easy, honey. Here, sit down."

"I'm sorry, Nell. I haven't heard from Calvin in months. I'm so worried. Ned hasn't written in a while, either. He says they've been really busy. Why can't this all end?"

"It will, honey. It will. We have to be strong," Nell assured her. "I'll get you some coffee."

Bonnie sat at the table wiping her face, trying to get control of herself. Just then, she saw a man on crutches trying to get through the Lunch Room doors. Quickly, she jumped out of her chair and ran to his aid.

"Let me get that for you," Bonnie told the sailor.

"Thank you, ma'am. If this foot don't get better soon, these crutches are going to grow on me like another set of arms."

Bonnie laughed. "Where would you like to sit?" she asked.

"Well, actually, I'm looking for a girl I think works here. Her name is . . ."

The sailor's conversation was interrupted by the sound of coffee cups crashing to the floor. Bonnie looked up to see Nell standing by her table with her hands to her face, glass cups strewn around her feet.

"Joey?"

"Hi ya, babe," the sailor answered, grinning.

"Joey!" Nell said as she ran to him, wrapping her arms around his neck. Joey dropped his crutches to the floor, precariously wrapping his arms around her. He kissed her right there in the middle of the Lunch Room; Nell kissed him back. Bonnie stood back, folding her arms in front of her, taking great pleasure in knowing that she had been right all along. Nell did still love him.

"Joey, you're okay!" Nell said, stroking his face.

"Yeah, babe. I'm okay. Just a bum foot. It should heal okay," he said as Bonnie handed him his crutches. Everyone in the Lunch Room began to applaud. Nell kissed him again.

"Oh, I should hate you," she whispered, her lips brushing lightly across his.

"You could never hate me. I've been trying to find you, Nell. Sally finally fessed up and told me where you were. Why wouldn't you let her tell me before?"

"Oh, shut up. I don't want to talk about that. You're here now."

"I gotta ask you something, Nell," Joey said as he fumbled for the pocket of his jacket and pulled out a box. He managed to open it and showed Nell a gold band. "Will you marry me, babe?"

Nell took a step back, aghast, then caressed his face in her hands. "Yes," she said as she kissed him softly. "Yes. I'll marry you."

"Oh, God," Joey exclaimed. "I was so afraid you'd say no!" Tears surfaced on his lower eyelids as he fumbled with the box.

The crowd cheered again. Bonnie pulled her handkerchief out and wiped her eyes. Nell took hers out, wiping her own.

"Oh, Joey, this here is my friend Bonnie."

"I'm so pleased to meet you. I'd like to say I've heard all about you, but your fiancé here is very secretive."

"Proud is probably more like it," Joey added.

"Well, that, too."

"Okay, you two. No ganging up on me," Nell said as she helped Joey to a table. She sat down and immediately began to fire questions at him.

"Where were you stationed? In the Pacific?"

"Yeah, that's a long story. I spent a year in hell, and I never want to go back."

"I'll get you something to eat," Nell said as she bolted from the table. Customers congratulated her as she made her way behind the counter. Bonnie sat at the table with Joey.

"You sure have made her happy," Bonnie told him. "I've known Nell for almost ten years now, and I've never seen her like this. She told me a little about you. I had a feeling she was still in love with you. I told her so."

"I sure am glad she is. I thought about her that whole time I was over there. Swore if I ever made it back, I wasn't going to stop until I found her."

Bonnie put her hand over his. "I'm so glad you did. I'm sure we'll get to know each other better. I've got to get back to work and leave you two alone to catch up," Bonnie said as she stood from the table. "Tell Nell I'll see her later."

"Sure thing," Joey said as he watched Nell from across the room. Bonnie smiled and walked out into the lobby. She leaned back against the wall. Memories of Calvin's leaving flooded her mind. She was unable to stop the flood of tears rolling down her face. She dashed to the exit, hoping no one would see her crying.

CHAPTER THIRTY-ONE

"He just didn't have the courage to follow his heart."

"MR. BASS," MISS Cooper said into the intercom.

"What is it, Miss Cooper? I'm busy. I'm running late for court."

"Yes, sir. There's a long-distance call from Washington. The gentleman says he needs to speak with you."

The elderly Mr. Bass turned ashen. The reminder of the cause of his recent irritability and distraction suddenly came rushing to the surface.

"Would you excuse me?" he said to the young associate whom he'd been trying to brief on an upcoming case. His business had more than doubled over the past year and with Ned overseas, it was all he could do to keep up with it. Even though the workload was more now than it had been in years, one thing had changed drastically; every day at five o'clock, Albert would pick him up and go straight home to Claudia. Not to the country club for drinks, not downtown for a drink before dinner, but straight home.

Claudia still didn't know about his call from Washington, although Carlton suspected something. He believed it was a woman's intuition, but he thought Claudia knew something was wrong.

As the young lawyer shut the door behind him, Mr. Bass laid his hands on the receiver, trying to steady himself as he picked it up.

"This is Carlton Bass."

"Carlton, this is Colonel Appleby in Washington."

"Colonel Appleby. I thought it might be you," he said, then a silence permeated the telephone line. Neither man seemed to want to fill it.

"Have you any news of Ned?" Carlton asked finally. "We haven't heard a thing."

He heard the Colonel clear his throat. "Carlton, I'm afraid I'm calling with bad news."

Mr. Bass held the phone to his chest as he covered his mouth with his free hand, closing his eyes tightly as he fought hard to gain control. Slowly, he lifted the receiver back to his ear.

"Carlton? Carlton . . ."

"I'm here, Ed."

"I'm sorry, Carlton. I just received word this morning. It seems he was with another group of ground soldiers that the Germans had stripped. We just got IDs on all of them. The report I received says that Ned bailed out just inside the German offensive line. A platoon had circled around, trying to surround a small pocket of German soldiers, when they were overrun with artillery. Some were taken prisoner." Colonel Appleby paused a moment to let Carlton catch up with the story.

"Carlton, we believe that the fall killed Ned. We believe he was already gone when he . . . well, when he landed. He never saw the Germans. He'd been cut out of the trees, but he never saw them. He was a brave Airman, Carlton. Ned held the plane together while his crew got out."

Mr. Bass' hands began to tremble as he fought to maintain his grip on the receiver.

"Carlton, Ned will receive the Congressional Medal of Honor in a ceremony here in Washington as soon as he gets to the States. We want you to be here. Listen, I'll have someone call you back in a couple of days with the details."

"That will be fine, Ed. Thank you very much for your extra effort to let me know personally."

"You're welcome, Carlton. I'm really sorry. I'll have someone call you soon. Take care of yourself."

"Yes . . . thank you. Good day, Colonel Appleby."

"Goodbye, Carlton."

As Mr. Bass placed the receiver onto its cradle, his head suddenly felt heavy. He put his hand to his brow trying to steady himself. He knew Miss Cooper was standing outside the door, holding her breath and waiting as well.

Carlton Bass stood, turning to look out his window, which over-looked Broadway. He'd thought about all the times he had stood there in the past, looking over Nashville, the city that had afforded him the opportunity to have the life he had always wanted for his family. His family; Claudia and Ned. Now his son was gone.

Dead.

No one to carry on his business.

He wasn't coming back.

Outside Mr. Bass' door, Miss Cooper leaned close, listening for some sign when she heard him crying. She backed slowly away from the door, leaning against the opposite wall of the hallway clutching her arms close around her waist. Ned Junior was gone. She knew many parents who had lost their sons, and even their daughters, in this war, but it was different for Carlton Bass. He was one of those men who put much emphasis on making a name for himself that he had bulldozed his way into the making of Nashville and the circle of society that sur-rounded it all of his life. His son was always in the background, both the reason for his ambition and suffering from it. Mrs. Cooper felt sad for her boss, the stoic, proud Carlton Bass. He had only come to know his son in recent years. Now, he was gone.

Slowly, she moved from the hallway to her desk. There would be things to do. She'd have to call the courthouse, talk to Judge Whitaker, and tell him what had happened. He'd take care of court today. The rest she'd just have to rearrange. The other call would be to Albert. That one would come first.

"Yes, Miss Cooper. I'll be right there," Albert said.

"Who was that, Albert?" Mrs. Bass asked as she entered the kitchen with her coffee cup.

Startled, Albert tried to hide from her how shaken he was.

"That was Miss Cooper, ma'am. I'm to go to the office early today."

"I thought Mr. Bass had a full load today. Is he well?"

"Probably just needs me to run some errands. Can I get you anything while I'm out?"

Mrs. Bass set her cup down on the counter looking hard at Albert. His face was white, and he refused to meet her eyes as he fussed around the kitchen. She stood, still holding onto the counter for support.

"No . . . no. I don't think I need anything, Albert. I'll be fine."

"Are you all right, Mrs. Bass?"

Claudia Bass smiled. You couldn't live with someone as long as Albert had and not know him as well or better as he knew himself.

"Albert?"

"Yes, ma'am?"

"It'll be okay. I'll be fine," she assured him.

Albert blinked back tears and choked the lump in his throat down as he finally looked up at Claudia. They didn't need to speak.

He put his hand on hers. "I know."

Back at the office, Carlton Bass quietly picked up the phone and called Reverend and Mrs. Parker to inform them of the news so that they could pass it on to Bonnie in the privacy of their home.

The old man sat in his office, waiting for Albert to come and get him, waiting to go home and tell his wife the worst news any mother could ever hear. How could he tell her? How would he break the news to her? All these years, while he was so busy building a business and a place for them in the community, while he was never at home, Claudia had given her all to her son. He had been her whole life for so many years. Carlton, meanwhile, had put both she and Ned on the back burner to his career. Now Ned was gone. His and Claudia's life together might even be over. How could she forgive him for letting Ned go, for agreeing with him to go to war?

At that moment, he wasn't sure she would.

"Bonnie, that was Mrs. Bass on the telephone. She wanted to know if you wanted her to send Albert over to pick you up for the services. I assured her that we were going to be with you today."

"Thank you, Annie," Bonnie replied, never diverting from the crackling fire.

"It was kind of her to think of you. This will be a difficult day for the both of you," Annie said, moving next to Bonnie to get her attention. She placed her arm around Bonnie's shoulders for comfort.

"Miss Annie. I just feel like I don't even deserve to be at Ned's funeral. I feel like I've betrayed him like I'm betraying his family now. Oh, I don't know. I know I haven't done anything wrong. I just can't help this feeling of guilt."

"Bonnie, we've had this conversation before. You've got to quit beating yourself up over this. Your feelings for Calvin only surfaced again after you saw him leaving for war. I know you would never hurt anyone intentionally. This is going to be a difficult day, Bonnie. Let this go. Mrs. Bass is going to need you. You've got to be strong."

"You're right, Annie. I know. It's just so hard to believe Ned isn't not coming back. He was so brave," Bonnie said as she dabbed at her face with her handkerchief.

"He was, and today we're going to honor that bravery. You were his fiancé. He loved you, and you loved him. Now, you go to that funeral and hold your head up high and be proud that you had the time together that you did."

Bonnie smiled gratefully at Annie. "Of course, you're right. You know, I did love him, Annie."

"I know you did, dear. Now let's go. It's going to be a long day."

The masses of people who attended the funeral services of Carlton

Netherly Bass, Jr. was assuredly a testament to the numbers who called themselves his friend. Hundreds passed through to pay their respects at the funeral home. The procession to the gravesite stopped traffic for hours on the west side of town. People from all over the country came to pay their respects.

As the crowd began to gather, Bonnie noticed someone she hadn't seen earlier in the day. It was the woman from the train station, the woman who was with Ned that day when Bonnie returned from Smithville, the one who was leaving on a train with him. Even though her collar was pulled close around her neck and she wore black sunglasses, Bonnie could see who she was; Della Houston.

Bonnie watched her over the shoulder of one of the many well-wishers who was speaking to her, a quaint, frail little lady whose blood was probably as blue as her hair. Bonnie hadn't heard a word the little old lady had said to her. She was too busy watching this woman. Who was she? More important, who was she to Ned?

On Bonnie's first encounter with her, it seemed as if she were going somewhere with Ned. They were boarding a train. The second time Bonnie saw her, she was watching from the top of the stairway that led to the train shed. If Miss Houston had been there to see Ned leave, she had to have known he was in town and that he was leaving at that time on that day.

Bonnie's legs suddenly became weak. Perhaps Ned had been visiting Miss Houston on that night he'd gone out.

She felt faint. The only thing she could see was this woman. Everything else blanked out. Della was speaking to Albert now. He knew her! Albert would know who she was. Bonnie walked toward Albert. Quickly, she stepped between them offering Della her hand.

"Hello. I don't believe we've met. I'm Bonnie McCaverty."

Startled, Della nervously offered her hand.

"No, I don't believe we have. My name is Della, Della Houston. I am . . . I *was* an old friend of Ned's."

"Really. I'm not sure I ever heard your name before."

"Well, as I mentioned, we were *old* friends. I hadn't seen him in quite some time. You must be Ned's fiancé. I heard he was getting married."

Bonnie studied the woman's face. Her dark hair was pulled back in a tight chignon at the nape of her neck, which only showed more of her exquisite face. She was striking. Maybe it was the way she carried herself. She seemed quite a proud woman. If only she would remove those dark glasses.

As if reading her thoughts, Miss Houston removed her dark glasses. She was the same woman Bonnie had seen at the station. Her eyes were swollen and dark, solemn. The sadness in this woman's soul poured out from the look in her eyes. As Bonnie's eyes met hers, she knew in her heart that Della had been more to Ned than just an old friend.

More than jealousy or curiosity, Bonnie felt compassion for the woman. She watched her as her eyes inadvertently looked toward the coffin while the gravediggers lowered it into the ground. Miss Houston's gloved hand went to her mouth, unable to contain her emotion.

"I was nice to meet you, Miss McCaverty. I'm sorry about your loss . . . I must be going now," she choked out the words as she put on her glasses and began to hurry away.

"Wait . . ." Bonnie said as Miss Houston quickened her pace, trying to lengthen her distance from Bonnie and Albert.

Bonnie quickly turned to Albert. "Who is she, Albert?"

"Miss McCaverty, I . . ." Albert replied as he shook his head.

"Albert, I need to know."

"Miss McCaverty . . . I can't."

Bonnie strode back to him, allowing Della to slip farther and farther away from her. She faced Albert, placing her hands on his arms.

"Albert, she was at the train station watching as Ned left the last time he was home. She was with him when he boarded a train long ago before Ned and I got together. I know there's more."

Albert was silent. He looked her in the eyes.

"It's hard to break a confidence," he said, "especially a promise to Mr. Bass."

Bonnie smiled. "He won't mind, Albert. I believe he was in love with her. I want her to know that.

Albert smiled back. "Ned loved you very much, Miss Bonnie." He looked up to Della hurrying away. Bonnie looked, too. "He just didn't have the courage to follow his heart."

"Then I'll do it for him," Bonnie said to Albert as she kissed his cheek and patted his back. He pulled his handkerchief from his coat pocket as Bonnie ran after Della Houston.

CHAPTER THIRTY-TWO

"We all make mistakes, Mr. Bass, but sometimes
God makes the most amazing gifts from them."

A RAY OF LIGHT slowly crept across the room as the sun made its way higher in the sky. As it crossed the soldier's face, lying on the small bunk shoved against the wall, the warmth stirred him to consciousness. He slowly opened his eyes, sliding over, following the warmth.

The window, too high to see out of, provided the only warmth and illumination in his small cell. That is, on the days that the sun shined. Most of the time it was gray; gray days followed by dark nights.

The German soldier passed a plate of what he considered food through the cell door across the floor, waking the soldier out of his daydream.

"Frederick, don't go yet," Calvin said to the young soldier. "You have a girl, Frederick?" The soldier stood, staring at Calvin. Every day he brought Calvin's plate, and every day Calvin would try to talk to him. Every day, the soldier would just stare at him. He would stay as long as he could, but he never spoke. Calvin didn't even know whether he understood him.

Calvin pulled himself to sit up against the wall. The ringing in his ears persisted, and the wounds from which they had removed the shrapnel hurt so bad, he could barely move. He had yet to understand why they fixed him up and didn't just let him die. Why was he here?

There were others, too; a colonel a couple of cells down and a lieutenant. Calvin was just a sergeant. The only thing he figured saved him was his age. They must believe that he was more than a sergeant, only wearing a sergeant's uniform.

"Hey, Frederick. Here's a picture of my girl," Calvin said as he reached into his shirt pocket for the one item the Germans hadn't managed to strip from him. "Bonnie. Pretty, ain't she?" Calvin thought he saw the German smile.

"No, no!" a voice screamed from the end of the row of cells. Frederick's face turned gray with fear. He stood at attention. They were bringing the colonel out for questioning again. They dragged him out over and over, torturing him and pelting him with unrelenting questions. They were in Berlin, and Berlin was being closed in on. The Germans were desperate.

"Where are they taking him, Frederick?" Calvin asked. He picked himself up and made his way to the bars of the cell. He could see that Frederick was scared. He was a boy, not more than sixteen. The prison Calvin was in seemed to be run mostly by young men. Calvin guessed that, wherever they were, the older men must be off fighting. They must be close to the front because there was constant shelling. Mortars crashed near the prison numerous times. Either the Americans or the Russians had to be closing in.

Frederick stood perfectly still, at attention with his back to Calvin, until the soldiers dragged the colonel past him and out of the cell block. His shoulders relaxed as he turned around to face Calvin.

"The Russians are here," he whispered to Calvin in a thick German accent. "They are coming into Berlin." Calvin smiled. He had reached the kid after all.

"I know you're scared," Calvin whispered. "Where's your family?"

"They are here," he whispered. "I believe we die today."

"That doesn't have to happen," Calvin whispered. "Can you get them out?"

"I do not know. We talk about it. We have family in Sweden. They left before it got bad." The shelling began to hit closer. Both soldiers instinctively flinched.

"Give me your keys, Frederick. Run to your family. Get them out of here," Calvin urged. He was pushing his luck. He knew that. Frederick was scared, but he was still a German.

"My keys? I cannot do that."

"Why not, Frederick? Why not? What good would it do to stay? I've been here for a while now, Frederick, and I know the shelling is getting closer. If we're in Berlin, it's over. They're here. Berlin will be destroyed."

"They will fight. We will not lose Berlin," the boy said distantly.

"It's over. You know it's over. You can still get out. The leaders will only leave you." Just then, the sound of running and yelling from below their cellblock made its way to upper floors. Frederick ran to look over the railing.

"I will be back."

"Frederick . . ." Calvin called as quietly as he could.

The shelling sounded closer. Calvin moved to the end of his cell.

"Mick? Mick? You there, Mick?"

"Yeah," came a voice from another cell. "What's going on?

"The guard said the Russians are closing in. Pass it down," Calvin instructed. "Be ready to move."

"Got it," Mick said.

Frederick appeared at Calvin's cell door again.

"The soldiers who took the colonel. They have gone."

"What do you mean?"

"They are all leaving."

"Give me your keys, Frederick," Calvin said as he held his hand out between the bars of his cell door waving his fingers, urging the boy.

"I have a girl, too," he said, trying to muster a smile. "Her name is Anna."

"Frederick, go get Anna and your family and get out of here. Just hand me your keys, Frederick, and get out while you can." Calvin could hear the desperation in his own voice.

Frederick reached into his pocket, pulling out his keys. He stared at them for a moment, then tossed them to the floor in Calvin's cell.

"I wish you and Bonnie much happiness," Frederick said with a smile. That act of dropping his keys brought life to the young boy's face.

"Thank you, Frederick. I wish the same for you and Anna, also."

"The colonel is downstairs. He is bad hurt."

Calvin reached between the bars of his cell and held out his hand to Frederick. Slowly, as if afraid of what might happen, Frederick clasped Calvin's hand. Calvin smiled and shook his hand heartily.

"I go now," Frederick said.

"Godspeed, son," Calvin said to the young boy as he disappeared down the cellblock.

"I'll get it," Annie called from the dining room as the front bell rang. "Bonnie, where are you going? You promised you'd rest today," she asked Bonnie when she realized that the younger woman was in the entranceway preparing to leave the parsonage.

"I'm going down to the station, Annie. It'll only be for a bit. I promise I'll be back in time for church this evening."

"You're not going anywhere," Annie said reaching for the front door. "You're going to rest today."

As the door opened, Annie saw Mrs. Carlton Bass standing on the other side. "Mrs. Bass . . . it's so good to see—"

"Mrs. Bass!" Bonnie chimed in. Both of the women stopped short as they realized at the same time that Mrs. Bass was still dressed head to toe in black.

"May I come in?" she asked. Bonnie stepped slowly away from the door backing into the foyer to allow entry.

"Yes, yes. I'm sorry. Come in. I didn't mean to appear startled. We were just not expecting any company today." Mrs. Bass's eyes remained glued on Bonnie's.

"May I speak to you, Bonnie?" Bonnie nodded and stepped into to the living room, where the Reverend was already on his feet ready to greet his guest.

"Frank, you remember Ned's mother, Mrs. Bass."

"It's a pleasure to see you again, Reverend."

"Frank, let's give Mrs. Bass some time with Bonnie," Annie interjected.

Bonnie slowly removed her hat, laying it on the table as the Reverend and Mrs. Parker left the room.

"Bonnie, I have something for you," Mrs. Bass said as she took a seat. "Please come sit down with me, dear." She motioned to the seat next to her on the sofa.

Bonnie sat next to Claudia Bass and tried her best to look at her. Bonnie's eyes met Mrs. Bass' sad, gray ones. It looked as if all the life had drained completely out of them.

"Bonnie, Ned wanted you to have this," she said as she retrieved a velvet box from her purse.

"I can't take it, Mrs. Bass."

"Why not?"

"Because I don't deserve it. You don't understand, Mrs. Bass. I disappointed Ned so much," she said, standing. "All he ever wanted to do was get married and I . . . and I . . ."

"Bonnie, I have some things I want to say to you, and I want you to listen," Mrs. Bass said commandingly. "Come sit back down."

Bonnie pulled out her handkerchief, dabbing at her face. How would she tell Mrs. Bass about Calvin? Should she? It wouldn't be honest if she didn't. Once again, her mind raced. Another decision.

"Bonnie, my son was quite a different person when he met you. He was wild, to say the least. He hadn't much care for the things a woman cares for. He had all the things a man usually has to fight to get. His father did that for him. So Ned went through life in a rather destructive way. Oh, he wasn't a bad person; he just didn't want anything. He didn't want a family, he didn't want to follow in his father's footsteps. All he cared to do was drink, carouse around town, and develop a bad reputation.

"But when he met you, that all changed. He became the man I always knew he was inside. You gave him that. You came along with your beliefs and your courage, and your innocence, and Ned had finally met someone who didn't want him for what he had, but for who he was. I'll be forever grateful to you for that.

"He loved before he died.

"He knew what love was. You made him be responsible to that love, and it changed him." Mrs. Bass turned to look at Bonnie. "I know there was some reason why you didn't marry Ned when and how he wanted to, and it doesn't matter now," she said. "I want you to have this." She opened the velvet box. "It was my mother's. It was to be your wedding ring."

Bonnie's anguish broke through. She stood, pacing the floor, and began to cry. "You don't understand, Claudia. You don't understand! I loved Ned, but I had made my mind up that I wasn't going to marry him." She stopped to look at Mrs. Bass. "I just couldn't tell him while he was over there. I just couldn't!"

Mrs. Bass stood and faced her. "*You* don't understand, Bonnie," she said. "I knew that. I knew there had to be a reason why you wouldn't marry him. It's okay. How many women do you think would have had the courage to do that? How many women would have married Ned Bass regardless of whether they loved him or not just to be the widow of Carlton Netherly Bass, Jr.?

"It's a war, Bonnie. I respect your decision. I'm not angry with you, dear," she said as she put her hands on her shoulders.

Bonnie looked at Ned's mother, who stood there forgiving her without knowing. Bonnie squared her shoulders and looked at her.

"I was in love with someone else," she explained. "It's not that I didn't love Ned. Oh, I loved him. But I knew it wasn't enough. He didn't deserve to not be loved as much as he loved." Slowly she moved from Mrs. Bass to the window. "I loved Ned. But since he first asked me to set a date, I . . . I don't know. Something bothered me, and I didn't know what it was.

"You see, there was this boy back home. His parents died, and he grew up with my family until he was old enough to go back to his farm. He's eleven years older than me. He was sort of like a brother. Then, as I got older, I knew I loved him and I told him so, but he turned me away. So, I left and came here almost fourteen years ago. I thought I was over him. I did. I met Ned and fell in love with him, and I wanted to marry him, but I just couldn't make myself.

"I thought it was because of the way everything was happening with the war and all. I thought that maybe I just wanted it all to be so right because I had waited so long for everything to be right! Last year, Calvin came through the train station. He had joined up, too." Bonnie turned away from the window to face Mrs. Bass. "I saw him standing there in that uniform getting on that train and . . . oh, Mrs. Bass, I wouldn't have hurt Ned for the world!" She burst into tears.

Mrs. Bass led her over to the sofa to sit down. She grabbed Bonnie's hands forcing her to look at her. Strangely, she was smiling.

"You knew you still loved him, that this man was part of you and you were part of him. That all of this time, your life hasn't been complete because he wasn't in it."

Bonnie tilted her head as she looked at Mrs. Bass in disbelief. "Yes," she said, "that's it exactly."

"Listen, many marriages have been committed when one or the other was in love with someone else. The best thing you can do is to follow your heart. Believe me, if you don't, it's not what your life was meant to be. You're not wrong to follow your heart, Bonnie," she said with a smile.

Bonnie leaned forward, wrapping her arms around Mrs. Bass. "I'm so sorry, Claudia. I know you didn't want him to go," Bonnie said as she pulled away to look at her.

"He died a hero, Bonnie. He held his plane together as all of his men bailed out. Ned had to join up. He wouldn't have been happy if he had stayed even though he didn't have to go." She looked off somewhere Bonnie couldn't see. "He did so love to fly . . . but, anyway, it would be Ned's wish for you to have this. I know so. He told me before he left."

"But it doesn't belong to me. It belongs to someone else."

"Whatever do you mean?" Mrs. Bass asked with a puzzled look.

Bonnie's heart was racing as she thought about Della. It was only fair. Ned should have known, so should his mother. It could only ease her sorrow. Bonnie decided that there had been enough secrets.

"Would you go somewhere with me? There's someone I'd like you to meet."

"What do you mean? Where?"

"Mrs. Bass, would you do this one thing for me? Please?" Bonnie asked softly. "It's important to me. Ned meant so much to me, and I have to do this one thing for him. Will you go with me?"

Mrs. Bass sighed and reluctantly agreed. "If it means that much to you."

"It does. I promise it won't take long," Bonnie said, picking up her coat and hat and heading toward the front door.

"Albert can take us. He and Mr. Bass are waiting in the car."

"That's even better," Bonnie said as she helped Mrs. Bass to the front door.

As they walked to the car, Mr. Bass and Albert got out and met them on the sidewalk.

"Bonnie is taking us to meet someone, Carlton."

Albert's eyes quickly met Bonnie's.

"Will you drive us there, Albert?" Bonnie asked.

"Yes . . . of course," he stuttered as he opened the front door for Bonnie. Mr. Bass helped his wife into the back seat as Albert shut the door and took his place at the wheel.

"Miss McCaverty . . . do you think . . ."

Bonnie leaned over placing her hand on his arm. "It's what Ned would want."

"Yes, ma'am," he said with a smile.

"Number 5 Rutledge Street."

As they pulled up to a large Victorian house on Rutledge Hill, Mr. Bass was still asking questions that Bonnie wouldn't answer.

"Who lives here?" he said as he helped his wife out of the car.

"You'll see in a minute," she said as they all made their way to the front door. Bonnie rang the bell. The door opened slowly.

Millie stood at the door to greet Bonnie.

"Hello, can I help you?"

"Hello. Millie, isn't it?"

"Well, yes," she said as she looked at Albert, her eyes widening with panic.

"Millie, tell Miss Houston that Miss McCaverty is here to see her."

"Miss Houston?" Mr. Bass asked. "Look here, Miss McCaverty. What are you up to?" Bonnie didn't answer. She led them all inside the house. Della was coming down the stairs but stopped halfway.

"Hello, Della," Bonnie said.

"Bonnie . . ." she stammered, nervously smoothing her hair into place, straightening her dress. "What are you doing?"

"Della, this is Mr. and Mrs. Carlton Bass. Ned's parents. Mr. Bass, Mrs. Bass, this is Della Houston."

Mrs. Bass looked confused. "Did you know Ned?" she asked.

"Know him? Bonnie?" Della looked at her, pleading for an explanation.

"Mr. and Mrs. Bass, why don't you wait in the living room."

"What's going on here?" Mr. Bass asked.

"I'm sorry. Please come in," Della said showing them into the living room where everyone found a seat, then she returned to the hallway to speak with Bonnie.

"Why did you bring them here?" she cried. "Why? Why now?"

"Ned loved you, and you loved him. That's the way it was supposed to be. Now their son is dead. They deserve to know."

"I can't, Bonnie. I can't! It won't work!"

"Mommie!" Carl cried as Millie helped him down the stairs.

"Oh, son."

"What's the matter, Mommie?" he asked as he made his way to Della's side and motioned for her to pick him up with outstretched arms.

"Nothing, darling. Mommie's just sad for a friend, that's all."

Mr. and Mrs. Bass were on their feet again moving slowly toward the stairway. "Miss McCaverty, I demand to know what's going on," Mr. Bass said. Bonnie turned to face them. She folded her hands in front of her and smiled.

"Mr. and Mrs. Bass, this is Carl. This is who I wanted you to meet," Bonnie said as she blinked tears from her eyes. Mrs. Bass never stopped walking as she looked at the little boy. He scampered out of his mother's arms to get to the floor. Mrs. Bass knelt to look at him eye to eye.

"Carl, this is Mr. and Mrs. Bass . . . your grandparents." Bonnie said slowly.

"Carl?" Mrs. Bass asked, her eyes wide, looking at Della.

"Yes, ma'am. It's short for Carlton."

"Carl?" Mr. Bass whispered.

The little boy ran over to the old man and looked up at him. "You have a funny nose," he said. Mr. Bass pulled his handkerchief out to wipe his eyes. He tried to speak, his voice shaking and lilting between his voice and a higher pitch

"My grandson?" he whispered.

"Yes, Mr. Bass. He's your grandson," Bonnie said as she helped Mrs. Bass to stand. Albert helped Mr. Bass as he went down on one knee to get a better look. He reached out and ran his hand through Carl's sandy hair.

"I don't . . . I don't understand," he said quietly.

"It's a gift," Bonnie said, kneeling down beside the old man. "We all make mistakes, Mr. Bass, but sometimes God makes the most surprising gifts from them."

The old man looked down at the boy as tears rolled off of his face and onto the floor. All he could do was nod in agreement. Bonnie stood to face Mrs. Bass, who had reached out to take Della's hands.

"Why didn't you tell us?"

"I . . . I," Della stammered.

"Mrs. Bass, I just recently found out myself. I saw Della at the train station years ago with Ned, then I saw her again when he left the last time watching us all say goodbye to him. I knew there was something to it, so I came and asked her. I don't think Ned realized until he left how much he loved Della."

"Did he know?" she asked Della.

Della shook her head. "I couldn't tell him. He was going to marry Bonnie, I thought."

"You poor dear. If we had only known."

"You couldn't know, Mrs. Bass. It wouldn't have helped anything. I loved your son. I've loved him for years and years, but I knew I didn't belong in his life. I didn't have the upbringing—"

"Nonsense," Mrs. Bass interrupted. "Anyone who Ned loved is good enough for me."

Della began to cry. "He's not coming back."

"No, but he'll never be forgotten," Mrs. Bass said. Mr. Bass carried Carl off to the living room with Albert's help.

Mrs. Bass moved closer to the mother of her newly discovered grandson. She reached for her bag.

"I have something I believe belongs to you, my dear," she said as she pulled the ring from its case.

"Whatever could that be, Mrs. Bass?" Della said as she tried to dry her eyes.

"It was the wedding ring my son was going to give to the woman he loved and truly wanted to marry," she said as she slowly took the ring from its case placing it in Della's hand. She curled her fingers around it and looked at the older woman incredulously.

"Thanks to Bonnie, I now fully understand my son. He was a fine man. His son will be a fine man, too. Bonnie was right. This belongs to you."

Della glanced quickly at Bonnie, who nodded back to her with a smile.

"I can't accept this, Mrs . . ."

"Nonsense. Any daughter-in-law of mine will have it. You're part of the family."

Slowly, Della slid down to sit on the steps with the rings clasped tightly in her hands. She held it against her face and closed her eyes.

"Oh, Ned."

Mrs. Bass moved to her side to comfort her. Bonnie backed out of the room, making her way to where the gentlemen were playing with their new companion.

Mr. and Mrs. Bass dropped Bonnie off at the parsonage that evening after a quiet supper with their new grandchild. Mr. Bass was already making preparations for their grandson's future. There would be certain mistakes he had made with Ned that he wouldn't repeat. Bonnie's sense of accomplishment was heightened by Della's quiet thank you on the porch after supper. They would remain friends. Ned would want it that way.

Bonnie waved goodbye to them as Albert drove them back to their home in Belle Meade. She couldn't wait to get inside and tell Annie what had happened.

"Miss Annie," Bonnie called bursting through the door. She found her and the Reverend in the living room. "I can't wait to tell you what happened today," Bonnie exuberantly announced, then she noticed the sullen expressions on their faces.

"What's wrong?" Bonnie asked.

"Bonnie, come sit down," Annie said.

"What's wrong, Annie?" she asked quietly.

"I received a call from Lizzie this afternoon."

"Is she all right? Is it Daddy?"

"No, Bonnie. They received a notice today since they're Calvin's next of kin."

"No!" Bonnie screamed. She covered her face with her hands.

Annie stood quickly to steady her.

Reverend Frank stood as well. "Bonnie, they've received notice that Calvin is missing in action. They don't know what's happened exactly. It appears it happened some time ago, during a hard-fought battle in Belgium. They haven't declared him dead, Bonnie, just missing."

"I don't understand! Missing? How can he be missing? He's either dead, or he's there. How can he be missing?"

"It's confusing over there, Bonnie. You have to understand. There are men spread out everywhere and sometimes . . . well, it just takes time to locate them all. He could be hiding out somewhere. They just haven't been contacted by him."

Bonnie spun around on her heels to face the both of them, the horror of what had occurred evident in her face. "He could have been captured?" she asked.

Reverend Frank lowered his face to avoid her terrified look. "Yes . . . it's possible."

Bonnie sank slowly into the chair nearest to her. "Captured."

"There's just no way of knowing. All we can do is wait," Reverend Frank added.

"All I ever do is wait," Bonnie said quietly to herself.

"Now, Bonnie. You know it's best not to guess at these things. There are a hundred things that could have happened."

"I have to go home. I have to go see Mama and Daddy."

"We'll leave tomorrow," Reverend Frank said.

"I'll call Mrs. Greenfield and let her know," Bonnie said as she moved toward the phone.

"I'll do that, Bonnie. You go up and try to rest," Annie instructed her.

Trancelike, Bonnie followed orders and walked slowly upstairs to her room.

"Blast this war!" Reverend Frank screamed. "How much more of this can this country take? How much?" He paced the room. "All these young men . . ."

"Frank, they're close, aren't they? Won't we win this soon?"

"They have to capture Hitler. It'll never be over until they capture him and put an end to this bloody mess," he said, walking out of the room. He snatched his hat from the rack and stormed out of the door.

He needed to pray for Calvin Wade.

CHAPTER THIRTY-THREE

"Awfully young, isn't he?"

ONNIE SAT ALONE in the lobby after a shift of relative quiet. Union Station was steadily growing busier these last few weeks since the announcement of Hitler's demise. Men who could were returning home as quickly as possible, although it would take months to wrap up what had taken years to accomplish. There was much to do still in Europe, and the sheer volume of men who had to be transported to various places would surely take a long time. Unfortunately, many of these men, battle-worn and weary, would only be rerouted to the Pacific Theatre with no time for home.

Mrs. Greenfield approached and sat next to Bonnie on the bench. "Rather quiet in here tonight. Isn't it?" she asked Bonnie.

Bonnie stared at the floor and nodded.

"Bonnie, don't you get tired of being down here? The worst is over. Go home to Smithville. Start living again."

"I can't."

"Why not?"

"If Calvin comes home, he'll have to come through here."

"That's possible. But do you know if he's coming back?"

"What?" Bonnie said, surprised at the directness of Mrs. Greenfield's question.

"Do you know if he's coming back? Have they found him yet?"

"Well . . . no," she answered, trying to figure out what point that Mrs. Greenfield was trying to make.

"Bonnie, you're incredibly talented. These men react so well to you. You put all of your pain behind you when you see a soldier, and you make him feel like he's the most important person in your life at that moment. Can you imagine how they feel? What they've been through? What they've seen? The years in the mud and the snow and the heat, never knowing where they are or where they are headed, just to push forward and kill the enemy, all for the sake of God and country.

"Then they come back and their first contact with home is you, and you smile and make them laugh, bring them a cup of coffee, write a letter for them. Then, they know they're home. They make a connection. I've seen it in their eyes so many times as you talk with them.

"It's like they're coming out of a bad dream, and here's this pretty redhead who reminds them of all that's good, reminds them of exactly what they were over there fighting for. Then they're glad, proud even.

"I've seen them when you walk away from them. They nod like they're assuring themselves that they did the right thing. It's a gift, and you need to share it. I'm not saying to forget your pain. I'm saying to face it head-on. You've had your time here, and you've done your share.

"Go home."

Mrs. Greenfield stood slowly, the strain of the last four years showing in her movements. She turned to look at Bonnie. "Then again, if you don't want to go home . . . there's a Red Cross vessel that's leaving port in two weeks for Europe. They're sadly understaffed. There are going to be many wounded crossing the ocean in the months to come. They do need help," she said slowly, carefully baiting Bonnie's curiosity. "You would be perfect. You never know. Calvin might be one of them.

"Good night, dear," she added as she made her way out of the empty station.

Mrs. Greenfield left Bonnie sitting alone on the bench, stunned at what she had just heard. Mrs. Greenfield rarely complimented anyone. In her field, there was much to be done, and getting it done was the primary objective. She had no time to pamper anyone. What she had said to Bonnie meant more to her than anything anyone had ever said to her.

She had made a difference. These past years had meant something.

She often wondered if what she did there at the station made any difference at all. Now, after all of this time, knowing that she had . . . Bonnie smiled, quietly knowing what Mrs. Greenfield's intentions had been.

The next day, she bombarded Mrs. Greenfield with questions about the trip to Europe. She'd been up all night thinking about it. She could sit here and wait, or she could go and help and in the process maybe find Calvin. It was a long shot, but even if she didn't find him, at least she wouldn't be sitting, waiting for news. She'd be doing something.

"Now, now, Bonnie, let's not be hasty. I think it's a good idea, but you can't go alone. I insist you have a traveling companion."

"Mrs. Greenfield?" Henry said as he stuck his head inside the door. "I don't mean to eavesdrop, but I heard you talking to Bonnie about going over to Europe on that Red Cross ship. I'll go with her, ma'am."

"Oh, Henry!" Bonnie shouted as she hugged his neck.

"It would be my privilege," Henry added.

"Now, Henry, how could I manage here without you?"

"There's plenty of guys already coming home. You'll have plenty of help. Besides, I don't have no one here and, well," he added as he looked down at his feet, "Miss Bonnie's done a lot for me, Mrs. Greenfield. I'd like to return the favor."

"All right," Mrs. Greenfield said. "It's settled then. I'll work it out to get you two to Boston before the ship leaves. We'll talk about it later. Now both of you get to work," she said, escorting them out of the office.

As they stood outside the door, Bonnie looked at Henry. "Thank you, Henry. I'm not sure anyone has ever done a kinder thing for me."

"No sweat, kid. Just make sure I get plenty of those cookies when I get back. Oh, and the peach preserves and the cider."

"Henry, you'll just have to move to Smithville."

"Sounds like a mighty swell place to me."

"Speaking of home, my mother isn't going to like this at all."

That night, Bonnie wrote a letter to her mother and father, hoping they would understand. She'd give it a little time to sink in before she called, then she wrote another letter to Calvin, like all the other letters she had written. She mailed it, hoping it would reach him—hoping and praying they'd find him soon.

"All right, boys, listen up!" Bonnie shouted above the din in the make-shift tent. "Tonight, we have a special treat for you. We have a movie!" The hoots and hollers of the men interrupted her speech. It had been a long time since any of them had seen a movie.

"It's *The Princess and the Pirate*, starring Bob Hope. It will be in the main tent at exactly 1900 hours. Get there early for a good seat."

"Hey, Red, be my date tonight for the picture show?" one of the soldiers playing cards at a table nearest to the door said.

"Sorry, Soldier, I'll be the one passing out coffee and doughnuts," Bonnie answered.

The soldier reached up, slid his cap off his head, and held it to his chest. "Ma'am, please have a date with a poor, destitute soldier. Please, ma'am."

"I don't think it would be fair to the others. Do you?"

"To hell with the others, ma'am!" the soldier said, as the others at the table joined in the laughter.

Bonnie rolled her eyes at them and left the tent.

"Man, oh, man. Wh.h.h.e.e.w.w.w . . ." the corporal whistled. "She's a looker."

"No use," the sergeant said as he dealt the cards. "She's taken."

"How do you know? I didn't see no ring."

"Word is she's over here looking for somebody. He's been missing in action for months."

"She came all the way over here to find him?"

"Yeah, you dope. That's what I said."

"Man, oh man. What a lucky guy."

At 1900 hours, chairs were set up, and the men from the hospital who were well enough had been escorted to the tent. The film was ready. The coffee and doughnuts were being passed out, and soldiers were still packing into the smoky tent.

"Cut the lights!" someone yelled from the back of the tent.

As the room went dark, Bonnie waited for her eyes to adjust before she attempted to hand out any more coffee. As soon as the light from the projector hit the screen, the men began to shout. Bonnie stayed back, pressed against the wall of the tent until they calmed down. A newsreel began the film as more cheers and shouts went up. Bonnie finally started handing down coffee to the next row.

"Private, pass this down," she whispered to the first man at the end of the row of chairs, then, one at a time, she passed the rest of the coffee down until her tray was empty.

"Look, it's Berlin!" one of the soldiers nearest the front shouted. More shouts went up at the sight of Nazi prisoners being loaded into a transport truck. Bonnie glanced up as the scene changed to a group of American officers talking. She walked to the back of the room for a tray of doughnuts.

"Today, a soldier who will no doubt be a hero in his hometown was honored in the American sector of Berlin," the announcer began. Bonnie passed down the tray of doughnuts.

"Even though the Russians captured Berlin, our boys were there to help. This soldier managed to escape a cell where he and other American, Russian, and British soldiers were being held. He freed Colonel Ralph Comstock and others and managed to hide them safely until Allied troops had taken the city.

"Lieutenant Calvin Wade will be decorated with the Distinguished Service Cross for distinguishing himself by extraordinary heroism in action against an enemy of the United States . . ."

Bonnie froze. Slowly, she turning toward the screen, the tray of doughnuts held precariously in her trembling hands. There he was. Bonnie walked in a trance toward the screen.

"Calvin," she whispered. Her eyes drank in the sight of him as he smiled looking nervously at the camera, shaking hands with a general. Through her tears, Bonnie smiled back at him. "He's alive," she assured herself quietly. "He's alive."

Henry had been leaning against the service table at the back of the tent with his arms crossed, watching as the servicemen were enjoying themselves. He was looking at the screen as the announcer said Calvin's name. Pushing himself away from the table, he immediately began looking for Bonnie. He saw her moving slowly toward the screen. He made his way through the crowd to catch her for fear she might faint. Henry placed his big hands on her shoulders from behind her.

"It's him, Bonnie," he said. "He's alive."

"He's alive," Bonnie repeated as the film clip moved on to another subject. She turned slowly to look at Henry. "He's alive, Henry!" Henry then realized she was in shock.

"I know. I told you he would be!" Henry said over the noise of the soldiers. He took the tray from Bonnie's hands, handing it to one of the other girls who had made her way down the aisle. They all knew the name, they all looked up at the same time, and they all came to her side to congratulate her. A big smile formed across Henry's unshaven face. He bent down to look at Bonnie eye to eye. "He's alive!"

Her shock became exhilaration. "Oh, my God, Henry! There he was. He was on the screen! Did you see him?" Bonnie asked as she grabbed him by the shirt.

"You bet I did!"

"Henry, it was Calvin!" she said, throwing her arms around his neck. He twirled her around and sat her gingerly back on her feet. Her green eyes were aglow in the darkened room. The other girls grabbed on for their own hugs.

"Henry, I have to see it again. Make them back it up," Bonnie said from the midst of the other women. Henry was already making his way to the back of the room. Word of what had just happened began to spread around the tent.

As the projector turned off, angry shouts from the soldiers began to fill the room. Henry quickly made his way to the front.

"Calm down. Calm down, everybody," Henry said, motioning for everyone to sit back down. "The film is fine. We're just going to back it up and see the soldier shaking hands with the general again. It's Miss Bonnie's fiancé. He was missing in action, and this is the first time she's seen him. She wants to see it again," he said as the men's eyes turned toward Bonnie. Whistles and shouts of congratulations went up from the room. The film began to roll again. Henry took his place next to Bonnie.

The newsreel began again and there he was. Thinner and grayer, but it was him. One of the women handed Bonnie her handkerchief. It finally hit her. After all the months of waiting, wondering, praying, there he was—alive. Bonnie buried her head in Henry's shoulder. He gently shepherded her toward the entrance and out of the tent.

By ten o'clock, the wounded had been escorted back to the hospital tent, and the rest of the men had wandered off to do different things. Bonnie sat quietly in the first row of seats as Henry backed up the film again. She'd already seen it again three more times and begged for just one more look. After the fourth time, Bonnie stood wiping her hands across her face. She pushed her hair back and made her way to where Henry was rewinding the film for the final time.

"Henry, how long ago do you think this was? Bonnie asked.

"I don't know. In the morning, we'll find out what we can from the CO. We'll find him, Bonnie. He might even be back home by now."

"Home? Do you think?"

"I don't know. Maybe not. He might be making his way back to England. I know they'll be able to tell you more tomorrow. Now," he said as he put his hands on her shoulders, "I insist you go get some sleep, okay?"

"All right, Henry. I won't sleep a wink, though! I know I won't." She smiled.

"Yes you will," he said, kissing her on the forehead. "Sweet dreams."

"Thank you, Henry. Goodnight," Bonnie said as she wandered outside under a clear June sky. She looked up at the stars, stretched her arms out to her sides, and began to twirl slowly as she looked up, just as she used to do out in the fields on clear summer nights at home. The stars began to make circles in the sky. She stopped abruptly and fought to stay on her feet. Suddenly, Bonnie realized she felt happy; sweet, overflowing happiness. It was a strange sensation. It rose from her drunken feet all the way to her dizzy head.

Suddenly, she felt like running. She had so much energy! Bonnie leapt into the air as she threw her cap toward the sky. She grabbed it on its way back to earth, then ran the rest of the way to her tent.

The first thing the next morning, Bonnie was in the commanding officer's headquarters, bombarding them with questions.

The CO's secretary attempted to calm her down. "All right. All right!" the staff sergeant said. "I can't do anything until you sit down and give me some details. "What division was he with? Do you know?"

Bonnie unfolded a scrap of paper she held in her hands. "30th Division, 117th Infantry Regiment, Company F."

"You're prepared, aren't you? You say he was in the film?"

"That's right," Bonnie answered happily. "I looked up, and there he was, shaking hands with a general right there on the screen!"

"Well, what are the chances of that happening again?"

"I don't know." Bonnie shrugged. "Can I find out where he is?"

"Okay, here's what's going to happen. I'll run it by the CO. He's probably going to tell me to put in a call to the headquarters of the 30th. I don't know if they went on to Berlin or were sent back. They could have even been sent to the Pacific by now."

"The Pacific?"

"Yes, Miss McCaverty. We've only won part of this war. We're still at war with the Japanese. The guys who can are being rerouted to the Pacific."

"No, he can't have been sent there."

"Calm down. I didn't say he was. Look, I'll talk with the CO, and you check back with me at the end of the day. Maybe I'll have something to tell you."

"You're not going to let me speak with the CO?" Bonnie asked.

"Look, Miss McCaverty. I know you want to find your fiancé.

I want to help. But I know the CO. He's not going to have me drop everything to find him. Please be patient."

"But you don't understand. I've been waiting so long. It seems like a lifetime," Bonnie pleaded.

"We've all had to do a lot of waiting, Miss McCaverty. Anyway, look on the bright side. At least you know he's alive. That's better news than a lot of others are getting."

Bonnie felt a pang of guilt at that, recalling Della, Carl, and Mr. and Mrs. Bass. "I understand," she said. "I'm sorry to be so impatient."

"It's okay. Just come back this afternoon."

Boarding the *Queen Elizabeth* for his voyage across the Atlantic, Calvin waited at the end of the boarding steps, watching for a glimpse of her. Her letters were delivered to him during his debriefing, all at once. He had put them in chronological order and read each slowly, over and over again. Now it was time for him to go home, and her last letter informed him that she was on her way to Europe to help with the Red Cross. He had orders to go back to America. He had done his tour and wasn't going to be rerouted to the Pacific.

Calvin felt lonely. He had none of his old pals with him. They had either died in the war, were sent home in pieces, or were sent home while he was in a German prison. Because of what had happened in that prison camp, he was now on his way to a celebration, where he would be decorated with honors.

He found that he didn't care about that. He just wanted to get home and wait for Bonnie. If it was true and she was actually somewhere here in Europe, there was a good chance that she might board this boat headed for New York.

So, he waited.

He waited until the last of the passenger list had been accounted for.

There was no Bonnie McCaverty, Red Cross volunteer.

Calvin extinguished his smoke, grabbed his bags and strode up the gangplank. He stopped to peer one more time at the crowd of people, trying to force himself to see a wild redhead racing for the boat from afar. No such luck today. Again, he would have to wait. Calvin took comfort that, at the end of this journey, he would finally be at his home—their home. He knew that if all else failed, she would find him there.

The CO's secretary eventually informed Bonnie that the men of the 30th Infantry had made it as far as Magdeburg, Germany. Most had been routed through France to wait for a ship to take them home. Some were resting there, waiting for ships that would carry them to the Pacific.

The secretary's information only had the 30th going as far as a camp near Sisson, France that had been lovingly deemed *Camp Oklahoma* by the troops. There, the wounded were patched up. Some rested before catching a ride stateside.

Bonnie reached *Camp Oklahoma* in record time thanks to Henry's rather reckless driving. Immediately upon arrival, she asked about Calvin's platoon. They had all been sent different directions, she discovered. The only way she could find out who, when, and where was from the adjunct general's office. The list he kept would know who loaded what ship.

In her heart, she feared Calvin might have reenlisted for the Pacific, especially if any of his men were to go. She hoped upon hope that this time he would have done the right thing instead and gone home.

"Look, Henry. Did you see that?" Bonnie indicated the adjutant's list. "Look here. Calvin Wade. He was here! He's gone on to England to catch the ship home. Home! We have to catch the next Red Cross ship leaving for New York. Can we do that?"

"Yes, I'll check on that, Kitten. You stay here."

Bonnie walked outside and looked around the camp. It was a busy place. There were men everywhere, packed and ready to go. The mood appeared quite happy, for the most part. Some of the later enlisted were being sent to the Pacific. She could tell which ones. It was written on their faces. Most were young; too young. Oh, how she wanted to tell them to go home, not to follow those orders. To just go home to their girlfriends, wives, and mothers, but she knew, just like those who had come before them, why they did it. She understood now. Driving through the French countryside that had been utterly destroyed, seeing the children living outside of shell-torn homes and sleeping on stacks of rubble and hay, the men in the Red Cross Camps, torn to shreds by the war, some of them delirious, some past the point of no return. She understood, even though she'd only born witness to a fraction of what they had seen.

Bonnie thought about Ned, how proud he had been to sign up and fly for his country, even though he didn't have to. He had gone for her and for Della and, without knowing it, for Carl; for their freedom.

Smithville, Tennessee was a long way from France, well removed and safe now. Calvin was safe. He was alive and on his way home. Buttermilk and Shorty would be so glad to see him, she thought, as she walked along through the men, some bandaged, some limping along on crutches, some being carried. She smiled at a young boy as he passed her. He smiled at her through his sadness and tipped his hat. He reminded her of Joshua McAllister, the boy who shot her so long ago. She wasn't mad at him anymore, just sad. She thought about his father, Ben, and how sad he must feel. He lost all three of his boys.

"Excuse me," Bonnie said to the boy as he passed by.

"Yes, ma'am?" the young soldier said as he turned and removed his hat.

"What's your name?" Bonnie asked as she offered her hand.

"My name's Matt, ma'am. Matt Lester."

"Matt Lester. You sound like you haven't been out of the South very long," she said in her best Tennessee accent. "Where you from?"

The boy's eyes lit at the sound of Bonnie's voice. "Well, I'm from Tucker, Georgia."

"You don't say!" Bonnie said. "I'm from Tennessee near Nashville. A little place called Smithville. I bet you've never heard of it."

"No, ma'am, I can't say as I have," the excited young man said, clutching his hat to his chest. "But I know about Nashville! I been wanting to come there to see the Grand Ole Opry. One of these days I will."

Bonnie placed her arm over his shoulder as they began to walk. "I've been to the Grand Ole Opry."

"You have? Who'd you see? Hank Williams? Oh, I'd love to see him. I've got all of his records."

"Well, I actually went to a gospel singing there, but they have all kinds of folks come through.

"Where you headed?" Bonnie asked.

"I came here from Belgium. I'm shipping out again to the Pacific to fight the Japs," Matt said quite sadly. "Maybe it won't be long, and we can get that over with, and I can get back home."

"How long have you been over here?"

"Since last Christmas."

Henry walked out of the adjutant general's office surveying the area for Bonnie. He scanned the crowd and found her walking away, talking to a young soldier. Henry trotted off to catch up with her. Just as he drew near to them, Bonnie stopped and turned to face the young man to whom she was talking. Henry stood off a bit and waited for them to finish their conversation.

"Now, Matt, it'll all be over soon. You just pray every day that you get back home safely and remember that everyone at home is proud of what you're doing for them. More proud than you'll ever know," Bonnie said as she reached up and kissed him on the cheek.

"Thank you, Miss McCaverty. I'll remember that. Goodbye."

"Goodbye, Matt," Bonnie said as she watched him walk away from her. Henry walked up behind her.

"Awfully young. Isn't he?" Henry asked.

"Yes," Bonnie answered. She continued to watch him as he disappeared into the crowd. "We can't go, Henry," she said, still craning to catch a last glimpse of the young boy.

"What?"

"We can't go just yet."

"Miss Bonnie, there's a boat leaving tomorrow. We could be home in no time. What do you mean, we can't go just yet?"

Bonnie spun around to face him. "We just can't go. There's too much that needs to be done."

"But, what about Calvin?"

"Calvin is safe. He's alive," she said, smiling. "He'll wait for me to get there. I . . ." Henry was grinning at her. "Oh, Henry, don't look at me like that."

"He got to you, didn't he? That young soldier. You can't help yourself. Been doin' it too long," he said as he pulled out his tobacco and rolled a cigarette.

"Don't be silly. There's just so many men here, and they need our help. Besides, that's what Mrs. Greenfield sent us over here for, wasn't it? I'm going over to the Red Cross headquarters and tell them we're staying so they'll know where to put us." Henry laughed and shook his head as she walked away.

"I guess I'll cable home and tell them we're not coming," he said as he flipped his cap over his head and lit his cigarette. "Mrs. Greenfield won't be surprised."

CHAPTER THIRTY-FOUR

"The minute she sets foot off the train."

THE PARADE IN New York was overwhelming. Calvin had never seen so many people in one place. Every time a ship came in, everyone dashed out to meet it. They were making him out to be some kind of hero, which made Calvin uncomfortable. From here, he was to go to Washington, where there would be another parade, then he was supposed to get another medal of some kind. He didn't care. He just wanted to go back to Smithville.

That night, when he finally had a moment to himself, he called the parsonage.

"Reverend Parker, it's Calvin," he yelled into the receiver.

"Calvin, Calvin! Annie, it's Calvin. It's so good to hear your voice. Where are you, son?"

"I'm in New York. They had a big parade here today. Then I'm off to Washington for some parade there before they let me go home."

"Yes, I'm sure. We heard all about it, you being the hero and all. Congratulations, Calvin. We're all so proud."

"Well, I just want to get home. I got Bonnie's last letter before she left for Europe. Do you have any idea where she is?"

"Yes. She's in France at a place called Camp Oklahoma."

"Yeah? I went through there. She must have gotten there after I left. When's she coming home?"

"Well, she knows you're okay, son. Seems the strangest thing happened. She saw you on a newsreel."

"You're kidding. The one from Berlin?"

"She was headed straight for home after that."

"When will she be back?"

"Well, Calvin. We don't know. We got a cable not long ago. Seems she's staying for a while to help with the wounded coming through the camp."

Calvin smiled, laughing out loud. "Well, that would be what Bonnie would do."

"I'm sorry, Calvin. I wish I could say she was on her way."

"Well, I guess she's going to make me wait this time."

"So it seems," the Reverend replied, laughing along with him.

"Well, I've got to go call Lizzie and Jessie. I'll phone you when I reach Nashville."

"That'll be fine, son. We'll pick you up at the station."

"Thank you, sir."

"No, thank you, Calvin. Thank you for all you've done for us."

"Yes, sir. Thank you, sir. Well, give Miss Annie a kiss for me. Goodnight."

"Goodnight, Calvin."

Calvin hung up the phone in the lobby of the hotel and shook his head. He tried to remember how old he was. He couldn't remember exactly. It had been well over a year since he'd seen Bonnie at the train station. He guessed he could wait another month or so.

"I think it will be a long month," he said to himself.

It was another week before he reached Nashville. The Reverend and Annie picked him up and drove him all the way to Smithville themselves. They wanted to be there when he returned to Lizzie and Jessie.

As they drove through Smithville, Calvin began to see familiar faces. The Parkers slowed, stopping along the way for handshakes and hugs, but Calvin couldn't wait to get home. Finally, they pulled into the drive that led to Calvin's house. He leaned as far forward as he could.

"Stop the car, Reverend."

Frank pulled the car to a stop as Calvin opened the door and got out. "I'll walk the rest of the way," he said, never taking his eyes off the house. The Reverend put the car into gear and pulled down the road to the front of the house.

Calvin stood there, surveying his home. The trees were a bit taller, but it still looked the same, only better. He slowly put one foot in front of the other and walked down that familiar road he'd walked so many times before.

The sound of the car brought everyone outside. Calvin watched as they all poured out of the house. There was Buttermilk and Shorty, Pippin, Emma and Sam, Nettie and Tom, all the kids, Jessie and . . . Lizzie. Two of the kids helped Lizzie down the porch steps as Calvin made his way toward the house. Lizzie silently made her way toward Calvin. The others stood back, letting them have this time together.

"There's my Calvin," she whispered to herself as tears trickled down her worn face. "It's really him."

As they reached each other, Calvin buried his face in her neck, lifting her frail body off the ground. Tears streamed down his face for the first time in years. Gently, he settled her back on the ground, straightening the shawl around her shoulders. She reached up, cupping his face in her hands.

"I knew you'd come back. I just knew you'd come back."

"Lizzie. I missed you so much."

"I'm so proud of you. John and Sarah would be proud, too. Oh, son, I'm so glad to see you," she said, wrapping her arms around him again.

"I'm glad to be home."

"Well, here he is," she announced to the others, stepping back so they could all see him. Calvin kissed all the girls and hugged all the kids, then there was Shorty and Buttermilk, standing beside the porch steps and crying all over each other.

"Mr. Calvin, we so happy you home in one piece," Shorty said.

"Don't say nothin' like that to Mr. Calvin after he been through what he been through. We sho is glad you home, Mr. Calvin," Buttermilk added.

"You two. Oh, it's so good to see you!" Calvin said as he reached down, hugging them both.

"We just thought about you every day, Mr. Calvin," Shorty said.

"We sho did. We done took good care a the farm while you were gone. She looks good, don't she?" Buttermilk said, grinning from ear to ear as he waved his hat over the landscape of his home.

Calvin followed the hat over his land. "Boys, you have no idea how good she looks."

Calvin turned to face Jessie, the man who was, by all rites, his father. He was old now. He sat smoking his pipe, waiting. He leaned forward, motioning for someone to help him up. When he was on his own two feet, he lifted his right hand to his forehead, standing straight as he could, and saluted Calvin. Calvin returned the salute.

"It's good to have you home, son," Jessie managed before the tears that ran down his face made him reach for his handkerchief. Calvin ran to him and helped the old man inside. He sat him down in his favorite chair, next to the fireplace, then knelt to be eye to eye with him. "You know," the old man said slowly, "I stayed alive so's I could see you again." The emotion overcame them both. They held on to one another for some time. "Your father would be proud of you, son. Just as proud as I am."

"I fought a long way to come back and hear you say that. Thank you."

"Well, all right now. All the cryin's done for a while. Let's get this homecomin' a goin'," Lizzie instructed as Emma, Nettie, Buttermilk, Shorty, and Pippin fell in and followed her to the kitchen. Reverend Parker sat down and lit his pipe. Annie joined the others in the kitchen. The kids knew it was their turn at Uncle Calvin.

They all piled on top of him as soon as he sat down, then came the questions.

"How many Krauts did you kill?"

"Can I see your gun?"

On and on they went until Annie announced that supper was ready.

After the food had been blessed by Reverend Parker, they all dug in.

"Well, we got a letter from Bonnie Girl yesterday," Jessie said matter of factly.

Calvin's heart skipped a beat when he heard her name spoken like that by her father.

"Seems like that girl ain't ever going to come home again."

"Oh, I think she'll be home pretty soon, Jessie," Lizzie said, smiling.

"Have you heard, Lizzie? Do you know when she'll be home?" Annie asked.

Lizzie looked at Calvin. "From the cable, seems like she should be home sometime in the next couple of weeks."

"Reckon you two could possibly find the time to get married before I leave this earth to meet my maker?" Jessie asked. Everyone at the table laughed at his impertinence. As soon as the ruckus died down, there was silence. Calvin answered.

"The minute she sets foot off the train."

Everyone clapped and hollered. Lizzie stood and hugged Calvin. Jessie shook his hand. The girls cried.

"Well, finally! We're goin' to have ourselves a wedding!" Lizzie added.

As the sun was setting, Calvin walked outside to have a smoke on the front porch as he had done so many times in his life. The Parkers had gone home with Lizzie and Jessie. Buttermilk and Shorty had retired to their house. The quiet hum of a country evening had fallen on the Wade farm.

For Calvin, it was a quiet like no other; a quiet he'd played over and over in his mind so many cold nights as he'd tried to sleep in a foxhole. It was July. The crickets were arguing with the bullfrogs about who could make the most noise. Over that, the whippoorwills called to one another. An owl screeched from his perch at the edge of the woods. A single hawk circled lazily above it all.

Calvin looked up to the spot where Bonnie used to wave to him, the cliff above the farm. His heart ached. Here he was. Back home, yet

Bonnie wasn't here. He looked toward the tool shed and thought about the day she had come to tell him how much she loved him. He thought about the times she'd come home to visit and how he wouldn't admit it to her. He shook his head. Lizzie was right. How much time had he let get away from him? How many times did he let her go? Until they were separated by something neither of them had any control over. He'd never let it happen again.

It had been three weeks since Bonnie's letter to Lizzie and Jessie. Three weeks without a word. Calvin had gone right to work as before, tending to his farm. It was almost the same. Almost. His anxiousness grew daily as he waited to get word when Bonnie would return. She hadn't phoned to say when she'd be home and Calvin was beginning to worry.

It was Sunday. There was church, then dinner afterward at Lizzie's. Calvin stayed to help do some work on the house that afternoon. He sat outside on the front porch with Jessie till late that afternoon before starting home through The Dark Forest.

It was a warm night, and the sun was just beginning to set as Calvin stowed the old horse away in the barn and headed for his house. He stopped on the front porch for one more smoke before he went in to read his paper. He surveyed his farm as he had every night since he had been home. He drank in the sounds, the smells, looking around just to ensure once more that it was all true. Then he heard a truck coming up the drive. He hiked a leg up on the porch and rested an arm on his knee, waiting to see who the visitor might be.

As the old truck got closer, Calvin realized it was Doc Morgan's boy, Chad. He pulled the truck to an abrupt stop and hopped on out.

"Hi ya, Calvin. I got a letter here from Bonnie McCaverty. Weren't sent to her house, but sent to yours," he said as he handed the letter over to Calvin, who glanced at the return address. Cesson, France. A smile surfaced on Calvin's face as he opened the letter and carefully withdrew its contents.

"I hope this letter is to tell us she's on her way," he said to Chad.

"That what it says, Calvin?"

"I'm not sure. Let's see," Calvin answered opening the letter and read:

August 10, 1945

Dearest Calvin,

If I never thought miracles could happen, now I know they do. I was serving the men at the post I was at in Belgium while we were getting ready to show a movie. As the Movietone Newsreel played and I was handing out coffee, I heard a name coming from the screen, and it was yours! Calvin Wade. I looked up, and there you were, larger than life on the picture screen. You were alive! All these months of not knowing and there you were. I made Henry play it back five or six times just so I could see your face.

Immediately, we headed for Camp Oklahoma where I understood your outfit was being sent to the Pacific and some were going home. I just missed the boat you were on, Calvin. Just missed you.

So, as we were walking through this camp seeing all these sad faces knowing they are going to be shipped out immediately to the South Pacific, my heart broke. These are kids, Calvin, just babies. There are so many wounded that they are bringing through here, I just can't seem to leave them with no one to cheer them up. Please don't be upset with me. You are on your way home. I know you are safe, and I know it will take me some time to get back there to be with you, but I must stay just for a little while to help out. I promise the next Red Cross ship that gets loaded with wounded going home, I'll be on it. I promise. I just feel like they need me here, just for a while.

This horrible wait that we have both had to endure will all be over soon. I have seen what you went through over here, Calvin, and I know many aren't going back with you. That's why I need to stay and help just a bit, for those who might give up living if someone don't come by and tell them how good living is after what they've done for us. I can't turn my back on these poor boys.

So tell Mama and Daddy. I know they won't be happy. But I will leave on the first ship I can. They're coming in every week.

I can't wait to see you, to hold you, to kiss you. I have so much to tell you. I'm sure we'll have plenty of time for that.

Well, I love you with all of my heart and soul.

Love,

Bonnie

"Well, whad it say?" Chad asked.

Calvin just smiled as he folded the letter and stuck it into his shirt pocket. "Bonnie's just being Bonnie. She's going to stay on awhile at a camp over there in France and help with the wounded. I hope she makes it home in time to see her daddy." He said the latter mostly to himself. "Listen, thanks for bringing this out. How much do I owe ya?

"Awe, nuthin, Calvin. I don't mind. I'll see you at the Square this weekend, and you can buy me a Coca-Cola."

That's a deal, son. Tell Doc thanks for everything."

Chad loaded himself into the old truck, turned, and headed back into town. Calvin let out a pronounced sigh and plopped himself down on the steps of the front porch. He propped his elbows on his knees and began to rub his face in his hands as if to wipe away the exasperation from his face. He wrapped his big hands around his neck and tried to relieve the tension in his shoulders.

When will this war ever end? he wondered. It had been over a year since he had seen Bonnie at the station in Nashville. It had been a year since he had declared his love for her. Since then, he had fought hard in the cold, the mud, and the snow. He'd been captured, had escaped, and had sailed back across the ocean. He'd been in a parade, had been made to go to Washington and, finally, had made it home, only to find out that he would have to wait again to see Bonnie.

Then, he wondered about Jessie. The poor old man was doing everything he could to wait for his little girl before he leaves this world. How could he let Bonnie know her father was ill? In that instant, Calvin decided to go to Nashville and talk to the Red Cross. It was time for Bonnie to come home.

CHAPTER THIRTY-FIVE

"I've waited long enough."

U PON CALVIN'S VISIT to the Red Cross headquarters in Nashville, an urgent message was sent to Bonnie McCaverty at Camp Oklahoma in France. Calvin waited outside Mrs. Greenfield's office.

"Mr. Wade, everything has been taken care of. We've cabled Bonnie's chaperone in France and informed him of Bonnie's father's condition. He'll get her home as soon as possible without alarming her. You're right, Mr. Wade. It's time to retire this volunteer. She has definitely done her duty."

"Thank you, Mrs. Greenfield. I knew you'd understand. It's just that her father has held on so long. He's so weak. I just don't know how much longer he can hold out."

"Certainly, son. It'll take a while for them to get home. I shouldn't have let the two of them stay in France. I certainly didn't mean for Bonnie to stay so long. She actually went over there in hope to find you, you know."

Calvin looked up suddenly at Mrs. Greenfield.

"Yes," she added. "She would sit in the station night after night. Every time a train was due in from New York or Boston, Bonnie would be there. She didn't want to take the chance of missing you coming home. I thought she would do more good over there helping out after the in Europe was all over. You know, I thought that because I knew there wasn't much of a chance of you coming home. I knew that many of the soldiers who landed on D-Day never saw the end of the war.

"Bonnie didn't know that. She didn't keep up with the fighting much. That wasn't her job. She knew her job and did it well. Her job was to smile. Her job was to let that soldier know when he stepped off that train that he was home and there was someone here who was proud of him.

"Mr. Wade, you should have seen the way those men would light up when she spoke to them. No one hid her personal hardships better than Bonnie. Even after Mr. Bass' funeral and finding out that you were missing, she never took time off. Always, Bonnie was here to deliver a cup of coffee, a pat on the back, and a warm hug to any given soldier coming off a train. She has a heart of gold, you know."

Calvin looked down at the hat he held, trying to choke back the lump forming in his throat. "Yes, I know."

"Her happiness is long overdue."

"I agree," Calvin said as he stood, "and I plan to make up for that."

"Very good," Mrs. Greenfield said as she extended her hand to him and smiled. "We should hear from her soon."

"Thank you for your help, Mrs. Greenfield."

"You're very welcome, Mr. Wade."

"I'll be staying with the Parkers until you hear back from Mr. Boyd. Would you call me there as soon as you hear something?"

"Certainly. I'll let you know as soon as possible. It could be tomorrow."

"That's fine. I'll wait. Thank you again."

"You're welcome, Mr. Wade."

Calvin made his way back down to the street and climbed into his truck. He decided he would stay with the Parkers until he heard some news he could deliver to Jessie. As he turned toward the west end of town, Calvin saw the tower of Union Station standing sentinel above Nashville. Something drew him to it, to the place where Bonnie had spent so much of her time, the place where she had waited for him.

As he walked in the side door of the cavernous building, it seemed strange and foreign to him. The few times he'd been there, the place had always been bustling with people. With the war in Europe at an end, the pace had calmed a bit.

Calvin scanned the area where Bonnie had first spotted him the day he shipped out. He could see her now, leading Roy and Bill from wanting to kill each other to being best friends. They wouldn't have lasted as long as they did had they not had each other to rely on over there. Now they were gone.

He watched as people passed in and out of the Lunch Room. He pushed the door open and looked around. Nell raised her head at the sound of the door opening, ready to greet the new customer.

"Calvin! Calvin!" Nell said as she quickly made her way out from behind the counter. "Oh, it's so good to see you again." She extended her hand to him.

"Hello." Calvin faltered, trying to remember her name.

"It's Nell. It's been a long time."

"Yes, it has. It's nice to see you again, Nell."

"Are you here to get Bonnie? Is she coming home?"

Calvin looked down at the hat he unconsciously twirled in his hands. "No, not yet."

"Blast her! Why doesn't she come home, Calvin?" Nell asked as she folded her arms in front of her. "I don't understand why they let her stay over there. Hasn't she done enough? Hasn't she done more than her share?"

"Yes. She has and more."

Nell's face softened a bit when she realized how much Calvin must miss her. "I'm sorry, Calvin. I'm sure you want her to come home more than anyone. Here you are home, and she's the one overseas. I haven't even asked who you're here to see."

"No one," Calvin answered. "I just came from the Red Cross office. I went to see Mrs. Greenfield."

"What's happened?"

"Nothing yet," Calvin answered as he pulled his tobacco out to roll a cigarette.

"Can you sit for a minute?" Nell asked as she motioned to an empty table.

"Sure."

"So, you went to see Mrs. Greenfield?"

"Bonnie's father isn't well. I don't know, he's in his eighties somewhere. No one really knows. He's just holding out to see his little girl again. He loves her very much. It's no secret Bonnie was always his favorite. He was none too happy when she moved to Nashville to begin with. I just decided she needed to know so she could get home."

"Well I, for one, am glad," Nell said as she stood and walked to the counter. She poured them both a cup of coffee and set them down on the table. Someone needs to take charge of that girl. She just tries to do too much."

Calvin licked the paper of his cigarette, rolling it back and forth between his fingers. He looked up at Nell. His clear, blue eyes began to fill with his pent up emotions. "Miss Nell, I can't wait another . . ."

Nell put her hand on his arm. "It's okay, Calvin. She'll be home soon. It will all be over. They just have to make her come home!"

Calvin put his hands to his face and rubbed the tiredness from his eyes. He picked up his cigarette and lit it. "They're trying to contact Henry Boyd now. Mrs. Greenfield will let me know as soon as they hear anything."

"Oh, Calvin, will you let me know as soon as you hear? I've missed her so much," Nell said, choking back her own tears.

"Of course I will," Calvin said, laying a hand on her shoulder. He stood. "How much do I owe you for the coffee? I better get going."

"It's on the house. I'm so glad to see you again."

"It was nice to see you, Miss Nell. I'll phone as soon as I hear something. Thanks."

"Goodbye," Nell said as she watched Calvin shuffle from the Lunch Room. She stood there for a moment as bits and pieces of her memory played in her head. She could hear Bonnie's voice, see her face. She remembered when she dropped her Coke onto the floor the last time Calvin was in here. She thought about Ned and all the other boys who had been through here who weren't coming back. Nell blinked the tears from her eyes, yet they made their way down her face. She drew her handkerchief out and wiped them dry before turning around to face Charlie.

One hand went to the back of her apron and untied it. The other ripped it off the front of her dress. "Charlie," Nell announced, "I quit!" she said as she grabbed her purse and sweater and headed out to find Joey.

"What do you mean, you quit?" Charlie screamed from the grill. "Hey, get back here."

"Find someone else, Charlie. I'm going to have a baby!"

"A baby? Nell! Get back here!"

The next morning, the phone rang early at the Parsonage.

"Hello?" Annie answered. "It's for you, Calvin." She extended the phone toward the breakfast table at him. He removed his napkin from his lap and stood, slowly accepting the receiver from Annie.

"Yes, this is Calvin Wade."

"Mr. Wade," Mrs. Greenfield said on the other end of the line.

"Yes, good morning, Mrs. Greenfield."

"Mr. Wade, I just heard from headquarters about our Miss McCaverty. It seems they can't deliver our message because she and Henry Boyd are not there."

"What do you mean, not there?"

"Well, it seems they've already left to come home."

"She's on her way?" Calvin asked, a smile surfacing unbidden across his face. Annie clapped her hands together as the Reverend put his arms around her.

"Yes. They left days ago. They decided at the last minute to get aboard one of the vessels used by the Red Cross to deliver wounded back to the States. I guess they didn't have time to cable anyone. I don't know exactly how long it will take them to get here, but they should already be back in the States."

"Already back in the country?"

He could hear Mrs. Greenfield's smile on the other end. "Yes, Mr.

Wade. I'm sure the boat has made it to port by now. Maybe she'll call Reverend and Mrs. Parker."

"Yes, ma'am. Thank you so much for your help!"

"Anytime. And Mr. Wade?"

"Yes, ma'am?"

"Remember your promise to me. Take Bonnie back to Smithville. Have some children. Be happy."

"That I can sure enough promise, Mrs. Greenfield."

"Good enough. Good day, sir."

"Goodbye. Thanks again," Calvin said as he slowly put the receiver back down into its cradle.

"What did she say?" Annie asked.

"Well," Calvin said, trying to compose himself. "She said they had already left and that they should already be in the country by now and that they probably didn't have time to let anyone know they were leaving."

"Oh, Frank! Bonnie's coming home!"

"Yes, dear. Did she say when they might hear anything?" Reverend Parker asked.

"No, sir. They said she might call here first. I don't think they know any more than we do."

"That's fine, son. Just fine. She's on her way home," Reverend Parker said as he patted Calvin on the back and returned to his seat. "I guess all we can do is wait."

"I've waited long enough," Calvin said as he kissed Annie on the cheek. "Thanks for breakfast, Miss Annie. I'm going to the station to wait for her."

"But Calvin, she might not come in today," Annie called after him, but it was too late. He was already making his way down the walkway to his truck.

"It's okay, Annie," Reverend Parker said. "He's waited this long. He'll be fine."

CHAPTER THIRTY-SIX

"As me and my Bonnie together grow old . . ."

B ONNIE CRANED HER neck to look out the window of the lumbering train. "Look, Henry. We're home."

"Finally," Henry said, rubbing the back of his neck.

"It's the station. Look!" Bonnie pointed. "I never thought that station would ever look so good."

She leaned back in her seat. "Now I know what the look on all those men's faces meant. They never thought they'd ever pull into the station again," she said quietly.

"We're home now," Henry offered. "The war is over for us. It's time we start living again. You promised you'd quit thinking about it."

"I know. I'm sorry, Henry," Bonnie said, staring at her hands. She had taken ill just before leaving Europe and was still fragile. It was then that Henry made the quick decision to get her on the next ship home. The Red Cross had arranged everything. They were first taken to England and, in a few days, were on their way home. Henry hadn't even taken the time to cable. He left instructions for the Red Cross to contact Mrs. Greenfield in Nashville.

Henry looked at her. "Bonnie, we've seen enough sadness to last a lifetime. I've seen enough. I've done enough. You've done enough. You'll never get better if you don't put this behind you.

"You have the rest of your life. Mr. Wade is waiting on you. You got well enough for me to get you home. Now it's up to you. No one here knows about the things you've seen. You could never explain it to them. The men who depended on you to take care of them will never forget you, and you can't ever forget them, but you have to put it behind you. Your body can't take anymore."

Bonnie smiled at him through tired, darkened eyes. The light in them seemed all but gone. It made Henry sad.

"Henry," she said, "I want you to know something." She laid a gloved hand on his. "You've been the best friend a girl could have. For years you've watched out for me. You took me to see Polly. You were always there at the station for me. Then, you were there to go to Europe with me when I couldn't think of anything else to do. You were there again to get me home when I couldn't think for myself. I just want you to know, I don't think I could stand it without you around. I want you to come to Smithville with me."

"Miss Bonnie, I can't . . ." Henry started.

"No, I do. You're as much a part of my family as anyone. It's important to me. There's no reason for you to stay here alone."

Henry had thought about it a lot on the long journey home. He wasn't looking forward to being alone again. Henry had been Bonnie's protector for over fifteen years now. How would he go back to not having her to look after?

"It's time for me to take care of you now, Henry," she added.

All Henry could do was put an arm around her shoulder. She laid her head against his neck as they watched the station get closer.

Calvin walked up to the board at Union Station, checking for arrivals from Boston or New York, any train that might have Bonnie on it. There was one from the East Coast that had arrived earlier that morning. Evidently, Bonnie hadn't been on it. He checked with everyone; the women at the Red Cross station, the USO, even Mr. Nelms, the stationmaster, who, of course, knew Bonnie McCaverty well.

"Mr. Nelms. Hi, I'm Calvin Wade."

"Yes, yes. So you're Calvin," Mr. Nelms said as he offered his hand to Calvin.

Calvin blushed at the recognition. "Yes, sir. I hope that's a good thing."

"Yes, son. It is," he said, smiling, and added a friendly pat on Calvin's back as they moved to walk through the station. "We all know about you and our Bonnie. My, my. Well, all of Nashville knows about you, son. You're a hero around here," he said as they walked along. "We've all read the papers of your heroism in Berlin. We're all very thankful."

"Thank you very much, sir," Calvin answered.

"Bonnie sat here many nights after she heard the news you were missing. Scared she might miss you coming through the station. We all tried to get her to go home to Smithville, but she wouldn't hear of it. You know, she and Henry Boyd left to go to Europe to volunteer to help."

"Yes, sir. I know. Seems like we just missed each other over there," Calvin said. "I got word from Mrs. Greenfield that they've left England to come home, but she didn't know when they left or what transport they were on."

Mr. Nelms smiled as he pulled his pocket watch out, checking the time. "Mr. Wade, she's coming home. Go home and wait for her. It'll all be over soon."

"Yes, sir. Thank you, sir," Calvin said as he offered his hand to the stationmaster.

"Nice to meet you, Mr. Wade. Now, if you'll excuse me," he said.

"Yes, sir. I'm sorry to keep you. Thank you for your time."

"No bother at all, son. Nice to meet you," Mr. Nelms said, replacing his watch in his vest pocket as he turned to go about his duties.

Feeling frustrated, Calvin started toward the Broad Street entrance. He turned and looked around the train station, wondering if this was ever going to be over. He was tired. Finding a seat, slumping onto it, trying to decide what to do next, he thought about all the folks who must have sat on that same bench over the past four years. How many soldiers sat here waiting for their train that led them to their destiny? How many soldiers had napped here, or written a letter to their sweetheart or wife, but never made it home?

He put his head in his hands and rubbed his face, cradling his head in his hands, covering his ears from the cavernous sounds coming from the station. The noise bothered him now. The city was so loud; horns, cars, and buses. His ears were so sensitive.

At the other end of the station, at the entrance from the train shed, there was a small commotion going on. Everyone was rushing to greet a few new arrivals. Applause and shouts of joy rang out from the offices above. Calvin sat holding his head in his hands with his ears covered; his eyes closed.

As Bonnie and Henry made their way into the lobby, Bonnie instinctively looked up and saw Mr. Nelms appear from one of the offices on the second floor. She blew him a kiss. Mr. Nelms smiled and waved, then pointed toward the front of the station.

She looked to where he pointed. There was only a single traveler sitting alone. He sat with head in his hands.

Bonnie walked through the well-wishers toward the man, now leaning back on the bench, his hands in his lap. Her pace slowed as she came closer to him. Bonnie looked back up at Mr. Nelms, then back at the man sitting there. A step closer and she understood why Mr. Nelms had pointed him out.

It was Calvin!

Bonnie's hands went to her face as she tried to gain her composure. Henry watched to see where she was going. She was still weak. She lowered her hands to her sides, moving closer. Her heart beat heavily as tears made their way down her cheeks. She opened her mouth, but nothing would come out. Bonnie McCaverty was at a loss for words.

Finally recovering, she said the only words that would come to her mind. "As I get to the end of the meadow I'll see, a big, fine white house for my Calvin and me. We'll sit on the front porch and watch the sunset. A fine time we'll have that we'll never forget . . ."

Calvin's eyes fluttered open. He sat erect on the bench as those words made their way to his ears. He stood, turning slowly, facing her.

"We'll have ten fine children and all with red hair to match their mother's so bright and so fair. We'll sit on the rooftop and watch the moon glow . . ." Bonnie continued.

"As me and my Bonnie together grow old," Calvin finished as he rushed to her, burying his face in her neck, wrapping his arms around her. "Bonnie Girl . . . you're here," he whispered, pulling back to look at her face. He held her up sensing her weakness.

"Calvin . . . Calvin," she repeated as she placed her hands on each side of his worn face.

"I came to wait for you, Bonnie. I didn't know what else to do," he said softly. "I just couldn't stand it no longer." The emotion he'd held in for so long seemed to be stuck in his throat.

"I went to try to find you," Bonnie rushed to say. "I saw you on the screen during the movie, then I missed you in France," she explained as her voice gave in to the overwhelming emotion in her heart.

"Shhhhh . . . . It's okay. The waiting is over," Calvin said as he bent down and kissed her. All of their years apart disappeared in an instant. Everyone in the station seemed to be watching them. The women began pulling their handkerchiefs out. Everyone was cheering. Henry stood with his handkerchief in his hand, intermittently lifting his cap, wiping his eyes.

Calvin smiled at the sight of her. In a moment, all of those memories held captive in his mind came rushing to his consciousness. Here she was, this beautiful, fragile creature he now held in his arms. Calvin made another vow right then and there. He would never let her go.

"Bonnie, I have something to ask you."

"What is it?" she asked.

"Can you ever forgive me? Can you ever forgive me for making us wait this long?

"Oh, Calvin. I knew in my heart one day this would happen. It just took me a while to convince you."

"Fifteen years."

"It was worth every minute of it," Bonnie replied.

Calvin lifted Bonnie's frail body in his arms and headed to the entrance. Henry followed with their bags.

September 19, 1945 Smithville Courier

Bonnie McCaverty and Calvin Wade were married at the home of Calvin Wade, local Smithville hero who was awarded for bravery when he led fellow prisoners of war to safety as the Allied troops liberated Berlin. Bonnie McCaverty did her part in the war effort as well, tirelessly volunteering at Union Station in Nashville and in Europe during the war. They have waited long for this day, and we wish them all the blessings the world has to offer . . .

CHAPTER THIRTY-SEVEN

"She was made of the same stuff as her mother.
Strong as an ox, that little one."

"THEIR WAIT WAS finally over . . . them two," Pippin said, faltering a bit, the sound of her voice a mixture of quiet sadness and latent expectancy. "They was separated by superstition, pride, a war, an ocean, strange lands, and they finally found each other. They was so happy.

"They got back to Mr. Wade's, and Mr. Calvin nursed Bonnie back to health, with Mr. Henry's help, of course. Uncle Buttermilk and Uncle Shorty was so happy to have them back. I tell you, this farm went from being a sad and lonely place to a bright, beautiful home when Miss Bonnie got here. Even though she never quite got back to her old health, she got that garden back into shape, and things got whitewashed and clean, and oh, I tell you, ladies, it was a happy place."

Pippin looked down at her wrinkled hands. She reached inside her sleeve for her handkerchief, dabbing at her nose.

"Course she got to see her daddy 'fore he passed.

"They was so happy when they learned of Miss Bonnie's condition. Nothin' coulda completed them more than a baby. They was all so happy," she said, winding the handkerchief in and out of her stiff fingers nervously. She was working up steam to tell the women the rest of the story. Pippin knew it wouldn't be easy.

"It was a hard time Miss Bonnie had with that baby," she continued.

"She was weak already; her frail little body never having recovered from all that traveling and all that she done through the war. Doc put her to bed right early on. Mr. Calvin and Mr. Henry wouldn't let her so much as lift a little finger. Well, Miss Bonnie didn't take a shinin' to that much at all.

"One day, the men was all out tendin' the fields. It was a spectacular spring day, and Miss Bonnie had had all the bedridden she could stand. She wanted to get out in the sun, tend to her new garden. She made it to the garden, weak as she was, but when Mr. Henry got back to the house to check on her, she was nowhere to be found! He was frantic! He called and called and finally, he found her in her beloved garden down in the good dirt. She had tried to stand from weedin' and it was just too much for her. She was pale white, but still alive!

"Mr. Henry carried her upstairs and, in a state of shock, he found that the baby had decided it was coming out to meet this world. She didn't care what the circumstances. It was her time.

"And come out she did!

"Mr. Henry was there. He held the baby in his arms when Miss Bonnie gave him his orders of what he was to do next . . ." Pippin gazed again into the distance as if looking back in time.

Bonnie heaved as much air as she could into her lungs, drawing breath to speak the words she needed to say to Henry. In a labored whisper, she spoke direct and stern to him.

"Henry, Calvin ain't going to take this well," she whispered in a tired, coarse voice. "He ain't gonna know what to do. Watch out for him. Don't you let him go back to drinkin'. Hear?"

The baby wailed in Henry's arms, squirming and turning her little head to Henry's chest, instinctively looking for her first meal.

"Yes, Miss Bonnie, I understand, but you gotta save your strength. He'll be home in no time, and he'll get you to the doc. You're gonna be fine. You just gotta save your strength."

"Henry, I'm dying. I'm not going to be all right. Promise me." She tried hard to open her eyes and lift her head, but she hadn't the strength. Frustrated, she laid her head back down, opened her eyes wide glaring at the ceiling. Tears streamed out of the corner of her eyes. She panted hard, drew another deep breath, and forced herself to look at Henry. His head was down. His big brown hand stroked the baby's head, trying to calm her.

"Henry, you promise me now. You must promise me you'll take care of my husband. He's so fragile, and he waited so long for me and Annie. You can't let him fall apart. He has to be okay to take care of her."

"Annie?" Henry looked at her.

"Yes, Elizabeth after my mother." Bonnie drew another long breath. "Ann, after Ms. Parker. Tell him, okay? Tell him that's what I decided. Elizabeth Ann Wade. I want her to be called Annie. Okay, Henry?"

Henry nodded slowly, tears now rolling freely off his stubbly chin. Bonnie drew in another breath, but this time, it was slow and laborious.

"Put the baby here next to me, Henry . . . let me smell her," she instructed. Henry stood and lightly placed little Annie in the crook of Bonnie's arm. She immediately stopped squirming. Henry propped Bonnie up as best he could so she could see her. Annie's arms flailed about until she found Bonnie's chin with one hand. Her little hand cupped Bonnie's chin. She drew a breath and let it out slowly. Her little body relaxed and the edges of her tiny mouth turned upward into a smile.

"That's a good girl," Bonnie whispered to her daughter. "You're so beautiful, little Annie Girl. Your daddy is going to be so proud of you. And you have to be good for your daddy and help him as much as you can, okay?" Bonnie's head tilted back, squeezing her eyelids tightly together, trying to fight back the desperation.

"Henry, pick her up and take her downstairs. Wait for Calvin. Tell him I loved him very much, Henry . . ." she said with all of the strength left in her body. As Henry lifted the baby off the bed, Bonnie's eyes closed, the tension falling away from her face. Her head lolled slightly to her left.

Bonnie McCaverty was gone.

In the kitchen, Henry walked the floor, trying to calm the screaming baby. He bounced her lightly in his arms. Calvin burst through the door of the kitchen wide-eyed, having heard the baby's screams from outside as he approached the house. Buttermilk and Shorty were close behind.

"Henry, that's a baby!" Calvin said breathlessly.

Henry nodded, but couldn't look at him.

"Henry, what happened?" Calvin asked as she rushed to the man's side to see his new baby. "Where's Bonnie? How is she?"

All Henry could do was shake his head back and forth as tears continued down his cheeks.

Calvin backed away, glancing toward the ceiling. He ran, taking three steps at a time to the second floor. He drew a deep breath, turned the corner to the bedroom, stopping cold in the doorway. His hat dropped to the wooden floor. Calvin forced one foot in front of the other as he slowly made his way to the edge of the bed. He sat at Bonnie's side, lifting her pale hand to his mouth, kissing it softly. He cupped her hand around his face.

"My Bonnie Girl. Bonnie," he whispered as if waiting for her to open her eyes and speak to him. Calvin laid her arm down by her side, gathering her limp body as close to his as he could. That was where he stayed until the next morning when Henry and the doc came in and made him let her go.

Pippin lifted her specs again, wiping her tired, old eyes, swabbing her nose in one swift motion. She laid her hands back in her lap and turned her eyes to Polly and Cora, who had pulled out their own hankies and who were holding each other's hand.

Cora spoke up. "Pippin, did Annie live?"

Pippin lit up like a puppy at a new bowl. "Why, yes! Our little Annie Girl. Of course, she did. She was made of the same stuff as her mother. Strong as an ox, that little one. No one could calm her down but Calvin. Oh, Henry and Buttermilk and Shorty, they did their part. They fed her and cleaned her and played with her. But no one could calm her when she fretted like her daddy. He would pick her up and, no matter how fussy or how sick or how mad she was, she would just relax in his big ole arms.

"After Bonnie died, Calvin stuck to that baby. He never left her side. Almost like he was in fear that something might happen if'n he turned his back for one minute. He walked that house all night, some nights with her in his arms. Henry said he saw him many nights sitting in his chair, Annie curled up in the crook of his arm, just staring out into the night. He was totally devoted to her.

"Then, there were the Parkers. Miss Annie and Reverend Frank moved back to Smithville after Bonnie passed. Lizzie and Jessie were gone by then, and they were the only parents she had.

"So little Annie Girl growed up with a real grandma. That Miss Annie . . . she sho loved that little girl.

"Soon she was walkin' and talkin' and runnin' through the fields just like her mama did. Like Mister Calvin would say, 'hair the color of a wheat field in evening sun' streamin' out behind her, runnin' up to her papa. He'd scoop her up and whirl her around. Miss Bonnie is some kinda proud of them two. I just know she is.

"I came and lived with them shortly after Miss Bonnie died. All them mens . . . well, they had to have a woman to keep 'em all goin', you know? Uncle Buttermilk and Uncle Shorty, they both died on the Wade farm. They's buried down by the Caney. It was near and dear to both their hearts. And Henry; old Henry. He was a kind a man as you ever known in your life. Henry was everything to little Annie. She took it hard when he passed."

Polly spoke. "I remember Henry! He used to drive that rickety old truck, and he would bring Bonnie over to see us before Mama died. Miss Pippin, Bonnie wanted to be our mother. Even though she was just a young girl, she tried. She came out to see us in Nolensville after we were adopted. I missed her so badly for years. She never left my heart, even after all of these years."

"Honey, Bonnie McCaverty never left anyone's heart she came in contact with. She was an angel walked this earth in the skin of a woman. She was my friend. Lord have mercy how we played up there in those woods," Pippin said as she pointed toward the remnants of what once was The Dark Forest. "Uncle Buttermilk was like my daddy, you know? His brother, my daddy, died when I was just a little thing. Buttermilk and Shorty was my daddies, and Bonnie was my sister. I miss her still," The old woman spoke softly, lifting her glasses, wiping them again.

"Miss Pippin, we didn't mean to get you upset. We just never knew fully what happened to Miss Bonnie. Why, if it hadn't been for Bonnie, we would have never been adopted, and we would have never had the life we had with our brothers and our mother and daddy. We just wanted to know how her life turned out," Polly told her.

"Well," Pippin quickly responded, "Bonnie McCaverty had a good life. She was well loved and spent her whole life takin' care of others during that horrible war. She made it home and married the man she loved and left us with a beautiful reminder of her in Annie."

As Pippin spoke, a car pulled down the long rutted drive that led to the house. Pippin stood slowly. "There's my girl now," she said with her hands folded over her mouth as if she just might scream for joy.

A young woman with fair skin and freckles opened the driver's door and stepped out. She waved at Pippin. "Hi, Pip!" she yelled across the lawn as she ran to the other side of the car to help her father out of his seat. "Look who I brought to visit!" she yelled again, escorting Calvin to the front porch.

As he gingerly took one step at a time, Pippin leaned over the top of the steps, took his face in her hands, and kissed his forehead. "Mister Calvin, you lookin' good! Welcome home!" she said. She turned sideways when he stepped up to the top step. She put his arm through her's instinctively walk him to his favorite chair.

Calvin dropped down into the seat. "Oh, Pippin, it sure is good to be home."

"I knows it is, Mister Calvin. I knows it is. How 'bout some good old iced tea?"

"Pippin, that sounds like pure heaven."

"Well, okay then. You don't go nowhere. I'll be right back," Pippin replied as she turned to face Annie.

"And there's my grown up college girl! Mmm," she said as she planted a big kiss on Annie's cheek.

"Oh, get on with you, Pip. I haven't been gone that long!" She turned toward the two women who stood watching this mix-matched family come back together as natural as the sun that set over the horizon.

"Miss Annie, this is Cora and Polly. You remember the girls your mother tried to adopt when she was back in Nashville? They come to pay their respects."

Before Annie could speak, Calvin stood. He shuffled on unstable legs to stand in front of the two women.

"You knew my Bonnie?"

Polly spoke first. "Yes, Mister Wade. I remember her well. My sister Cora doesn't. She was just a baby. But, Mister Wade, we wanted you to know. We've had a wonderful life, and it's all because your wife helped us when no one else cared. She tried to take care of us herself, but—"

"I know," Calvin interrupted. "She told me. Judge Whitaker wouldn't give a single woman custody of the two of you. I often wondered what our lives would have been like if he would have and Bonnie would have returned home with you."

"Well, Daddy, you might not have had me!" Annie interjected.

"That's true, my dear," he replied, "so true." He kissed his daughter's cheek. She helped him back to his chair.

"It is so nice to meet you both," Annie said, extending her hand to them. "I brought Daddy back for the weekend to visit. I'm at Vanderbilt studying law in Nashville. He lives with me so someone can look after him.

"He's just a bit much for Pippin anymore," she added in a hushed tone that Calvin couldn't hear.

Polly spoke up.

"Miss Wade, what type of law do you practice?"

Annie smiled at the two women sitting in front of her.

"I specialize in family law," she said proudly. "Mother would have liked that don't you think?"

With that, the three women sat down and began to get to know one another. Pippin returned with iced tea for everyone.

Polly and Cora had now heard the story of Bonnie and Calvin's wait. They had heard the story of a love that spanned the hardships of drought and the Great Depression, the superstitions of the times that had kept Bonnie and Calvin apart for more than a decade, and the war that finally brought them together.

Later in the afternoon, Annie took Calvin upstairs to rest before supper.

"I'll come get you before supper, Daddy," Annie said. "Take a little nap, and it'll be ready soon."

Calvin only shook his head upon entering the bedroom he once shared with Bonnie. The room hadn't changed in over twenty-five years. Bonnie's clothes still hung in the bureau; Lizzie's hairbrush and comb still lay on the faded Irish lace draped over her dressing table.

Annie watched as her father shuffled into the room. She knew he waited day upon day to get back here. It was the only part of his life he had to look forward to. She knew he waited patiently for her to have time to take him back there. Annie went back downstairs to help Pippin with supper.

Upstairs, Calvin stood at the window steadying himself on the window ledge looking out over his land, knowing one day he would have to part with it, but for now, he was home, close to his memories.

Calvin looked out over the farm. In his mind's eye, he could see Bonnie as a young girl always trailing behind him, running up to him, smiling. He saw her face the day he left her crying at the train station, the day he forced her out of the kitchen door in a drunken stupor, but no memory was clearer than the day she came to him in that dark tool shed with all her hopes and dreams and laid them at his feet, only for him to deny her. He could literally feel the pain hit his heart, squeezing like a vice at that memory. He placed his hand over his heart, trying to calm the pain, but it wouldn't subside, then Calvin felt warm arms surround him from behind. A smile spread across his worn face. He pulled her arms closer to him as he began to hear her speak familiar words; words that haunted him, yet now brought a strange comfort.

"As I get to the end of the meadow I'll see,
A big, fine white house for my Calvin and me.
We'll sit on the front porch and watch the sun set,
A fine time we'll have that we'll never forget."
Calvin turned to face her.
"We'll have ten fine children and all with red hair," he said, stroking her lovely, soft hair.
To match with their mother's, so bright and so fair,
We'll sit on the rooftop and watch the moon glow,
As me and my Bonnie together grow old."

He studied her face; those brilliant green eyes set within a canvas of creamy skin, a speckle of freckles still perched on her cheeks. She was so young, so beautiful.

"Bonnie Girl, you finally came for me."

"Calvin . . ." she whispered, burying her face in his chest.

"I waited for you, Bonnie Girl. I knew you'd come for me soon."

"I'm here, Calvin."

His Bonnie Girl had finally come for him.

Annie found her father lying on his bed with his arms folded around him as if he were holding on to something. His eyes were closed, a warm, sweet smile on his face. Calvin had gone to be with his beloved Bonnie. Their final wait was over. No war, no depression, no superstition no sickness, not even death would ever separate them again.

CPSIA information can be obtained
at www.ICGtesting.com
Printed in the USA
LVOW03*1916270417

532464LV00002B/3/P